ANGEL

Jessie grabbed her dress off the bed and held it up in front of her, backing away from Jake's measured approach. His eyes were filled with a warm light she was beginning to know all too well.

"I'd appreciate it if you'd wait outside while I dress," she told him frostily.

"So, my sweet Jessie has disappeared already. I have only my waspish partner," he said, continuing to walk toward her.

"I'm merely trying to put our relationship back on a businesslike basis," she said indignantly.

"By all means, Miss Taggart. We're partners, nothing more. That wasn't you in bed with me last night. It wasn't you with the soft sweet skin I kissed and caressed until you begged for more."

"Stop it, Jake! I don't want to hear it. You and I are partners, and that's all we can ever be. We can't let last night happen again."

He stepped closer, his flashing blue eyes pinning her where she stood. "You know we can't go back now, Boston," Jake said. He closed the space between them and took her into his arms, silencing her protests with his warm, urgent kiss.

Other Books in
THE AVON ROMANCE Series

TIN ANGEL

KATHY LAWRENCE

AVON BOOKS ⬥ NEW YORK

TIN ANGEL is an original publication of Avon Books. This work has never before appeared in book form. This work is a novel. Any similarity to actual persons or events is purely coincidental.

AVON BOOKS
A division of
The Hearst Corporation
105 Madison Avenue
New York, New York 10016

Copyright © 1989 by Kat Martin and Larry Martin
Inside cover author photograph by Roxanne Photography Inc.
Published by arrangement with the authors
Library of Congress Catalog Card Number: 89-91270
ISBN: 0-380-75735-4

First Avon Books Printing: November 1989

AVON TRADEMARK REG. U.S. PAT. OFF. AND IN OTHER COUNTRIES, MARCA REGISTRADA, HECHO EN U.S.A.

Printed in the U.S.A.

RA   10 9 8 7 6 5 4 3 2 1

Chapter 1

San Francisco, 1872

Jake Weston dropped his long, booted legs from the rolltop desk and stood up. After digging a coin from the pocket of his breeches, he flipped it to the towheaded boy from the Wells, Fargo telegraph office.

"Thank you, Mr. Weston." The boy grinned at the generosity of the tip and backed through the open office door. The etching on the frosted glass identified Jake as the proprietor—only a slight exaggeration in the past, and a fact now that Henry Taggart had died. Just two days ago, Willard Jensen, Henry's lawyer, had come to Jake with the news that Henry had left him half interest in everything he'd owned. Well, forty-nine percent. That was almost the same as half.

They boy turned to leave, and Jake closed the door behind him, shutting out the *plinkity-plink* of a cheap piano that mingled with the din of boisterous voices and high-pitched female laughter.

Jake had occupied the office above the saloon for the last four of the five years he'd been Henry's manager. Of course, the word *manager* was a bit misleading. *Ramrod* would probably be a more accurate description. Jake smiled at the thought.

He didn't hurry with the telegram. He knew who

it was from. Instead, he casually sliced open the ivory envelope with the edge of his pocket knife. Returning to his swivel chair, he propped his feet back up on the desk and leaned back.

Dear Jake,
I am stricken with the news of Father's death. Though we have never met, I am confident of your ability to watch after my affairs until I arrive. Please do not inter my father until I reach San Francisco.
Warmest regards,
Jessie Taggart

Jake ran a hand through his wavy black hair, then took a cheroot from his waistcoat pocket and bit off the end. Damned fool woman, he thought as he dragged a match across the bottom of his boot and lit up. The last thing he'd expected when he wired Jessica Taggart to inform her of her father's death was that the woman would come all the way from Boston to San Francisco. Now that she had inherited fifty-one percent of Henry Taggart's holdings, she was his partner—there was no denying that—but surely she didn't expect to get involved in the business!

Rupert Scroggins, the bartender, opened the office door and stuck his head in. "Hey, boss. You look like a fellow who just found out he was the guest of honor at a vigilante party."

"Worse, Rupert. Henry's daughter is coming to town. The last thing we need is a schoolgirl telling us how to run a saloon and bawdy house." She couldn't do any better with the freighting company or fleet of harbor scows they owned, he added to himself.

"Don't worry about it, boss." Scroggins gnawed on the stub of a cigar. "You can handle a schoolgirl."

"I'm heading for the telegraph office, Rupert. You keep an eye on things till I get back."

Jake followed the stocky little bartender down the stairs, worked his way through the gambling tables, and stepped through the swinging doors of the Tin Angel onto the streets of San Francisco.

Dodging a beer wagon clattering behind a team of matched grays, he weaved through throngs of Chinese coolies in long black robes, Italian immigrants, Sydney Ducks in canvas breeches, Peruvian miners with puff balls dangling from the brims of their flat hats, and myriad other minorities that made up the booming population of California's fastest growing and most prosperous city.

At the Wells, Fargo office Jake carefully composed a return telegram to Jessica Taggart.

Dear Jessie,
Impossible to preserve your father until you arrive. Will manage your affairs until then but your presence is not required. It is a difficult trip. Too much for a woman. Will be happy to sell your father's assets and forward funds to you. Please advise.
Jake Weston

The answer arrived before midnight. Jake sat at the bar, his expression grim as he scanned the wire.

Dear Mr. Weston,
I will arrive in twelve days. Have retained Horace McCafferty, Esquire, of your city to manage my affairs. Do nothing, repeat, do nothing until I arrive. Pack my father in salt and charcoal and store him in the icehouse. I will, repeat, will be in attendance at his funeral. I hope my father's trust in you was not misplaced.
Your employer,
Miss Jessica Taggart

Rupert Scroggins leaned over Jake's shoulder. "I suggest you circle the wagons, boss. Looks like an ambush to me." He chuckled softly until Jake stood up.

"Don't you have some beer mugs to scrub?"

Jake took the stairs up to his office two steps at a time. Sitting at his desk, he gnawed angrily on his thin cigar. Then he smiled. By the time that eastern bit of fluff got beaten and bruised on the twelve-day train ride through hundred-degree deserts and ten-thousand-foot peaks, she'd be softened up to jelly. She'd sell to the first man with gold in his pockets—and Jake would personally have enough ready to buy out her fifty-one percent of the Tin Angel and the other holdings Henry Taggart had left behind.

Jessica Taggart lifted the hem of her black faille traveling dress and climbed the iron steps to the train. Around her, the Boston station echoed with merchants hawking their wares, small children scampering excitedly toward the puffing engine, and uniformed baggage clerks hauling cartloads of luggage.

Feeling a thrill of excitement even under the grim circumstances, Jessie pushed open the heavy mahogany coach door.

"May I take your bag, miss?" A black-uniformed conductor hoisted her small carpetbag into a bin above her head as Jessie sank down on the plush dark burgundy seat. Her steamer trunks had been stored in the baggage car.

"All the way to California?" the man asked, perusing her ticket. "Quite a distance for a young lady."

Jessie controlled a surge of anger. After all, the man was only making conversation, not passing moral judgment. "I assure you, I'm looking forward to it."

The conductor just grunted, as if to say We'll see about that.

"If there's anything you need, miss, just ask." With that he waddled off toward a gentleman seated on her left.

Like the others in the salon car, the man was fashionably dressed and smiling. She glanced around, anticipating the journey ahead, then carefully tucked a strand of glossy dark hair under her narrow-brimmed, black-plumed hat.

With several shrill whistles and a bellow of steam, the Pacific Express rumbled from the station. Though Jessie had often traveled with her father as he traded goods and supplies along the eastern seaboard, and occasionally with her mother before her death two years ago, they had rarely gone in such grand style. Jessie ran her hand across the rich dark velvet seat. Why shouldn't she indulge herself? After all, she could certainly afford it. Her father had been a wealthy man.

Thinking of her father made a hard lump rise in Jessie's throat. The fact that she hadn't seen him in almost three years did little to ease her feelings of loss. Although he'd been moderately successful in Boston, he'd made his fortune in San Francisco, the city he called home.

"I've come to love the West," he'd once told Jessie. "I belong there. Your mother belongs in Boston. She wouldn't be happy anywhere else." In truth, Jessie knew the need for adventure was part of his nature—but also sadly, a means of putting some distance between himself and Jessie's mother, Bernice.

As a child, Jessie had been saddened by her parents' constant quarreling and the unkind remarks her mother often made about her father. Her father, although obviously unhappy, had always made certain that Jessie and her mother wanted for nothing. The schools Jessie attended were the finest, her clothing elegant and expensive. After he'd left three years ago on his third and final trip West, his letters spoke proudly of his growing prosperity and his life in San Francisco. She could join him, he promised, just as soon as she finished school.

Although in Jessie's opinion his letters were too few, she had read and reread the words until the pages were limp and torn. They were a symbol of her dreams—his adventures a way of escaping the prim and proper confines of Mrs. Simpson's Academy, her stuffy Boston school.

Jessie missed her father terribly, but even more, she missed the freedom she'd tasted, the richness of life she experienced whenever she was with him. Although her mother had preached propriety, her father had encouraged her independence and taken her with him on his endless journeys—as far north as Maine and as far south as Charleston. He'd even urged her involvement in his business ventures. By the time she was ten, she could cipher better than her father's bookkeeper, and she always had a new idea for turning a bigger profit.

A month after her eighteenth birthday, only three weeks before her graduation, Henry Taggart had died. Their dream of being together would never come true, but he'd left her another in its stead. She owned fifty-one percent of Taggart Enterprises. Although she wasn't completely certain what the businesses earned, or even, for that matter, how they were run, she intended to find out—the sooner the better.

Jessie was sure that no matter what she discovered in San Francisco, with continuing good management Taggart Enterprises would flourish. It was a challenge she relished. She only wished her father could be at her side.

As the train gathered speed, Jessie pushed sorrowful thoughts away and pondered for the hundredth time the wire she'd received from Jake

Weston. A flood of hot temper surged through her veins, just as it did each time she thought of it.

Of all the nerve! Did Weston think she was a complete fool? That she'd just lie down and let him run over her? Her father might have trusted him, but that didn't mean she did. For all she knew, Weston could have been stealing from her father for years.

Jessie straightened her spine. If Weston had any notion of taking advantage of her, he was in for a big surprise.

One thing was certain. No matter what awaited her out West, Jessica Taggart was ready to take charge of her future. And no one—especially not a man like Jake Weston—would keep her from doing just that.

Chapter 2

Although Jake owned a fine gray saddle horse and half interest in a dozen freight wagons, he hired a buggy for the trip to the Embarcadero ferry station. The six-foot climb to a freight wagon seat would be awkward for a lady, and Jake still harbored hope that Jessica Taggart was one.

The ferry that crossed the bay to San Francisco from Richmond, where the railroad terminated, was due in twenty minutes, and Jake didn't want to be late. He'd chosen a flat-bedded buggy out of practicality, knowing the girl would have a trunk or two, depending on how long she planned to stay. Jake grimaced at the thought.

He knew little about her since Henry had preferred to keep family matters to himself. However, from the bills Jake had seen for her schooling and clothes, it was obvious that Henry had catered to her every whim. Jake knew that Henry held his daughter on a pedestal above all other woman.

''My dear, sweet Jessie deserves only the very best,'' he once said. Henry tolerated little foolishness in his employees, but Jake imagined he'd put up with just about anything from his daughter. Jake felt certain that the woman who was raised with such indulgence would cause him endless grief.

Clucking the horse into a trot as he rounded the corner toward the wharf, Jake grumbled beneath his

8

breath. He could have taken the trip across the harbor to meet the girl at the Richmond train station, but after her sassy telegram, he wasn't eager to meet his new partner. To Jake, Jessica Taggart was nothing but a pampered schoolgirl. He intended to treat her as such and set the tone of their relationship right from the start.

Jake bit the end off a cheroot, touched a match to it, and smiled as he inhaled. After her long trip, she ought to be good and tired, he thought. Too damned tired to carry her baggage—and too damned tired to cause him any trouble!

Sitting near the edge of the wharf on the buggy seat, his tall black boot propped on the brake, Jake watched Chinese laborers busily moving the cargo around him, gulls circling above and the water traffic bustling in the harbor. About a quarter mile out in the bay, a fine two-hundred-foot clipper rolled quietly at anchor, her naked masts awaiting the sails that would speed her back to New England.

There had been a time, twenty years ago, when the harbor had bobbed with bare-masted ships. They were perfectly seaworthy, capable of the worst the Cape had to offer, but they couldn't sail without a crew. The men had all headed for gold mines. Even old man Taggart, then captain and owner of one of the brigs, had decided to batten her down and head for the Sierras. He hadn't had much choice—there weren't enough able-bodied men in San Francisco even if he'd shanghaied them.

Far out on the water, Jake caught sight of the ferryboat, its red paddle wheels churning sparkling foam against the blue bay waters.

During the past two weeks, Jake had been busy picking up chits for gambling and other debts people owed him. He had twenty thousand in cash stowed in the green-and-gold-trimmed safe in the corner of his office. It was twice what he should need to buy Jessica Taggart out of the Tin Angel, and, he

hoped, enough to take over the freighting company
as well.

He didn't give a damn about the harbor scows;
they were the least profitable part of the small but
money-making businesses old man Taggart had
built. The leaky, rock-a-bout scows never failed to
make Jake seasick, and he'd be damned if he'd own
a business he couldn't watch closely. Maybe he
could convince her to trade her half of the freight
company for some cash and his half of the scows—
or he could sell the damned boats altogether. That
would leave him with a good bit of money, the Tin
Angel, and the freight company—and *without* a finishing school, know-it-all female partner.

The red and white ferry tooted its whistle and re-
versed its massive paddle wheels, causing the sea to
roil and mist to fly. She slid smartly up along the
tall wharf and the Chinese laborers leaped into ac-
tion, affixing dock lines and adjusting ramps.

Several other wagons and two hansom cabs reined
up beside Jake's buggy as he waited. After climbing
down from the seat, he made sure the horse was
securely tied, then he walked to the passenger gate.
After taking a last deep draw on his cigar, he flipped
it into the bay.

Jake stood aside, watching men and women leave
the ferry. He had seen an old, beat-up daguerreo-
type of Jessica Taggart that her father had carried,
but now she'd be ten years older—a full-grown
woman. Old man Taggart had had a tendency toward a broad beam, and the picture had depicted a
round-cheeked child, so Jake figured Jessie Taggart
would be a bit plump. He started toward a young
woman who looked as if she hadn't pushed away
from a meal for years but stopped when he saw that
the girl was a blonde. Jessie was a brunette. Besides,
she would surely not be traveling alone. It would be
only proper that a maiden aunt or a hired companion would accompany a Boston lady.

The deck was almost empty when Jake spotted a young woman standing in the entrance to the main salon. Stepping through the bulkhead, she picked up a flowered carpetbag and started along the deck. She had dark brown hair, although he could see little of it under the narrow-brimmed, slightly wilted hat that also shaded her face.

Her once-black traveling dress was wrinkled and covered with the dust of her torturous trip, but her hips swayed enticingly, drawing his eye to the fashionable but slightly bedraggled bustle. When she turned toward him, her bearing so straight that she seemed almost regal, Jake stifled his lazy smile.

Beneath her wilted hat, the girl's face fairly glowed. Her complexion was as clear as spring rain, and her features were fine and delicate. Jake watched with fascination as she handed her bag to a Chinese porter who kowtowed and scurried behind her while she made her way along the deck.

Jake scanned the rails of the ferry and glanced over the people on the wharf, then back to the boat. Surely the woman walking toward him had only come from across the bay. Jessica Taggart should have dark circles beneath her eyes and be looking for a featherbed. Jake chuckled to himself. If this woman was looking for a bed, he'd be the first to help her find one—his!

Leisurely, he returned his attention to her rumpled traveling clothes. By the look of them, she'd sure as hell come from someplace far away.

The lady stopped as a fellow passenger—a tall, well-built blond man whom Jake recognized as Rene La Porte—tipped his hat in farewell. He said something that Jake couldn't hear and the woman's soft laughter rang out as she turned to descend the gangway. She can't be the Taggart girl, Jake thought. Old Henry would spin like a top if his daughter came West with no chaperon and a trainload of strange men—especially if one of them was Rene La Porte!

La Porte was a frequent customer of the Tin Angel, a competitor in the freighting business, a Frenchman, and an infamous ladies' man. Jake had heard he'd gone to Reno on business. At least he'd spent only hours with the girl, not days.

Still not certain he'd found the right woman, Jake stepped forward as she reached the foot of the ramp. She was even prettier up close, her eyes big and emerald-green and her cheeks rosy. Under different circumstances, Jake would have enjoyed just looking at her. Before he could gain her attention, Horace McCafferty, wearing a fancy velvet-collared split-tailed coat, stepped up beside her, doffing his black bowler and bowing effusively.

"Miss Taggart." The lawyer smiled, showing far too many teeth for Jake's taste. "I'm Horace McCafferty."

Before she could answer, Jake strode up and removed his white Panama hat. He extended his hand. "And I'm Jake Weston. Glad you arrived safely. I have a buggy waiting just over there."

"And I have the hansom cab you requested, Miss Taggart." McCafferty cast a disapproving glance at Jake and gave her another toothy smile. The lawyer was notorious for his shady dealings. Jake wondered how in the hell Jessie Taggart had managed to hook up with a skunk like McCafferty from three thousand miles away.

"Pleased to meet you both." Jessie regarded Jake with slight disdain and ignored his proffered hand. "I didn't expect you to meet me, Mr. Weston. I sent you the time of my arrival only as a courtesy. I hope I haven't put you out."

"The Tenderloin is not the safest district for a young lady, Jessie." Jake returned the Panama to his head. "Besides, I figured you'd like to get your affairs settled as soon as possible." He noticed Jessie stiffen at his use of her first name. Good, he thought.

He intended to let her know who was in charge right from the start—fifty-one percent or no.

"Mr. McCafferty is handling my affairs, Mr. Weston." She smiled tightly. "All except for the funeral arrangements. I left that up to you."

"The funeral is set for three hours from now. The trains are notoriously late, and I wanted to be sure you arrived in time."

"Three hours! Why I can't possibly . . . I have to freshen up! Surely it can be postponed."

"We've dragged things out too long already. There are city ordinances about this sort of thing. Your father is being buried in three hours, whether you're there or not."

Jessie's fingers tightened on her reticule and her pretty lips thinned. "Then I had better be on my way." She turned her back to Jake and accepted McCafferty's arm. "Will you be kind enough to escort me to the funeral?" she asked, although her tone left no room for refusal.

"Of course," Horace replied. "The service is being held at St. Joseph's Episcopal, if the newspapers are correct."

"That's right," Jake said. "But I think you'd better let me escort you, Jessie. I've had dealings with Mr. McCafferty. I suggest you consult your father's attorney, Mr. Jensen."

"It's my understanding that Mr. Jensen represents your interests, Mr. Weston."

"Well, he does, but—"

"Then, as I said before, Mr. McCafferty will be representing mine. He was kind enough to wire me at the Academy, offering me his assistance, and I accepted."

Jake wondered how he'd found her, but guessed it wasn't too hard, since the Academy was the most expensive school in Boston.

"I've made all the necessary arrangements,"

McCafferty added, throwing a hard look at Jake as he turned to leave.

"Just a minute." Jake stepped in front of the moon-faced attorney. "I don't like you, McCafferty, and I never have. As for you, Miss Taggart, there are things we need to discuss."

"I'm leaving with my attorney," she said firmly, and started to walk away.

"I've made arrangements for you at the Palace," McCafferty said, and Jessie nodded her approval.

Staring at her stiff back, Jake felt his neck grow hot, but he held his tongue. He wanted to whip the dandy lawyer and heave him in the bay, but it looked as though he'd have to wait and deal with the man later.

"One more thing," Jessie called over her shoulder, almost as an afterthought. "The business we need to discuss? I'd be pleased to meet with you tomorrow. For dinner perhaps?"

"Fine," Jake said gruffly.

"We can get together at the restaurant."

"*Which* restaurant?" Jake asked, more irritated than ever.

"Why, *our* restaurant, of course! The Tin Angel." Jessie smiled. "I presume you have been overseeing that part of our affairs, Mr. Weston?"

It was all Jake could do to not to burst out laughing. *Restaurant!* Old Henry had told his daughter he owned a *restaurant!* A soft chuckle escaped him.

"If you would be so kind as to take care of my trunks, Mr. Weston." Jessie looked down her small, straight nose as if she were speaking to a servant, and Jake's urge to laugh suddenly died.

Only his anticipated "dinner" with her at the Tin Angel soothed his irritation. "I'll have your things sent along, Miss Taggart." He broke into a broad grin. "And I'll be pleased to set a table tomorrow at the Tin Angel. The ladies will be thrilled to meet the other new owner." He chuckled again.

A severe expression came over Jessie's pretty face. "I don't know what you think is so funny, Mr. Weston—or are you merely being rude?"

Just as Jake was able to compose himself enough to answer, a circling sea gull released a white gob that landed with a plop across the broad brim of his Panama. He frowned as he removed the hat and looked up with disgust at the screeching bird. The heat at the back of his neck rose to his face. "So far, Miss Taggart, it's *your* attitude that leaves something to be desired."

"It seems all of God's creatures share the same attitude toward you, Mr. Taggart." Jessie turned a forced smile upon McCafferty as he helped her into the hansom cab. "Mr. McCafferty will be in touch," she called to Jake through the isingless window as the horse clopped away.

Jake snarled and sailed his hat into the bay. God put women, mules, and attorneys on the earth for the same damned purpose, he thought—to drive sane men crazy! He arranged for Jessie's trunks to be loaded on the wagon and paid a man with the ferry crew to haul them to the hotel and return the buggy to the livery. Then he began to walk uphill to the Tin Angel.

A soothing breeze ruffled his wavy black hair. Jessica Taggart might have won this hand but, pretty as she was, it was he who would win the game. He smiled to himself. Tomorrow night at the Tin Angel he would trump her queen of hearts with his ace of diamonds.

Meanwhile, there was Henry Taggart's funeral to attend. Jake had said his farewells two weeks ago when Henry died. He'd been a good boss and a good friend, but life went on. Jake was ready to get on with his.

Jessie slumped back against the leather seat. My God, what an experience! Why, the man was even more boorish than she'd expected. She took several deep breaths, trying to calm her ragged nerves. Jake Weston was irritating beyond belief—even if he was damnably handsome! Tall, rugged—virile is how she'd describe him—but also arrogant, pompous, dominating—and downright infuriating! He was certainly unlike any Boston gentleman she'd ever met.

"Miss Taggart?" Horace McCafferty's nasally voice interrupted her reverie. "There are a few things we had better discuss before your meeting with Mr. Weston."

"Fine, Mr. McCafferty. How about tomorrow? Shall we say around four?"

"I was hoping we could speak this afternoon." He seemed a little nervous.

"I'm afraid that's quite impossible. The funeral, you understand. Tomorrow will be soon enough." A gust of wind blew in through the open front of the carriage, ruffling the drooping feathers on Jessie's hat. One irritating plume refused to stay out of her eye. Smiling all the while, Jessie gave a quick jerk, plucking the offending feather from the crown and tossing it away. McCafferty only grunted.

Jessie stifled a yawn. "How much farther to the hotel?"

"It's at the top of the hill. I insisted on a room with a view."

"That was thoughtful. Your city is lovely." She glanced back toward the wharf. The ferryboat, now appearing toy-sized, was just leaving the dock.

"Maybe I could give you a bit of a tour tomorrow," McCafferty offered, "after our meeting." He reached into the pocket of his waistcoat and pulled out a small white card. "My address is on the bottom. Just give it to the hack driver. He'll know where it is."

The cab rolled up outside the hotel, an impressive gray-brick three-story building. McCafferty descended the hansom and hurried around to help Jessie down. "I'll see you to your room."

"That won't be necessary." Jessie picked up her carpetbag and extended her hand. "Until this afternoon, Mr. McCafferty."

"I'll call for you at two."

Jessie nodded.

McCafferty touched the rim of his bowler. "Until then."

Jessie lifted her skirt and, head held high, swept through the heavy brass and glass doors into the hotel. The rich Oriental carpet muffled her footsteps as she passed plush green velvet settees and delicate Queen Anne tables. Looking loftily down his nose at her, the desk clerk informed Jessie that her room was ready, and a uniformed bellman led her up the wide curving staircase to the second floor.

Like several of the other guests she passed, the bellman raised his eyebrows at her sooty clothes. He seemed relieved when Jessie ordered a bath and reminded him to deliver her trunks as soon as they arrived.

"Thank you," she said with a polite smile as she closed the door behind him. Then she collapsed against the frame. Thank God! San Francisco at last! One more day on that train and she would have been as wilted as overcooked greens. Every bone in her body ached, every joint and every muscle. She'd virtually destroyed the few dresses she'd worn on the trip—they were all covered with dust, soot, and grime. And although she'd traveled on a Pullman sleeper car, she hadn't had a decent night's rest in twelve days. It had taken every last ounce of strength to walk down that gangplank to meet Horace McCafferty—let alone Jake Weston.

Of all the rotten luck! She had hoped to dodge her new partner for at least a couple of days. She'd planned to rest up, have her garments pressed—but no, Weston had to show up at the dock. And having the funeral today! It was just like the arrogant brute. He knew how tired she'd be—he probably enjoyed making her miserable. She smiled as she thought of the fifty-one percent she owned to his forty-nine. More than likely, he resented her already. After all, in a way she was his boss—although it was obvious he wasn't ready to accept that fact!

In his telegram, and again today, Weston had tried to gain the upper hand. He hadn't succeeded—at least she didn't think he had. But he *had* destroyed her plans for some much-needed rest. First there was her father's funeral to attend, and somehow she had to make it.

Thank God she'd had the last two weeks to grieve. She refused to show any sign of weakness in front of Jake Weston.

Jessie stripped off her soiled traveling dress and donned a blue silk wrapper she carried in her carpetbag. Two young boys delivered a copper tub and filled it with steaming hot water. Jessie thought a bath never looked so good. She tipped the boys as they left, finished undressing with the help of a chambermaid, and climbed into the tub. With her body aching as it did, it was all she could do to lather her thick, dark brown hair and rinse it clean.

Jessie rested her head on the back of the tub, her eyes heavy with fatigue. Jake Weston. He was nothing like what she'd expected. Though she hated to admit it, he was far more handsome. Too handsome. From the tone of his wire, she'd envisioned a balding, grumpy old man. Her image of Weston had been about as wrong as her idea of a glorious trip to California. Weston was tall and lanky, whipcord lean, yet broad and muscular across the shoulders. His bronze complexion and wavy dark hair enhanced the vivid blue of his eyes. She didn't have to be an expert on men to know a fine example when she saw one.

Jessie frowned. He was damned attractive all right,

but he was also an arrogant, dominating bully. He was *nothing* like her father. Her father had treated her as an equal even when she was still a little girl. He felt that women were just as capable as men. He'd instilled that belief in her, then entrusted her with his businesses. He'd taught her enough to get started— how to read account ledgers, how to balance profits and losses, assets and liabilities. But mostly he'd taught her good business is a matter of common sense, and she had plenty of that.

Although the school she'd attended had been strict and proper, she'd had no parental guidance since her mother's death. Except for the overbearing school mistresses and the letters from her father, she'd been on her own for the past two years.

As it had ever since she'd received the news of her father's death, thinking of him brought a hard lump to Jessie's throat. She should have come West as soon as her mother died. Then she and her father could have been together, at least for a while. She'd wanted to come, but he'd been determined that she finish her schooling. She'd agreed.

Henry Taggart was the one person who had understood her completely. He hadn't criticized her liberal views the way her mother had, had never tried to force her to become something she wasn't. Her mother had expected her to behave like a lady, never to be outspoken or overly bold. Bernice had wanted her to marry well, to forget her views on equality of the sexes, her dreams of love, excitement, and adventure. But Henry had encouraged her to grow and develop her potential.

She was here in California because her father had had enough faith in her to believe she could run his businesses. And now, in the wild western town of San Francisco, she intended to teach her new partner something her father had never doubted—that Jessica Taggart was not easily intimidated, that nobody ran Jessica Taggart's life but Jessica Taggart.

With a deep sigh, Jessie slid farther into the copper tub and closed her eyes. She didn't wake up until the bellman knocked on the door with her trunks.

Jake pushed through the swinging doors of the Tin Angel and headed straight for the bar.

Rupert Scroggins, his chief bartender, eyed him over the top of his wire-rimmed half-glasses. ''You look like your best dog just died.''

''Not a dog, a dream,'' Jake growled. ''Taggart's daughter is just like Henry described her mother—meaner than a bitch wolf with her hair up.'' He raked a hand through his hair. ''Gimme three fingers of Who Hit John.''

''What's she look like?'' Rupert eyed him quizzically as he poured.

Jake downed the drink in a swallow. ''Not bad,'' he mumbled.

''What?''

''Prettier'n a frilly French whore,'' Jake said. ''But, by damn, pretty or not, she's mean as a rotgut hangover.''

Rupert laughed and filled his glass again. ''Well, that oughtn't to be a problem for you. I never saw a looker you couldn't handle.''

''Worst of it is,'' Jake added, ''her attorney is no better. She's hired ol' Whore Ass McCafferty.''

''She picked a real sorry cuss with that one.'' Rupert's bushy brows came together.

''And he's a councilman. I'm surprised he hasn't joined up with that bunch pushing for the city to regulate the sporting houses.'' Jake broke into a grin. ''Speaking of houses, seems old man Taggart fell shy of telling his missus about the Tin Angel. Little Miss Boston Taggart thinks she's the proud half owner of a la-di-da restaurant.''

''A restaurant!'' Rupert guffawed. ''Well, we got pickled eggs and peanuts.''

"Well, chef, get ready to serve 'em, because Miss Jessica Taggart will be here for supper tomorrow night."

"No!" Rupert's jaw dropped. "You didn't!"

"Sure as hell's hot and this is the finest whorehouse on the Barbary Coast, I did." Jake laughed aloud. "And if this supper doesn't make Miss Priss Jessie drop this place like a hot coal, my name's not Jake Weston."

"Should be Jake the Snake," Rupert mumbled.

"You gotta do what you gotta do, old friend. And, for your information, you're gonna help."

The bartender bellied up to the bar as close as possible, and Jake lowered his voice.

"I want you to fetch old Wall Eye Wong to do the cooking. Tell him I want some of that fine green octopus and purple sea slug mixture he fixed the time Henry and I were invited to the Gum San tong meeting . . . and that bird he fixed with the head still on and looking at you . . . and whatever else he can conjure up."

Rupert wrinkled his nose and backed away from the bar. "Boss, you're just supposed to scare her off—not poison her! That stuff would choke a mule. I'd eat the tail end of a skunk before I'd touch Wong's cooking."

Jake ignored him. "Then you call all the women together. I want them to properly greet the new girl joining the crew of the Angel."

"Now, Jake," Rupert picked up Jake's glass and drained it. "I couldn't do a thing like that to a proper lady, an' for sure not to ol' man Taggart's daughter. She'll faint dead away . . . maybe have apoplexy. I couldn't—"

"If you don't want a Miss Priss checking your mugs for water spots every day, you will. If that Boston kitten gets her claws into this place, you'll be serving tea and finger food to the Ladies' Aid

Society on Sunday morning after they have their church service right here.

"And," Jake said, cocking an eyebrow at Rupert, who frequently enjoyed the girls' services, "she'll be reforming all the whores. We'll be out of business in a fortnight."

Rupert sighed resignedly, eyeing the mugs lining the back bar. "All right, I git your drift. Where's Wall Eye hanging his braid these days?"

"Just ask around Grant Street. You got time before the funeral. We're closing down from noon to six and hanging out the black bunting."

Chapter 3

Jessie spotted Jake Weston the minute he walked through the door. He stood taller than most of the men in the room, and his dark good looks and flashing blue eyes did not go unnoticed by the ladies.

Although the church was crowded and buzzing with quiet conversation, when Weston walked in, the room suddenly fell silent. Jessie watched him from beneath her black tulle veil. There was definitely something unusual about the man, she decided. He had a certain presence. That's what her father would have called it. He always claimed a man with presence was a man who could accomplish anything. Jessie wasn't so sure about that, but she was sure her tall partner commanded respect from the people around him. Considering his boorish manner, his arrogance, and the way he'd tried to bully her, the thought rankled more than a little.

Turning her attention toward the front of the room, Jessie pushed all thoughts of Jake Weston aside. Twisting the embroidered handkerchief she held in her lap, she wished the service would begin. Although she'd been grieving for her father for the past two weeks, seeing his casket and knowing he was lost to her forever renewed all her feelings of sadness. She fought to keep from crying and found herself almost wishing Weston would take a seat beside her.

Instead, Jake walked to the front of the church and sat down on the far right side. Scanning the room, he noted the familiar faces of Henry's friends and acquaintances over the years. Then his eyes came to rest on Jessica Taggart, who, along with Horace McCafferty, was the only one seated in the left-hand front row. The girl turned her head in his direction, but her heavy black veil hid her expression.

Straining to get a closer look, Jake watched her for a moment, trying to read her thoughts. When he finally leaned back against the seat, his pocket Colt .36, hidden at the small of his back under his coat, thumped against the walnut pew.

By the time the preacher stood at the pulpit, the back half was filled with workingmen and sailors, while Chinese and Californios, Sydney Ducks, even a few Peruvians, stood at the very rear. Every segment of the bustling city's diverse population seemed to be represented. Henry Taggart had been a universally well-liked man.

Jake glanced toward the back of the overcrowded room. Seated in the last row on the right-hand side were sixteen whores—including Lovey McDougal; her Chinese friend, Sugar Su Ling; a mulatto; two black-haired Californios; and red-haired Megan O'Brien—all dressed demurely in somber black dresses and veils. The people in the front section of the church had whispered noticeably when they had entered.

On the inside aisle of the right front row sat Tok Loy Hong, a wizened man in a flowing white silk suit—the Chinese color of mourning—and a white silk skullcap, his hair in a long braid. His wispy pointed beard reached to the middle of his bony chest. Behind him in the second row sat two huge, round-faced Chinese with matching curled-down mustaches, who dwarfed everyone but two equally large men at the opposite end of their row. All four were bodyguards. Two each for the most powerful—and opposing—forces in the city.

Across from Tok Loy, Chan Lee Sing, who called himself Charley, wore a somber Boston city suit of the latest fashion, his hair cut in the style of the country he'd adopted. A black bowler rested in his lap.

Jake, and anyone who knew anything about the powers in Chinatown, knew the two Chinese tong leaders. Tok Loy Hong, known more commonly as Red Silk for the garrotes found around the necks of his strangled enemies, headed the Gum San tong. Charley Sing headed the Auspicious Laborers of the Sea, an organization composed of the Chinese who worked in the Embarcadero. The AL of S was also a tong, but the group posed as a social organization, since any obvious attempt to organize Chinese labor would be met with instant retaliation by the merchants, bankers, and politicians of San Francisco.

Jake warily eyed the four huge bodyguards behind Tok Loy and Charley. He knew each one carried beneath his cloak an intricately marked, razor-sharp tong hatchet. An elaborate peace must have been declared for the funeral, because each tong leader had sworn a blood oath to kill the other—and each had accused the other of Henry Taggart's murder.

In his wire to Jessie, Jake had deliberately avoided mentioning the cause of her father's demise. Since Henry had had dizzy spells and chest pains for the past few years, Jessie hadn't been entirely surprised by his sudden death. Until he had received the wire telling him Jessie was coming West, Jake had hoped she would never find out that Henry had been strangled. His meeting with her at the ferry had gone so badly he hadn't had the opportunity to break the news gently, as he'd planned.

Now Jake was in a quandary. He'd have to tell her sooner or later. The case was still unsolved, and Isaac Handley, the sheriff, would want to ask her some questions. Taggart's body had been found behind the Tin Angel, garroted by a red silk rope, an Auspicious Laborers of the Sea hatchet buried in his chest—the marks of both tongs. The city had been in an uproar ever since the murder, and angry talk of running the Chinese out of town filled every bar and saloon.

Jake wondered how many of the Chinese in the back of the church and lining the streets outside were tong warriors and how many carried revolvers or hatchets beneath their full silk robes. Henry's funeral could easily erupt into a war.

As the preacher droned on, Jake remembered how Henry had first become involved with the two opposing Chinese leaders. A man of little prejudice, Henry had hired a number of Chinese workers when he made his first gold strike in the mountains above Jackson. The other miners hated the Chinese—for their industry, for their ability to go into an area the whites had abandoned and glean gold that they'd missed, and for their simple way of life.

Chinese Moving Day was a common occurrence in the gold fields. White miners would get liquored up and drunkenly decide the Chinese were the source of all their problems. The men would turn violent and run the nearest Chinese families out of their camps. Since the Chinese had no legal rights, if one or twenty of them happened to get shot or hanged in the moving process, the law looked the other way.

But Henry Taggart had liked and respected his Chinese workers. When white miners had decided it was time to move them out of Henry's mining camp, Taggart, standing alone, had met them with a double-barreled shotgun. When they had pushed him too far, he had dusted their Levi's with buckshot and sent them packing till they sobered up again.

Henry had intervened on behalf of the Chinese in San Francisco many times since then. He'd met Charley Sing when Charley had stumbled in the back door of the Tin Angel with a bullet in his side and the city marshals hot on his trail. Charley had sought the protection of Sugar Su Ling, one of Henry's most prized whores. When Henry discovered him, Charley had been sure he was doomed. But Henry didn't agree that Charley's effort to organize the Chinese in the Embarcadero was a crime, so Henry had hid him in the attic until things cooled down.

Charley owed his life to Henry, and in the Chinese tradition there was nothing Henry could not ask of him. But Henry hadn't asked for anything, and the obligation had passed on to Jessie, although of course she knew nothing about it.

The preacher finished the eulogy, and eight men took their positions beside the casket—Rupert, Charley, Tok Loy and five local politicians. Jake walked in front. Several times during the long service, he had glanced over at Jessie. She'd remained ramrod straight, never making a sound. What kind of a woman was she? Was she as hard as she seemed? Something told Jake that wasn't true, but so far, everything about her had surprised him. At least she hadn't protested the presence of the Chinese—or the whores—as most people did, even if they didn't come right out and say so. Even in death, Henry Taggart wielded enough power to keep them silent.

As the casket passed, Jessie rose and walked closely behind it. The Chinese bodyguards followed Horace McCafferty, ignoring him but watching each other with hands hidden beneath their cloaks. Horace glanced nervously over his shoulder, stepping on the hem of Jessie's black skirt. He apologized, then pushed up beside her on the pretext of offering his arm. Jake figured he wanted to get as far as possible from the four massive Chinese men.

The coffin passed through the tall carved doors of the church, and Jessie looked down into the street. She hesitated at the top of the steps, unable to believe her eyes. Drawing on the last of her strength, she fought to suppress the lump in her throat and tears that threatened to spill down her cheeks. She glanced around for Weston and found him standing behind her, holding his hat in his hand. He seemed as taken aback as she by the people crowding the street below. Jessie had always believed her father was a man of vision, a man of greatness. It was obvious now that she wasn't the only one who thought so.

The street was filled to overflowing with a bewildering variety of people, the men holding their hats, the women's heads covered by bonnets or scarves. All were stone silent. At the intersection half a block away, a gang of Chinese, dressed somberly in white, waited to join the procession, beating brass gongs and trailing white banners. Many carried pots of steaming food, a traditional offering to the ancestors.

As the casket slid into a gleaming black ebony hearse with etched glass windows, the San Francisco Fire Department Band issued a booming brass and drum funeral dirge, while the Chinese, one group leading, the other following, began playing their own funeral march on their strange brass and wooden instruments. The street erupted in a din of noise.

Jessie turned to face Jake.

"I've arranged a carriage for you," he said. His expression was grim, his eyes distant and bleak.

She nodded and, hoping he wouldn't notice, reached discreetly beneath her veil to brush the tears from her cheeks. Jake caught her surreptitious movement, and his features softened, making him look even more handsome than before. His hand, warm and strong, slid beneath her elbow, and Jessie was grateful for his support. He escorted her to the only other vehicle in the roped-off street—a glossy black buggy with a black-plumed, two-horse team. He helped her up on the seat and Horace McCafferty climbed in beside her.

Up front, the hearse rolled away, pulled by six black horses in plumed bridles. Jake walked directly behind the hearse, and four rows of somber-suited pallbearers followed. When Horace slapped the reins lightly against the horse's rump, Jessie leaned back against the seat, and the carriage rolled away.

"Thank you, Horace," Jessie said as they climbed the curving staircase to her second-floor room at the Palace Hotel, Horace holding her arm. "I appreciate everything you've done."

Though he'd said little, she wasn't sure she could have made it through the day without him. The funeral had exhausted every last ounce of her strength. Thankfully, much of the ceremony had passed in a blur, but Jessie would never forget it. Not once in her life had she experienced anything as moving as her father's funeral. Seeing the crowds of people in attendance, all come to pay their last respects, had given Jessie new insight into her father's character. More than ever, she wished she had come West to live with him.

Even Jake Weston had surprised her. He'd been solicitous, which she had expected. What she hadn't expected was the haunted look in his eyes, his genuine grief. He'd tried his best to hide it, and maybe from some people he had—but not from Jessie. For Weston, too, she'd gained a new respect.

"Get some rest, Miss Taggart," Horace said, tipping his bowler.

"Thank you, I will. I'll see you tomorrow at four." Jessie closed the door softly behind him.

After summoning a chambermaid to unfasten her buttons, she readied herself for bed. She had cried her last tear for her father. He would want her to go on with her life, to be happy, not sad. She intended to do her best to be strong, for his sake.

Overcome with fatigue, she slid between the cool cotton sheets.

Jessie slept like a child—until six o'clock the following afternoon. A sharp rapping on her door finally roused her. She shrugged into her wrapper and peeked out to find the thin young bellman standing in the hall.

"Got a message for you, Miss Taggart. Thought it might be important."

Jessie accepted the envelope and, digging into her reticule, she found a coin and handed it to the boy. "Would you happen to know the time?"

"Six o'clock, miss."

"Surely I've been asleep for more than a few hours."

"It's six o'clock Friday, miss. You got here on Thursday."

"What! But that can't be."

" 'Fraid it is."

"Oh, God, I've missed my appointment, and it's almost time for dinner! Could you please send up a bath? I've got to be clearheaded tonight."

"Yes, ma'am." The boy smiled as if thinking that, with two baths in a row, Miss Jessica Taggart must be the cleanest, sweetest-smelling lady in all of San Francisco.

Jessie read the message, then dashed wildly around the room. She had a dress sent out for pressing, and when the tub arrived, she took a quick, refreshing soak. By the time the dress returned, Jessie was already in her chemise, corset, and petticoats. She wished she had time to coif her hair more extravagantly; as it was, she merely pulled it up and arranged it in a crown of ringlets.

Her gown was a rich plum silk brocade. It was suitable for mourning, which she planned to observe for only a few weeks, yet the color enhanced her green eyes and revealed the high swells of her bosom. So far Weston held the advantage. He knew the city, the current state of their businesses, their assets and liabilities. Jessie's first priority was to even the odds. Newfound respect aside, she'd use every trick in the book, every feminine wile she'd ever learned to put Jake Weston in his place.

Jessie reread the message she'd received. It was from Weston, suggesting they meet at eight at the Tin Angel and giving the address, which Jessie already knew. Slipping into her matching plum high-heeled pumps and grabbing her beaded reticule, Jessie calculated that she had just enough time.

Chapter 4

From the window of his room, Jake looked down on Wall Eye Wong, who was working in the makeshift kitchen he'd set up on the boardwalk below.

Wong's huge belly, wispy beard, and droopy mustache made him look more like a Chinese warlord that the king of San Francisco's Cantonese cooks—which, in fact, he was. As Wong bent to his task, cleaning two small octopi and a host of purple sea cucumbers, his long black braid danced beneath his skullcap. A golden pheasant, now skinned and cleaned, lay beside green and yellow vegetables, only some of which Jake recognized, on the wooden planks that Wong was using for a table.

Jake smiled, satisfied that his plan was proceeding on schedule, and glanced down the street toward the two smaller gambling halls that vied with the Tin Angel for customers. Though the hour was still early, several drunken sailors were standing out front, singing a bawdy song. Across the street, three more saloons also rang with noise, including the Golden Thorn, the Tin Angel's toughest competitor. They all teemed with business, but the Tin Angel was queen.

She was the largest and oldest saloon in the section between Chinatown and the Italian district, standing more than two stories tall and covering half a city block. Both the second floor and basement housed cribs assigned to the girls. The second story also accommodated Jake's bedroom and his roomy office. He kept another, smaller office at the freight terminal.

Jake stood in front of an oak-framed mirror and adjusted his four-in-hand tie. Smoothing his black frock coat, he winked at himself in the mirror. Jake, my friend, he thought, little Miss Priss Taggart will soon be begging you to take her interest in the Tin Angel. He loved the old saloon. He'd be damned glad when his "partner" was on her way back home and things returned to normal.

He combed his curly black hair a second time, then splashed lilac water along his jaw, flicked a piece of lint off his ruffled white shirt, and headed for the door. One stiff shot of Who Hit John and he'd be ready to greet a wide-eyed, very surprised Boston lady. Hell, he decided, he'd have a snifter of Napoleon Brandy. This was a special occasion.

Jessica Taggart waited anxiously beneath the awning in front of the Palace for the doorman to hail her a carriage. Once inside, she relaxed against the hard leather seat, but she couldn't calm her frayed nerves. She'd missed her appointment with Horace McCafferty, which meant she had missed getting any information she might have gleaned about Jake Weston and her father's businesses. Well, she'd just have to play it by ear. She'd been making her own decisions for the past two years—she'd manage this time.

Feeling a little more confident, Jessie adjusted the silk skirt of her fashionably low-cut gown, then leaned forward to get a better view of San Francisco, the city she was determined to make her home. It was almost dark, and the fog rolling across the lower parts of the city blocked her view of the harbor. Friday night traffic crowded the streets, hansom cabs and hacks vying with fine carriages emblazoned with the crests of the city's *nouveau riche*. Jessie wondered where such people lived and who they were. She wondered if she'd ever be accepted among their ranks, although she wasn't certain she really wanted to be.

If her father's funeral had been any indication, he certainly had not been constrained by the conventions of society, and there was no finer man than he. Although her upbringing demanded that she seek social approval, Jessie had to admit that just like her father, she'd rather have the freedom to be herself than the privilege of belonging to the upper crust of society.

First and foremost, she wanted her father's enterprises to prosper—she owed that much to him—and the idea of being a businesswoman fascinated her. It was a step toward equality, both for herself and for all women. The money would give her the means to experience life and the freedom to discover more of what living was all about. She just hoped Jake Weston wouldn't be a problem. If she had to, Jessie decided, she would simply drag him to success along with her.

Jessie smiled at the thought. She couldn't wait to see the restaurant her father had written about. He'd described it in exquisite detail, from the elegant crystal chandeliers to the thick Persian carpets. The Tin Angel, she was sure, was the main source of her father's money.

The pungent odor of decay drew Jessie's attention to the streets outside her window. The carriage clip-clopped through Chinatown, a section of the city Jessie had read about, and now, after her father's funeral, found even more fascinating. Its streets bustling with people, rickshaws, and animals, Chinatown captured her imaginaton. She leaned out the open window, determined not to miss a single thing. She was enjoying herself immensely until the car-

riage turned down a side street that looked more
than a little sinister. For the first time, Jessie began
to worry.

"Driver," she called, leaning further out the window. "Are you sure you're going the right way? I
thought you said you knew the Tin Angel."

"Not much farther, ma'am," he replied. "You
sure that's where you want to go?"

"Of course I'm sure. Why wouldn't I be?"

"Just askin'." The man clucked the horse into a
trot. They continued down the street, then turned
into an even seedier-looking area. The sound of raucous female laughter mingled with the tinkle of a
cheap piano. Several drunks burst through the double doors of a nearby saloon and staggered, arm in
arm, along the board walkway. One man looked
askance at her, then mumbled something to his
mates. As the carriage rolled by he laughed loudly,
doffing his hat and bowing deeply. Jessie turned
away from them, trying to ignore their rude catcalls.

As the carriage clattered farther into the decrepit
neighborhood, Jessie felt a sinking in the pit of her
stomach.

"Pull up, driver," she instructed. "I believe
there's been some mistake."

The man did as he was told, and Jessie leaned out
the window to look at him. "I think you must know
another place. The Tin Angel I'm speaking of is located at the address on this paper." She handed
him Jake's message. "It's one of the finest restau-
rants in the city."

"Yup," the driver said, "Nine-eighteen Montgomery Street. That's where we're headed. But she
sure ain't no restaurant. The Angel's the finest gam-
ing saloon and bawdy house this side of the bay."

"What!"

"Beggin' yer pardon, ma'am, but that's about the
size of it."

"But surely you're mistaken."

"Ain't no mistake, ma'am. Been there more'n a few times myself—course only to the saloon, you understand. My missus wouldn't approve of the other."

Jessie sank back against her seat, feeling the knot of despair tighten in her stomach. A whorehouse! Oh, God, had her father lied to her? How could he? He must have been ashamed to admit the truth about his business. That was what Weston had been laughing about on the dock and why Horace McCafferty had been so insistent on meeting with her. Damn them! Damn them all!

"You want me to take you back to the hotel, ma'am?" the driver called down.

Jessie twisted the folds of her skirt. If she didn't show up, Weston would think she was a coward. A whorehouse wasn't the sort of business she'd bargained for, but it was the one she had.

Another of her girlish dreams had just withered and died before her eyes. So what? she chided herself. So you feel let down and disappointed—well, you've been disappointed before. Jessie stiffened her spine and felt a little of her spirit return. She'd just make the best of it, she decided. Her father would expect no less. No doubt Weston believed she was incapable of handling her share of the business. That, she vowed, would not be the case. There was only one way to handle a man like Weston, and that was with fortitude. Jessie squared her shoulders and took a deep, calming breath. She'd get through the evening, no matter what Weston had cooked up. She'd show him just what a Taggart was made of.

"No, driver. Take me on to the Tin Angel. I have a dinner engagement."

"Whatever you say, ma'am." With a light slap of the reins, the carriage rolled away.

Jake paced restlessly, his thumbs hooked in his waistcoat pockets. It was dark outside, and Jessie was already fifteen minutes late. He should have picked her up at the hotel, but she'd wanted to play the businessman, so he'd let her call the shots. Besides, he'd been so damned mad yesterday morning that he'd forgotten to act the gentlemen. He was paying for it now.

The Tenderloin after dark was no place for an innocent girl. But then, just how innocent *was* Jessica Taggart? She'd traveled across the country unchaperoned and had arranged for McCafferty to represent her, without consulting Jake or anyone else. She was stubborn and spoiled—and alone in a dangerous city.

After glancing out the swinging double doors for the twenty-fifth time, Jake forced himself to take a stool at the bar. Hell, maybe she'd pulled up in front, seen what the Tin Angel really was, and hightailed it back to the hotel—to send McCafferty a message telling him to sell, he hoped. Still, if she didn't get there in the next fifteen minutes, he'd head over to the Palace and track her down himself.

After ordering a stiff shot of whiskey, Jake again strode to the door. He released a long breath of relief when a carriage rolled up and the door opened to reveal an elegantly dressed young lady. Now that he knew she was safe, he could relax and enjoy himself—and get on with the business of convincing her she had no place running her father's "restaurant." With a satisfied smile, Jake buttoned his coat and strode forward to greet Jessica Taggart.

"Why, Mr. Weston," Jessie said, stepping lightly from the carriage. "It's nice to see you again."

"I assure you, Miss Taggart, tonight the pleasure is all mine." The odor from Wong's cooking pots wafted over them as they crossed the boardwalk to the door. Jessie looked askance at the makeshift kitchen but said nothing. Jake watched her closely, awaiting her reaction to the boisterous, odorous scene.

"Lovely evening," she said.

"Perfect night for dinner at the Tin Angel," Jake replied with a self-satisfied grin. As determined as he was to one-up Henry Taggart's prissy schoolgirl daughter, Jake had to admit she was a beauty—far more lovely than he ever would have imagined when she first arrived in her rumpled black traveling dress. The plum-colored gown she wore this evening made her large green eyes look impossibly wide and sparkling. The dress revealed more of her creamy skin than Jake felt proper—although he could hardly tear his eyes away from the delectable swells straining at the tight-fitting bodice. He groaned inwardly. Why couldn't she have been the dowdy little dumpling he'd imagined?

Still, it was imperative that he put her in her proper place—immediately. He had to let her know just who ran the show, and he had to let her know *now*.

Jake offered his arm, and Jessie accepted with a smile that was far too winning and insincere to suit Jake. Something wasn't right. At the very least, Miss Priss Taggart should be having vapors about the Tenderloin.

"Shall we go inside?" he suggested.

"Why not?"

Jake held wide the bat-wing double door, anticipating her reaction with relish. The raucous noise in the place suddenly dimmed to a hushed roar. It was unusual, to say the least, for a *lady* to be visiting a place like the Tin Angel, and it was unheard of for a woman of Jessica Taggart's obvious breeding. Jake smiled to himself, beginning to warm to the game.

Lovey McDougal, the Angel's oldest employee and unofficial madam, strolled toward them through the smoky oil-lamp haze. Hands resting on her ample hips, massive breasts stuffed precariously into a tight red satin bodice, Lovey sized Jessie up with a single knowing glance and grinned broadly.

"Well, Lordy be, Jake Weston, you said the new girl was a beauty, but I never expected anyone the likes of her!"

"How do you do," Jessie cut in, apparently determined to appear unruffled. "I'm Jessica Taggart, half owner of the Tin Angel, now that my father has passed on."

Lovey crossed herself in respect. "God rest his soul."

"Amen," Jessie added.

"I thought you said she was the new miss," Lovey snapped at Jake out of the side of her overrouged mouth.

"You must have misunderstood." Jake looked at her hard. "I said the new *mistress*."

"Pleased to make your acquaintance, ma'am. Sorry for the misunderstandin'." Lovey smiled politely, but she frowned and pursed her lips at Jake before she hurried back to the three sailors she'd left at the bar. Jake surreptitiously waved away three other girls who started over to greet the new girl. He decided that playing up that particular ruse would be pushing things a little too much. Plan B ought to be enough to send Jessie screaming into the street.

"What do you think of her so far?" Jake asked, indicating the Tin Angel's long carved bar and the high-ceilinged room crowded with faro tables. An ivory roulette ball rattled in the wheel as the noise level in the saloon returned to its usual riotous din.

Jessie smiled sweetly. "That will depend on the profit she produces, Mr. Weston." Jessie wanted desperately to say, *I think the place is a vulgar, indecent display of sin and debauchery.* She wanted to rail at him and scream at her father. Instead she picked at the ruffle flirting with her breast and waited for Weston to make the next move.

"Would you like the grand tour, or would you prefer to wait until after dinner?" he asked with a lazy smile she wanted to slap off his arrogant face.

Of all the nerve! Jake indicated a roped-off section in a front corner of the saloon where a table had been set with gorgeous exotic flowers and magnificent china and crystal. Had she been anywhere but the middle of a gambling hall, Jessie might truly have anticipated the meal. As it was, eating under the stares of fifty men who crowded the long bar and filled the tables would be like dining onstage.

Well, fine, she fumed. It would be the grandest performance of her life! Controlling her fury with a will of absolute iron, Jessie smiled up at Jake.

"I think we should dine," she said. "I haven't had a bite to eat since yesterday. The table looks beautiful."

"Fine," he said, gallantly escorting her into the roped-off circle.

Jessie could feel the smiling eyes of the customers, hear their muted laughter. For Weston's sake, she was glad she didn't own a gun. She let him seat her, hoping her counterfeit smile appeared sincere.

Once he sat down, Jessie forced herself to look at him. Instead of wanting to shoot him, she was surprised to find she was again noticing how astoundingly handsome he was. Lamplight flickered on the shiny black hair that curled across his forehead, and his blue eyes seemed even more vivid against his tanned skin. His jaw was lean and hard and his mouth sensuously curved. Angry though she was, it was hard not to be drawn to the man—and that thought only made her madder.

Jessie forced herself to concentrate on the conversation, which was strained at best. Fortunately, two Chinese waiters arrived with glasses of wine and the first course of the meal, an excellent clear soup laced with shavings of local abalone.

The soup tasted delicious and she ate ravenously. Jake ate too, but his mischievous smile betrayed his anticipation. Jessie didn't like it one little bit. Her resolve strengthened. Whatever he was up to, she would not be caught off guard. Nothing he could do or say would force her to lose control. Nothing!

"I hope you're enjoying the meal," Jake said. "It was prepared by one of San Francisco's finest chefs." He took a sip of wine. "Wall Eye Wong. We brought him in special, just for the new partner in the city's finest sporting house."

"How charming," Jessie said, her voice syrupy sweet.

They finished their soup, and the waiters served another wine, then brought them each an ebony-lacquered platter. Dark purple sea cucumbers were artfully arranged in the center of the plate, a small octopus atop them, each of its eight legs precisely curled. Watercress circled the rim of the platters. The steamed octopus had taken on a delicate pink-trimmed white color.

Jessie felt her stomach roll. The food was beautifully prepared, but she'd never eaten anything even remotely similar. She tried to remember her mother's teachings: *A lady is never so rude as to reveal her distaste and is never afraid to try something new.* With great determination, Jessie quelled her uneasy stomach and picked up her fork.

Jake watched her closely. Glancing at his plate, he turned a little pale, but he looked up at Jessie with feigned relish. He fully expected her to run screaming from the table, but to his surprise, she beamed with delight.

"This looks absolutely lovely." She smiled prettily at the waiters. "Please give Mr. Wong my compliments."

She daintily speared a small chunk of sea cucumber and, looking at Jake over the exotic centerpiece, tentatively took her first bite.

Jake slugged down his wine.

Jessie dabbed her lips with the cloth napkin. To her surprise, the food had a wonderfully delicate flavor. She smiled again, almost genuinely. "Jake, this is just delightful. I *may* call you Jake . . . ?"

"We're partners, aren't we?"

"But of course." She glanced pointedly at his untouched plate. "You haven't tried your . . . your . . . What did you say it was?"

"Some kind of deep sea worm," he grumbled, amazed that she'd picked up her knife and was busily sawing away at an octopus tentacle.

"And you say this is not even the main course," Jessie said, obviously savoring each bite. "I'll have to be careful not to fill up."

"Me too," Jake muttered, stabbing a piece of sea cucumber with his fork. "How do you like the painting over the back bar?"

Jessie turned to look at the eight-foot reclining nude, and Jake managed to knock the piece off his fork and onto the napkin in his lap. When she turned back, he was diligently chewing air, the plate craftily rearranged to look half empty.

"The artist is quite good. I believe he could have used a bit more restraint with his subject matter, but I suppose it's appropriate to the setting."

One of the waiters quickly swept the napkin from Jake's lap and replaced it with a fresh one. Jake gave the man a withering look. "Thanks."

Relieved that he'd managed to get past the first dish, Jake glanced across the table at the woman chewing her food with such enjoyment.

"You're right, Jessie, we shouldn't fill up on this course." He shoved his plate away. The glassy-eyed bird would be next, and Jake could hardly wait. Jessie took several more bites, and Jake watched her closely as he sipped from his refilled glass of wine. This damned woman, he thought, is either the best actress I've seen, or she has a stomach like cast iron. Hell, maybe she really does like this stuff. Well, let's see how much she enjoys eating a bird that's looking her right in the eye.

A waiter arrived carrying a huge, cloth-covered silver platter which he placed carefully in the center of the table. Jake nodded, and the man pulled off the cloth with a flourish. The roasted pheasant's golden-brown body, precarved and reassembled, glistened in the candlelight. In its proper place, the neck and head rose from the platter, fully covered with white and gold feathers that were vibrant in the lamplight. The wings and brilliant red body feathers were arranged down each side, and the golden tail rested with breathtaking splendor in its proper position, so long that it flowed off the plate and over the edge of the table.

Another platter arrived, this one holding assorted steamed vegetables, each carved in the shape of an animal or fish and arranged by color, along with other beautifully prepared dishes—each more exotic than the last.

Jessie's eyebrows shot up.

By God, I finally got her, Jake thought smugly. She'll run out of here straight to old Whore Ass McCafferty, and she'll order him to make any kind of deal.

Jessie turned to the waiters and graced them with another brilliant smile. "Please tell Mr. Wong that this is the most magnificent show of culinary talent I've ever had the pleasure to witness.

"Mr. Weston," she said, turning back to Jake, "I had no idea San Francisco would be so sophisticated, nor you such a connoisseur of fine food and wine."

Thoroughly disgruntled, Jake sighed wearily. "Well, Miss Taggart, sometimes I even amaze myself."

The waiters served the pheasant with silver utensils, while Wong tottered to the table to receive Jessie's praise in person, bowing his head in such rapid succession that his pigtail bounced across his pudgy back. After taking the first bite, Jake had to admit the bird was tasty—if you didn't really look at the damned, glassy-eyed thing.

"Do you think we could get Mr. Wong to cook for us full-time?" Jessie asked. "We could build a small kitchen where the roulette table is." She looked at Jake pointedly. "I'm sure our clientele would be upgraded considerably."

Behind his napkin, Jake began to cough until the waiter had to pound him on the back.

"Okay, okay," he growled at the little man.

"It's not *his* fault." Jessie smiled up at him. "You're just eating too fast because the food's so good."

Chapter 5

Jessie finished the rest of the meal with the same gusto she'd shown from the start.

Once she'd gotten over her shock at its appearance, she found the meal was really quite good. Of course, she wasn't serious about turning the saloon into a restaurant—nobody in his right mind would venture into such a neighborhood just for a meal! But the look on Jake Weston's face when she'd suggested it made the whole evening worthwhile.

Jake excused himself for a moment when Lovey called him away to attend to a minor problem somewhere upstairs. While he was gone, Jessie decided to take her first real look at the inside of a saloon. After all, she owned the place, didn't she? Why shouldn't she take a walk around? Shoving back her chair, Jessie marched purposefully toward the bar. She hadn't gone three steps outside the roped-off circle when she was pulled roughly against a wide masculine chest.

"Well, little lady, you're just about the purtiest piece I've seen around here. What say you and me go on upstairs?"

"Of all the ridiculous—unhand me this minute!"

"Money's no object, little lady. I got a ten-dollar gold piece, and you're just what I been lookin' for."

The huge man pulled her along effortlessly, although she fought mightily to resist him. Her slen-

45

der arm was lost in his meaty hand, and she had to take two steps to his one just to keep from falling down.

"I'm warning you," she said as he approached the stairs. When he didn't let her go, Jessie felt a tremor of fear shoot through her. Where was Jake? Wasn't someone going to stop him? Was this just more of the entertainment Jake had planned for the evening? Maybe he would just look the other way and let this man, let this man . . . Oh, God, she couldn't even say it. Jessie grabbed the banister and held on for all she was worth.

"Somebody do something!" she yelled, but with all the hubbub in the bar, no one seemed to notice her—or care, for that matter. "I own this place!" Jessie shrieked. "Let go of me!"

The man roared with laughter, his massive chest and heavy arms rippling with the sound. "Yeah, and I own the Taj Mahal!" With that he tossed her over his shoulder like a sack of flour and continued up the stairs.

Jake shoved Megan O'Brien's customer out of her room ahead of him. "You've got to buy another token for a second turn, my friend."

"I jus' wanna little more poontang," the man muttered drunkenly.

"And you can have it, but you've got to buy another token." Jake was used to this scenario. Usually, Lovey handled these situations with ease, but this time the man had been too drunk for the big woman's boisterous tactics to work. The two oversized gentlemen Jake employed to handle matters were nowhere to be found.

Jake cursed beneath his breath. The new man was probably in a room with one of the girls. He made a mental note to tell the bouncer that the door swings both ways, and if he didn't start doing his job, he'd be out on the street looking in.

The old bouncer, Paddy Fitzpatrick, had been with Jake for five years. Paddy had come to town to fight a heavyweight match. He took a hell of a beating in the forty-seventh round of the bare-knuckles bout, but his bulldog toughness had impressed Jake, so he'd hired Paddy as soon as he healed. Tonight Paddy was in his cellar room sick with a fever.

Jake walked down the hall to the head of the stairs. A round, silk-clad rump faced him from atop Bull Haskin's muscular shoulder. Bull was taking the stairs two at a time, while his wriggling load kicked and screamed and beat at his back. The smile froze on Jake's face when he realized the plum-colored bottom belonged to none other than Jessica Taggart.

Jake met them halfway down the stairs. Sizing up the situation, he stopped Bull with a hand to the middle of his chest. First mate of the China clipper *Fair Wind*, Bull spent only a week or two in the city each year, but that was more than enough. Bull had come by his nickname honestly.

"Bull, you know better than to treat our ladies like that," Jake said, trying to handle the situation with finesse. He didn't want to see Jessie hurt. Jake had watched Bull fight three men at one time, bloodying each, then knocking them through the window into the street. Bull had just wiped his hands on his duck pants and come back to the bar for another drink.

Bull scowled at him. "I got tokens in my pocket and meat on the hoof. Stand aside."

"Bull, set the lady down. She can walk up."

"The hell you say, Jake Weston!" Jessie screamed beating at Bull's broad muscular back with no apparent effect.

"She's a spitter and kicker," Bull said, smiling with anticipation. "Stand aside, Weston. I'm a-haulin' her up."

"I said, she can walk. Now set her down and show me your tokens."

"Are you crazy?" Jessie broke in. "I'm not going anywhere with this maniac!"

"Shut up, Jessie," Jake told her, with a coldness she hadn't expected. The gravity of the situation struck her like a blow. With concerted effort, she held her tongue and stopped struggling.

Bull set her on her feet. As Jake had hoped, he dug his right hand into the pocket of his duck pants, the whole time watching Jessie from the corner of his eye. She looked as though she might bolt at any second. "Don't you be running away, now."

Jake steeled himself. Bull had made up his mind, and there was no getting around it. Jake put everything he could muster into a driving punch that hit the huge man smack between the eyes, knocking him backward. He rolled head over heels down the wide staircase with Jake right behind him. The fall would have killed the average man, but Bull was definitely *not* the average man.

He landed on his belly facing the bottom of the stairs, and was nearly to his feet by the time Jake reached him. Another punch snapped Bull's head up, and a straight right rocked him backward.

Bull just stood back and grinned. "I need to work off a little of your cheap whiskey, Weston, before I pleasure your new girl."

Jake stepped into the man with an overhead right. This time Bull easily blocked the punch and drove his own right to Jake's midsection. The blow winded him. He gasped for air and saw stars. Jake side-stepped a vicious left and dove to his right, ducking under a table and out the other side. As he gained his feet, Bull swept the table away and sent it crashing into the spectators. Jake groaned as he heard bets being placed by the crowd. One man held a pocket watch.

"Two to one Bull knocks him out in thirty seconds."

"Yer on!"

Jessie clutched the banister at the bottom of the stairs, the blood pounding in her ears. She had never seen a fight before, and Weston seemed completely overmatched. Good God, what would happen to her if he lost?

Jake paused and took a deep breath. He looked tired and hurt, and against her will, Jessie felt a surge of compassion for him. He was trying to protect her, and though she found the knowledge a little surprising, she also found it strangely comforting. Jessie held her breath as Bull lowered his head and charged. Jake kicked an overturned chair into his path and scooped up another while Bull tripped over the first. When Jake smashed the chair across Bull's broad back, shattering it, Jessie stifled a scream. Bull hit the floor hard, but quickly got to his feet once more.

"Boss!"

Jessie glanced at the bartender the same instant Jake did. The man flipped Jake a short wooden bat he had pulled from beneath the bar. Jake caught it in mid-air, and in the same easy motion, he cracked it across Bull's head. This time, Bull went down in a heap.

"Sonofabitch tore my ruffled shirt," Jake grumbled as Rupert and another man grabbed Bull by the arms, hauled him up, and started for the door.

"Wait," Jake said, "don't throw him out. He'll just come back. Take him upstairs. When he wakes up give him three free tokens."

Jessie raced up to him, a shiny dark tendril dangling across her cheek. "Wh-what?" she sputtered. "You're not going to throw him out? He tried . . . he wanted to . . . he would have . . ."

"So would the rest of these men." The look in Jake's blue eyes silenced her. "He's a good customer, but a bad enemy. If we threw out every man with a difference of opinion, we'd find ourselves drinking and gambling alone. I just hope he'll forget this little incident after he wakes up and has a few—*tokens*."

Jessie turned a furious red. "You could have solved the whole problem by explaining who I am."

"If you like, Miss Taggart, I'll take you up to Bull's room, and you can have a little talk with him when he comes to."

Jessie fought to control her temper. Any compassion she'd been feeling abruptly fled. "I wouldn't talk to Mr. . . . to *Bull*, here, or anywhere else for that matter! But I most certainly wouldn't talk to him with a club, Mr. Weston. That wasn't exactly Queensbury."

"And this isn't England, Miss Taggart. *Or* Boston—as I've been attempting to show you."

Jake glared at her, and she glared back. Neither spoke.

Finally, as the crowd scattered to the bar and tables, Jake put a hand on her waist and firmly escorted her toward the door. "I think you've had enough fun for the evening. I'll take you back to your hotel—it's a far more proper place for a lady."

Jessie stiffened. "Propriety has nothing to do with this, Mr. Weston. And next time, kindly refrain from breaking *our* chairs—since you have a bat for such things."

Jake gritted his teeth, but he didn't say a word. In truth, he was so damned glad she hadn't been hurt it was hard for him to stay angry. Watching Bull Haskin manhandle her had fired a surge of fury he hadn't expected. She was his partner, by God! If anyone was going to put his hands on her like that, it was going to be Jake Weston—though the thought that he wanted to do just that irritated him no end.

By the time they neared the Palace, Jessie had worked herself into a terrible temper.

"I promised myself I wouldn't let you goad me, Mr. Weston, but I find I cannot contain myself a moment more. That was a despicable thing to do. You could have told me Father owned a—a—"

"Whorehouse," Jake supplied.

"Well, yes. Instead you let me think it was a restaurant. We're supposed to be partners. You apparently think this is some kind of a game."

"If anyone sees this as a game, Miss Taggart, it's you. Your father's businesses need a man's hand. You have no place trying to run a saloon and bawdy house. Surely after tonight you can see that."

"What I see, Mr. Weston, is that you're trying to scare me off. For all I know, you paid that horrible man to maul me. You'd like nothing better than for me to sell out. And I'll just bet you'd be the first one in line with an offer."

Jake felt a twinge of guilt. "I *was* hoping you'd sell, Jessie, for your own good. But not at an unfair price. I mean to offer you ten thousand dollars in gold for your share of the Tin Angel, and six thousand dollars for the freighting business. I figured we could sell the river scows. They don't make much money anyway."

"You mean Father really did own some legitimate businesses?

"Like I said, Taggart Freighting and Yuba City Riverboats."

"Why, that's wonderful! After tonight, I assumed he had made those up as well."

"He owned 'em all right. Now *we* own them." The driver halted the horse in front of the Palace, and a doorman helped them down.

"Consider my proposal, Jessie," Jake said after they'd reached the front door. "You belong in Boston. You're a fine-looking woman. Plenty of men would be glad to take you as a wife. You should be raising a passel of kids instead of brawling in a whorehouse."

Jessie could barely contain her outrage. If she had ever considered selling to Jake, his words had put an end to that notion. "You just made up my mind, Jake Weston. I'm staying right here. I own fifty-one percent of Father's businesses, and that gives me the controlling share. From now on, you take orders from me. I'll meet you at the Angel at eight o'clock tomorrow morning. I'll expect a full accounting at that time."

"You can't be serious. We don't even close till four. Nobody's up that early."

"You'd better be, Jake. And starting tomorrow night, I intend to be there at closing. Four, you say?"

"Jessie, you can't possibly be out on the street at four in the morning. Bull Haskin's attentions will seem like a parlor dance compared to what you'll get from the rowdies out at that hour."

"I'll manage just fine, I assure you. Now if you'll excuse me, Mr. Weston, I believe, as you said, I've had enough fun for the evening. I'll see you at eight."

Furious, Jake watched her march haughtily through the glass hotel doors. Damn that woman! She'd be the death of him yet! But he didn't look away from her trim waist or the seductive sway of her hips until she disappeared from his view.

Jessie closed the door to her room and slumped against it. Lord, what an evening! It had been ten times worse than anything she could have possibly imagined. And that horrible man, Bull Something-or-other! Her face flamed again just thinking of the familiar way he'd touched her, the places he'd put his beefy hands. It was simply appalling. And Jake Weston was to blame.

Jessie stormed across the room, exhausted yet strangely keyed up. She'd have trouble falling asleep, she was sure. Her mind would replay the scene with Weston, and she'd get angry all over again.

Jessie fought the buttons at the back of her dress,

then stepped out of her clothes and into an embroidered cotton nightgown. After her battle with Bull, she'd love to have a bath, but she was just too darned tired. Instead, she slid beneath the sheets and wished fervently she could soothe her jittery nerves.

After tossing and turning for an hour, Jessie decided the only thing that would calm her down would be slapping Jake Weston's too-handsome face. How could her father have made a man like that her partner? Weston was a rogue and a bounder—and probably worse.

Even as she thought the words, Jessie remembered the concern she'd seen in Weston's eyes when Bull Haskin had dragged her up the stairs. She had to admit he'd saved her. From what exactly, she couldn't be sure—and she refused to guess. Unbidden, an image of Jake Weston hauling her up those same stairs slung over his broad shoulders flashed through her mind, followed by a warm, hollow sensation in the pit of her stomach. In contrast, she remembered Benjamin Keefer, the very proper young man she'd left in Boston. Ben was slim, fair-haired, and handsome. He'd courted her, held her hand, and finally kissed her. The sensation hadn't been unpleasant, so she'd allowed him to do it again on several other occasions.

On her trip West there'd been other men who had paid her court, but none had stirred the emotions Weston did. The tall blond Frenchman, Rene La Porte, had made his interest clear, although she hadn't seen him since. She'd enjoyed her conversation with Monsieur La Porte, but she most certainly hadn't considered kissing him—which, she discovered, was exactly what she'd been thinking about Jake.

What would it feel like? she wondered, and experienced another rush of warmth. Different, she was certain, but *how*, she couldn't be sure. Damn you, Jake Weston, she silently cursed, wishing he didn't occupy so much of her thoughts. And damn Henry Taggart for putting her in this position.

Thoughts of her father cooled Jessie's ire. Henry Taggart had been no fool. He'd had a reason for throwing them together. Maybe some good would come of this arrangement yet. Tomorrow she would know more. Yes, tomorrow at the Tin Angel her work would begin in earnest.

Tok Loy Hong sat in a huge carved chair on the top floor of the Gum San joss house, headquarters of the Gum San tong. His chair faced the broad windows at the rear of the fourth floor, overlooking the bay and the city below Grant Street. A warm glow bronzed the eastern sky. Tok Loy had always enjoyed the morning. The rising sun was the harbinger of things to come—new trials and new joys. But Tok Loy wasn't enjoying the view.

The tong could be in trouble.

Tok Loy sighed. His friend, Henry Taggart, had been murdered. But unlike most people, Tok Loy was certain that Henry hadn't been killed by one of the tongs. If Charley Sing had killed Taggart, he might have tried to place the blame on the Gum San, but he would never have left an Auspicious Laborers of the Sea hatchet buried in Taggart's chest. There were other tongs in San Francisco and across the bay in Vallejo, but none of them would have profited by the murder. No, the killer had to be somebody else. Someone who wanted to stir up trouble between the tongs—a white devil. No Oriental would have been so obvious. Simple clues for simple white minds—Tok Loy was *almost* certain.

Chapter 6

"I've been knocking for fifteen minutes!" Jessie said, her face flushed with the early-morning chill.

"Sorry, Miss Taggart." Rupert Scroggins stifled a yawn as he unlocked the front doors of the Tin Angel. "We don't normally open till ten."

"Where's Jake Weston?"

"Well, I suppose he's upstairs, but he's—"

Ignoring him, Jessie marched over to the stairs and started climbing, lifting her skirts away from the littered floor. Below her, Rupert gaped in amazement as she walked straight to the office, opened the door, and went in. Finding no one, she returned to the top of the stairs. "He's not in his office."

"Next room is his, but—"

With an indignant glare that cut him off, Jessie strode to the door and began banging away. It was just too bad if Jake Weston didn't want her interrupting his sleep. She beat on the door one last time, then turned the knob and shoved it open. In the sparsely furnished room, Jake sprawled across an old iron bed, his sensuous mouth curved in a contented smile. Beneath a red Navaho blanket that served as a quilt, he stirred a little, his dark hair curving against the pillow. His strong, suntanned hands rested atop his blanket-covered chest.

"You're late, Jake Weston," Jessie said. She was

already sorry she'd burst into his room but she was determined not to let him know it.

At the sound of her voice, Jake bolted upright and the blanket fell away. For a moment he seemed disoriented, unable to believe Jessica Taggart was standing in his room. He just sat there staring at her, then he growled and raked a hand through his rumpled hair.

"What the hell—"

"Don't curse at me, Jake Weston. I told you I'd be here at eight o'clock, and it's already eight-fifteen." It was all she could do to keep her eyes fixed on his face. She'd never seen a man's chest before, and Jake's seemed wider and darker than she could possible have imagined.

He reached onto the marble-topped table beside his bed and fumbled for his pocket watch. "Damned if it's not," he grumbled.

"I'll wait for you in your office."

"Very considerate." He threw her an icy glance and watched as her full lips tightened. She stopped at the doorway and glanced back just as he dropped the blanket, stretched, and yawned. A blotch of color brightened her cheeks, and her brows shot up.

"Apologize to your friend for my intrusion," she said curtly, abruptly turning away.

As she pulled the door shut, Jake looked quizzically in her direction, then back at the bed. Two of the four feather pillows he slept with formed a softly curving lump that looked decidedly female beneath the covers. He chuckled softly to himself and swung his long legs onto the hard wooden floor.

Serves her right, Jake thought as he poured cold water into the milk-white basin on the lowboy. With a tortoiseshell comb, he slicked back his hair, dressed, and crossed the room to the door. As he walked into the hall, he turned and loudly addressed the vacant bed. "You go on back to sleep, sweetheart. I'll join you again just as soon as Miss Taggart leaves.''

Fighting a grin, he entered his office.

Jessie didn't miss the smug amusement in Jake Weston's bright blue eyes. She should have expected something like that from a man like him! Still, it bothered her to think of him with a woman—and the fact that it did fired her temper even more.

''I'll expect you to keep our appointments in the future, Mr. Weston,'' she said, sitting ramrod straight in the side chair next to his rolltop desk. ''*If* we have a future.''

''You agreed to call me Jake.''

''I've decided to reserve my decision about that until we've had this meeting, Mr. Weston.''

''As you wish, *Jessie*,'' he said. Stifling a yawn with his hand, he rolled up the desk top, reached into a humidor, and removed a thin cigar.

''Must you smoke?'' she asked waspishly, desperately fighting the hurt and anger she had no right to feel. Why should she care *who* Jake Weston took to bed? He was her partner, nothing more. The memory of his wide muscular chest, lightly covered with curly black hair, flashed across her mind. A scar marked one shoulder, and she wondered how he had gotten it. She could easily recall the way his body tapered, vee-shaped, to his narrow waist.

Jessie shoved the image away. Why, the man was probably as heathen in bed as he was everywhere else! Still, she felt a second sharp stab of jealousy. God in heaven! What in the world is the matter with me?

Jake paused as he brought a match near the tip of his cigar. Damned sassy schoolgirl, he thought. Busts into my room, accosts me in bed, and now she's telling me not to smoke!

With grand ceremony, he held the match to the end of the cigar and drew the flame in several times. Then he exhaled, expelling the smoke across the five-foot distance that separated them. As it billowed around Jessie's face, he smiled, enjoying her displeasure. "Now, Jess, what brings you out so early?"

"I . . . I . . ." Unable to control herself, she coughed discreetly behind her hand, then dug into her reticule to fish out a handkerchief, which she held beneath her nose.

Jake smiled with satisfaction.

Jessie ignored him. Instead, she rose and walked over to the window. Determined to make her point, she tugged at the latch, discovered the window was stuck, and dropped her reticule in the process. Jake shoved his cigar between his teeth and strode over to retrieve her cloth bag, but he didn't open the window.

Throwing him a furious sidelong glance, Jessie went to a chair in the far corner and sat down. Tilting her chin for effect, she dabbed at her nose several more times with the hanky.

"If you must smoke those foul things, we'll be forced to communicate from a distance," she said frostily.

Jake returned to his swivel chair and sat down. Crossing his legs, he tossed her a satisfied look. Extending the cigar at arm's length, he smiled at her and explained, "Breakfast."

Jessie's eyes grew wide. "I figured you for a man who breakfasts on beer or whiskey," she retorted, purposely flashing him her most insincere smile. He grinned.

"Good idea. Too bad I don't have a raw egg to crack in it." Reaching for the decanter of brandy resting atop the desk, he poured a dollop into one of the miniature snifters beside it. As he settled back in his chair, his eyes sparkled with mischief.

"I warn you, Mr. Weston, you'll need a clear head for this conversation."

"I'll keep it to less than a quart," he promised.

Rising, Jessie clasped her hands in front of her and began to pace. "I'm the first one to realize that a woman is at a . . . a certain disadvantage when it comes to doing business." She glanced at Jake, who nodded smugly but said nothing. He obviously hoped she had come to her senses and was about to accept his offer. "Mr. Weston, I want you to know I have an excellent education, the best money can buy."

Jake's smile began to fade. He took a deep swallow of brandy.

"Also, my father often allowed me to travel with him. He taught me a lot about business. Granted, I was young and inexperienced, but with a little time and effort on my part, I believe I can do as competent job as any man."

With a single long gulp, Jake drained his glass and came to his feet. "Jessie, this is no schoolgirl game. The time you spent with Henry couldn't begin to prepare you for the business world, to say nothing of *this* sort of business."

"Will you at least hear me out? I've come a long way, Mr. Weston. I think it's the least you can do."

Jake smiled thinly. "I'm sorry. From now on you have my undivided attention." How could she not? She was the finest-looking woman he'd seen in years. He was hard-pressed not to admire the fiery determination in her lovely green eyes, the stubborn set to her chin. She was something, all right—proud, intelligent, beautiful. Just for an instant, he hoped she wouldn't sell out. Then his common sense returned.

"My father wouldn't have left me the businesses if he didn't have faith in my abilities," she told him. "He would have instructed his attorney to sell my share of Taggart Enterprises and forward the proceeds to me. I know in my heart he wanted me to carry on. He believed that I *could* do it."

Jake kept his expression carefully blank.

"Now, as to our relationship." She began to pace again. "You may assist me in that endeavor, or you may continue to act at cross purposes. But Mr. McCafferty has informed me that I have every right to remove you from the premises if you don't offer me your full cooperation."

Jake felt heat rise at the back of his neck. Unconsciously, he balled his hands into fists, but he didn't say a word.

"As I said, you may assist me, or you may leave the management up to me. I realize I have a great deal to learn. I know nothing of the freighting business, of the riverboat operations, and certainly nothing of the saloon and . . . and . . ."

"Whorehouse," Jake supplied.

Jessie glanced away nervously. "I prefer to think of them as ladies of the evening." She fiddled with a long shiny strand of mahogany hair. "To put it bluntly, Mr. Weston, I could use your help."

Smiling dryly, Jake thought that had to be the understatement of the year.

"But it has to be just that," Jessie continued, "help, not hindrance."

"Jessie, you don't realize what this means."

"My mind is made up, Jake. I'm going to carry on—with or without you."

"You won't consider my offer to buy your half—to relieve you of this burden?"

"Absolutely not." She paused. "As a matter of fact, at breakfast this morning, Mr. McCafferty offered me considerably more money for my share."

Jake's head shot up. "McCafferty offered to buy you out?"

"Yes, he did. He was representing a client who wished to remain anonymous. But you don't have to worry, I turned him down, too."

Jake felt a second surge of anger. This was a development he hadn't considered. Horace McCafferty and whoever he represented were the last people

Jake wanted for partners. Even Jessica Taggart would be better than that two-faced lawyer—at least he hoped so. "If that's your final word, Jessie, then I guess you leave me no choice."

"No choice at all," she said, meeting his eyes squarely.

Jake stubbed out his cigar and walked to the window. Below him, the street was beginning to bustle with morning activity. Horses pulled wagons loaded with supplies, flatbeds rolled down the lane loaded with lumber, a milk wagon rumbled by. Jake watched the procession for a moment. Then he turned to face Jessie and extended his hand. "Partners?"

She smiled genuinely for the first time since she'd arrived, and Jake grudgingly confirmed that she really was a beauty.

"Partners."

When she wet her lips before speaking again, Jake felt a jolt of heat that went all the way to his boots. She was something, he repeated to himself—a pretty bit of baggage that he found himself more and more attracted to.

That thought fled as she marched purposefully toward his desk.

"Let's get to work," she said. "Unless your *pleasure* comes before your business."

Jake thought of the lump of pillows in his empty bed that Jessie had thought was a woman, eyed her full round bosom and wisp of a waist—and began to question his decision to continue working with her.

Jessie worked with Jake all morning. He yawned continually, and even nodded off once while she was working on the ledgers, but overall he was helpful, even fairly congenial. As she questioned him about the Angel's earnings—which endeavors made the most, which the least, how the earnings were spent and why—she could have sworn he began to answer with a little less smugness, a little more sincerity than he had ever shown her before.

"Your daddy always said you were more than a pretty face," he told her with a teasing grin when she discovered an error in the bank account that even he had missed. The error was in their favor, and Jake seemed pleased. "I guess all that money Henry spent on your education paid off after all."

"Thank you," she said. "I think." They laughed together for the first time, and Jessie was struck by how handsome Jake looked when he relaxed and lost his scowl.

By the end of the morning, they'd finished only half of the books, but they'd made a good start. Jake then showed Jessie around the Tin Angel, a tour that went smoothly until they passed one of the girls in the hallway. Wearing a flimsy negligee that clearly revealed her rosy nipples, the girl flirted brazenly with Jake, running a hand along the inside of his thigh in an unmistakably lewd gesture.

"Mornin', Jake darlin'," she said, wetting the corner of her red mouth with the tip of her tongue. "Anything I can do for you today?"

With a wry half smile, Jake just shook his head. "I'm busy, Rosy. Maybe next time."

"You better watch out for him, Miss Jessie," she said. "Jake's a wolf in wolf's clothing. He looks like a scoundrel—and he *is* one." Rosy laughed huskily and winked at Jessie.

Jessie blushed from head to toe. "I'll remember that, Rosy," she said, looking askance at Jake, who leaned casually against the doorjamb. He was wearing a loose white shirt open at the throat, his thick black chest hair curling suggestively against his bronze skin. His legs were long and lean, and he was so tall that the top of his head barely cleared the doorway.

"I take it Rosy is another of your early-morning friends," she said peevishly.

"For your information, Miss Taggart," he answered just as tartly, "I don't dip my pen in the company ink."

"What's that supposed to mean?"

"It means running the Tin Angel is my job. I keep business strictly business. As for the way Rosy talks, if you're going to own a whorehouse, you'd better get used to a little rough language. It's a way of life for them. They don't mean anything by it."

"Then you're not a wolf?" she pressed.

Jake just grinned. "Wouldn't be much of a man if I was completely immune to the ladies' charms, would I?"

Jessie didn't answer. She wondered why it irritated her so much that women found him attractive. There was certainly nothing she could do about it. Refusing to dwell on thoughts of Jake Weston, Jessie continued her tour. She met Paco, a dark-skinned Peruvian boy about nine years old who smiled shyly at her, and Jake explained that the child lived in the basement and helped with the cleaning.

"Mr. Jake give me job," the boy said, careful to keep his eyes cast down. When he looked up at her, she read his uncertainty. "I work hard, señorita. Very hard. Mr. Jake tell you."

"I'm sure you do, Paco. I'm glad you're here." His face lit up in a smile of relief.

"Thank you, señorita. You need anything, anything at all, just call Paco." Turning, he raced off toward the stairs.

Jake smiled down at her with something akin to approval. "I think you've made a friend," he said.

"He seemed to think I was going to toss him out in the street," Jessie said.

"He's had a hard life. He still doesn't trust most people."

"He trusts you, I think." Jessie said as Jake's blue eyes fastened on hers, his gaze unwavering.

"I hope you'll come to trust me, too," he said softly.

Jessie turned away without answering, but she didn't forget the gentle note in his voice.

After her tour, she went back to work on the books. She left several hours later, vowing to return that night, although Jake tried to talk her out of it.

"You keep showing up around here, and people will get the wrong idea."

"They'll get the idea that I own this place as much as you do."

Jake groaned aloud, his temper beginning to build. "Damn it, you're a woman! Didn't your mother ever teach you that?"

"My mother tried. My father never attempted to mold me into something I'm not."

"What you are, Miss Taggart, is a spoiled little girl who hasn't learned her place."

"Talk like that will get us nowhere, Mr. Weston. I'll see you tonight." Jake just scowled as Jessie walked away.

From the railing that ran along the second floor, Jake surveyed the long bar teeming with boisterous patrons and the satin-clad ladies who entertained them. Saturday night was the biggest night of the week at the Tin Angel.

Most of the men working the Tenderloin and the waterfront had been paid today, and some of them were already so drunk that Paddy Fitzpatrick had to break up their fights and throw the more recalcitrant ones out into the street. Although the evening had just begun, the upper level of the room was already darkened by the haze of smoke.

Adjusting his four-in-hand tie, Jake started down the stairs.

Five Chinese merchants sat at the closest table, while several more stood around the outside. The upside-down bowl in the center of the table was righted as Jake approached, exposing a pile of coins. Most of the saloons forbade the game of fantan in their establishments, since it encouraged a Chinese patronage, but old man Taggart had allowed it, occasionally even joining in.

Beyond the group of Chinese several faro tables were set up, house dealers deftly moving the cards from the boxes. In some houses, the dealing boxes were referred to as tell boxes, for with the right mechanical manipulation, the dealer could tell what the next few cards would be. But Henry Taggart had insisted on an honest deal for the players, and Jake was determined to carry on that tradition.

Even this early, the floor was littered with peanut shells and eggshells, and Paco hurried from spot to spot with a whisk broom and scoop. Against the wall near the rear door, Mormon Pete, the piano player, banged out an impromptu rendition of "Buffalo Gals."

Moving from table to table, Jake spoke with dealers and players, wishing his patrons luck even though he knew the odds were in the house's favor. He skirted the roulette table, working his way instead through the group of men lining the long bar three deep.

"Rupert," he called down the bar as he approached. Glancing up, Rupert made his way back to where Jake stood, one shiny black boot propped against the gleaming brass rail.

"Yeah, boss?"

"Where's Paddy?"

"He just assisted a gentleman out into the street. He'll be back in a minute." Rupert swirled a towel over a puddle of beer. "The sheriff's at the other end of the bar asking for you."

"Pour him a whiskey on the house and tell him to join me upstairs. And send Paddy to my office as soon as he gets a spare minute."

"Yes, sir."

Jake headed toward the stairs through a circle of women in brightly colored, low-cut dresses and tantalizing black net stockings. He climbed to the landing, where he watched the sheriff—a tall, angular-faced man with a floppy-brimmed hat and a cigar that stuck out from under his handlebar mustache—make his way through the crowd. His narrow-set eyes searched the room looking for Jake as Isaac Handley moved along, one barrel-shaped deputy parting the crowd ahead of him, another walking behind.

After motioning his men to stay below, Handley reached the midpoint landing and extended his hand to Jake. They shook. From the corner of his eye, Jake caught the bulge of the ivory-handled Colt .44 the sheriff carried under his coat. Both deputies carried shotguns across their shoulders.

I sure as hell wouldn't want his job, Jake thought as he and the sheriff climbed the stairs side by side. "I've got some fine Franciscan brandy in my office," Jake told him. "You deserve better than bar whiskey."

Isaac nodded and flashed a grateful smile.

"What brings you to the Tin Angel?" Jake asked.

"Thought I might run into your new partner." The sheriff's eyes crinkled with amusement. "Rumor has it she'll be takin' an active hand in ramrodin' the place."

Ignoring the jibe, Jake opened the office door and stood aside as the tall man entered. Handley had taken on the Taggart murder case, although normally the city marshal would have handled it. Isaac had been dealing with the Chinese problem at the mining camps and since Henry's murder investigation involved the tongs, the sheriff had been assigned the case.

Handley took a seat while Jake poured them each a snifter of brandy, then perched on the edge of his desk.

"Jessie Taggart is a strong young woman, Isaac," Jake said, "and she seems a decent one. I don't think she'll be spending much time around the Tin Angel."

"Well, I need to have a chat with her, so the next time you check with your boss," he said, his eyes crinkling again, "tell her to drop by my office."

Jake nodded. He didn't mention the trouble he'd taken to shield Jessie from learning about her father's murder. He'd been worried as hell someone would say something at the funeral, but for once folks had used the good sense God gave them and kept quiet.

"Anything new turn up?" Jake asked.

"The track is colder than a whore's heart and getting colder. Maybe the daughter can be of some help."

Jake drained the snifter. Now that Jessie had decided to stay in San Francisco, there was no way around it. He'd have to tell her the details of her father's death. The chore would not be a pleasant one, but the news would sound a helluva lot better coming from him than from a stranger.

"I'd best be gittin' back to business," Isaac said, finishing his drink and heading toward the door.

Jake just nodded. Absently, he pulled his gold watch from the pocket of his waistcoat to check the time. Where the hell is she? he wondered, beginning to worry. She'd said she was coming, but now he was glad that she'd missed Isaac.

As the sheriff opened the door, Paddy Fitzpatrick stepped in, his huge bulk filling the door frame.

"You wanted to see me, boss?" Noticing the sheriff, Paddy stepped aside.

"I'll be right with you," Jake said. As he and Handley entered the hall, Jake slapped the lanky sheriff on the shoulder. "Isaac, you take care now," he said, then waved Paddy inside.

"I'm getting worried about the Taggart girl," Jake

told him. "She should have been here by now. I want you to go to the Palace Hotel, find her, and stick with her. I don't want her coming into the Tenderloin alone."

Paddy shook his head, his massive shoulders hunching forward and straining at the frayed blue jacket he wore. Beads of perspiration glistened on his balding pate and crooked nose.

"She as pretty as they say, boss?" Paddy grinned and raised his right eyebrow, which was bisected by a vertical scar. After an overhand punch, the brow hadn't healed correctly. The inside half was a quarter inch lower than the outside, giving Paddy a look of perpetual surprise.

"She's pretty, all right. That's one of the reasons I want you to watch out for her. In fact, I think it would be a good idea if you took Miss Jessica Taggart under your wing for a while."

Paddy glanced from one massive arm to the other, as if to see if he were growing wings.

"What I mean," Jake explained, "is to sort of watch over her . . . like a big brother."

Paddy rubbed a cauliflower ear and cocked his head like a pug-faced bulldog watching his master. "All the time, boss?"

"Except when she's sleeping. Paddy."

"I shouldn't watch when she's sleeping, boss?"

"No, Paddy. She might think that was watching a little too close."

"Okay, boss. Whatever you say."

Paddy lumbered to the door, stopped and turned back. "Should I sleep outside her door, boss?"

"I don't think that'll be necessary, Paddy. You can sleep in your own bed in the basement. You just make sure she gets safely to her room at the hotel, then be back outside her door before she leaves in the morning."

Paddy let the information soak in a moment. Then, with a grin, he pulled the door closed. Jake shook his head. Paddy was as loyal as a puppy, as big and strong as a bear, but he'd been hit a few too many times. Jake had seen him fight dozens of men, taking blows from chairs, mugs, bottles, and fists—but he'd never seen Paddy lose his temper. He just did what he had to do, over and over again.

With Paddy watching over Jessie, it would take a small army to do her harm.

Jake walked down the hallway and over to the rail, surveying the hall as Paddy made his way back down the stairs. Damn, he thought, spotting Jessie near the front doors talking with the sheriff. Even from a distance he could see the color drain from her cheeks. She suddenly swayed on her feet, and the tall man reached out to steady her. She shook off his hand and squared her shoulders, as if denying his words.

Jake wasn't sure whether he should go to her now or wait until the sheriff had answered her questions. Damn, he thought. I should have told her in the first place. Now there'd be hell to pay, and I probably deserve it.

He didn't have long to wait. Isaac spoke to her a few minutes more, then Jessie turned and headed toward the stairs. There was no mistaking the angry set to her shoulders, the determination in her stride. Even as grim as she looked, the swing of her slender hips turned the head of every man in the saloon.

Paddy met her halfway to the stairs, spun around, and followed her. She glanced up toward the balcony, and her eyes flashed fiery green sparks as they locked with Jake's.

Jake removed a cigar from his waistcoat and bit off the end. He could see what kind of a greeting this was going to be.

Chapter 7

Her eyes bright with tears that she refused to shed, Jessie stormed toward the stairs. How could he have failed to tell her the truth? How could he have been so cruel? She had almost reached the bottom step when she stopped and turned back, heading instead to the bar.

"Rupert, I'd appreciate it if you would kindly pour me a drink." She was surprised her words came out so evenly. A little uncertain, Rupert filled a shot glass with whiskey and handed it to her. Jessie closed her eyes and took a sip, feeling the fiery liquid burn her throat and warm her stomach. A little of her control returned.

"Thank you," she managed, stifling a sudden urge to cough. She took another sip and set the glass back down on the bar. Taking a deep breath, she lifted her black silk skirts up and continued toward the stairs. She would not let Jake Weston know how much she ached inside. She refused to reveal her weakness.

"Why didn't you tell me my father was murdered?" she demanded when she reached his side.

Jake took a deep drag on his cigar and let the smoke roll slowly out over the rail. "I would have, Jess, but you had enough problems to face. I wanted to give you some time."

"Do you know who killed my father?"

His blue eyes darkened. He clamped down hard on his cigar, working a muscle in his jaw before he spoke. "If I knew who did it, Jess, they'd be crow bait hanging from the eaves of the Tin Angel."

"I notice you've got quite a Chinese clientele. The sheriff said that the tongs might be involved, which seems quite convenient for you. If I were Sheriff Handley, I would think Jake Weston had the most to profit from my father's murder."

Jake's mouth tightened in a narrow, angry line. "And if I were Jessica Taggart, I'd realize that I was not too old to get my backside tanned in front of a saloon full of men and whores. If you were a man, you'd already be arse over teakettle down those stairs and out in the street."

Jessie backed up a step, but her eyes still flashed. "Don't you dare try to throw me out of my own place, Jake Weston."

Jake took a long slow breath, obviously fighting for control. "Henry was my friend, Jessie. Almost a father to me. I don't know who killed him, but the whole town knows I've offered a thousand-dollar reward for information leading to the man who did. I didn't tell you how he died because I wanted to spare your feelings."

He watched for her reaction, which she carefully kept blank, then his features softened. "This is a tough town, Jess. Paddy here"—he indicated the brawny Irishman who stood beside him and Jessie turned, assessing the man for the first time—"is going to stay close to you . . . sort of watch over you."

"I don't need watching over," she said stonily.

"Tell Bull Haskin that."

Jessie felt the heat creep into her cheeks while a corner of Jake's mouth tilted in an amused half smile. Paddy stood aside, his knotted hands folded in front of him. Jessie watched him briefly, then returned her attention to Jake.

"Is he supposed to watch me, or spy on me for you?" she asked curtly.

"You are the most infuriating—"

"Which is it?" Jessie demanded.

"He's working for *you*, Miss Taggart."

"Then pay him out of my half of the Angel."

"Done."

"You're working for me now, Mr. . . . ?"

"Paddy," the brawny man said slowly, as if she weren't too bright.

"Paddy. Do you understand?"

"Yes, mum."

"Only me."

"Yes, mum."

"I'd like to take another look at the ledgers," Jessie said to Jake. Just how much longer she could maintain her careful self-control she wasn't sure, but she was not about to break down in front of Jake. Without waiting for his reply, she spun on her heel and headed down the hall toward his office.

Paddy hesitated a moment. "You shouldn't ought to talk to a lady about her backside, boss—er—is it Mr. Jake now?"

"Call me anything you damned well please," Jake snapped.

Paddy just nodded and followed Jessie down the hall.

"Damn," Jake muttered. He watched her go into his office as Paddy took up a position outside the door. I'll be a sonofabitch, he thought. Pairing Jessie's brain with Paddy's brawn—I hope I haven't created a monster.

Jake entered his office to find Jessie sitting at his desk opening one drawer after another.

"I don't suppose you think I deserve a little privacy?" he asked.

"This was my father's office too, wasn't it?"

Jake didn't answer. Instead, he pulled open a heavy oak drawer and lifted out the leather-bound volume containing the Tin Angel's records. "You can go over these till the cows come home, but you won't find any inconsistencies."

"I hope that's true, Mr. Weston, for your sake."

Jake shut his jaw against the biting retort he wanted to make. "I'll be downstairs if you have any questions," he choked out instead.

"As you found out this morning, I am quite capable of reading these without any help from you," Jessie said without looking up.

Jake just glowered at her as he turned and stalked out of the room.

Hearing the door slam, Jessie let her shoulders sag. The tears she'd fought so hard to hold back welled up and rolled down her cheeks. Her father dying because of a failing heart she could have accepted—but murder was a far different matter. Leaning over the desk, Jessie buried her face in her folded arms and sobbed out her grief.

As he headed down the hall, Jake remembered a second volume of records containing payments to local politicians he kept in a secret compartment of his desk. Grumbling at the thought of another scene with Jessie, he returned to his office and pulled open the door. The sight that greeted him stopped him dead in his tracks. Prim and proper Jessica Taggart, in her high-necked black mourning dress, was slumped over his rolltop desk crying her heart out.

Jessie's slender frame shook with the force of her sorrow, and Jake realized for the first time how much of her grief she'd kept locked up inside. With a soft click of the latch, he closed the door behind him. As he crossed the room, his boots rang on the oak plank floor, and Jessie's head shot up. Like a guilty child, she sprang to her feet, quickly brushing the tears from her cheeks.

"What do you want?" she asked. Her voice was defiant, but he didn't miss the undertone of despair.

"I forgot to give you the second ledger. Are you all right?"

"I'm fine," she replied stiffly. "I just got something in my eye."

Jake moved closer. "Listen to me, Jess. It's all right to show your feelings. Your father was a good man. We're all going to miss him."

A tiny sob caught in her throat, the sound unmistakably feminine, and her bottom lip trembled. "It's just that . . . it's just that . . . Oh, God, it was such a horrible way for him to die!" The last of her composure fled, and a fresh flood of tears cascaded down her cheeks.

Without thinking, Jake pulled her into his arms, one hand slipping into her thick mass of shiny dark hair as he cradled her head against his shoulder. Jessie didn't resist. She leaned into him, sobbing violently, her fingers clutching the front of his coat. Her tears fell until they dampened his shirt, and, although he fought against it, he felt a surge of protectiveness for the feisty dark-haired girl.

"It's all right, honey," he said softly, pressing her tighter against his chest. "He's beyond hurting now." Jake's hand moved soothingly over her back, trying to ease her pain.

For the first time in days, Jessie let her guard down. It felt so good to be held in a man's strong arms, to feel protected and cared for, as if she weren't so all alone. She wanted to forget about her father's murder, forget the Tin Angel, forget that she was by herself in the world and more than a little bit lonely.

As her sobs quieted to a series of soft hiccups, Jessie realized one of Jake's hands was caressing her back, while the other gently massaged the tense muscles in her neck. Leaning against him, she felt his powerful muscles flexing as he worked, and a sudden warmth ignited in the pit of her stomach.

Like rain on a picnic, the thought came unbidden.

Was she seeking comfort from her partner—a man her father trusted and admired? Or was Weston a crook—a criminal who had cheated and murdered her father for a share of his businesses? Although her instincts told her she could trust Jake, it was far too soon to tell.

Taking a shaky breath, Jessie forced herself to pull away. "I'll be all right now. Thank you, Jake."

"My pleasure," he said with a smile that touched her heart and made her think of things other than her father's death and her growing list of problems.

Was that exactly what he meant to do? Disarm her with kindness and his too-handsome face? Suddenly Jessie remembered with vivid clarity the woman in his bed just that morning. She squared her shoulders and moved away from his reach. "I apologize for acting so childishly. I assure you it won't happen again."

"There's nothing childish about loving someone, Jess." Jake's softly spoken words nearly unsettled her again.

"You can go back to work now," she told him, forcing a hardness into her voice she didn't feel. "I have a lot of work to do before I'm satisfied there are no errors or oversights in our accounts."

"Fine," Jake said, his voice suddenly matching hers in coldness. He left abruptly, and Jessie watched him close the door.

It was as if the gentle interlude between them had never happened, and Jessie breathed a silent prayer of thanks. The last thing she needed was kindness from Jake Weston. She didn't want to be indebted to him, or anyone else.

Sunday night wasn't much different than Saturday, Jake thought as he wandered around the saloon in the early evening. He spoke to the players and the men drinking at the bar, but his thoughts kept drifting to Jessie and the mixed emotions she stirred in him.

Holding her in his arms the previous night had felt good—too damned good. He could easily recall the silky feel of her hair, her incredibly tiny waist. The last thing he needed was to get involved with a Boston schoolgirl, especially the daughter of his best friend. Yet he couldn't help wondering what it would be like to kiss those full lips, or how her breasts would feel in his hands.

I need a woman, he decided. A flesh and blood woman, not just a lump of pillows. After Jessie finally left for the evening, he'd go over to the Golden Thorn and visit Monique. If anyone could make him forget Miss Boston Taggart, Monique Dubois could. Jake smiled and felt a whole lot better.

While the ivory ball on the roulette table clattered to a halt, he slowed to watch the players at one of the poker tables. Horace McCafferty and Rene La Porte sat playing seven-card stud with Kaz Bochek, the manager of the Wells, Fargo and Company San Francisco freight station, and Don Ignacio Gutierrez, once a wealthy California landowner. McCafferty's patronage had never been on the top of Jake's list, and was even less so now that he had involved himself in Taggart business. Jake liked Bochek and La Porte little better, but he'd learned a long time ago that one man's money was as good as the next's.

Nearing the table, he realized Kaz Bochek was speaking to him. "How about joining the game and giving us a chance to win back a little of the money you charge for your watered-down whiskey?" A big, brawny, hard-faced man, Bochek rarely had anything good to say.

"I don't water the whiskey, Bochek, but I'll be happy to take your money—whether it's for booze or cards doesn't make a tinker's damn to me." Though he rarely joined a game anymore, Jake took the last of the five chairs at the table.

"It's a ten-dollar limit, three raises, jokers wild with aces, straights, and flushes," McCafferty told him.

"How is your pretty new partner?" La Porte asked with his soft French accent. "Or is it *boss?*" He curled one side of his mouth in a lazy smile, never taking his eyes off his cards.

"It's partner," Jake replied, a little irritated by La Porte's intimate tone. He'd be damned if he'd discuss Jessie with the slick-talking Frenchman. Instead he calmly placed his bet and picked up his cards.

By the end of the first few hands, Jake began to suspect that McCafferty and Bochek were somehow communicating their hands. It gave them little advantage in a five-handed game, but it was just the sort of cheap trick Jake figured them for.

In the next hand, Bochek raised heavily and Jake called. Bochek turned over three kings and reached for the money.

"Not so fast, Bochek." Jake smiled, turning over his cards to reveal his full house, aces over threes. Bochek's expression grew sour. He flashed a murderous glance at McCafferty, who looked back at him sheepishly.

The next few hands were won alternately by Jake and La Porte, even with Bochek and McCafferty's shoddy attempts to cheat. Don Ignacio continued to lose, a fact that didn't surprise Jake, since the old man rarely won. By the end of the first hour of play, Jake had amassed a sizable pot and was beginning to enjoy himself. As the cards were dealt again, La Porte turned the conversation in Jake's direction, fingering the large diamond pin in his ascot.

"So, Monsieur Weston, how are the other Taggart businesses doing?"

"We've had our share of trouble lately, but aside from that, the scows are carrying more and more of the river traffic, what with the new gold strike up near Marysville. And thanks to Alec Abernathy, Bochek gives up a little more of the freighting business out of Jackson and Stockton every month." A hard-working station manager, Abernathy had been steadily gaining Wells, Fargo business.

"Only what we don't have room to handle," Bochek snarled at Jake.

"I thought perhaps," La Porte put in, "you might be ready to sell either the scows or the wagons by now."

"Or maybe both," Bochek added with a raised eyebrow.

The table grew quiet, as if they were all interested in Jake's answer. "As Horace here knows, my partner hasn't indicated any interest in selling out. And if she did, I'd be buying. My interest is not for sale, gentlemen."

"Mr. Weston is quite correct," Jessie said from behind Rene La Porte's wide shoulder. "I find I'm beginning to enjoy being a businesswoman."

Jake shoved back his chair and rose to his feet, as did the others at the table—all except Bochek. "Gentlemen, please meet my partner, Miss Jessica Taggart."

"Miss Taggart and I became acquainted on the train," La Porte said with a predatory smile. "For me, the journey from Reno was far too short."

Jessie laughed softly.

"And I, of course," Horace put in, "represent Miss Taggart's business interests."

"Please, gentlemen," Jessie said, "don't let me interrupt your game." The men sat back down, and Bochek began to deal. "Oh, and Mr. Weston, before I forget," she added, "I was hoping you could take me to see the Yuba City Riverboat operation tomorrow."

Spreading his cards, Jake answered without glancing up. "I'm afraid I've got plans for the next few days. I've arranged for you to see the operation next week. Monday, if that's all right with you."

"I suppose I have plenty to learn around here in the meantime," Jessie said, "but I would like to take a trip along the delivery route up the river."

Jake stifled a groan. The last thing he wanted was to take a boat ride on one of those leaky old tubs. His stomach rolled at the very thought. "Paddy can take you."

"I'd rather you went along," Jessie said. "I might have some questions."

"I've got plans," he told her evasively. She looked disappointed, but he'd be damned if he'd let her find out he got seasick.

La Porte won the next big pot. With a smile, he looked up at Jessie, who still stood behind him. "You have brought me luck, *chérie.*" La Porte caught her fingers and brought them to his lips.

Jake's jaw tightened. Jessie pulled her hand away, her cheeks flushed, and La Porte gathered up the pot that included a hundred dollars of Jake's money and the last of Don Ignacio's.

Kaz Bochek reached into his pocket, pulled the old man's marker out, and threw it on the table. "How are you going to pay this, Don Ignacio?"

"Come to my hacienda, Senor Bochek. We will discuss it there." The old man looked tired as he stood and shuffled away from the table.

"That's the fourth marker I've taken from that old greaser in the last two months," Bochek said. "The first time I was paid in cattle. About all he's got left is a few scrubby acres and an old adobe. Looks like I'll have to take a mortgage on that."

"He keeps trying to win back his losses," Jake said.

"It's a pity," Rene added. "A few years ago, the Gutierrez land grant comprised thousands of acres."

"Hell, if you can't hang on to what's yours, you deserve to lose it," Bochek said.

Jake clamped down on his thin black cigar. "Why

don't you just deal, Bochek, and stop flapping your jaws?''

"What's the matter, Weston?'' Bochek snapped. "Can't wait to lose your money?'' He shuffled the cards, his eyes boring into Jake.

"I believe I will sit this one out.'' Rene La Porte stood and offered his arm to Jessie. She smiled up at him and let him guide her to a table in the corner.

After a glance in their direction, Jake lost the next four hands, one after another. "My luck's run dry, gents,'' he said, shoving back his chair with a rough grating sound.

"Give me a call, Weston,'' Bochek said, "when you're ready to sell. I might know an interested party.''

"Don't hold your breath.'' Jake turned from the game and took a step toward the bar.

"Better to sell while you're ahead.'' Leaning back in his chair, Bochek took a drink of his whiskey.

"What the hell is that supposed to mean?'' Jake asked, suddenly wary.

Bochek shrugged. "Don't mean nothin' special. It's just that old man Taggart died before he could sell out and enjoy his money. Smart fella would consider gettin' out . . . while the gettin' is good.''

"Not for sale,'' Jake said slowly, stressing each word. He cut his gaze to McCafferty. "Not for sale.''

Both McCafferty and Bochek shrugged and studied their cards. Jake turned on his heel, strode to the bar, and ordered a whiskey. Jessie and Rene La Porte sat in a far corner, laughing over a bottle of champagne.

"Gimme three fingers of Who Hit John,'' Jake said to Rupert, downing the fiery liquid in a single gulp. "Now, give me another.'' He slammed down his shot glass, and Rupert hurried to refill it.

As Jake lifted the glass and studied the amber liquid, Lovey McDougal walked up beside him. "Somethin' not goin' right, Jake?''

"Not something—everything."

"Seems like Miss Jessie and that handsome Frenchman is gettin' on real well. Now, if she was to up and get married, a husband wouldn't want her hanging around a place like this. Might solve all your problems."

"Don't you have some customers waiting?" Jake tossed back his second drink.

"No," Lovey snapped, "but those five drunken Chinamen are better company than you, Jake Weston." Raising her chin proudly, she started toward the fantan table.

Jake grabbed her plump arm. "I'm sorry, Lovey. You're right, I don't know what's gnawing at me."

"I do, but you wouldn't believe me if I told you." Lovey leaned over and gave him a peck on the cheek. "You're still my favorite fella."

"Thanks, Lovey." Jake managed a smile, then bristled again. Kaz Bochek and Horace McCafferty had stopped playing cards and were talking to Jessie and Rene La Porte. La Porte poured them each a glass of champagne, and they all toasted to something.

As Kaz and Horace drained their drinks and tipped their hats to Jessie, her clear laughter echoed above the noise of the saloon. She leaned over the table to catch something La Porte was saying, and Jake's stomach curled into a hard, tight ball.

"You're not only as grumpy as a kicked cat," Lovey said, "you *look* like a kicked cat." With a knowing glance, she flounced away.

"That's it," Jake said to no one in particular. Slamming his glass down on the bar, he headed in Jessie's direction.

Chapter 8

"So, *chérie*, you will dine with me tomorrow night?'' Covering Jessie's fingers with his manicured hand, Rene smiled down at her.

Jessie smiled back. "I think that would be—'' Before she could finish, Jake strode up to them. His jaw was tightly clamped, and he had a dark expression on his face.

"We need to talk," he said to Jessie through clenched teeth. "Now.'' Grabbing her arm, he hauled her to her feet.

Rene's softly accented voice stopped him. "The lady was speaking to me, Monsieur Weston. I believe you are interrupting.''

"Stay out of this, La Porte," Jake snapped. "This business is between my *partner* and me.''

"I believe that is for Mademoiselle Taggart to decide.'' Shoving back his chair, La Porte rose quickly to his feet.

"It's all right, Rene," Jessie said, glancing at the Frenchman, who looked ready to do battle for her honor. "I'm becoming accustomed to Mr. Weston's saloon manners.'' Jake just glared at her and began tugging her toward the door at the back of the room.

By the time they were inside the storeroom, among whiskey barrels, crates, and boxes, Jessie was fuming. "What on earth do you think you're doing? Take your hands off me!''

"What the hell do you think *you're* doing? Just how well do you know that Frenchman, anyway?"

"What I was doing was accepting a supper invitation. As to how well I know Monsieur La Porte"—she pronounced his name in perfect French just to irritate Jake—"that is none of your concern."

"Well, I'm making it my concern. La Porte is nothing but a fancy-pants dandy. He's the most notorious ladies' man on the Barbary Coast. He's after only one thing, and any decent woman would be smart enough to know it."

Jessie's face paled. "Are you insinuating . . . Are you implying—"

"No," Jake cut her off, his voice softer. "But everyone in town will assume just that if you're seen out with La Porte. If you intend to be accepted into polite society here, you had better stay away from La Porte. For that matter, you better stay as far away from the Tin Angel as you can get."

"I don't give a fig about polite society," Jessie told him. "Mr. La Porte is a gentleman. We spoke for several hours on the train, and he has asked me out to supper. I intend to go."

"The hell you do. You are going to go back out there and politely decline his invitation."

"And if I don't?"

"If you don't, you'll find yourself upstairs in my office, hog-tied and gagged."

"You wouldn't dare—and if you did, Rene wouldn't stand for it."

"No. He probably couldn't stand—he'd be flat on his back! Now, if you want to try me. . . ." Jake's flashing blue eyes pinned her, his challenge unmistakably clear.

Jessie squared her shoulders and tilted her chin. "You can't threaten me, Jake Weston. I'll do what I please, when I please. Even if I decline his offer tonight, sooner or later I'll get another opportunity to go, and I will."

"No, you won't. Because unless you give me your word that you won't go out with him, I'm going to cart you up those stairs the way Bull Haskin did and tie you up just like I promised. Sooner or later, you're bound to see reason."

"Of all the overbearing, domineering . . . You have no right to make decisions for me!" Furious, Jessie glowered at him, but she didn't want to cause trouble between the two men. She'd glimpsed the derringer Rene had tucked in his waistcoat pocket, and God only knew what kind of weapon a man like Weston carried.

Still, Jake Weston wasn't about to run her life— nor would any man! Jessie hesitated for a moment. Then, with a furtive glance to the door, she made a dash for it. Jake caught her in two long strides, his hard arm going around her waist as he pressed her up against the wall.

"Oh no you don't, you little minx. You're not leaving this room until I have your word."

"And just what makes you think I'll keep it?" Jessie demanded.

"You're a Taggart, aren't you?" Jake shot back.

Jessie glared at him, knowing he was right. If she gave him her word, she would keep it. "I can't believe Rene is all that bad."

"When it comes to women, he's as bad as they get. He'll take what he wants, and when he's had his fill he'll toss you out like so much dirty laundry."

"And what about you?" Jessie pressed. "When it comes to women, are you any different?"

Jake's grim expression softened, one corner of his mouth tilting into a lazy half smile. "Probably not. But I'm not inviting you out."

Jessie's brows shot up, her temper flaring again. "Why not? Because I'm your partner, or because you don't find me attractive?"

Jake's gaze settled on the curve of her full breasts.

"Oh, you're attractive. There isn't a man in this saloon who won't vouch for that. But you're also a spoiled little bit of baggage, and nothing but trouble. What you need is a husband to take you in hand, but where you're gonna find someone crazy enough to tackle the job is beyond me—not that La Porte or any other man out there wouldn't mind playing at husbanding awhile."

Jessie's mouth fell open. "Why, you uncouth, good-for-nothing, womanizing . . . bastard! How could my father have been so cruel as to pair you up with me?"

"Maybe I am a bastard," Jake said with a look she couldn't quite fathom, "and maybe most of those other things, too. But that doesn't make a fiddler's damn. I want your word you won't keep company with La Porte."

"Go to hell!" Jessie cried, unable to control her anger any longer.

"It's what your father would have wanted, Jess."

"My father knew better than to try to bully me."

Jake leaned closer, pinning her against his chest. "I want your word."

Jessie jerked her hand free and drew back to slap him, but Jake grabbed her wrist before the blow connected.

"Damn you, Jess," he said, his eyes dark with suppressed anger.

Without even thinking, he pulled her closer, dipped his head, and kissed her—a fiery touch that left Jessie stunned. She could feel the warmth of his breath, the softness of his lips as they burned against her flesh. Jake's hand cupped her chin, and the kiss deepened. When she opened her mouth to protest, his tongue slide inside, capturing her completely.

What was happening to her? With a tiny whimper, Jessie swayed against him. Even when Jake released her wrist, she clung to him. Her hands moved of their own accord along his back and across his shoulders, until they touched the silky strands of his hair. She felt shivery all over, and there was a warm tingling in the hollow of her stomach.

Although part of her knew she should break away, another, secret part wanted the kiss to go on forever, wanted to know where the fiery sensations were leading—wanted to succumb to the yearning she felt deep inside.

While his lips moved over her mouth and his tongue teased hers, his hands slid along her back and down her hips until they cupped her bottom to pull her more firmly against him. Jessie whimpered softly. Even through the folds of her skirt, his palms felt big and warm as they caressed her softly. Goose bumps rose on her skin and she trembled.

When she felt something hard and insistent pressing against her body, Jessie's eyes flew open. With a startled gasp, she jerked away, her face scarlet and her heart hammering wildly.

Jake appeared as stunned as Jessie felt. The door burst open, throwing a bright beam of light into the lamplit room. Rupert stood starting at them in surprise.

"Boss, er, sorry to interrupt. One of the customers is accusing Stubby of handling a tell box. It's that drover who carries a boot gun. Paddy is out in the necessary, and that new man has disappeared again. Think you'd better come see about it, afore things git outta hand."

"I'll be right with you." As Rupert backed out the door, Jake took a steadying breath and turned to Jessie. She looked a little disheveled, but her eyes were wide and intent as she stared at him. "I'm sorry, Jess. I didn't mean for that to happen. That it did just proves my point."

Jessie's head came up. "Oh?" Though she tried to sound nonchalant, one hand clutched the folds of her skirt while the other held the base of her throat, where she could feel her pulse beating wildly. "And just what point is that?"

"That you're a naive little schoolgirl who's far from ready to handle the appetites of a man like La Porte."

"I am not naive!"

Jake stepped forward menacingly. "If you need more proof, I'll be happy to give it to you."

It was all she could do not to back away, but Jessie held her ground. "You're a devil, Jake Weston."

"And La Porte's a scoundrel. I want your word."

Telling herself that her heart was only pounding with anger, Jessie glared up at him. "All right," she finally conceded, "I won't see La Porte—at least for a while."

"Not good enough."

"I won't see him until I've discovered more about him."

"Try again."

"I won't see him for the next two weeks."

Jake smiled indulgently. "Give it a month, Jess. If you still want to see him after that, it's your business."

Wondering if what she read in his eyes was really concern for her welfare, Jessie finally agreed. "All right, a month," she said.

"He's a scoundrel," Jake repeated, a touch of his usual humor returning to his tone, "but he's got an eye for the best-looking woman on the Barbary Coast." Jake's glance roamed over her, his mouth set in a lazy smile. Then, as if a sobering thought had suddenly occurred to him, his smile faded and he stalked from the room.

Jessie sank down on a nearby sack of sugar. My God, what had happened? Felling shaky all over, she touched a finger to her lips. Her mouth still tingled from the rasp of Jake's late-evening beard and the warmth of his mouth over hers. It certainly wasn't like kissing Benjamin Keefer! Ben's touch had been sweet and gentle. Jessie had encouraged his kisses because they made her feel desirable. Jake's kisses, on the other hand, stirred a far more powerful desire.

Worst of all, she'd enjoyed every moment. In truth, she hadn't really wanted him to stop. God in heaven, Jake Weston was a rogue and a bounder of the worst sort. He had probably cheated her father, and he might be cheating her right now. He might even have had something to do with her father's death—and all she could think about was the feel of his body against hers and the warmth of his lips!

With a determined shake of her head, Jessie came to her feet. Damn him! Damn him to hell! As if in emphasis, she kicked the sack of sugar, managing only to bruise her slender foot. He'd made her promise not to see Rene, but would Rene have taken the liberties Jake just had? So far, the handsome Frenchman had been nothing less than a gentleman, but she didn't know him well enough to be sure. Still, she wondered how a man who behaved as Jake did had the nerve to criticize another!

Thinking of the intimate way Jake had touched her, Jessie groaned in embarrassment. The nerve of the man! What in God's name had her father been thinking?

With a sigh of resignation, Jessie headed for the door. She found Paddy standing guard just outside and wondered what the big Irishman would have done if she had called for his assistance.

"I'm going home," she told him, and he nodded. Forcing herself not to look at Jake—or at Rene La Porte—she followed behind Paddy as he cleared a path through the crowded room. She wouldn't be back tomorrow, or the day after that. She needed some time to think. She needed to stay as far away from Jake Weston as she possibly could.

* * *

Jake awoke early the next afternoon with a pounding headache. He'd dreamed of hatchets and red silk garrotes—and making love to his pretty new partner.

Jessie had left right after the incident in the storeroom—without so much as a backward glance. Jake's conscience smarted sorely. Old Henry would have shot him if he knew Jake had taken liberties with his daughter. Hell, he hadn't *meant* to kiss her. Getting involved with the Taggart girl was the *last* thing he wanted. But she'd made him mad—as she had the damnedest habit of doing—and kissing her had just seemed the most natural, and certainly the most pleasant, way to shut her up.

Sitting on the edge of his bed, Jake remembered the bottle of Franciscan brandy he'd drained last night in a futile effort to get the girl off his mind. He'd tried for hours to forget the feel of her slender body, the way her bosom had pressed against his chest, the firm round curves of her bottom. Jake cursed beneath his breath.

His head still pounding, he shaved, dressed, and headed downstairs. Wandering behind the bar, he cracked an egg into a beer mug, filled it with beer, and drained the mug in one gulp. The slippery concoction made him feel a little better, so he topped the mug off and walked down the bar to help Rupert hoist a keg of whiskey onto the back bar.

Five years ago, when he'd first met Henry Taggart, Jake had been the one serving drinks behind the bar. He'd worked his way to California after a stretch in the Confederate army that had taken him from Texas to Richmond. His mother had died in a cholera epidemic before the war, and he'd never known his father. The knowledge that his father had been married, with a family of his own, had never set well with Jake.

To Jake marriage meant lying, sleeping with one woman while the bulge in your breeches made you ache for somebody else. Jake had decided at an early age that marriage was an institution he'd prefer to avoid.

"Thanks, boss," Rupert said as Jake put a shoulder to the barrel. "Them damned kegs is gettin' heavier every year. You don't suppose they're making whiskey weigh more, do ya?"

"I don't know, Rupert. This damned business is starting to gnaw at me. Everything seems heavier, and tougher, and meaner."

"Kinda like them Yankee guards back at Elmira?"

Jake smiled. "Damned near." He'd been a captain in the calvary, leading a charge at Hatcher's Run, when his horse was shot out from under him. With a bullet in his shoulder and one in his thigh, he'd been transported to New York. The scurvy, the rats, and the dying Confederate soldiers had made his stay in Elmira prison the worst six months of Jake's life.

"Being partners with Miss Jessie gettin' you down?"

"She's a handful, Rupert, no doubt about it. But she's a whole lot smarter than I thought, and damned determined. If you'd told me a woman with Jessie's upbringing could show enough grit to get this far, I'd have said you were spending too much time smoking that Chinese heavenly pleasure."

"That's the same thing La Porte said last night," Rupert told him. "He said she was smart as she was pretty, and he wouldn't mind bein' her partner one bit."

Jake threw Rupert a hard look and muttered an oath. "I'm going over to the Golden Thorn to check on the competition." Turning on his heel, he headed for the door.

Monique Dubois would get rid of his hangover. In fact, she'd drain all the poison out of his body, especially the unwanted thoughts running wildly through his head.

* * *

Unlike the Tin Angel, which relied mostly on the girls, the Golden Thorn used entertainment to entice customers. The saloon was a narrow two-story building with a raised stage at the far end. Bars lined both sides of the theater, and a row of velvet-curtained cribs above allowed customers to watch the show when they weren't involved in more exciting pastimes.

The saloon was owned by Nob Hill Kate, who ran the place along with Monique Dubois, Kate's "adopted" daughter. Jake had been seeing Monique off and on for the past two years. With a waist as trim as Kate's was ample, the pretty little French girl had long black hair, a porcelain complexion, and flashing turquoise eyes.

Monique entertained only the men she chose. She never entered a crib—there wasn't enough money in the world to entice her to do that. She was the princess of the Golden Thorn, and Kate, the queen, was smart enough to keep her there. Kate knew the wisdom of providing something just out of her customers' reach, something for them to dream about—and Monique was that something.

Shoving open the swinging doors, Jake shouldered his way through the already crowded saloon. Damn, he thought, old Kate really got on to something when she hired that belly dancer. With a hip shake that could make the building tremble, Fatima had men lined four deep at the bar, and all the tables were full.

The world-renowned belly dancer was the Golden Thorn's hottest attraction. When the woman had first performed, the crowd had been struck silent, and Kate thought that the men hated her. But at the close of the show, after Fatima's sensuous moves and voluptuous gyrations, the crowd's thunderous roar had changed Kate's worry to fear that the mob would tear the house down.

Searching for Monique, Jake looked over the

crowded saloon. Careful to keep his visits to a minimum, he hadn't seen her all week. Spending too much time with her would be an admission of interest beyond that of a privileged acquaintance—and commitment of any kind wasn't something Jake Weston was willing to make. Though Jake didn't encourage her, Monique paid an occasional visit to his room across the street, usually right after closing. She was always gone before sunup.

Spotting her at a table near the stage entertaining two city politicians, Jake headed in her direction. Since he was taller than most of the men in the room, Monique noticed him almost immediately.

"*Bonjour, chéri*," she greeted with her pretty French accent, kissing him on the cheek while her bosom pressed softly into his chest. "You 'ave met Councilman Peterson and Judge Fenderman, no?"

"Gentlemen." Jake shook hands with the two men, ignoring, as his profession dictated, the fact that Fenderman was one of his best late-night customers. "Will you be tied up long, Monique? There's some . . . business . . . we need to discuss."

"No, *chéri*, I was just making certain these gentlemen 'ad a good seat for the show. Why don't you 'ave a drink, and I will join you at the bar as soon as the entertainment begins."

"Gentlemen." Jake nodded and excused himself, pushing through the throng at the bar. He was neither surprised nor offended by Monique's attention to those particular customers—the votes of the councilmen and the rulings of the judges were the lifeblood of the Tenderloin. Keeping their goodwill was no easy task, since the politicians received continual pressure from the city's churches to reform the Tenderloin.

The plinking sound of mideastern stringed instruments drifted over the saloon, and the men at the tables quieted as all attention focused on the stage. Bedecked in glittering bracelets and transparent silk, an arm slid from behind the curtains, moving like a charmed snake in time to the music. The curtains parted, and Fatima whirled onto the platform. Soon she was well into the gyrations of her trade, and even Jake's eyes were transfixed. He hardly noticed when Monique appeared at his side.

"*Chéri*," Monique said with a pout, "I see you too are taken with the charms of Fatima."

"Fat is right," Jake teased, turning his attention to the beautiful French girl. "You make her look like a mule skinner."

"*Oui*, I do, don't I?" Although her smile appeared confident, her expression betrayed a hint of doubt.

When Jake looked into her turquoise eyes, he thought Monique made Fatima look like a common bar girl—although few could come close to the way the dancer moved. Unbidden, Jessie's great green eyes appeared in his mind, filled with a mixture of hurt and disapproval. Jake pushed the image aside. Why the hell would Jessica Taggart care what he did? And why the hell should it matter to him if she did care?

"I 'ave a bottle of fine champagne on ice in my parlor. I 'oped you would visit today."

You hoped one of the two or three men granted access to your room would visit, Jake thought, but he accepted her offer. "Let's go see how fine it is."

Heading up the stairs, he looked back over the room. Today, the usual jealous glances he got were missing, the men's eyes fixed instead on Fatima.

"She moves like that only on the dance floor," Monique said petulantly, "but if you prefer to watch 'er . . ."

As she turned to leave, Jake caught her arm. "No you don't, Frenchy." Pulling her into his arms, he kissed her hard. As her lips parted beneath his, he noticed they felt cool and smooth, not full and warm like Jessie's. With skilled expertise, her tongue circled his, darting in and out while her fingers drew tiny patterns on the skin of at the back of his neck.

He hadn't been disappointed with her practiced touch before, but compared with the honest, innocent response he'd received from Jessie, the kiss felt somehow lacking. Suddenly a little unsure that making love to her was what he really wanted to do, Jake broke away. Monique smiled up at him, entwined her fingers with his, and pulled him into her room. He followed halfheartedly.

Afterward, Jake lay sated, his headache gone but his thoughts in turmoil. At the end of their lovemaking, it hadn't been Monique he'd felt he was kissing—it had been Jessie. In his mind, it was her body arching beneath him, her breasts he caressed. He'd come to Monique to sweep away thoughts of the green-eyed girl, but his efforts only made them stronger.

Monique's finger slid along the side of his neck and onto his chest. When she spoke, there was an undercurrent of an emotion he couldn't quite discern.

"You said something, *chéri*, when we were making love."

Jake cringed inside. Surely he hadn't said Jessie's name out loud.

"I don't remember," he said.

Monique rolled to her side. "What name did you call me?" she persisted, her voice turning cold.

"Honey. I called you honey."

Monique came to her knees beside him, her bosom rising and falling with each agitated breath. "Who is Jessie?"

Jake felt his face flush. "Maybe I called you *hussy* . . . you know how I like to tease."

Monique got up and pulled on a fine silk wrapper. "Who is Jessie?" she demanded.

"I'm sure I didn't say Jessie, Monique." Her face

began to redden. Despite all her attributes in bed, she had one well-known failing—her raging temper.

"You . . . said . . . Jessie!" She reached for a half-full champagne glass beside the bed. Jake hoped the liquor would calm her down, but instead of taking a drink, she hurled the glass in his direction. Jake ducked as the glass crashed against the wall behind him.

"Monique, that was good champagne."

"You bastard!" Her lips curled, and Jake reached for his breeches. He had one leg in when she hurled a perfume bottle at him. His movement constricted, he failed to dodge the bottle that glanced off his shoulder and bruised his cheek.

"Cut it out, Monique." Jake's own temper began to flare.

"You are the sonofabitch," she spat, and went for the champagne bottle.

Cursing, Jake stuffed his other leg into his pants, hitched them up, and started on the buttons. Clutching the bottle, Monique launched herself at him. Jake caught her wrists as the bottle began its descent toward his head.

"Calm down," he ordered, shoving her back on the bed and pinning her beneath his weight. "I thought you didn't care where I got my appetite."

"I 'ope you starve, Jake Weston!" she shouted, trying to hit him again.

Jake wrenched the bottle from her hand. "You little spitfire! Take it easy. If you don't like what I say, you can always find a replacement."

Monique watched him with flashing eyes, but she relaxed in his grip. Jake dressed in silence while she curled up on the bed, looking highly offended. Furious at himself for the turn of events, he walked to the door and opened it.

"I'll see you in a couple of days," he called back over his shoulder, not really meaning it. He'd had enough of Monique to last him a good long while.

"Go see Jessie!" she spat at him, sitting up.

"Monique—" he started, but quickly slammed the door as the champagne bottle came sailing toward him. It crashed with the sound of shattering glass. Women! he thought as he strode away. If one of them wasn't giving him trouble, another one was.

As he passed through the buzzing saloon, he ran into Kate. "Well, if it isn't my favorite competition," she said. "How are you, Jake?" Hands on her broad hips, gray hair dyed an uncommonly dark shade of brown, Kate was still an attractive woman. She gave him a hug, then held him at arm's length. "You don't look so good. What happened to your face?"

"I'm fine, Kate." He absently touched his cheek while one corner of his mouth curved upward. "I finally figured out how you named this place—you're the gold and Monique's the thorn."

Kate laughed. "Even roses have a few thorns."

Jake just nodded. He made his way out of the smoky saloon, then stopped in the street and took a long deep breath. If roses had thorns, he decided, he'd find himself an orchid.

Chapter 9

After a long, productive visit to Madame Delaine's, recommended as the city's finest seamstress, Jessie returned to her hotel.

She hadn't been to the Tin Angel in two nights, but she had decided that her evenings there required a different mode of dress, something a little more daring, while still retaining an air of class and elegance. Her mourning clothes of plain black bombazine just would not do.

Her first few nights at the Tin Angel had shown Jessie that her presence there would not go unnoticed. As she had in the past, she would use the looks God had given her to her best advantage. Although she hated to admit it, she also hoped to set Jake Weston on his too-smug ear!

Strolling across the hotel lobby beneath the crystal chandeliers, Jessie headed toward the sweeping staircase that led to her room.

"Miss Taggart?" the desk clerk called out, stopping her in mid-stride. "Mr. La Porte was here looking for you. I believe he said he'd stop back in an hour or so. That ought to be just about now."

"Oh no," Jessie muttered.

"Is there some problem?" the young man asked.

"Oh, it's nothing like that. It's just that—"

"Mademoiselle Taggart?" Rene's soft voice drifted across the lobby as he strode toward her, looking quite handsome in a cream-colored suit. "I was hoping I might see you."

"Hello, Rene." She extended her hand, and the handsome Frenchman carried it to his lips.

"Might I have a moment?" he asked.

"Of course." Rene led her to a settee in front of the great marble fireplace that dominated one end of the lobby. Jessie sat down, and he took a place beside her, a little closer than he should have.

"You left so quickly the other evening, we were unable to finish our conversation," he said.

"I . . . I'm sorry about that. I wasn't feeling well."

"I see." He flashed her an appraising glance. "And how about today? Are you feeling well enough to join me for supper?"

Jessie smoothed the folds of her skirt. If she hadn't given Jake her word, it would be very easy to say yes to the handsome man. She didn't believe he was really bad. Besides, she wanted to make her own judgments about people—right or wrong. She was a full-grown woman, on her own at last, with no one to answer to but herself.

Still, there was something about Rene . . . something she'd first noticed on the train, but brushed aside. Now, as she watched him from beneath her lashes, she sensed a predatory air that she hadn't quite recognized. She'd felt a similar undercurrent of danger in Jake, but for some reason it only made him more attractive.

"I've decided it's too soon after my father's death to be socializing," she said, making the obvious excuse. "I appreciate your kindness, but for now I'm afraid I must decline."

"You are certain your . . . partner . . . has nothing to do with your decision? He and I," he said, shrugging, "we have had our differences."

"Over women?" Jessie asked, and Rene smiled.

"Women, yes. Business also. Maybe we are too much alike."

"Both rogues, I think," Jessie teased.

Rene took her hand. "I am a patient man, Jessica. Far more patient than Jake Weston. I will wait until you are ready. And when you are, I will not be far away." His eyes, usually a soft brown, had darkened. "There is much I can teach you. In time, you will see what I mean."

Jessie pulled her hand away, beginning to think Jake's warning had not been overly harsh after all. "I appreciate your *friendship*, Rene." She emphasized the word. "But right now that's all I want from anyone." Jessie stood up, effectively ending their conversation.

"As you wish, *chérie*," he said, bowing to her wishes. But, his eyes said he had no intention of ending his pursuit. Jessie found his attentions both intriguing and unsettling. Time would tell, she decided.

"Thank you for stopping by, Rene."

"It is always a pleasure to be in the company of a beautiful woman. If you need anything, do not hesitate to let me know." With a last brief smile, he headed toward the door.

Jessie released a sigh of relief. Although Jake Weston had kissed her—manhandled her would be a more apt description—he'd made it clear he wasn't interested in her. Rene acted the gentleman, but he looked at her with such obvious intentions, she got goose bumps. Which of the men was the more dangerous, she had yet to discover. Wondering how she'd gotten herself into all this trouble in the first place, Jessie again vowed she'd control her own destiny one way or another. Jake Weston and Rene La Porte could both go straight to Hades!

Kazimir Bochek paced the length of the Persian carpet in his third-floor office.

The room overlooked the Wells, Fargo and Company staging area, where men unloaded, sorted, and reloaded the day's freight, some of which had originated in the Sierra Nevada mountains, some as far away as the East Coast or even distant countries.

Kaz spat into a brass spittoon near his big oak desk and dropped his heavy-boned frame into his leather swivel chair. As he turned to look out on the yard below, only the hard knotted muscle in his jaw revealed his anger. He lifted a powerful hand and smoothed his thick mustache, his brow furrowing as he saw one of the men below sneak behind a shack and roll a smoke. The man glanced hesitantly up at the window, as if wondering if Bochek was watching, then hurried back to his job without lighting up.

The hostlers, muleteers, and freighters who toiled below knew they worked for a tough man—one who'd cracked many a head proving he was boss. Bochek had come up the hard way, through the ranks of Wells, Fargo and Company. He considered himself personally responsible for the company's rise to the number one position in freighting, particularly in transporting gold bullion. When he had come to California in '54, the company was third behind Page, Bacon and Company and Adams and Company.

With Bochek hustling business, in three years Wells, Fargo had become number one. Kaz had been promoted to station manager in the fastest-growing terminal in the system—San Francisco.

But he hadn't moved up since, and Kaz knew the reason. Poles weren't considered good enough to rise above the level of station manager. Every young man who had been promoted was either related to the company owners or to the investors. Sam Youngerman, Kaz's new boss, had been given a vice presidency because his father was a top executive at American Express. Though Wells, Fargo and American Express weren't directly related, they had common investors and even some of the same board members—and they took care of their own.

Youngerman had received the promotion instead of Kaz, who was much more qualified. But Kaz hadn't been surprised, not this time. Long ago he'd decided that his fate and that of Wells, Fargo would never be one and the same. If Kaz Bochek was to become a rich man, he would have to do it on his own.

And Kaz knew how. As station manager, he was in a position to know everything that was happening in the city. The company hauled goods, people, and mail. Over the years, Kaz had taken an interest in what was being transported and by whom—an interest that didn't stop him from steaming open correspondence. He knew more about who made money in the city than most of the bankers did, and more importantly, he knew how they made it.

Throughout his career, he'd used that information wisely—strategically dropped hints bought special favors from businessmen who didn't want their more nefarious activities known. Some of the favors were merely rewards for his discretion; others were a result of threats to reveal their operations to the local constable's office. Those businessmen called it blackmail. Kaz preferred to think of it as an investment in silence.

Kaz flipped his cigar butt into a spittoon and stuffed a pinch of snuff between his lip and lower gum. Although he'd accumulated thousands of dollars over the last few years, as well as precious silks, fine European liquors, and ivory, Youngerman's promotion was the slap in the face that had pushed him over the edge.

One more big hit and he'd quit this ungrateful company. To hell with them. He had one of the city's most powerful attorneys under his callused thumb, and his plans were moving forward.

Kaz smiled, and his jaw relaxed. He spat again and wiped his mouth with the back of his hand. Kazimir Bochek was glad he hadn't changed his name to Carl Bowen, as a friend had suggested when he'd first arrived in San Francisco.

Poland had been a land of kings, and Bochek intended to carry on the tradition.

Deciding that she'd stayed away long enough, Jessie showed up at the Tin Angel on Wednesday night, Paddy in tow. She was determined to learn the business. If that meant putting up with Jake Weston, so be it. She didn't mention the incident in the storeroom, and neither did Jake, but she stayed well out of his way.

Jake treated her respectfully, but he also kept his distance. Jessie watched him as he worked, noting how efficiently he handled the help and kept the place in order. She wondered how he'd gotten the fading purple bruise beside his eye.

"What happened to you?" she couldn't resist asking as she passed him on the stairs. "Bull Haskin pay you a visit while I was away?"

"A case of mistaken identity," he answered gruffly, but he wouldn't meet her eyes.

She wondered if he regretted the way he'd treated her in the storeroom, then decided that a man like Weston probably didn't regret anything.

Jake watched Jessie's retreating figure as she gracefully climbed the stairs. She'd given him a wide berth all evening, and Jake had to admit he deserved the treatment. He shouldn't have kissed her—he owed that much to Henry. But what irritated him the most was the guilt he felt over visiting Monique. Damn it! Jessie was his partner, not his keeper. He owed her nothing. But his niggling conscience would not be silent.

For most of the evening he stayed away from her. Then he decided, hell, she was Henry's daughter and half owner of the business. He ought to set things right between them. She was going over the day's deposits when Jake brought the night's take into the office.

Jessie glanced up at him, then returned her attention to the books. "There's an entry each month that I don't understand," she said over her shoulder as he set the bag of money on the desk. "It says Redemption, and it's always for fifty dollars. There are no invoices from them, either. Who are they, and why are we giving them money?"

When she turned to face Jake, she was surprised to see that his cheeks had reddened, while his eyes remained carefully fixed on the toe of his boot. "It's the Sisters of Redemption Orphanage," he mumbled.

"It's what?"

"It's an orphanage," he repeated so softly that she still wasn't sure she had heard correctly.

"Would you mind speaking up?"

"I said it's an orphanage, damn it! If it bothers you, we can take the money out of my share."

Jessie had to forcibly close her open mouth. For seconds she just stared at him. Then she smiled. "I wouldn't want to do that. I think contributing to an orphanage is a wonderful thing to do. There's no need for you to be embarrassed about it."

"Who says I'm embarrassed?" Jake tried to look forbidding, but he couldn't disguise a hint of uncertainty. Touched by this rare glimpse of his vulnerability, Jessie fought a second smile.

"How did you happen to get involved with an orphanage?"

Running a hand through his hair, Jake released a slow breath and sat down on the edge of the desk. "It started about three years ago. Some food was missing from the kitchen one day. The next day a pie was gone. At first we thought it was one of the girls, or maybe a cook, but it turned out the thief was a little Peruvian boy who'd devised a sort of lean-to shelter behind some wooden crates in the basement.''

"Paco?" Jessie asked.

"Paco. He was too small to work here then, so I took him to the orphanage. He was a scrappy little thing, so skinny you could see his ribs. He fought like a banty rooster, but with Paddy's help we finally got him over there." Jake glanced off in the distance. "It was the first time I'd been to a place like that. The nuns worked hard, and the old brick building was clean, but it was obvious there wasn't enough food to go around. I talked to Henry about it. The year before, your father had given me a piece of the profits instead of a raise, and I was making damned near five hundred a month—sometimes more. I figured five percent wouldn't hurt me so much. I told him I'd put up twenty-five a month if he'd match it. Now the sisters have a bed for each of the kids, and enough to eat." Jake smiled. "Ol' Henry always was a soft-heart."

"And you're not?" Jessie said, watching his face. Jake didn't answer.

"How did you and my father first meet?" she asked. Now that she'd gotten him talking, she wasn't about to let him quit.

"I met Henry a little over five years ago. I'd been drifting ever since the war. After a six-month stretch in a Union prison, I was really enjoying my freedom."

"You were a Confederate soldier?"

Jake flashed a mischievous grin. "An active participant in the late unpleasantries. Just think, Boston, you've been kissed by a captain of the Rebel hordes."

Jessie blushed at the memory and saw Jake's blue gaze turned dark. When it fastened on the curve of her breasts, Jessie felt a rush of warmth, and her heart began to pound.

"You were telling me how you met my father," she reminded him softly.

"Since there wasn't a whole lot to do in prison except wait for my shoulder to heal and play cards, I—"

"You were wounded?"

"Hit in the thigh and the shoulder at Hatcher's Run. Anyway, while I was biding my time, trying to figure a way to break out, I played a lot of cards and—"

"You escaped?"

Jake nodded slowly, as if uncertain. Then he said, "I hid under six dead soldiers in the back of a wagon. Took off while the burial detail was on its way to the gravesite. It still gives me nightmares." He shook his head as if to banish the painful memory. "I joined up with some Southern sympathizers who gave me the Leech and Rigdon .44 that hangs on my bedpost and helped me start back to my unit. I was in Maryland when Lee surrendered.

"After that, I hostled and freighted and swamped my way through Kansas, Colorado, and Nevada, and wound up gambling and tending bar over at the Golden Thorn. Henry had just bought the Tin Angel. He was getting ready to go back to Boston and was looking for a ramrod. I was tired of moving around, so I applied for the job. First thing you know, I was running the Angel, then the freighting company, and finally the Yuba City Riverboats."

"My father must have been impressed."

"As you may recall, your father had a pretty mean temper. Sometimes it worked against him. When it did, he looked to me to smooth things over a little."

"From what I've seen, you've got a pretty sizable temper yourself."

Jake grinned. "You have a way of bringing out the worst in me," he teased.

Jessie laughed softly.

"Actually, your father and I made a darned good team."

"I can imagine."

"I miss him, temper and all," Jake said, his voice betraying the depth of his feelings.

Jessie looked up at him, beginning to understand why her father had thought so highly of him. "So do I."

Jake held her gaze a moment more, then he glanced away. "You want to check the take?"

She shook her head. "I'm a little tired. Why don't you go ahead?"

Jake smiled, aware that she'd just bestowed upon him a little more trust. "Paddy's waiting to see you home."

Jessie nodded. "He really is a comfort. I suppose it was pretty silly of me to think I could come down here alone."

"Maybe naive is a better word," Jake said.

"I guess I should thank you for trying to look out for me."

"You don't have to thank me, Boston. You're my partner. Partners are supposed to look out for each other."

She just nodded.

"Good night, Jake."

"Good night, Boston."

After that, she came each night at closing. Jake marveled at the way she maintained her ladylike demeanor while keeping the girls and the male employees in line. The night they had talked about Paco, they'd developed a kind of rapport. Although he hated to admit it, Jake found himself looking forward to her arrival every night. He had the feeling Jessie felt the same way.

"Excited about your boat ride?" Jake asked, the morning Jessie was to visit the Yuba City boats and take a trip on the *Callie Sue*. Across the room, Rupert was busily escorting the last drunken cowhand out the door. The gray light of dawn lit the windows with a dusky glow. The air outside was still cool, but the late-summer day would be warm.

"I'd enjoy seeing the bay even if we didn't own the boats, but I really don't see how I can get much insight into the way the business operates if you don't come along."

Jake pulled a cheroot from the pocket of his waist-coat and lit up. "I've got a meeting over at the freighting office." He took a drag on the cigar and blew a plume of smoke into the room, refusing to meet Jessie's gaze. If she'd asked him to do any-thing but ride those damned rockabout boats, he'd have been happy to oblige.

"So you said." She tossed him a doubtful look. "It's getting late—or rather, it's getting early. I'd better be going." Paddy rushed ahead of her as she turned and headed toward the door. The big Irish-man held it open for her.

Against his will, Jake's eyes fastened on the gentle sway of her hips, the tiny waist he could almost span with his hands. "Do you really want me to go?" he finally called after her.

Surprised, Jessie turned. "Don't misunderstand me, Jake. It just makes good business sense, since you manage the company."

It made good sense if he gave Jessie's interest in the businesses serious consideration, which he had only recently begun to do. "I guess if you look at it that way, you've got a point."

"It would certainly help me understand what's going on," she said persuasively, her pretty green eyes locked with his.

Jake felt a rush of warmth. Damn, he'd like to kiss her again. "Tell you what I'll do. I'll make other arrangements for my meeting—on one condition."

As if she expected him to ask for something totally improper, Jessie stiffened.

"I'll go with you," he told her, "if you'll convince the cook to bake some pies for the orphanage."

Jessie flashed him such a radiant smile that Jake felt the blood rush through his veins.

"You've got a deal," she said.

A little unnerved by her effect on him, he forced a smile in return. "You'd better hurry to the hotel. You won't get a whole lot of sleep. I'll pick you up at eleven. The *Callie Sue* leaves for the second part of her daily run at eleven forty-five sharp."

"Thank you, Jake. I really appreciate your help."

Jessie extended her slender hand, and Jake took it, holding it a little longer than he should have. Her skin felt smooth, and her fingers were slim and delicate. The blood in his veins rushed to his loins.

He felt her hand tremble just before she pulled it away, and the look on her face told him that his touch had affected her, too. With a slightly hesitant smile, she headed out the door, Paddy trailing behind her.

As soon as she was gone from sight, Jake groaned and tossed his cheroot into the nearest spittoon. What the hell had he done? Those blasted boats would be the death of him yet. The damned woman could charm a cobra. With a sigh that sounded more like a grunt, Jake headed for his room. At least he hadn't had much to drink. His stomach would be queasy enough without a hangover to contend with.

Arriving at the wharf at exactly eleven-fifteen, Jessie looked across the glistening bay. Jake's expression seemed harder than when she'd left him at closing, and she wondered at his thoughts. Almost absently, he swung her down from the carriage, his strong hands on her waist. Only when she steadied herself against his chest did he look at her; then his expression changed.

"Thank you," she whispered, slightly breathless at the heated look in his eyes.

"You're welcome," he said, but he didn't remove his hands from her waist. They felt warm and strong, even through the fabric of her dress.

"We'll be late," she said softly, trying to ignore the tingling sensation creeping up her spine.

Jake nodded and his hands fell away. As they walked along the pier, crying gulls winged overhead. The sun felt warm against her face as she tilted her head back to watch them. Chinese coolies worked the busy landing, while the rigging on ships of every shape and size clanked and clattered.

Jake held her hand as they descended the steep gangplank to the deck of the low-riding, forty-five-foot scow and searched the crowded deck for a place to sit. Hemp line, lumber, sacks of flour and sugar, canvas, and kegs of square nails were stacked on the bow of the *Callie Sue*. Cases of Cyrus Noble's Fine Old Whiskey and kegs of beer shared the aft with barrels of pickles and crackers—and two Chinese and three Peruvian passengers.

"They're headed for jobs in the mines," Jake told her, apparently reading her thoughts. "They're good workers, but some folks won't hire them because their skin's a different color."

"And you think that's wrong?" Jessie asked.

"Don't you?"

"Of course," she said and was pleased by his look of approval.

The passengers found seats where they could. Jake explained that the cargo was lashed down with triple braided lines secured to cleats near the rails. Every step across the cluttered deck required great care.

"Those two barren masts fore and aft support booms set at a forty-five degree angle," he said. "That heavy block and tackle hanging above is used to load and unload the scow." Stays and rigging from the booms added to the intricate spiderweb of lines that crossed and recrossed the deck.

As Jake finished his explanation, he felt the deck shift beneath his feet, and his stomach turned. God, he hated the ocean!

"It's a lovely day for a boat ride, don't you think?" Jessie flashed him a brilliant smile.

"Not in one of these stink buckets," he muttered, unable to stop himself. As if to add validity to his words, the steam engine belched smoke. Jake coughed and his stomach churned again.

"Are you all right?" Jessie asked.

"As good as I'll be till we're back on dry land." Concentrating on the tiny waist he circled with his hands, Jake lifted her onto a bale of hemp rope. The warmth of her body and a whiff of her perfume almost made him forget the queasiness in his stomach. Almost, but not quite. He moved a little forward in order to get as far as possible from the stench of the smoke.

Finn Engstrom, the skipper of the *Callie Sue*, took the wheel just in front of the squat deckhouse that covered the steam engine, and yelled to his Chinese deckhand to cast off.

"Steam's up. Chop chop, Ling Ling. You best watch we don't kiss de udder boats." Only an occasional word betrayed Finn's Norwegian heritage. For the past twenty years, he'd lived and worked in the West. Finn shouted a second command, and the pony engine came to life, giving power to the eight-foot paddle wheels on either side of the boat. As the wheels began to churn, the captain nodded his approval.

Standing next to Jake, Paddy stretched his arms wide and inhaled. "Makes a man feel good. Like a drink a' Irish whiskey."

"And a fly thinks a pile of cow dung is paradise," Jake growled. Paddy gave Jake a confused look and scratched his head.

As the deckhand cast off the line and Finn began the intricate job of maneuvering the small sidewheeler through the various steam- and sail-powered craft that crowded the wharf area, Jake watched Paddy make his way back to where Jessie sat atop the bale.

She seemed enthralled as she watched the deckhand lean forward and use a ten-foot boat hook to help fend off the other boats. Jake tried to help him, hoping the work would keep his mind off his stomach, but within minutes after the top-heavy scow headed into the rolling swells of the bay, he was feeling sick in earnest.

The last thing he wanted was for Jessie to notice. Cursing beneath his breath, he wondered how the fetching little baggage had gotten him to come along.

Chapter 10

On her perch above the deck, Jessie talked to the captain and admired the ships they passed as they headed into the bay.

The *Callie Sue* rolled and dipped beneath her, but all she noticed was how blue the sky was, how green the hills in the distance. Although she hoped Jake would join her and explain some of the boat's workings and the shipping operation, he made his way to the bow instead. Only an occasional glimpse of his blue-checked shirt betrayed his location between the crates and barrels.

"Excuse me, captain," Jessie finally said as her temper began to rise, "I think I'll see what's keeping Jake."

Captain Engstrom helped her down from the seat with a warning to be mindful of the cargo-strewn deck, and she headed toward the bow of the boat. Lord in heaven, she'd asked Jake along because she wanted him to explain the business. The way he was acting, he should have stayed home!

Lifting her skirts, Jessie picked her way along the deck. Just before she reached the spot where Jake sat behind a wooden crate, she heard a groan and a curse and the sound of someone retching.

"You no look so good, Mr. Jake," the little Chinese deckhand said from beneath his conical straw hat as he peered around the crate.

"Keep your mouth shut, China boy," Jake growled, "or I'll throw you to the sharks."

The little Chinese bobbed his head and backed away. "Ling Ling have much work," he said, and quickly disappeared.

Not certain just what was going on, Jessie stepped around the crate. Jake was leaning against the side, his face deathly pale, his long legs stretched out in front of him.

"Oh, Jake," Jessie said, kneeling beside him. "You're not seasick, are you?"

"What the hell are you doing here?" he snapped, struggling to his feet. "I told you to stay put. It's dangerous for you to be walking around the deck in those damned high-heeled shoes." Turning away from her, Jake leaned over the rail, scooped up a handful of water, and washed his face.

"What I'm doing here is trying to find my partner. You're supposed to be explaining the riverboat operation to me—or had you forgotten?"

Jake ran a wet hand through his hair, but he wouldn't meet her eyes. "I haven't forgotten, but I'm afraid the captain's gonna have to do the explaining."

Noticing the lack of color in his lips and the way his hand shook, Jessie's annoyance fled. "Why didn't you tell me you got seasick? I would have understood."

"Who says I'm seasick?"

"I do."

"Well, for your information, Miss Taggart, I just drank too much whiskey last night. Not that it's any business of yours."

Jessie's temper flared, but before she could make a suitably biting retort, the captain walked up.

"Finn," Jake said, "I'm afraid I'm snakebit. I'm gonna have to go ashore at Richmond."

Jessie took a good long assessment of him. His skin looked almost gray, and his eyes, usually a crystalline blue, appeared bleak and dull. He could say what he wanted, but she knew when someone was seasick! Then for the first time, she noticed the defiant set to his jaw, the stiffness in his broad shoulders. Her anger faded as she realized he was just too proud to admit it.

"Sorry, Jess," he said, his tone a little softer, "you and Paddy will have to go on without me."

"Is there anything I can do?"

"No, I'll be fine."

"It's nothing to be ashamed of."

"I told you before, I'm not seasick."

"All right, you're not seasick. Do you want us to turn around and head back?"

"No, this is a work trip. Finn has freight to deliver, same as any other day. I can make do alone. You go on with Paddy, just like you planned. Besides, Finn knows practically as much as I do about the riverboat operation."

When the captain flashed an expression of doubt, Jake threw him a warning glance. *Men!* Jessie thought as Jake excused himself and made his way to the opposite side of the boat. But when he settled himself out of sight behind a barrel, Jessie couldn't help feeling sorry for him. The Richmond stop was still a quarter of an hour away.

By the time they reached the dock, Jake looked a little better, but Jessie was still concerned.

"I'm going with you," she said as he started up the ladder.

"The hell you are," he growled. "You've been looking forward to this trip, and I'm not letting a little indigestion spoil it for you."

"A little indigestion! Why, Jake Weston, you're positively green. I'm the one who suggested you come along; now it's my responsibility to see that you get home all right."

Jake muttered a low curse. "Damn you, woman. When will you ever learn to mind? Paddy," he called over to the big Irishman. "You see Miss Jessie stays aboard."

"Yes, boss." Paddy stepped in front of her.

"Need I remind you, Paddy, that you work for me, not Jake?"

"Yes, mum. I mean, no, mum." Careful to keep his eyes on the deck, Paddy stepped away.

A muscle worked in Jake's jaw. He looked so determined—and so pale—Jessie gave in.

"All right, Jake, you win. The way you're acting you deserve a good dose of the miseries."

Grumbling something she couldn't hear, Jake climbed the ladder, and Jessie headed back toward the stern. Then, remembering Jake's words, her temper rose again. *When would she learn to mind?* Why, the nerve of the man! When would *he* learn to treat her as an adult instead of a child? Jake Weston was the most overbearing, pigheaded man she'd ever met. Still, she wished he'd let her accompany him back to the city. Now she'd be worried about him the rest of the afternoon.

Taking her place on the bale of hemp, Jessie sighed in resignation. At least he was right about the *Callie Sue* continuing on schedule. Customers were expecting the freight on board, and, as Finn had pointed out earlier, punctuality was the backbone of the freighting business. Deciding Jake probably didn't deserve all the fuss, Jessie made her mind up to learn everything she could about the business the two of them owned.

During the trip from Richmond to Benicia, she asked Finn all about the boat, the operation of the engine, the steering system, and the booms. The rest of the time she spent with Paddy, studying the passing landscape.

As the scow turned into the Sacramento River, the going got slower. When Finn swung the bow of the boat toward the old town of Benicia, he pulled his pocket watch out and flashed Jessie a ruddy-faced grin.

"Four twenty-five," he said. "Right on time." Because the *Callie Sue* was one of the smallest scows in the fleet, her freight runs were mostly short hops between the towns surrounding the bay.

Their arrival came none too soon for Jessie, who was ravenous. For the first time, she invited Paddy to dine with her. Holding on to his arm, she let him guide her up the narrow gangplank from the deck to the wharf. As they negotiated the town's busy streets, Jessie admired the quaint shops. Benecia, Finn had told her, was named for the wife of Governor Vallejo, one of the most powerful men in Spanish California. His family still held a large land grant to the north of the river, and were one of Yuba City Riverboats' biggest customers.

Strolling along the wooden boardwalk away from the river, Jessie spotted a respectable-looking establishment called the First Lady Chop and Oyster House, and they headed in that direction. Paddy held the door open, then seated Jessie at a small table near the corner—courtesies he'd learned from Rupert, he told her proudly. He failed to remove his bowler, however. Smiling into his battered face, Jessie decided that his slight indiscretion was hardly important.

The waiter solved the problem. "May I take your hat?" he asked, extending a hand while the other remained politely folded against his green cloth apron. A white shirt topped by a small bow tie peeped from beneath.

"Why?" Paddy asked, eyeing him suspiciously. Jessie fought to keep from smiling as the waiter stepped back a bit hesitantly.

"Why, to put it on the hat rack for you, sir," the man finally managed.

Paddy removed the bowler, but watched the man

carefully to make sure he actually placed the hat on the bentwood rack.

Jessie surveyed the small menu, then glanced across to Paddy, who was carefully studying the contents of the other customers' plates. "What looks good to you, Paddy?"

"You choose, mum."

With a flash of understanding, Jessie realized that Paddy couldn't read. "How about the pork chops? They look like enough for a man your size."

"Anything you say, mum. Is there potatoes?"

Jessie smiled. "Lots of potatoes. And I noticed a delicious-looking apple pie."

"That would be fine, mum."

To the waiter's surprise, Jessie ordered, then she discreetly passed a gold piece to Paddy when the man left. "You pay with this, Paddy."

"Yes, mum," he said, leaving the gold piece on the table.

"You know, Paddy, my father didn't learn to read or cipher until he was twenty. He told me the story many times." Jessie tried to be as diplomatic as possible, but she hated the thought of anyone going through life without being able to read. "I noticed you didn't take note of the menu," she added by way of explanation.

"I . . . I left the old country when I was a lad, mum. Me blessed mother taught me all she knew about learnin', but I guess it weren't much."

"Would you like to learn?"

"A man oughta better hisself, mum. That's what me blessed mother always said . . . before she went on to her reward."

"I'd be proud to teach you. It would only take an hour or so a day."

"If it would please you, mum."

Jessie's smile broadened. "It would please me, Paddy."

When the waiter brought the soup, Paddy stuffed

his cloth napkin into his stiff white collar and they ate in silence. Finally, Jessie looked up, studying the quiet man Jake had assigned to watch over her. "Have you known Mr. Weston long?"

Paddy put down his spoon and folded his hands in his lap. "The boss . . . I mean Mr. Jake, was at a fight five years ago—I was a professional fighter, you know." Paddy grinned proudly, then his smile faded. "The fight went forty-seven rounds, and I was beat bad. The promoter, man named Stokes from New York, found me in the mines in Pennsylvania. We fought our way across the country. I'd lost the last three fights so Stokes left me lying there, hurtin' so bad I couldn't get up. Mr. Jake took me back to the Tin Angel and give me a bed till I got better, then Mr. Taggart and the boss offered me a job taking care of the place. Your daddy and Mr. Jake was real good to me, mum."

"So you think highly of Mr. Weston?"

"He's a fine man, mum. He does what he says he's gonna do, expects the same of other men, and he's always treated me kindly."

"And my father?"

"As long as a man did his job, he'd have no trouble from Henry Taggart. Everybody liked Mr. Taggart." Paddy glanced away. "It was a terrible thing they done to him, mum."

"Were you there . . . I mean . . . when it happened?"

"No, mum. Me and Mr. Jake was in Stockton lookin' after some trouble in the freightin' business."

Jessie ate her single lamb chop and sipped her tea in silence, considering what Paddy had told her. Paddy attacked his two thick pork chops, a pile of mashed potatoes, and a gallon of coffee. While Jessie finished her tea, Paddy ate a quarter of an apple pie.

"Do you think the *Callie Sue* will be loaded yet?" Jessie asked.

"If you're finished, mum, we could walk back down to the wharf and find out." Paddy retrieved his bowler even before he paid the check.

As they headed down the boardwalk, Jessie laid her hand on his arm. "I'm pleased you want to read, Paddy, and that you thought so highly of my father. And, of course, Mr. Weston."

"I'd die for Mr. Jake, mum . . . and for Mr. Taggart's daughter." Paddy didn't look at her when he spoke, but his neck turned red, and Jessie was convinced he meant exactly what he said.

In the shadows of the alley across from the First Lady, a stocky, olive-skinned man watched from a shadowy doorway as Jessica Taggart and the heavy brute who watched over her made their way down the boardwalk.

Rubbing his whiskers with a muscular hand, the man narrowed his hard gray eyes. Pulling his slouch hat lower, he stepped onto the boardwalk and followed them, acting as if he were admiring the goods displayed in the store windows. Beneath his arm he carried a rolled-up coat, in which he concealed a short-barreled scattergun.

It would have been simple to walk up behind the two and let the scattergun do its deadly work, but his employer had said that their deaths should look like an accident. It wouldn't be the first time Portigee Santos Silva had murdered for pay—and it probably wouldn't be the last. But this assignment was by far his most interesting. Silva chuckled to himself.

The pair ahead of him reboarded the loaded *Callie Sue* for the return trip to the city, while Portigee Santos Silva headed toward a nearby wharf. The *Memphis Cloud*, two hundred twenty feet of stern-wheeled splendor, had arrived from Sacramento City bound for San Francisco while the Taggart girl and her bodyguard had dined.

Silva knew the schedule of both the *Callie Sue* and the *Memphis Cloud*. The scow would depart at five-thirty, making the return trip to San Francisco via Richmond and Oakland, arriving an hour after the stern-wheeler. The *Cloud* would depart at six, overtake the scow in the narrow channels of the river, and be in San Francisco just two hours after departure. The *Cloud* would average the trip from Sacramento City to San Francisco at over seventeen knots, running with the current until she entered the fickle waters of the bay.

Silva purchased a deck passenger ticket with a five-dollar gold piece, received three dollars in silver as his change, and boarded the ship. Having served as second mate on the beautiful stern-wheeler soon after his arrival in California, he was familiar with the elegant, flat-bottomed boat. But he held no love for her. He'd been discharged for beating a Chinese stoker half to death when the man didn't kowtow as Silva approached. No, his plan held no consideration for the *Cloud*, or its owner, Rene La Porte.

Along with the other passengers, Silva boarded via a broad, canopied stageplank that led onto the main deck. Although the cabins and staterooms on the *Cloud* were as fancy as any fine hotel, she was still basically a work boat. The main deck was filled with bails and boxes and wagons, stock of all kinds, and low-fare deck passengers. In the center stood the housing for the boilers and engines, and below the deck were holds for additional freight. Wood was stacked in high piles on the deck—the *Cloud* burned a cord an hour.

Silva stared up the ladder to the second level. He hadn't eaten yet, and he was hungry. Soon a table would be set for first-class passengers, who would be served five different kinds of beef, fowl, several vegetables, warm home-baked breads, and exotic fruits—accompanied by the best liquor.

Hearing his stomach growl, Silva clenched his jaw. It angered him that he couldn't show his face among the officers and passengers of the *Cloud*. He couldn't afford to be recognized. And he couldn't afford the price of a first-class ticket.

Silva ran his tongue across his lips. When he finished this job, he told himself, he would have money to burn.

Jessie stood beside Finn and watched the big stern-wheeler in the distance, the beautiful bow skimming the surface while the great red paddle wheel churned up the water behind it.

"Isn't she beautiful, Finn?" Jessie said wistfully.

"Not to me," he replied, starting straight ahead as he guided the scow to the far right side of the channel so the big boat would have room to pass. "The *Cloud* belongs to our competition, Rene La Porte."

"Mr. La Porte owns her?"

"He owns her and a half dozen udder boats. He even has a fancy steam-driven yacht named *Le Gran Dame*. She's the fastest ship in the harbor."

"My, but he certainly sounds successful," Jessie observed.

"I guess you could say that. He and your fadder were often at odds, and Mr. Weston doesn't much care for him either, but I don't think he's really so bad. Maybe a little too pushy sometimes."

"Yes," Jessie agreed, thinking of the way Rene had talked to her at the hotel. "I believe I know what you mean."

"Considering the power Mr. La Porte wields," Finn said, "Jake and your fadder did a damned fine job—beggin' your pardon, ma'am—building up the riverboat business and Taggart Freighting."

"From what I've seen of the books so far," Jessie

said, "I'd have to agree. Jake seems to be a fairly good businessman."

"He's a sight better'n fair, ma'am. He didn't have a whole lot to work with when Henry hired him on . . . no disrespect, ma'am. It was the two of them working togedder that made a go of things. One seemed to have whatever it was the udder lacked, if you know what I mean."

Jessie was only beginning to understand, but she didn't say that to Finn.

"I think your fadder thrived on adversity," he said. "He and Jake both. They were really making headway when old Henry's luck ran out. Even before he died, the businesses had begun suffering one mishap after anodder."

"What sort of mishaps, Finn?"

"Oh, shipments mixed up, orders canceled—nothin' you could really put your finger on. But each one created minor havoc and ate into the company's profits. Funny thing, now that I think about it, maybe you're good luck."

Jessie smiled. "How so?"

"Since you got to town, things have been running smooth as silk." Returning Jessie's smile, Finn glanced over his shoulder at the approaching *Memphis Cloud*.

Jessie followed his line of vision and again thought how beautiful the big ship was. "Let's hope things keep running smoothly," she told Finn. If she had any say in the matter—which she did—there should be no more problems.

In a concealed spot between some crates near the outside rail where he could watch the wharf activity, Portigee Santos Silva adjusted the scabbard of the knife he carried at his waist. He unfurled his coat and checked the loads in his scattergun. Then he carefully unrolled a copy of the *Alta California* that hid two cylindrical tubes of dynamite. Cautiously, he inserted a cap into one of the sticks.

As the *Cloud* headed downstream, Silva made his way aft to the massive stern wheel, where he hid his dynamite between bundles of ricking. He lit the long fuse, then checked his pocket watch. Most of the blast would be absorbed by the ricking, causing little damage to the ship, but attracting plenty of attention.

Silva climbed an outside ladder up to the hurricane deck, making his way forward to the texas deck.

From the front of the forward cabin, ports faced forward, providing a view of the river second only to the wheelhouse above. In the rear of the forward cabin, in the back of a closet, extended the lower half of the twelve-foot teakwood wheel that controlled the boat. By entering the closet, the wheel could be turned as readily as it could from the wheelhouse above. If his timing was right, his *accident* would happen.

Silva checked the closet and pulled out some hanging uniforms, which he discarded in a pile on the floor, exposing the lower half of the wheel. With a confident smile he moved to the window, leaning against a bulkhead so he could view the river ahead.

In the distance he spotted the *Callie Sue*, rapidly being overtaken by the much faster *Memphis Cloud*, and he smiled again.

"What de hell?" Standing just inside the open cabin door, an old waiter stared at the discarded pile of starched white uniforms. "Sorry, mister, but what are dese uniforms doin' throwed all about? Cap'n raise all kinds of billy joe hell if we gots spots an' such on our uniforms."

"I'm checking the steering. You go on about your business. You can clean up here later."

"Yes, sir," the man said, but he continued to look

at Silva. "I don't reckon I seen you hereabouts. You new on de boat?"

"I told you to go about your business," Silva warned.

"I think I find the cap'n an' see 'bout dis." The old man got midway to the door before Silva reached him and caught him in a viselike grip. He pulled out his knife and stabbed the man in the heart, killing him with ruthless efficiency. Silva quickly shut the door and went through the old waiter's pockets, gleaning half a dollar of tip money for his effort.

Hurrying back to his spot, he checked the distance between the two boats. Less than a quarter mile separated them, and the *Cloud* was closing fast. Silva drew out his pocket watch and flipped open the cover. In ten seconds, the dynamite would blow.

Satisfied that his timing was right, he pulled the huge wheel a half turn to larboard and jammed it fast with a ladder-backed chair. In the same instant, the dynamite went off, the explosion followed by the screams of terrified passengers and the sound of running feet.

In the wheelhouse above, the pilot raced toward the door, but his co-pilot, unable to move the wheel, frantically called him back.

"My God, man, what have you done?" the captain shouted as they tried in vain to straighten the course of the *Cloud*.

"I did nothing, sir." The young man's face was pale as he put all his weight into the wheel. "She turned herself, sir, I swear—"

"Pull, man! We're bearin' down on that scow, and the river's only a fathom deep beyond."

"I'm pulling my hardest, sir. She's jammed tight."

"Full speed astern!" the pilot called through the voice tube to the men in the engine room, but he knew it was too late. Again the two men pulled desperately at the wheel. "Hang on, boy," the pilot said as the great ship's momentum carried it forward, "and pray for those poor lost souls on the *Callie Sue.*"

Chapter 11

"Hold on, Miss Jessie!" Finn shouted as he frantically fought the wheel. "She's gonna ram us for sure!" The huge *Memphis Cloud* loomed above the little scow, its horn blasting wildly and its paddles churning the river in a mad attempt to slow its momentum.

"Can't we do something?" Jessie yelled back at him, but her words were lost in the roar of racing engines. Only the sound of her pounding heart seemed louder. Struggling to remain calm, she grabbed hold of one of the booms and steeled herself for the impending collision.

The last thing Jessie saw before she heard the crash of wood slamming against wood was Paddy's bulky figure dodging crates and barrels as he raced toward her. Then her head hit something solid and pain shot up her arm. The world spun into blackness.

Portigee Santos Silva clapped his hands, rejoicing at his success. The smaller boat splintered; its timbers snapped beneath the bow of the *Cloud* as the larger ship continued on its deadly arc. With a sharp jolt that threw Silva to the floor, the big, flat-bottomed boat hit a sandbar in the shallows of the river. The ship itself had sustained little damage, but the scow was lost, just as he'd intended.

Uninjured, Silva quickly regained his feet. Pulling the chair from between the wheel and the floor, he replaced it in its proper location. He returned the uniforms to the closet, but left the door ajar. With a grim smile, he looped his crowning touch—a red silk garrote—through the bottom spokes of the wheel, knotting it. When the wheel was spun in the pilot-house above, the bottom spokes would display the red garrote to tell its grim tale.

It was time to leave, and Silva hurried to complete his grisly task. He rolled the waiter's body in a blanket to hide the blood and hoisted the man across his shoulders, carrying him out of the forward cabin. He hurried past the center cabin where waiters and deckhands were talking excitedly and looking out at the wreckage of the *Callie Sue*.

"What happened?" one challenged as Silva passed.

"Must have fallen. Takin' him to the purser's cabin to be treated."

"You need any help?"

"You better get forward and see if they need assistance there."

Cursing the bad luck that someone had seen him, Silva continued down the ladder to the main deck. He was pleased to see that all the passengers were crowded in the bow, trying to see what had happened. Near the rail, between cases of freight, Silva slipped the old man's body overboard. It landed with a quiet splash, then sank out of sight.

Once again he was simply a deck passenger. It would be easy to make his way ashore among the people departing at the next stop—as soon as the *Memphis Cloud* was freed from her sandy perch. Glancing out at the flotsam that was once the *Callie Sue*, Portigee Santos Silva felt sure his boss would be pleased with the job he'd done.

Jessie forced her eyes to open, although she felt a great unwillingness to come awake. Clenching her teeth to keep them from chattering against the cold, she realized her head was throbbing. Her clothes, wet and heavy, clung to her body as she lay atop a floating chunk of wood that was once part of the *Callie Sue*. For a moment she felt so dazed she could hardly recall what had happened. Then, groaning aloud, Jessie lifted her head and saw that dusk had begun to fall.

Peering into the twilight, she realized the water was littered with debris, drifting with the current just as she was. Behind her and far upriver, she could barely make out the shadowy outline of the *Memphis Cloud* where it had run aground. The stern of the boat had drifted downstream, but the beautiful ship appeared to be lodged against some hidden obstruction near the shore. Another dark object along the shore might be the remains of the *Callie Sue*, but Jessie couldn't be sure. She silently prayed it was, hoping that Paddy and the captain had fared better than she.

At least she was alive, Jessie told herself as she scanned both distant banks and the river that stretched for miles into the fading sunset in front of her. She was sprawled gracelessly atop the scrap of decking, her legs dangling in the water, her water-soaked petticoats weighing her down. When she tried to pull herself farther up on the makeshift raft, she winced in pain and discovered that her arm was bleeding from a deep cut near her shoulder. At least the cold had numbed the pain somewhat.

Forcing herself to remain calm, Jessie glanced around again, hoping to spot some means of rescue. Surely someone would see the *Memphis Cloud*, and send word of the disaster. There would be rescue boats sent out; people would soon be searching for her. Thoughts of rescue reminded her of Jake. She wondered what he was doing now. She was grateful he had left the boat when he did. Maybe he would hear about the accident and come for her. Jessie clutched that hope as tightly as she did her make-shift raft.

Then she saw another figure bobbing in the water some distance ahead. She felt a tightening in her chest, and her heart began to pound.

Squinting against the rapidly falling darkness, Jessie tried to decide what the bulky object was. It's just another piece of debris, she told herself firmly, but her female intuition said it was a man, a desperate man, Jessie realized, as she heard him thrashing around in the water.

Lowering herself into the river, her arm still hooked over the raft, Jessie kicked her feet and aimed the raft downstream toward the other shipwreck victim. The closer she got, the more certain she was that the lump clutching the tiny piece of wood was Paddy. The chunk of debris wasn't large enough to support the huge man's weight, so he had to kick continually to force himself to the surface again and again.

"Paddy!" Jessie called out. "Paddy, is that you?"

The reply was so weak she almost didn't hear it. He coughed and spat water. "It's me, mum." Again the massive head went under and Jessie kicked frantically toward him.

"Hang on, Paddy. Just a little longer." Jessie fought the current, fought down her fear of the vast river, fought her heavy petticoats and the impending darkness, and kicked for all she was worth. Paddy either was hurt or couldn't swim. If the latter were true, and Jessie left the raft to tow him in, he'd probably drown them both. Instead she forced herself to be calm, and kept the raft in the swiftest part of the current. Little by little she overtook the heavy man.

Paddy's head went under just as Jessie got near enough to touch him. She grabbed his soggy wool coat at the back of the neck and pulled him to the surface. He broke the water sputtering.

"Climb up here with me," she ordered him.

Paddy choked and spat out a great stream of water. "I can't swim, mum," he said with the quiet desperation of a man resigned to die.

"You don't have to swim, just climb up." Jessie clutched his arm, keeping him afloat, but his heavy weight tilted the raft precariously.

"No, mum," Paddy persisted. "I'm not sure I got the strength, and I might tip you over. Then we'd both drown. Save yourself, mum."

"Paddy Fitzpatrick," Jessie commanded, "while I'm paying your wages, you'll do exactly what I say! Now you climb up on this raft this minute—and we'll both be just fine." She wished she felt as confident as she sounded. "And don't worry," she added, when he still seemed dubious, "I *can* swim."

For the first time Paddy smiled. Even in the thickening darkness, she caught the flash of his white teeth.

"Hold on tight, mum," he told her. Then, with a last great heave that tilted the decking at such a sharp angle Jessie was sure it was going to tip over, Paddy pulled himself up on the floating debris. His great chest heaved as he lay on his back, catching his breath. Jessie was hoping he'd be able to pull her up too, but she decided to wait till he'd regained a little of his strength.

As if reading her thoughts, he rolled to his side and stuck out a hand, but the raft pitched precariously, threatening to dump him. After fighting to stay alive and nearly losing, Jessie didn't think he'd have the strength to get up on the raft again.

"Stay where you are, Paddy. There isn't enough room up there for both of us, anyway."

"You can't hold on like that till they find us—we might be out here all night."

"I'll manage," Jessie said with a halfhearted smile.

Three more times, Paddy tried unsuccessfully to haul Jessie up on the raft. Each time he moved the slightest bit, Jessie was certain that the piece of deck was going to topple over. She finally let him pull her partly on the raft, as she had been before, her legs dangling in the water. Her arm was still bleeding, but the cold water kept the pain to a dull throbbing.

Exhausted and shivering, Jessie was grateful that at least she no longer had to hang on. As she stared out across the water searching for a boat, she began to accept the fact that they might be on the water until dawn. Shuddering more from fear than from the creeping cold, she smiled up at Paddy, who lay on his back clutching the sides of the raft for dear life, and said a silent prayer for their rescue. Resting her face against the soggy planking, Jessie suddenly realized the water tasted brackish and salty.

They had drifted into the shark-infested waters of the bay.

In the midst of the Tin Angel's usual noise and laughter, Jake checked his watch. It was nine o'clock. Jessie should be back by now, but after her long day on the water, she'd probably decided not to drop by. Hell, he didn't blame her. If she felt half as sick as he had after the first half hour, she was most likely home in bed, thanking God she was back on shore.

Still, the boat trip hadn't seemed to affect her the way it did him, and he found himself almost hoping she'd stop by with her usual round of questions or, even better, to make sure he was feeling all right.

Forcing his mind back to business, Jake strode toward the stairs, but before he reached the first step, he felt a tug on his arm and turned to see Rupert standing behind him, his face crestfallen.

"Boss, we got trouble."

Beside Rupert, Sheriff Handley stood, hat in hand. "Got some bad news for you, Jake. Seems the *Callie Sue* had an accident. Mid-river collision a' some sort with the *Memphis Cloud.* Boat's a total loss, and Finn Engstrom's been killed."

For a moment Jake just stood there, unable to accept the sheriff's words. "What about Jessie and Paddy?" he asked, and heard the hollow ring in his voice. His heart was pounding against his ribs, and the room seemed suddenly hot and airless.

"What about 'em?" the sheriff asked, looking a little confused.

"They were aboard the *Callie Sue.*"

The sheriff's expression grew grim, and he shifted his gaze to the toes of his boots. "Haven't heard a word about either one of 'em. Deckhand made it back to the *Memphis Cloud,* but things were so confused that nobody seemed to know much about what happened. We thought he and Engstrom were the only ones aboard. Deckhand said the rest of the passengers got off in Benicia."

"All but Jessie and Paddy." Jake turned to Rupert, trying to ignore the buzzing in his ears and the knot in the pit of his stomach. "Watch the store, Rupert," he said tersely "and send a man to fetch Burton James to the *Cairo Illinois Queen.* She's the fastest scow we've got." Taking the stairs two at a time, Jake disappeared into his office. When he reappeared, his arms were full of rolled-up charts.

"Come on," he told the sheriff. Refusing to succumb to his worst fear, he set his mind on his task and headed out the door. Hailing the first hansom cab they could find, he and the sheriff climbed aboard. Jake handed the cabbie a silver dollar. "The money's yours. Wharf fifty-seven, at a gallop, man."

"Yes, sir." The man cracked his whip above the horse's head.

While the cab careened toward the docks, the sheriff told Jake what he knew about the disaster. Once they reached the wharf, they discovered that within the past hour word had filtered back of the two missing people, and Rene La Porte had already set off in search of them in his steam-driven yacht.

Jake said a silent prayer that the two had indeed survived. He'd never been a particularly religious man, but in those few quiet moments in the cab, he'd have made any deal with God to save his friends. *Friends*, he repeated to himself, although in that instant he knew that Jessie Taggart meant a whole lot more to him than that.

"I shouldn't have let her go by herself," he said to Handley as the *Cairo Illinois Queen* was quickly readied for departure.

"She wasn't by herself," the sheriff said. "Paddy was with her. Besides, you couldn't have known this would happen. Stop blaming yourself." Handley laid a hand on his shoulder. "Somebody'll find them, Jake. Just keep believing that." Handley turned away and headed back to the carriage.

Jake climbed aboard the *Queen*. He'd be seasick again, but Jessie and Paddy were out there somewhere . . . if he wasn't already too late. The thought of Jessie drifting facedown in the river, her thick mahogany hair floating like a grim wreath around her head, ripped through Jake's heart like a blade. She couldn't be dead, he told himself, trying to be rational in the face of his overwhelming emotion. He'd already lost one partner this month. By God, he wasn't about to lose another!

Setting his jaw against the first roll of the ship, Jake lit a coal-oil lantern, spread his charts on top of a crate, and began studying the tide tables. Even though he'd never been much use on board the leaky old scows, his knowledge of the bay was thorough. After careful study, he had cut the fleet's wood consumption by thirty percent by rescheduling the scows to take advantage of the prevailing tides and currents. Now, he prayed, all his work would serve a more vital purpose.

At this hour, the tide was flowing out, racing past

San Pablo and Pinole Points at almost six knots. Jake checked his watch. *If* the accident had happened at six-thirty, as the sheriff had said, the debris should be rounding Pinole Point about now. By the time the scow reached the north end of the bay, *if* Jake's tables were absolutely correct, the debris would be rounding San Pablo Point.

That's valuable information, Jake thought, setting his jaw, *if* Jessie had survived the crash, and *if* she had managed to find a crate or piece of wreckage to cling to, and *if* she hadn't made it to shore somewhere between Port Costa, where the accident was reported to have happened, and Carquinez, where the river dumped into the bay.

So many *ifs*.

Even with a full head of steam, it took the better part of an hour to near San Pablo Point. The trip gave Jake time to study the river charts. At Port Costa, where the collision had occurred, the river was over a mile wide, the main channel over a hundred yards. There should have been plenty of room for the *Callie Sue* and the *Memphis Cloud* to pass each other easily.

The sheriff had reported that the damage to the *Cloud* was minimal, as Jake was sure it would be. Two hundred fifty tons against twenty tons was no battle at all.

Other accidents had befallen Taggart Enterprises these past few months, but until now Jake had believed them to be just that—accidents. Tonight he began to wonder. . . . Would Rene La Porte purposely order the *Callie Sue* run down? The Frenchman wanted very much to buy out Taggart Enterprises; he'd made that clear. Destroying Taggart assets would serve him no purpose, unless he'd decided that if he couldn't buy them out, he'd just as soon ruin them.

La Porte had known about Jessie's planned excursion aboard the *Callie Sue*; Jessie and Jake had discussed it while he and the others had been playing poker. Her death would leave La Porte another opening, since her reluctance to sell would die with her.

Jake forced his mind from thoughts of Jessie. Even the *why* was unimportant. The crucial thing now was *where*. Find Jessie, he repeated over and over, forcibly blocking out all other thoughts. Signaling to one of the deckhands, he began barking orders. He'd find them, he vowed. He wouldn't stop looking until he did.

The deckhands suspended four reflecting lanterns from the bow of the *Queen*, and Jake and two others leaned over the rails to search the water while Burton James, the *Queen*'s skipper, steered the scow back and forth across the outgoing current. The night was dark and moonless, making their task even more difficult.

As Jake watched the water flash by beneath the lantern, he suddenly realized he wasn't seasick. I'll be damned, he marveled, silently giving a prayer of thanks.

When the light of San Pablo Point lay directly to the starboard of the *Queen*, Jake spotted the lanterns of another boat bearing down on them. As she neared, he recognized the rakish lines of the eighty-foot *Le Gran Dame*, Rene La Porte's flagship and personal yacht.

She too carried search lanterns, and several deckhands, resplendent in spotlessly white, gold-trimmed uniforms, hung over the rails as they scoured the water.

"Come about, Burton," Jake called to the skipper of the *Queen*. "I want to talk to them."

The captain swung the scow around, and the *Dame* began to slow when Jake waved a lantern. As the ship neared, Jake busied himself rummaging through one of the deck lockers.

They were only twenty feet apart and traveling at

the same speed when Rene La Porte, wineglass in hand, walked out of the deckhouse and over to the rail. La Porte's mouth dropped open when Jake swung a four-pointed grappling hook across *Le Gran Dame*'s teakwood rail, the sharp prongs digging into the polished wood. Hurling his glass into the water, La Porte grabbed the railing just a few feet away from the hook and stared in disbelief.

While one deckhand pulled on the first line, bringing the scow in closer, Jake walked to the rear of the boat and let fly with another grappling hook, handing the line to the second deckhand. In moments, the old scow was rubbing her rusty rails against the gleaming white hull of *Le Gran Dame*. Jake climbed onto the deck and vaulted the rail.

His fists balled at his sides, Rene La Porte faced him. "You fool!" La Porte spat, his face a mottled red. "You've marked *Le Dame* with that . . . that garbage scow! Order her away this instant!"

"Not until you and I have a little talk, La Porte. How the hell did your stern-wheeler manage to run down the *Callie Sue*?"

"Get that scum bucket away from my yacht." La Porte stepped up to Jake. "Or I will have my man put a six-pounder through her hull. She will wind up on the bottom of the bay—along with the *Callie Sue*." Near the bow of the *Dame*, a rail-mounted swivel cannon was manned and trained on the *Queen*.

"Answer my question, La Porte," Jake said, ignoring his threat.

Looking from Weston to his crewman, Rene removed his coat and handed it to a steward. "On second thought, monsieur, I think I shall thrash you here and now."

"Why didn't the *Cloud* search for Jessie and Paddy?"

"The *Cloud* ran aground. There was an explosion aboard that no one has explained. The blast destroyed thousands of dollars in cargo, Weston, and a crewman was lost. She had her own problems.'' La Porte raised his fists in the classic Queensbury tradition. ''Now, monsieur, if you please.''

''I wish I had time to stomp that pretty white suit of yours into a grease rag, Frenchy, but I've got a partner to find, thanks to you. Get back to your Bordeaux.'' Jake vaulted the rail and ordered the lines cut.

''This is a long way from finished, La Porte,'' he yelled over the rails as the boats pulled apart. ''After I find Jessie, I'll look you up.''

Rene turned to his first mate and scoffed. ''A spittoon of a boat with a milksop for a master.'' The first mate laughed. ''Get those hooks out of my rails,'' La Porte ordered, ''and we will continue the search.''

The much faster *Dame* soon left the *Queen* far behind.

''Mum! Mum!''

Jessie forced her eyes open to find Paddy shaking her.

''Miss Jessie, there's lights up ahead. A boat, I think.''

Jessie rubbed her eyes and felt pain shoot through her arm. ''Oh,'' she moaned quietly.

''Are you all right, mum? You aren't hurt, are you?''

''I'll be all right if we can flag down that boat, Paddy. Yell. Yell for all you're worth.''

Both of them shouted as the lights approached, and continued yelling until they faded away. The ship had gotten no closer than half a mile, Jessie guessed as she sagged dejectedly down on the wet planking. She felt incredibly weak all of a sudden. In fact, she could hardly stay awake.

''Don't worry, mum,'' Paddy said. ''Mr. Jake will find us. You'll see. Mr. Jake thinks a lot a' you. He'll be awful upset when he finds out what happened. He'll come—I know he will."

"I hope so, Paddy," Jessie said. Closing her eyes again, she recalled Jake's ruggedly handsome features, his amused grin and his tousled black hair. Where are you, Jake Weston? she thought as she drifted back to sleep.

During the next hour, Paddy spotted two more boats. He yelled until he was hoarse, to no avail. Jessie thought they'd seen one of the boats before, but she couldn't be sure. Paddy kept asking how she felt, his worry apparent. She tried to reassure him, but she was just too weak.

"Hold on, mum," he told her, his voice sounding far away. He kept looking out across the water toward the few yellow lights along the shore. "There's a light, mum," he suddenly whispered. "It's comin' our way."

Jessie opened her eyes and squinted into the darkness. She could just make out a ship with lanterns hung at her rails. Although the boat was still too far away to hear his calls, Paddy bellowed into the damp evening air. As loud as he was, Jessie heard him only as a muffled echo.

Frantic to make their position known, Paddy continued to holler, although he dared not raise too far up on his tenuous perch. Eventually Jessie was dimly award of voices answering his calls.

"Over here!" he yelled back to them. "We're over here." He touched her with gentle concern and she opened her eyes. "Miss Jessie," he told her, "Mr. Jake is comin' just like I said."

"Jake?" she whispered. But when the ship pulled alongside, it wasn't Jake Weston but Rene La Porte who stood at the rail. For all Jessie cared, their savior could have been the devil himself.

"Where am I?" Jessie asked, opening her eyes for the first time in what seemed hours.

"Rest easy, *chérie*," came the soothing French voice she recognized as Rene's. "You are aboard my ship, *Le Gran Dame*, on your way back to the harbor. You are safe now, and so is your friend."

"I'm so tired," Jessie said, fighting to keep her eyes open as she took in her surroundings. Lamplight bathed the cabin in a soft yellow glow just bright enough to illuminate the sumptuous room: a canopied bed draped in ice-blue satin, a handsomely carved walnut bureau and matching armoire, and a small blue satin-covered settee. Jessie lay between satin sheets, and a soft down pillow cradled her head.

"You have lost a lot of blood, *chérie*. We have bound your wound and stopped the bleeding, but I am afraid the surgeon will need to stitch up your arm as soon as we reach the shore."

Jessie managed a weak smile. "Paddy's all right?"

"Your big overprotective friend is just fine. Worried about you, but fine. He is below, drinking his second gallon of coffee, laced with a little Napoleon brandy."

"Thank you, Rene. You saved our lives. I don't know how I'll ever be able to repay you."

Rene's pale blue eyes took on a hungry cast Jessie couldn't miss even in the dimly lit room. "I believe I know a way, *chérie*."

Ignoring his look, Jessie glanced at her bandaged arm and for the first time realized her soggy garments had been replaced by a man's white cotton nightshirt. "How did I get undressed?" she asked, suddenly wary. One look at Rene's roguish expression gave her the answer and sent a rosy blush all the way to her toes.

"Do not be embarrassed, *chérie*. You are not the first woman I have seen. One of the loveliest, I will admit, but not the first."

Jessie licked her lips. "Couldn't you have waited until we reached the dock?"

"Your safety was far more important than your modesty, do you not agree?"

Knowing he was right, Jessie lowered her lashes. "I suppose so," she admitted reluctantly, trying to fight the warmth in her cheeks.

"I had no choice, I assure you. Besides, with a figure as lovely as yours, there is no need to be ashamed."

"Please, Rene," she said, still unwilling to look at him.

Rene laughed softly. "Get some rest, *chérie*. We will be back on land very soon." He brushed her lips with a feather-soft kiss as he rose from his place on the wide berth beside her.

Jessie's eyes slowly closed. When she opened them again, it was to the sound of voices raised in argument just outside her door.

Chapter 12

"Be sensible, Weston. You have no quarters suitable for the lady's recovery, and she certainly cannot stay in the hotel alone." La Porte stood facing him, his white suit still immaculate, while Jake's white shirt and black breeches were damp and stained with engine grease.

"I will have her taken to my house," La Porte continued. "She will have servants to attend her, and a housekeeper who can act as chaperon."

"A housekeeper—that's a good one, La Porte. She wouldn't be safe in your house with a small army to protect her. Now get out of my way."

After hours of unsuccessful searching, Jake had returned to the dock to get more wood for fuel. He'd arrived just minutes before La Porte and *Le Gran Dame.* Paddy had spotted Jake immediately and lumbered aboard the *Queen* to tell Jake about the Frenchman's rescue.

"He's taking care a' Miss Jessie, boss," Paddy said. "She don't look so good, but he says she's gonna be all right."

Jake felt such an enormous surge of relief it made him dizzy. "Let's go," was all he said.

Now, as he stepped around La Porte and swung open the cabin door, he stopped short, content for a moment just to look at her. Lying on the bed, Jessie stared back at him, her expression one of relief and something else. Her eyes shimmered with tears.

Swallowing past the sudden lump that lodged in his throat, Jake moved into the room and knelt beside her.

"You're gonna be fine, Boston." Her face was as pale as the white satin sheets, and her trembling hand felt like ice. "You've just lost a little too much blood, that's all. You'll be good as new, soon as you get rested up."

Jake swept loose strands of dark shining hair away from her face. Without thinking, he leaned down and gently touched his lips to hers. They felt cold as marble, and a rush of tenderness surged inside him.

"Paddy told me how brave you were. He said you saved his life."

A single tear slid down her cheek. "I'm tired of being brave, Jake. I just want to go home."

Jake felt a tug at his heart. "I shouldn't have let you go alone."

Jessie shook her head. Although it took most of her strength, she couldn't take her eyes off Jake. She'd never seen him this way, his features soft with concern, his gaze full of tenderness. It touched her heart as words never could. She wished he would hold her, make her forget her terrible ordeal. She wished he would look at her that way each day for the next fifty years. "It wasn't your fault," she said softly.

"I've never been so damned worried in my life," he admitted gruffly, and Jessie smiled.

When she tried to sit up, Jake gently pressed her back down, but not before the sheet fell away, and he saw the soft cotton nightshirt she wore, the full breasts the shirt revealed. His look turned hard as it dawned on him that Rene had probably been the one to remove her garments.

"I . . . I was injured," she explained, reading his

thoughts. "My clothes were wet and . . . Rene—Mr.
La Porte—he . . . he had to undress me."

Jake tilted her chin, forcing her to look at him, and
saw the embarrassment in her eyes. "You leave La
Porte to me," he told her. "First we're gonna get
you to a doctor. Then I'm taking you back to the
Angel."

From over Jake's shoulder, La Porte's voice carried clearly into the room. "You will be taken to *my*
home, *chérie*, where you will receive proper care."
Jake turned to La Porte, who stood in the open doorway. "A saloon is no place for a young lady."

When Jake glanced back down at Jessie, she
looked beseechingly at him. "Can't I just go back to
the hotel?"

"You're in no condition to be left alone," he said.
"Lovey and the girls will look out for you back at
the Tin Angel." Jessie nodded, and her eyes drifted
closed.

"Don't be ridiculous," La Porte insisted. "You
have no suitable place for her there."

Although he cursed La Porte for his interference,
Jake had to admit the Frenchman was right. For the
second time since he'd walked into the cabin, he
berated himself for not buying a home of his own as
he'd started to do time and again over the years.
Still, he couldn't leave Jessie with La Porte.

"I'll hire a nurse to stay with her at the hotel,"
he said finally.

"Jake?" Jessie's lids fluttered open again, her
lovely green eyes drawing his attention like a mag-
net. "I want to go with *you*."

Jake felt a tightening in his chest and an ache
around his heart. It was all the encouragement he
needed. "You heard her, La Porte. She's going with
me."

Bending over La Porte's wide bed, Jake tossed
back the covers, threw a blanket over Jessie, and
scooped her into his arms. Her hands went around

his neck, and her still-damp hair brushed against his cheek. When she nestled her face in the hollow between his neck and shoulder, her skin felt as smooth as his good silk shirt. How would her breasts feel? he wondered, then he cursed himself for the rogue he was. She was injured, damn it! She trusted him, and aside from that, she was Henry's daughter. The last thing she needed was a man like him. With a silent prayer for strength, Jake strode toward the door.

"You are being a fool, Weston."

"Get out of my way, La Porte." Jake's gaze turned cold. "You're beginning to annoy me. I appreciate what you did for Jessie and Paddy, although I'm not sure you didn't take advantage of the situation. Miss Taggart's my responsibility, not yours. I'll see she gets the proper care."

Brushing past the Frenchman, Jake ducked through the open hatch, then strode along the deck and down the gangplank. A carriage waited at the dock; Paddy, at Jake's orders, had commandeered it.

"Let's take her straight to the Angel," Jake told him. "Rupert can fetch Doc Bedford."

Dressed in a steward's white uniform at least two sizes too small, Paddy held the door open as Jake climbed into the carriage, then the big Irishman mounted the seat beside the driver.

As Jake carefully positioned Jessie on his lap, she rested her cheek against his shoulder and he felt the warmth of her breath against his neck. Her skin was still cold, so he tucked the blanket more closely around her. Jessie smiled up at him, so sweetly that he thought his heart might stop. When had the little baggage insinuated herself so solidly into his affections? he wondered as he tightened his hold on her.

"Jake?" she finally asked, her voice barely rising above the quiet *clip-clop* of the horses' hooves on the hard dirt streets.

"Yes, Boston?"

"Were you looking for us?"

"I started looking as soon as I heard about the accident." Jake closed his eyes, trying not to remember the knot of despair that had tightened in his stomach when he'd first heard of the accident. It had taken a shipwreck to show him he cared about the girl—a helluva lot more than he wanted to admit.

"Paddy said you'd be looking," she said softly.

"I had to find you," he teased. "I don't have time to break in another partner."

Jessie smiled and snuggled against him, content, it seemed, to stay right where she was. Jake could feel the shapely curves of her bottom pressing against his thighs, the points of her breasts as they teased the fabric of his shirt. Although he tried to fight it, the blood surged to his loins.

"Sit still," he growled as she wriggled again. Any moment now she was going to feel his arousal. Jake groaned inwardly at the thought. After her experience with La Porte, she'd think both of them were cads.

"We're here, guv'nor," the driver called out as he pulled up to the back door of the Tin Angel. Jake said a silent prayer of thanks. Paddy pulled open the carriage door, and Jake stepped down, holding Jessie carefully. He carried her up the back stairs, and by the time he reached his room, the hall was filled with concerned faces, Lovey and Rupert among them.

"Go get Doc Bedford," Jake instructed Rupert. "Tell him he's got some stichin' to do."

"The poor, dear child," Lovey said as she helped Jake put Jessie to bed. "She looks pale as spun glass, and her arm is hurt." The bandage had turned red, the wound beginning to bleed again from the jouncing carriage ride. Cursing, Jake wondered if he should have left her with La Porte after all.

"Don't you worry, Miss Jessie," Lovey told her. "Doc's office ain't far. He lives above it, so it won't take Rupert long to fetch him. Soon as he gits your arm fixed up, you'll be good as new." She said the words with confidence, then glanced at Jake for reassurance.

"She's lost some blood," he told her, pulling a chair to the side of the bed. "Let's see she doesn't lose any more." With that he took hold of Jessie's arm and applied an even, steady pressure over the wound. She moaned softly.

"Sorry, Boston. I know this hurts, but it'll all be over soon."

Jessie nodded weakly and relaxed against the pillow. Jake was taking care of her—everything would be all right. She was glad he hadn't left her with Rene. Although La Porte had saved her life, she still had mixed emotions about him. She'd wanted to go with Jake—more than she should have. She liked the way she felt in his arms, the way he looked after her. It seemed so long since anyone had cared for her . . . so long since she'd felt safe and protected.

The pressure on her arm tightened and she dimly heard Jake barking orders. She could tell he was worried about her, and she found the knowledge comforting. Even the pain in her arm couldn't destroy her feeling of contentment. With a soft smile on her face, Jessie drifted off to sleep.

Although it seemed to Jake that he had waited for hours, Doc Bedford arrived in twenty minutes. Pulling a pair of spectacles from the pocket of his rumpled black suit, he set them on the end of his narrow nose and shooed Jake away, taking a seat beside the bed. Jessie woke up and gave him a weak smile. After a cursory examination of her wound, he dug through his bag and pulled out needle and thread.

"I got Annabelle boilin' ye some water," Lovey

said to him just as the buxom girl hurried through the door, steaming pot in hand.

"Just a little sewin'," the doctor said in a slow Virginia drawl. "No need for all the bother."

Jake caught the thin man's arm. "Use the water, Hiram."

The doctor shrugged his skinny shoulders and did as Jake said, cleaning the instruments as best he could. Jake poured some brandy into the steaming water as the doctor worked.

"Give her a shot of that before I start," Bedford instructed.

"What about some laudanum?"

"She's awful weak, Jake. I'd rather not take the chance."

Jake set his jaw, knowing the doctor was right. He walked around the foot of his old iron bed and sat down on the other side, taking Jessie's clammy hand between his warmer ones.

"Listen to me, Jess. You gotta hold on just a little longer. Doc's gonna stitch up your arm, then you can get some rest."

Lovey handed him a snifter of brandy.

"Drink some of this," Jake ordered. For once Jessie didn't argue, although she coughed and sputtered as the fiery liquid burned a path down her throat. "Finish it," he said, propping her up with his hand, his voice a little gruffer than he intended.

Jessie downed the last of the liquid. Sagging back against the pillow, she closed her eyes. She didn't realize that Jake had her shoulders lightly pinned down until she felt the first sharp jab of the needle, and her eyes flew open.

"Hold on, Boston. Lovey, give her something to bite on." Lovey handed him his razor strop, and Jessie bit down hard. As the doctor continued to pull the stinging thread through her skin, beads of perspiration popped out on her forehead, but she didn't cry out.

"Damn it, Doc," Jake swore, holding her as steady as he could without hurting her. "How much longer?"

"Almost done, Jake." The doctor made the final few stitches, drew the thread taut, knotted it, and clipped the ends. Everyone sagged in relief.

Jake removed the razor strop from between Jessie's teeth, admired its new set of perfect tooth marks, then leaned over and kissed her forehead. When he straightened he saw the strangest expression on Lovey MacDougal's face.

The absurdity of the situation hit him like a blow. What the hell was he doing? Coming down with calico poisoning? He was a gambler, a trader, a whoremonger, and a rogue. Jessie Taggart was his partner, nothing more—and that's the way he wanted to keep it. The last thing he needed was to get involved with a woman—any woman—especially a Boston schoolgirl who had no more in common with a man like him than a Baptist preacher did with a Chinatown whore.

"Well, what are you all staring at?" Jake snapped. "Let the girl get some rest." Catching his change of mood, Lovey, Rupert, and Annabelle all slipped quietly from the room.

Jake flipped the doctor a five-dollar gold piece. "Thanks, Hiram."

"Thank *you*. At my age it would take a month to take this out in trade."

They both smiled, then Jake's expression turned serious. "Anything special we should do for her?"

"Keep her warm and comfortable, and watch her close for the next day or two. I don't think she'll have any trouble." The doctor snapped the latches on his black leather bag. "You may be right about cleaning those instruments. German fella named Ferdinand Cohn claims little bugs called bacteria, smaller than the eye can see, cause infection."

"Now there's a new one." Jake clapped the gray-ing doctor on the back, and Bedford picked up his bag. "If you're thirsty, the drinks are on me."

The doctor grinned, licking his lips. "You're readin' my mind, friend. In fact, I've got cause to celebrate. I'm a citizen again."

"How's that, Hiram?"

"Congress passed the amnesty act today. We Southerners are officially welcomed back into the Union."

"I guess that's as good an excuse to celebrate as any."

"Jake?" Jessie called from the bed.

"I'll be right down," he told the doctor, who nod-ded and stepped into the hall, closing the door be-hind him. Jake returned to the chair beside the bed. "What is it, Jess?"

"I just wanted to thank you."

"You don't have to thank me. That's what part-ners are for. Besides, I didn't find you, I'm sorry to say. La Porte did."

"I know, but still . . ." She smiled up at him.

"Get some sleep, Jess."

"Jake?"

"Yes?"

"Would you mind kissing me good night?"

"What!"

"I said would you mind—"

"I know what you said, damn it." Jake ran his fingers through his hair.

"Well?" she whispered.

"Well, what?"

"Well, will you kiss me good—"

"Damn you, woman," he burst out. "You are without a doubt the biggest handful of trouble a man could be unlucky enough to run across." Knowing he should turn and run, Jake bent down instead, cradled her face between his palms, and kissed her. It was just a sweet, brotherly kiss at first, but when her cool lips parted beneath his mouth, Jake forgot all about his vows, forgot how ill-suited they were, nearly forgot his name.

As his tongue slid inside her mouth, he heard her soft mew of pleasure and deepened the kiss, sinking down on the bed beside her. He nibbled her tempting bottom lip just as he'd dreamed of doing, and ran his tongue into the corners of her mouth. His lips tracing a path from her jaw to her ear, he nibbled the petal-soft lobe while his hand drifted down the slender column of her throat to her breast. With a soft moan, her arms went around his neck, and she clung to him, her fingers laced in his hair.

As if by magic, Jake felt the fullness of her breast in his hand, her cotton nightshirt the only thing separating his thumb and forefinger from the nipple he teased to a hard, taut peak. Then the buttons at the front of the nightshirt came free, and his hand skimmed across her silky skin until her breast again filled his hand.

Shivering at his touch, Jessie sucked in a trembling breath and pulled away. "Jake?" she whispered uncertainly, suddenly bringing him to his senses.

With a strength of will he didn't know he possessed, he drew back and rebuttoned the front of her nightshirt. Glancing down at Jessie, he saw her huge green eyes staring at him with something close to awe.

"I . . . I . . . we shouldn't have done that," she stammered.

Fighting to control his ragged breathing and the telltale swelling in his pants, Jake glared down at her. "You're damned right, we shouldn't have," he snapped. "One of these days, Miss Boston Taggart, you're gonna get yourself in more trouble than you can handle."

Jessie touched her lips, still swollen from his kiss, blushed, and glanced away. "Good night, Jake."

"Good night, Boston." Without looking back he stalked out the door, closing it harder than he intended. A good night for her maybe, but she'd left him with a case of lover's blues that even Monique couldn't cure. Besides, he didn't want Monique. He wanted Miss Boston Taggart. She wasn't any safer with him than she would have been with La Porte.

"What the hell!" he cursed aloud. What was he going to do? Maybe after what happened in the river, she'd be ready to go back to Boston. Then again, knowing her as he was beginning to, that didn't seem likely. She had too much grit for that, too much damned stubborn Taggart pride. He had to give her credit. Young or not, naive or not, Miss Jessica Taggart was one helluva woman.

What she needed was a helluva man.

Tired though she was, Jessie lay awake, sleepily thinking about what had happened between her and Jake. Remembering his kiss and the bold way he'd touched her, she felt a warm blush rise to her cheeks. Then she thought of the way he'd made her feel— shivery all over, warm and languid, yet strangely keyed up. Her nipples still felt heavy, and there was a tender ache in her secret, womanly place.

What in heaven's name had possessed her to ask Jake Weston to kiss her? Even before she completed the thought, Jessie knew the answer. That one light touch of his lips on the yacht hadn't been enough. As she'd watched Jake standing in the open cabin door, she'd never been so happy to see anyone in her life. And the look on his face—she remembered every line, every detail. He cared about her, she'd seen it. Just how much, she couldn't be sure.

Jessie had discovered something about herself as well. There wasn't a minute she'd spent in the water that thoughts of Jake hadn't been with her. She'd been glad he hadn't been aboard the *Callie Sue*, glad to know that wherever he was, he was safe.

What was there about him that made her feel different than she did with other men? Womanly, desirable, and at the same time protected and secure. When she was near him, her emotions were in turmoil.

Jessie groaned aloud. In truth, she was becoming more and more attracted to Jake—and that could be fatal.

Oh, he cared all right. But there were other women, she was sure. He was a scoundrel, not the kind of man to settle down. Jake had taken liberties with her that no man ever had, kissed her as no man had . . . still she couldn't say she was sorry. To be honest, she had enjoyed it, though the notion was unseemly.

What in God's name was she going to do? she asked herself, not for the first time. She should have stayed in Boston. She'd have met some nice successful Bostonian, married him, and had a flock of children. Dull, dull, dull.

No matter how pampered she would have been, she wouldn't have been happy. Not when she compared that existence to all she had experienced since deciding to come to San Francisco: her trip West, her ownership of the businesses, her plans for the future. Besides, she wasn't at all ready for marriage. She wanted to savor the freedom she'd been granted. A husband would never allow such a thing.

She would stay right here, and Jake Weston could just go hang! She'd stop this foolish infatuation once and for all. She knew she could do it. If there was one thing Jessica Taggart had plenty of, it was willpower.

Still, as she remembered Jake's kiss, the warmth of his hand on her breasts, the heady way he made her feel, she wasn't completely convinced she could resist him—and she wasn't completely sure she wanted to.

Chapter 13

Having slept for over twenty hours, Jessie awoke to find Sugar Su Ling sitting at the foot of the bed, quietly mending a blue silk dress.

"Good morning, Su Ling," Jessie said drowsily. "It is morning, isn't it?" The girl leaped to her feet and hurried to Jessie's side.

"It is morning. You sleep long time. You wish water, Miss Jessie?"

"Yes. Thank you." Su Ling helped Jessie sit up while she sipped a glass of water.

"Mr. Jake say when you wake up, you have breakfast. Fruit and mush and eggs and—"

"Wait a minute, Su Ling. I'd like a little juice, but nothing else. First maybe you could help me . . . ?"

"Sure, sure Miss Jessie." Su Ling assisted with her morning ablutions and helped her change out of La Porte's nightshirt into a soft ruffled nightgown Annabelle had fetched from her room at the hotel, then put her back to bed.

"Have you been here long?" Jessie asked when the tiny Oriental woman pulled open the door.

"All night, Miss Jessie. Mr. Jake say I am to watch over you and not fall asleep."

"That's not fair. How does he expect you to make a living?"

"I am *mui jai*. My living is only for you and Mr.

Jake." Su Ling bowed her head and hurried out, pulling the door quietly closed.

What a strange thing to say, Jessie thought as Su Ling padded down the hall. The girl returned with a glass of orange juice and the latest copy of the *Chronicle*. She laid the paper on the bed and handed Jessie the glass.

"Thank you, Su Ling." Jessie savored the sweet juice while Su Ling returned to her mending. "Don't you need to get some sleep?" Jessie asked.

"Mr. Jake say to sit by you until someone else come. I am to sit with you every night until you are well."

"That's silly." Jessie glanced at the girl, who merely smiled and continued with her mending, making no effort to leave.

"You said something earlier . . . something I didn't understand. You said your living was only for Mr. Jake and me. What did you mean?"

"Why, Miss Jessie, I am *mui jai*. You own Su Ling. Understand?"

"No, Su Ling, I don't."

The little Oriental looked at her as if she wasn't too bright. "My life belong Mr. Jake and you. From Mr. Henry you have inherited Su Ling along with the Tin Angel."

"Surely you don't believe that!" Jessie was dumbstruck. "Since Mr. Lincoln's Emancipation Proclamation no one is allowed to own anyone in this country."

"Maybe that so in rest of Union. Here, China girls belong. Mr. Taggart, your honorable father, buy Su Ling at barracoon."

"Barracoon?"

"How you say? Queen's Room."

"I'm afraid this is all so new to me. Please go on."

"It is terrible place, Miss Jessie. China girls arrive on boat and all go to barracoon. Auction man sell girls to highest bidder. Honorable Mr. Taggart buy

Su Ling, and Su Ling very happy. This good place for Su Ling. Some girls not so lucky.''

''Why, that's the most outrageous thing I've ever heard. Su Ling, you don't belong to *anyone* but yourself.''

''I belong to Mr. Jake and Miss Jessie, now.''

Jessie pondered that for a moment. ''Su Ling, would you fetch Mr. Jake . . . I mean Jake. Then go and get some rest.''

A few minutes later, sleepily tucking his shirt tail in, Jake walked into her room and sat on the chair beside her bed. Even with his night's growth of beard he looked handsome. She remembered the warmth of his kiss, the intimate way he had touched her, and she forced herself not to look away. The man had the most astounding effect on her—she wondered what effect she had on him.

''Good morning,'' Jake said. Spying her glass of juice, he added, ''Where's the rest of your breakfast?'' He turned a scowl in Su Ling's direction. ''I thought I told you to feed her.''

''It's all right, Jake. Su Ling tried, I just wasn't hungry.''

''You've got to eat something. How about some biscuits and coffee? Su Ling—''

''Maybe a little later,'' Jessie said softly. He acted as if their encounter the night before had never happened. Jessie wasn't sure whether she should be grateful or disappointed.

Su Ling stood quietly by the bed until Jake looked at her again. ''All right Su Ling leave now, Mr. Jake?''

''Yes, Su Ling,'' Jessie answered for him, ''go get some sleep.''

''Yes, mistress,'' Su Ling agreed, but she waited for Jake's nod of approval before she hurried out.

''I understand that Su Ling is our slave,'' Jessie said accusingly.

Jake's mouth curved upward in amusement.

"Your father bought her contract a year or so ago. She is *mui jai*. Either her parents, her husband, or a former owner in China sold her as an indentured servant. Some of the Chinese sell their own indenture for passage. Buying them is common practice here."

"Why, that's barbaric, Jake! Do you mean she works for free?" When Jessie sat up, Jake gently pushed her back down and fluffed the pillows around her.

"I see you're feeling a whole lot better. Maybe you'd like to get up and go through the books?" He flashed his mischievous grin.

"No," she said, and smiled in return. "But I would like an answer."

"Su Ling works just like any of the other girls. She gets paid the same as the others, and she repays us for her contract. Henry paid six hundred and seventy dollars for her. In a few years she'll be free."

"Six hundred dollars?" Jessie's brows shot up. "How long was her contract?"

"Ten years. When they're sick, or it's time for their"—Jake rubbed the back of his neck and glanced away—"monthly miseries, or they find themselves with child, that time is added to the contract. But if one of the other brothels or one of the tongs had bought her, she probably wouldn't live long enough to pay off her debt. It's a tough life for the China Marys. Some of them are no more than ten or eleven years old."

"That's horrible!" Jessie bolted up, and again Jake pushed her gently down, his hand warm on her shoulder.

"Henry knew Su Ling had been a concubine in China. He wouldn't have been a party to it otherwise. Your father also bought four of the younger girls—"

"No! Don't you dare tell me that, Jake Weston." This time she did manage to sit up.

"He paid over four thousand dollars for them."

He grinned at her horrified expression. "Then he turned them over to the Women's Occidental Board. It's run by the Methodists and Presbyterians. They're doing just fine in the orphanage school."

Jessie fought back tears of relief. She shouldn't have doubted her father. "What will Su Ling do when her contract is repaid?"

"Whatever she wants. That's the deal Henry made with her."

"This 'barracoon' Su Ling told me about, does it still exist?"

"It exists all right."

"My God, Jake, in Wyoming women have had the vote for three years. In California they're still being sold into bondage. Isn't anyone doing anything to stop them?"

"Just before you got here, old battle-ax Margaret Culbertson and Donaldina Cameron of the Women's Occidental Board busted in the front doors of the Tin Angel, hell-bent on rescuing all of our 'Celestial slaves.' Poor old Rupert almost had a coronary, and Paddy didn't know what to do. He could handle ten Cornish miners, but two caterwauling women carrying placards were way beyond him."

Jessie smiled, thinking of Paddy's backing away from two elderly women.

"I was surprised they came here," Jake was saying. "I guess after Henry died, they didn't think I'd be quite as open-minded about the Chinese problem as Henry was. Or maybe they heard about Sugar Su being here, and just presumed she needed saving. I brought Su Ling right down and told them she was free to go. When they tried to haul her out, she screamed like a banshee and ran back upstairs. They still weren't real sure she wanted to stay, but they finally gave up and went home."

"It seems to me those women meant well," Jessie said. "And the practice *is* barbaric."

"It's gone on for years, Jess—since the big rush in

'49. You have to understand, it's against the law for a white woman to . . . well, be in the same bedroom with a Chinese man, much less marry one. There are seventy-five thousand Chinese men in the West, and only five thousand Chinese women. And most of those are whores.''

''I've seen Chinese men with Negro and Indian women.''

''It's legal for them to marry other races, but not whites.''

''I want to give Su Ling her contract, Jake.''

''As far as I'm concerned, you can burn the damned thing. It's down in the safe, written in that Chinese hen scratchin' with Su Ling's thumbprint on the bottom. Now, can I go shave?''

Jessie smiled, thinking that in some ways Jake reminded her of her father. He was gruff on the surface, but underneath it all, he really cared for the people around him.

Walking to the door, Jake paused. ''I hope you're feeling better.''

''Much better, thank you.''

Then, as he eyed the softly ruffled sleepwear that had replaced La Porte's cotton nightshirt, his mood turned dark. ''About last night,'' he said. ''You were injured and upset. I was worried about you. It shouldn't have happened, but circumstances weren't the best.'' Jessie's smile faded. ''Anyway, I've got to get to work.'' He turned, but Jessie's voice stopped him.

''Jake?'' He paused. ''Thank you—for Su Ling, I mean.''

''You're welcome. Henry would have given her contract to her anytime she asked for it. But keeping face is a big thing with the Chinese, Jess. Even if you give her the contract, she'll want to repay us.''

''That's fine, if she wants it that way.''

''Let her wait on you, Jess. Those girls are trained to be the very best . . . at everything.''

"Only if she *wants* to, Jake."

"Fair enough." He pulled the door quietly closed, then quickly opened it again. "By the way," he said, his jaw tense, "Lovey's waiting to see you. She's got a present for you from La Porte. Mark Twain's new volume, *Roughing It*, hot off the press. Knowing La Porte," he added with a scowl, "I'm surprised he didn't send you lacy French underwear."

Lovey brushed past Jake as he stormed off down the hall. Jessie could feel the reverberation of the door slam as he returned to his office, where he had set up a cot. Good, she thought, I hope he's jealous! But she didn't really think he was. *Circumstances weren't the best*, he'd said. He didn't like La Porte, that much was certain. But was he actually jealous? Just the hint of an idea began to take shape in her mind.

"Here you are, dearie." Standing beside the bed, Lovey handed her the book, bound with a pink satin ribbon and decorated with a rose. "Rene dropped this off first thing this morning. He was real disappointed when I told him you were still sleepin'."

"I owe him, Lovey, for saving Paddy and me. How is Paddy this morning?"

"Better than the half a ham and dozen eggs he just laid to rest." Lovey grinned. "Now, how about me bringin' you up a plateful?"

"Thanks. I think I would like some coffee and maybe a biscuit or two. Then I think I'll read my book. The next time Mr. La Porte stops by, be sure to send him up."

Tok Loy Hong sat ramrod straight in his intricately carved teakwood chair.

Shining through the windows behind him, the morning sun gave him the aura of a celestial deity as he watched the trembling man on his knees in front of him. Two of Tok Loy's most trusted bodyguards had brought the coolie from the Embarcadero. The man, a stoker on the *Memphis Cloud*, had just told him about the sinking of the *Callie Sue* and the discovery of the red silk garrote.

Tok Loy scowled down at the quaking man. "If there is any more news of the accident, you come to me. There will be a small reward, and you will shine in the eyes of your ancestors. If I do not hear news of the *Cloud* before it is common knowledge, you will *join* your ancestors. Do you understand?"

"Yes, Honorable One," the man whispered through trembling lips.

"Let him go," Tok Loy ordered his bodyguards, watching as the man kowtowed to the door, then turned and ran for the stairs. His black robe trailed behind him while his sandals slapped against his callused heels.

Silence swept over the room, thick and tense. The only sign of Tok Loy's anger was the drumming of his long nails on the arm of his ornate teakwood chair.

Again someone had tried to bring the wrath of the white devils down on the Gum San tong. It wasn't bad enough that the whites had passed the Cubic Foot Act, which allowed only so many residents per cubic foot in the city's structures—a law aimed directly at the crowded Chinese section. Or that they'd passed the Short Hair Ordinance for "health reasons," then had great fun catching coolies and cutting off their valued braids, shaming the Chinese in the eyes of their ancestors.

First Henry Taggart had been murdered. Now an attempt had been made on Henry's daughter. Were the Auspicious Laborers of the Sea attempting to discredit the Gum San tong? The *Memphis Cloud* had been crewed with AL of S tong members. One of them could have killed the old waiter who had been found by one of the search boats, and placed the sign of Gum San in the room where the old man's blood spotted the floor.

Tok Loy and the Gum San tong owed Henry Taggart, and that obligation had been passed on to his daughter. If the Auspicious Laborers of the Sea were responsible, they should be punished. Their leader, Charley Sing, himself a traitor to his Chinese ancestors with his Occidental suit and Western ways, should answer to these crimes.

Still, Tok Loy's instincts told him that Sing and his followers were not guilty of these acts. Who would want Jessica Taggart dead? Tok Loy asked himself. Who would benefit by stirring up problems in Chinatown? No answers came to him.

"Call the tong together tonight." Tok Loy came to his feet, his wizened body stooped as he stood before his chair. "Maybe someone will have information that will help us." The guards moved quickly to summon the runners who would alert the tong's three hundred local members to the coming meeting. Tomorrow he would pay a visit to Jessica Taggart.

Kaz Bochek stood at his office window and surveyed the work taking place in the yard below. As he spotted Portigee Santos Silva talking to the guard at the wide front gate, he felt a jolt of anger and clenched his fists. Following the guard's instructions, Silva picked his way between boxes and crates and disappeared into the stairway across the yard.

Bochek rapped his knuckles angrily on the desk, then flipped open his humidor, pulling out an expensive cigar and biting off the end. By the time he had the long nine puffing, a sharp rap sounded at his door.

"Come in," Kaz snapped, and the door swung wide.

Silva, short, but with shoulders that filled the opening, gave Kaz a satisfied grin. He carried the rolled-up coat Kaz knew contained his scattergun.

"I come to collect my money."

"I told you never to come here, Portigee. Besides," Bochek grunted, "you didn't do your job."

"What do you mean?" Silva crossed the room and stood in front of the desk, his feet spread cockily, his half-unbuttoned shirt revealing kinky black chest hair, his thumbs hooked into his pockets.

"I mean just what I said." Kaz clamped down on his cigar, scattering ashes across his desktop. "You didn't do your job. They brought the girl in. She's safely tucked away at the Tin Angel like the Queen of the May."

Silva looked stunned. "I saw the *Callie Sue* crunched under the bow of the *Cloud!* She couldn't have lived through that crash."

"Well, she did."

"I should still get my money." Silva leaned across the deck, his expression ominous. The folds of the coat fell away from the scattergun as Silva rested it casually on the desktop.

"Did you leave the red silk garrote?"

"Right in plain sight."

"And the *Callie Sue* is a total loss." Bochek pondered a moment. "I'll pay you half, for half a job."

"You sonofabitch," Silva hissed.

As if to wipe the ash from his desk, Kaz slid the drawer open, and his hand disappeared inside. A shiny, nickel-plated .46 appeared, and the hammer's ratcheting echo widened Silva's eyes. "You keep that coat rolled tight," Kaz warned. "You want your half in gold, Portigee, or would you prefer lead?"

Silva looked sheepish. "Gold, I guess."

Kaz counted two hundred and fifty dollars in gold double eagles onto the desk with his left hand, his right gripping the Colt. As he flipped the last ten onto the pile, Silva greedily scooped the money up.

"I need the other two fifty, Bochek. What can I do to get it?"

"Well, there *is* something I had in mind." Bochek's huge shoulders hunched as he leaned forward across the desk. "If you think you can do it right this time."

Jake paid four dollars to the Brooklyn Lottery runner for two numbers, one of which he bet for himself, and one he bet for the girls.

Megan O'Brien, a wisp of a girl with round hazel eyes that gave her an expression of constant wonder, wiped the table while Paco stood nearby, his small arms loaded with tin containers of food.

Jake settled back for his meal with Alec Abernathy, the local station manager of Taggart Freighting. Though the girls ate in the kitchen behind the saloon, Jake usually had his early noon meal with Alec, the food brought in from Tadich's Cold Day Restaurant just down the street. They met each day at the same hour so they'd have time to discuss business before the noontime rush began. Paco fetched and served the food for them.

As Jake dug into his Hangtown fry, a mess of oysters, potatoes, bacon, and whatever else the cook had left over, Alec began his report of the prior day's business.

He beamed. "We finally beat Wells, Fargo out of the Consolidated Jackson mining account, Jake. We start shipping next Monday. We got the contract for a month. If things go well, they're bound to renew us for at least a year." Alec sipped his coffee. "That's a wagonload of supplies every other day, plus their bullion. Should amount to over a thousand a month in additional revenues for the freight, and four percent of the bullion."

"How much bullion?" Jake asked.

"Well, they haven't shipped for a couple of weeks, so the first load is several thousand dollars' worth, maybe as much as twenty-five. Then it will be five or six hundred a shipment, sometimes over a thousand.''

"How come they haven't been shipping?''

"Apparently Wells, Fargo lost a critical load of freight, some gears they had ordered. They were able to keep smelting from their stockpile, but their whole mining operation was shut down.'' Alec beamed. "Those boys were mad as hell. Seems those gears are on their way to Mexico on a Pacific Express steamship.''

"How many guards will we need?'' Jake asked. "I'd hate like hell to have a loss right away.''

"From Jackson down into the valley, we've got a man riding shotgun and a man on horseback both front and rear. The mounted guards drop off at Bridge House and ride back to Jackson, then another pair pick up the wagon in Sacramento City and stay with it all the way into San Francisco.''

"May I sit in on this?'' Jessie walked up beside Jake, her bandaged arm hidden beneath her sleeve. The men stood up.

"You should be in bed,'' Jake said, looking concerned.

"I've been in bed until I'm about to go crazy. Lovey told me about your meeting when I asked for you. Since I haven't met Mr. Abernathy yet, I thought I'd come down.''

Alec snatched his slouch hat off his head and held it in front of him. "You must be Mrs. Taggart.''

"*Miss* Taggart,'' Jessie corrected him, extending her hand. Alec hesitated, then shook it.

Although he was unhappy about it, Jake resigned himself to her presence and pulled up a chair for her. Megan hurried over with a cup of coffee, which she set in front of Jessie with a curtsy. As briefly as possible, Jake explained what Alec had reported.

"We've been trying to break into that Jackson area mining business for years, Jess.''

"Why do the guards drop off at Bridge House?''

she asked. "Then the wagon's not guarded again until Sacramento City."

"There's still a guard riding shotgun," Jake answered patiently. "Much of the trip is on the flatlands, and most holdups occur in the mountains. But you're probably right. We should have the guards go all the way to Sacramento."

"Wouldn't it be best to haul the first load in a way that was less conspicuous? I mean, if half the country knows that Consolidated hasn't shipped for a while, they're going to know it's a big shipment."

Jake pushed his plate away. "This is the way we've always handled it, Jess."

"Does that make it the best way?" She locked eyes with him while Alec sat in embarrassed silence.

The saloon was beginning to fill with employees: girls making their way downstairs, dealers entering through the bat-wing doors on the street. Jessie saw Rupert take up his place behind the bar. Before long, the saloon would be full of patrons.

Jake cleared his throat. "Why don't you go on back upstairs and—"

"Keep quiet?" Jessie broke in. "This is an important piece of business, Mr. Weston. If you don't mind, I think I'm entitled to offer my fifty-one percent."

"Jessie, you're still not well enough. You should be upstairs resting."

Jessie got slowly to her feet, lifting her chin and squaring her shoulders. "I swear, you are the most condescending man I have ever had the *dis*pleasure of meeting."

Alec stood up. "I've got to be getting back."

"You stay right here, Mr. Abernathy," Jessie ordered, and Alec sat down as quickly as he'd risen.

Jake stared at her in stoney silence.

Jessie returned to her seat. "Now, let's discuss the Consolidated Jackson shipping contract like reasonable businessmen . . . business *people*. Why shouldn't we take special precautions to make sure this first load gets through safely?" Neither man offered an objection. "In fact," Jessie said, encouraged by their silence, "I think it would be wiser if . . . say . . . a woman was on board that wagon, and it was loaded with household goods."

"A woman?" Jake snapped.

"Yes. And her husband, of course. With all the appearance of a poor homestead family on their way across the state."

"And no guards, I suppose." Jake shook his head in disbelief.

"The Trojans proved that a little deception is worth an army of fools, Jake Weston . . . and a woman's as good as a wooden horse. Guards mean bullion; a homestead wagon means a few pounds of beans and some worn-out furniture. Which do you think would attract the least attention from potential thieves?"

"And just what woman do you suggest we hire for such a job?" Jake pressed.

"We don't have to hire one. I've been wanting to see the freighting operation. What better opportunity? Paddy and I—"

Jake shoved back his chair, the sound grating on the worn pine floors. "You must have lost more blood than I thought. It's time you got back to bed."

"Well," Alec said as he stood up, "when you two get this thing settled . . ."

"Sit down, Mr. Abernathy," Jessie ordered, and Alec again dropped into his seat.

"Get on back to work, Alec," Jake ordered. "We'll settle this matter later."

Alec stood up.

"Mr. Abernathy," Jessie snapped, and Alec sighed, then obediently sat down.

Jessie and Jake glared at each other.

From a few feet away, Jessie heard Lovey say to

Rupert, "They got poor Alec bobbin' like an apple in a barrel."

"And what about poor ol' Jake?" Rupert said with a grunt. "He don't know whether to spark her, or spank her, or light a shuck out a' town. He looks at her like a man looks at a woman, and she acts like a partner; he treats her like a partner, and she pouts like a woman."

Lovey planted her hands on her ample hips. "And that's so much hogwash, Mr. Rupert Scroggins."

"Alec!" Jake raised his voice loudly enough so that everyone in the room stopped and turned. Alec jumped to his feet.

"Wait a minute, Alec," Jessie called after him as he fled the room, almost running for the door.

"Just hold on, Jessie Taggart," Jake ordered. "We'll settle this out of earshot of this whole damned place. After you." Jake motioned her toward the stairs.

Her fists balled at her sides, Jessie lifted her chin and marched past him. She had almost reached the landing when the first wave of dizziness struck her. Blinking hard, she tried to focus, but her head spun and she couldn't see the next step. She reached out blindly, then fell backward into darkness.

Jake's arms went around her even before he realized what had happened. "Damned fool woman," he grumbled, swinging her into his arms. "Lovey!" he shouted as he carried her up to his room.

Watching Jake's retreating figure, Rupert turned to see Megan O'Brien wiping down the chairs and tables near the bar. The girls were expected to help out until the customers arrived, which from the sound of things wouldn't be long. Flashing him a smile, Megan finished her chore, smoothed her curly red hair, and walked over to where he stood drying glasses.

"Rupert, me love, will ya be steering me all the big spenders today?"

Rupert smiled and tried to mimic her accent. "You attract them like bees to honey, Megan, me little Irish lass. You need no help from the likes o' me."

"Well, if you happen to see Kaz Bochek, tell him I've got somethin' special for him." She winked suggestively.

As she walked to the swinging double doors to greet the first of the day's arrivals, Rupert watched her hips sway seductively beneath her green satin skirt. He released a long, slow breath and ran a finger along his suddenly too-tight collar, his imagination wild with what that special something might be.

Chapter 14

Jessie regained consciousness just as Jake used his boot to shove open the door to his room. Feeling more than a little foolish, she let him place her on the bed.

"I'm all right," she said softly, refusing to look at him.

"I should have carted you back up here when you first showed up downstairs. Doc said three or four days. That means another full day of rest. One way or another, I mean to see you get it."

"All right, I'll stay in bed on one condition."

"You'll stay in bed if I have to hog-tie you to it." Jake's expression suggested that wouldn't be a bad idea.

"Please, Jake."

"All right, what's the condition?"

"Give my suggestion some thought. If that gold shipment is really as important to our profits as you say, we should do everything in our power to protect it."

"It's just too dangerous for you to go along, Jess."

"Not with Paddy there."

"I'll tell you what I'll do," Jake said. "I'll consider the idea, as long as the woman on the trip isn't you. There's bound to be another female within a hundred miles who's as crazy as you are."

"I'm not crazy!" Jessie cried, sitting up.

Jake pushed her back down. "All right. You're not crazy. Just a little stubborn, and a whole lot willful."

Jessie's retort was interrupted by Lovey bustling into the room. Jessie rolled her eyes. Even when she'd lived with her family, she hadn't received so much attention.

Lovey glanced from Jessie to Jake and back again. "Mr. La Porte is here to see you," she told Jessie. "He's cartin' a load a' packages he says belong to you."

"Miss Taggart isn't feeling well," Jake snapped.

"Miss Taggart is feeling just fine," Jessie retorted.

Jake scowled and headed for the door. "He'd better not be bringing a load of frilly French drawers, or he'll find himself out on his ear."

Jessie fought a smile. "I really do need some new underthings. But surely Mr. La Porte couldn't know that—but then, I guess he could."

Jake's fingers tightened on the doorknob. His jaw clamped shut and a muscle worked in his cheek. He closed the door with a little more force than necessary, and Jessie heard him stomping down the hall.

"You're just itchin' fer trouble, ain't ya?" Lovey teased.

"Why, Lovey," Jessie said, wide-eyed, "whatever do you mean?"

Lovey just laughed. "Well, I say it's good fer both of 'em. They've both played cock a' the walk fer too danged long."

Jessie's laughter was stifled by a gentle knock. Lovey opened the door and ushered Rene inside. Then she headed down the hall, careful to see that the door remained properly open.

After setting a stack of boxes on the floor, Rene took the chair beside Jessie and drew her hand to his lips. "You look just as lovely as you did on board my yacht." His eyes told her he remembered exactly how she had looked that night—without a stitch of clothes! Jessie blushed and glanced away.

"Thank you, Rene. For everything."

"There will be plenty of time for you to thank me, *chérie*," he said, his words filled with meaning.

"Rene, I don't think it's a good idea for us to—"

"Later, *chérie*." He waved her words away. "For now, why don't you see if Madame Delaine's designs meet with your approval."

"How on earth did you know about the clothes I'd ordered?"

Rene smiled indulgently. "I often purchase gifts for my . . . companions. None so lovely as you, but they are not without certain . . . other qualities. Madame Delaine has frequently done work for me. She mentioned your visit the last time I was there."

Jessie felt her face flame again as she thought of Rene's *companions*. The man really was a hopeless bounder, just as Jake had said. Still, there was a side of him she found intriguing. Hoping he hadn't noticed her embarrassment, Jessie pulled the first lid off to find the lovely black and gold striped silk gown she had selected last week. The finished creation was far more spectacular than she could have hoped.

"If they're all as lovely as this, I'm sure to be pleased. I'll have a cheque sent over to the shop this afternoon."

"That has already been taken care of. Consider the dresses a gift."

"Oh no, Rene! I couldn't accept anything so expensive. We're only friends, after all."

"*Friends*, La Porte?" Jake repeated from the open doorway. "More like casual acquaintances."

"Hardly casual," La Porte said pointedly, and Jake stiffened. "I would say Miss Taggart and I know each other far better than that."

Jake stepped closer, a look of warning in his eyes. "Say one more word, La Porte."

Jessie jumped out of bed. "Jake, please. Rene is my guest."

Glancing at Jessie, Jake gave La Porte a second hard look, and stepped away.

"There will be a time for us, *mon ami*," La Porte said, "That much I promise you."

"You'll find full payment for the dresses in your office by this afternoon," Jake said.

"Thanks for stopping by, Rene," Jessie added. "I've enjoyed the book immensely."

La Porte purposely took his time kissing her hand. Then, with a slight bow, he left the room.

By the following evening, Jessie was up and feeling fine. So far Jake hadn't suggested she return to the hotel, and she was grateful. It would be lonely back at the Palace. With Lovey and Rupert and Paddy nearby, the Tin Angel felt to Jessie like home. Of course the setup was hardly fair to Jake, who was still sleeping on a cot in his office.

Jessie sighed, knowing all too soon she would have to leave. She began dressing to go downstairs. Tonight was the first time since the accident that she'd be in the bar in the evening. She could hear Mormon Pete plinking away on the piano, could hear the laughter and the gaiety, and she found herself looking forward to the excitement. Jake wouldn't like it, she knew. He preferred she stay as far away from the rowdy throng downstairs as she could get.

Jessie glanced in the mirror and smiled at her reflection. Jake wasn't going to like her black and gold striped gown either. She pulled the already revealing bodice a little lower, satisfied with the generous portion of her bosom the dress displayed. The devil with Jake Weston. She was a woman first, and his partner second. It was time he realized that.

Tucking a last stray tendril of thick dark hair into the curls atop her head, Jessie headed toward the door. As usual, Paddy waited at the head of the stairs.

"Evenin', mum."

"Good evening, Paddy."

"You sure do look pretty, mum."

"Thank you, Paddy." Jessie swept past him and headed downstairs. She hadn't gone more than a few steps when her eyes locked with Jake's. His hand, holding a half-full whiskey glass, stopped midway to his mouth. He tossed the drink back, slammed the glass down on the bar, and started in her direction. The confrontation was going to be worse than she'd thought.

"Just what the hell do you think you're doing?" Jake demanded, storming up beside her. His eyes swept down her body, from the crown of her up-swept hair to the breasts that swelled above the low-cut bodice. She could almost feel the heat that radiated from him, and against her will Jessie's heart began to pound.

"I'm going to work," she replied, keeping her voice even.

"Is that so? And just exactly what kind of work do you intend to do?" His eyes met hers briefly, then returned to her bosom. He seemed fascinated by the rhythmical rise and fall of her breasts as her breathing quickened. She could almost feel his hands caressing her, firing her skin as they had before. He looked handsome in his black frock coat and snowy white shirt. Denying an urge to run her fingers through his curly black hair, Jessie forced her mind on the problem at hand.

"I intend to help bring in business. I think I'd be very good at it."

"Oh, you'd be good, all right. Bull Haskin proved that beyond a doubt."

"I didn't understand the business as well back then."

"And now you do?"

"Now I have Paddy to protect me, and I intend to let the men know right away I'm not for sale. Since I own half of the Tin Angel, that shouldn't be too hard for them to comprehend."

Fuming with exasperation, Jake shook his head. "Just tell me why in the hell a Boston city girl wants to spend time with a bunch of rowdies in a Barbary Coast saloon."

"This isn't just any saloon, Jake Weston, this is *my* saloon. My father left it to me, and I mean to see that it's properly run. Once I'm assured that it is, I'll keep myself occupied, for the most part, with the freighting and shipping business."

Jake growled beneath his breath and dragged Jessie into the corner beside the bar. "Damn it, Jess. Can't you see that even a short time in here will ruin your reputation? No decent man will want you. You won't be able to hold your head up among society folks."

"Oh, now I see," she said haughtily. "It's okay for you to run the Angel because you're a man. I'm just supposed to sit back and watch the books."

"That's just about it, Jess. Your father never meant for you to get directly involved. He'd spin like a top if he knew I'd let things go this far."

"My father knew me a whole lot better than you, Jake. He knew exactly what I'd do with his businesses, and I don't intend to let him down. As for men wanting me, I'll be happy to demonstrate just how wrong you are." With that she smiled and waved at a big tall cowhand standing at the bar. When she started past Jake, he grabbed her arm.

"Oh no you don't. That's not what I meant, and you know it. These men want you, all right. They want you upstairs in one of those rooms. I'm talking about marriage—a husband and family. Don't you want that, Jess?"

Jessie's head came up, his unexpected question catching her off guard. "I . . . I . . . of course I want those things—someday. But I can't imagine myself sitting at home with my knitting while my husband's off in some saloon having fun. Maybe when I'm older I'll feel like settling down."

"By then it'll be too late. Those same men will know what you've been doing, that you've worked in a saloon on the Barbary Coast. They won't want to marry you, Jess. You've got to think about your future. You've got to decide today, Jess. Tonight. Right this very minute."

Jessie felt a hard lump rising in her throat. She blinked against a sudden sting of tears. When she glanced up at him, she could read the concern in his eyes, and it touched her heart. "I guess I made that decision when I ordered this dress," she said softly. "If I have to decide now, if I have to choose between living life, and watching others live it while I stand on the sidelines, then I choose to live it." Although she tried to stop it, a single tear slipped down her cheek. "If no man wants me, then I'll take care of myself, just as I'm doing now."

Jake watched her bottom lip tremble, and stilled it with his finger. He brushed away the tear. God, she was lovely. So tough on the surface, so soft underneath. He couldn't help but admire her. She knew what she wanted out of life, and she was willing to accept the risks involved in getting it.

He tilted her chin up with his hand. "Any man who felt that way would be a fool, Jess," he said gently, unable to look away from her clear green eyes. Her skin felt as soft as he remembered, and her low-cut gown aroused memories he'd been trying his damnedest to forget.

His own decision made as swiftly as hers, he offered his arm. "Why don't we make a pass around the tables? I'm sure some of the regulars have yet to meet my new partner."

* * *

The evening went better than Jessie expected. With Jake beside her, few words were needed to make her position clear. The men greeted her with deference, and maybe a bit of suspicion, but in time they'd get over that.

Jessie yawned and glanced at the clock. It was just past closing time. Only one or two diehard customers remained, and Rupert and Paddy were firmly assisting them to the door. Tomorrow she'd resume her conversation with Jake about the Consolidated Jackson gold shipment. She had no doubt she'd win that argument, too.

"Tired?" Jake asked, coming to stand beside her.

"Actually, I'm a little keyed up. I learned a lot tonight. Thank you, Jake, for making it easy."

"You made it easy, Jess. If I hadn't seen it with my own two eyes, I wouldn't have believed it could be done. There wasn't a man in the room who didn't treat you like a lady." He glanced pointedly at her black and gold dress, elegant yet revealing. "I guess being a lady either comes naturally to a woman or it doesn't."

Jessie smiled, feeling a spark of pleasure at his words. As he looked down at her, his features had softened. His lips looked warm and inviting, his eyes a darker blue. When he smiled, she knew what he was thinking, and her stomach felt a rush of warmth.

A woman's light laughter interrupted them. "Where 'ave you *been*, you naughty boy?"

Jake's jaw tightened as a beautiful, dark-haired woman swept up beside him in a swirl of expensive silk organdy. "I have missed you, *chéri*," she said. "Surely you aren't still mad at Monique for one tiny misunderstanding." She raised a delicate hand to his cheek, but Jake backed away.

"Aren't you going to introduce me to your friend?" Jessie asked, although she was fairly certain who the beautiful woman was. Everyone on the Barbary Coast had heard of Monique Dubois, but this was the first time Jessie had seen her. She studied the woman thoroughly. With her beautiful blue-green eyes, dark hair, and smooth olive skin, Monique Dubois was lovely—too lovely—with a figure men conjured up in their dreams. And the way she looked at Jake—Jessie felt an ache begin to build around her heart.

"Monique," Jake said brusquely, "this is my partner."

"I'm Jessica Taggart," Jessie put in, since Jake seemed unwilling to make a proper introduction. "I presume you're Mademoiselle Dubois."

"*Oui*, I am Monique."

Jake grabbed Monique's arm and tugged her toward the door. "I'm a little busy tonight, Monique. Maybe some other—"

"Jessica," Monique repeated thoughtfully, as if Jake hadn't spoken. "Now, *chéri*, I believe I understand." She ran a finger along Jake's cheek and her dark-fringed eyes flashed with anger. "*Bonsoir, chéri.*" Throwing a falsely brilliant smile over her shoulder, Monique tossed back her thick black hair and headed out the door.

"Could ya gimme a hand, boss?" Rupert called out, indicating one of the customers Paddy was about to toss out.

Jake glanced quickly at Jessie, then he nodded at Rupert and walked away.

While he was gone, Jessie said good night to Lovey and headed upstairs to her room. Although she kept her expression carefully blank, inside she was seething.

How could he? After the liberties he'd taken, and just when she was beginning to think he cared for her, his pretty French trollop shows up!

Sitting in front of the small oak-framed mirror atop the bureau in her room, Jessie pulled the remaining pins from her hair and brushed out her burnished curls with furious strokes. "Ohhh," she fumed, throwing down her hairbrush and springing to her feet.

Searching beneath the bed, she found her satchels. Tossing one of them on the bed and popping the latch, she thought angrily that she should have left long before now. She should have kept things strictly business. She shouldn't be feeling hurt and angry when she had no right to be. Jake had made no promises, nor did she expect him to. Still, if it weren't for her fury, Jessie knew she would be fighting back tears.

Emptying one drawer after another, she dumped her clothes into the bag. Twice a knock sounded on her door, but Jessie ignored it.

She was more than a little surprised when the knob turned and Jake strode into the room. It took all her strength not to look at him, but she'd be damned if she'd let him see her jealousy and pain.

"What the hell do you think you're doing?" he asked, when she didn't glance up from her packing.

"I think it's time I moved back to the hotel," Jessie answered, her voice surprisingly calm.

"At four o'clock in the morning?"

She folded a black bombazine day dress and tucked it in the satchel. "I never meant to cause trouble between you and your lady friend."

"Monique's nothing *but* trouble. You had little to do with it."

"Well, I'm sleeping in your bed. I assume that's somewhat inconvenient." Closing the satchel, Jessie picked up another and set it on the bed.

"I don't mind you sleeping in my bed," Jake said. He cleared his throat. "I mean, it isn't inconvenient." When she cast him a doubtful glance, he grumbled an oath she didn't catch. "What I'm trying to say is, I'm no longer seeing Monique."

Jessie's movements stilled, and she lifted her gaze to his face. He was watching her intently, as if gauging her reaction. She folded a sweater and put it away, determined to hide the rush of relief she wished she didn't feel.

"Do you really want to move back to the Palace?" he finally asked when she didn't respond.

Jessie folded an embroidered chemise with extra care. "I'll admit it's a little lonely," she told him, "but I'm used to being alone. Mama's been dead for the past two years, and my father had been living out here for three." She smiled wistfully. "I guess Lovey and the girls have spoiled me a little."

Jake released a long, deep breath that Jessie hadn't realized he'd been holding. As she laid the chemise on top of the clothes in the satchel, he grabbed her hand, refusing to let go even when she tried to pull away.

"What do you think you're doing?" she said as he tugged her toward the door.

"Come on. There's something I want to show you." Reluctantly, Jessie let him guide her down the hall. At the end, he pulled open a small door to reveal a set of wooden stairs that led up to the attic. "I was saving this for a surprise, but I think now's the right time." Still holding her hand, Jake led her up the steps.

The once dusty attic had been transformed into the most feminine room Jessie had ever seen. A canopied bed draped in pink cotton ruffles dominated one corner, while a thick tartan carpet covered the old pine floors. A dainty pink porcelain water pitcher sat atop a lovely old oak dresser, and lacy pink curtains that matched stuffed window seats hung at dormer windows that looked out over the city and the harbor. A small settee nestled in front of a tiny brick fireplace.

"Whose room is this?" Jessie asked, suddenly suspicious. *My God, did he have more than one mistress?*

"Yours," he told her proudly. "Rupert and Paddy helped Lovey and the girls. They all thought you'd be safer—I mean happier—here than back at the hotel. It's only temporary, of course. Just until things get settled and you find a permanent place to live."

Jessie felt the sting of tears behind her lids. She glanced around the room again, noting the feminine handiwork, the time and care her friends had shown. When she turned to look at Jake, he was smiling tenderly down at her, still holding her hand.

"And what about you, Jake?" she asked softly. "Do you want me here?"

Jake cleared his throat and glanced away. He released her hand. "As you said before, it's a little inconvenient sleeping in my office."

Jessie turned and started for the door. "I don't think it's a good idea."

"Because of Monique?"

"Partly."

Jake slid an arm around her waist and pulled her into his embrace. "I don't care about Monique, Jess. The woman means nothing to me—she never has." Jake turned her to face him. "Can't you see it's you I want?" His mouth came down over hers with such force it staggered her. Jessie wrapped her arms around his neck and clung to him for support as he kissed her cheeks, her nose, her eyes, the tender place beneath her ear.

"I've tried to stay away, but I can't anymore." He returned to her lips, driving his tongue inside her mouth, moving it in the most achingly sensuous manner. His insistence melted the last of her reserve. In minutes she was kissing him with equal passion, hardly aware of where she was, uncertain of what she should do, knowing only that she wanted Jake Weston more than she wanted to breathe.

She felt his arms beneath her knees, and smelled a hint of lilac as he lifted her off her feet and carried her to a place beside the canopied bed. He never stopped kissing her, and Jessie didn't want him to.

Her breasts seemed full and tingly as they strained against the fabric of her dress, and a rush of warmth moistened the place between her legs.

Jake set her on her feet, and her body slid the length of him until her toes touched the floor. Then she felt his hardened manhood, the warmth of his hand against her breast, and she experienced a moment of uncertainty.

"There's nothing to be afraid of, Jess," he whispered softly.

Jessie relaxed at his words. "I'm not afraid, Jake. Not when I'm with you."

Jake watched her for a moment, his vivid blue eyes caressing her face. Then, lowering his head, he kissed her. One hand kneaded her breast, sending shivers of desire down her spine and making her feel hot all over, while his other hand cupped her bottom. He fitted her perfectly against him, his legs warm against her own, his manhood pressing determinedly. When his hand slipped inside the bodice of her gown, Jessie moaned softly, but she didn't pull away.

"I want you, Jess," he whispered. Cradling her breast in his palm, he used his thumb and forefinger to tease her nipple, already pebble-hard.

"Jake?" she whispered against his mouth. "I need . . . I need . . ."

"I know what you need, Jess. God in heaven, I know I shouldn't, but I'm gonna give us what we both need." As he spoke, Jake unfastened the buttons at the back of Jessie's dress, and soon it and her petticoats fell into a frothy jumble at her feet. It was all Jake could do to free her corset laces, but he eventually undid the whalebone contraption.

Jake didn't miss her hesitant glance. He knew he should end this madness before it continued a moment longer. Instead, he untied the string that held up her lacy pantalets and pushed them down her thighs. He'd never wanted a woman more.

Forcing himself to move slowly, Jake pressed his lips against the fluttery pulse at the base of Jessie's throat. He moved to her mouth, using his tongue to taste every delicious line and corner, then pulled her simple chemise up over her head.

Exposed now, her rounded breasts pointed upward, inviting his touch. The rosy peaks looked swollen, yet each bud was hard, and so sensitive that Jessie moaned when his fingers lightly brushed them.

Lifting her onto the bed, Jake trailed kisses along her shoulder until his mouth settled over a pink nipple and he heard her soft cry of pleasure. At the touch of his tongue, she arched against him, but she did nothing to discourage his attentions, and Jake wasn't certain what he'd do if she tried.

He left her only long enough to pull off his boots, his breeches, and his shirt, and returned to the place beside her.

For the first time, Jessie wavered. "Jake?"

"It's all right, Boston," he said soothingly, lowering his mouth to the flat spot below her navel. Her skin felt warm against his lips, and he could smell her feminine scent. It was all he could do to keep from mounting her and driving himself roughly inside her. Instead, with a ragged breath and an iron will, he forced himself to go slow.

Hardly able to breathe, Jessie laced her fingers through Jake's curly hair. Her mind was a tangle of heated emotions. She wasn't certain what to do, but Jake was; she could feel his caring expertise in every touch. As his lips moved sensuously along her trembling flesh, she knew she should stop him, but she couldn't find the strength. She thought of the girls in the cribs below, remembered how he'd cast Monique aside, and felt a fresh wave of uncertainty. How would he look at her in the morning? Would he think of her as another fallen woman? Would he cast her aside, or would he still want her? She felt tears well up in her eyes.

"I'm frightened Jake," she whispered, and Jake's head came up. "I don't want to be like Monique."

He pulled her into his arms. "You're not like Monique. Don't ever say that. You're a lady, Jess. You'll always be a lady."

"Are you sure?"

"Nothing can ever change that."

"I want you," she whispered, and her words seemed to tear him apart.

"Stop me now, Jess, or it'll be too late."

"Please, Jake, give me what I need." He kissed her savagely then, ravaging her lips, forcing her response. He caressed her with his hands and his mouth, kneaded her breasts, teased her sensitive skin, slid his hands down her body. Kissing her all the while, he stroked her trembling thighs, then moved upward along her skin until his fingers sought and found entrance to the wetness between her legs. When he slipped inside, Jessie moaned and writhed against his hand. Barely able to think, all she could do was feel.

And Lord, the way he made her feel.

She bit her bottom lip to keep from crying out as his fingers worked their magic, making her tremble, driving all other thoughts from her mind. Then he was above her, the hardness of his shaft pressing against her, sliding slowly inside, filling her completely, and still she wanted more.

He stopped for a moment, hesitant, it seemed, as he pushed against the last thin barrier of her innocence. He was huge and throbbing, and she wondered for a moment if her slender body could possible accommodate his length. Jake seemed to be wondering the same thing, so Jessie made the decision for him. She arched her back and drove him farther inside, but she couldn't stop her tiny gasp of pain.

"It's all right, honey," Jake whispered. "It only hurts the first time. Just try to relax."

Reading concern in his eyes, Jessie did as she was told and found the pain receding. When Jake started moving again, she forgot her discomfort, feeling only the thickness of his shaft as it heightened her fiery passion, knowing nothing but the building desire that heated her blood. She could feel the tension in his body as he slid his hands beneath her hips, cupping her buttocks to drive himself more deeply inside her. Digging her nails into his shoulders, Jessie writhed and arched against him, meeting each of his pounding thrusts. She was torn between ecstasy and agony, needing that elusive something he'd promised, yet unsure of what it was.

Then, suddenly, she knew.

She was filled with such sweetness, such joy and utter fulfillment, that she was left breathless. Behind her eyes, silver pinpricks of light danced dizzyingly. Nothing she'd ever experienced had prepared her for this. No words could begin to describe the sensations she was feeling. Clutching his neck, Jessie cried out Jake's name and buried her face in the hollow between his neck and shoulder.

Jake's body tensed as he drove against her, finally reaching his own shuddering release.

Resting on his elbows, he leaned down and kissed her, just a feather-soft touch before he rolled to his side and pulled her into the circle of his arms.

Caught in a whirlwind of emotions, Jessie didn't speak for a long time. She could hear the soft tick of a clock somewhere on the wall, feel Jake's heartbeat and the hard muscles of his arms, warm and strong, around her. For the first time in her life, Jessie had no idea what to say.

Then, "Jake?"

"Yes, Boston?"

"What we did . . . It was the most . . . incredible thing that's ever happened to me."

Jake chuckled softly. "I'm glad I pleased you."

"Pleased me? I felt as if I were floating on a heavenly cloud."

He kissed the side of her neck. "It would be my pleasure to take you to heaven again," he teased, the words muffled against her skin.

Goose bumps raced up her spine and she giggled. Then her laughter faded, and she became serious. "I suppose we shouldn't have."

One corner of Jake's mouth tilted into a smile. "No, Miss Boston Taggart, I don't suppose we should have . . . so what do you propose we do about it?"

"Do about it?" she asked, confused. She rolled to her side to face him. "What *can* we do? We don't love each other, and we're obviously not well suited. You're a womanizer of the worst sort. You'd never be able to settle down. Even if you did, you'd probably be bored with me in no time at all."

"If there's one thing about you I've learned," Jake said, his voice suddenly gruff, "it's that you're far from boring."

"Well, you needn't worry about me. I enjoyed . . . making love with you. When I came West, I decided to experience life. Now I understand a little more of what it's all about. I appreciate your kindness, considering it was my first time and all. I'm sure it would have been better for you if I'd been more experienced."

"You appreciate my kindness?" Jake repeated, incredulous. He'd been prepared to do right by the girl, certain that she'd demand marriage. He would have complied—grudgingly, he admitted, since holy wedlock was about the last thing he wanted. Still, she was Henry's daughter, and he'd seduced her. He was man enough to pay the price. "Are you telling me we're just going to pretend this never happened? You'll continue to be my partner, and nothing more?"

"Well, I don't think we should do this very often," Jessie said. "There can be serious . . . consequences . . . you know."

"I'm very well aware of the consequences," he snapped, not at all liking the direction this conversation was taking. Jessie sat up and reached for her pantalets.

"What are you doing?" Jake asked.

"I think I'll go down to your room and get my things. That way you can have your bed back. That is, if you still want me to stay here. But then maybe . . . after what's happened . . . I should return to the hotel."

"You're not going anywhere." Jake grabbed her around the waist and hauled her back onto the bed. "Since you appreciated my *kindness* so much the first time, I think I'll give you a second dose. That way you can get a little more *experience*. You never know when it might come in handy."

Jessie squealed as Jake rolled on top of her, but she didn't protest when he kissed her, or when she felt his manhood pressing urgently against her thigh.

In minutes she was as breathless as before. She'd wanted to experience life, and this was one adventure she wouldn't have missed for the world. Tomorrow she would worry about the consequences. Tomorrow.

She only wished tomorrow was a few more days away.

Chapter 15

The sun was high in the San Francisco sky when Jessie awoke.

Her gaze fixed on the ceiling, she blinked several times, glanced around the room, then remembered the night she'd spent in Jake's arms. Jessie bolted upright.

A wave of relief washed over her when she discovered that she was alone in the room. At least Jake wouldn't be privy to the blush that stained her cheeks, or witness the uncertainty he was sure to see on her face. How would he treat her? What would he say?

Jessie lifted the sheet, ignoring the stains that evidenced her loss of virtue, and surveyed her naked body. Her skin looked rosy, but there were no visible marks, no telltale sign of their torrid lovemaking. She breathed a sigh of relief. At least she didn't look any different on the outside than she had yesterday.

She touched her lips, still tender from Jake's kisses. She didn't look different, but she certainly felt different—like a woman, Jake's woman. But she wasn't, and the sooner she faced that fact, the better off she'd be. She hadn't missed the expression of relief on his face when she told him she expected nothing in return for what had happened between them. For reasons she wasn't willing to examine, that look had twisted her heart.

Jake owed her nothing, she told herself firmly. He'd wanted her, she'd wanted him, and she'd given herself freely. So why did she feel so terrible this morning? Sort of hollow and empty all the way to her soul.

She wondered where he'd gone, and what he was thinking. She wondered if he regretted what had happened. As for herself, she didn't regret it—Jake had shown her passion and tenderness, and he'd given her a glimpse of love. No, she didn't regret it—but she sure as brimstone wasn't going to let it happen again! She wasn't about to be another of Jake Weston's Saturday-night amusements. If Monique was any example, he already had more than his share!

Several light raps at the door interrupted her thoughts. Hearing Su Ling's soft voice, Jessie beckoned her in.

"I have coffee for you, Miss Jessie, and you have an honorable visitor."

"Oh?" *God, don't let it be Rene.* "It's awfully early for visitors. Who is it?" Su Ling hurried across the room and set the steaming cup on the small oak stand beside the bed.

"Not so early, missy. It almost noon." Su Ling came closer and spoke in a reverent whisper. "The honorable Tok Loy Hong, ruler of the Gum San tong, awaits you."

"I see. I don't suppose you know why he's here?"

"Tok Loy Hong very powerful Chinese gentleman, missy. I just lowly China girl. You hurry now."

"I need my clothes, Su Ling. There's a satchel packed in my old room. Bring it to me, then go tell Mr. Hong it will be an hour before I'll be ready to receive visitors."

"Oh no, missy, please. Tok Loy Hong is not to be kept waiting."

"Su Ling, I just woke up. If Mr. Hong can't wait,

tell him I'll be happy to meet with him later in the day or tomorrow.''

"Oh no, oh no!"

"Just bring my things, and tell him what I said."

Shaking her head, Su Ling backed away, her eyes wide. Jessie could hear her tiny footsteps padding down the narrow stairway, then the door closing behind her. At least the poor thing had escaped having her feet bound like so many of her friends.

Jessie shoved a dark brown curl behind her ear and walked across the room to the dormer window that looked out over the city. The gleaming gold sign of the Golden Thorn was visible in the distance. Jessie thought of Monique and felt a wave of despair. Jake had said he was no longer seeing the pretty French girl. He'd spent the night in Jessie's bed, made love to her as if he really cared. But Jake was a rake and a bounder. Whose bed would he share next week? He'd called Jessie a lady, but she hadn't played the lady in bed.

Jessie groaned aloud. She wished she could crawl back under the covers and never get up again, never have to face Jake Weston and the smug look she was certain to see on his face. Instead, she squared her shoulders, lifted her chin, and moved toward the basin on the bureau. As she poured water into the bowl, Su Ling came in with her satchel and the message that Mr. Tok Loy Hong had decided to wait.

The saloon was beginning to rumble with the laughter and conversation of hostlers and drovers, clerks and tradesman, and a few of the girls from upstairs. Rupert worked behind the bar, and Jake sat at his usual table for his late-morning meeting with Alec Abernathy.

"I can't stress this enough, Alec. No matter what Jessie wants, she's not going on any freighting job as dangerous as that haul from Jackson. Do I make myself clear?"

"Very clear, boss, but you've got me between a rock and a hard spot. She tells me she's a partner and—"

"Partner or not, she's not going. If she tries to, you let me know. I'll handle Miss Boston Taggart."

"Her idea wasn't half bad," Alec said.

"As a matter of fact, it was damned good—but I can't agree with putting a woman at that kind of risk."

"You got a point there, all right. But Miss Taggart sure ain't gonna like it."

"She'll be just fine. We've got a new . . . understanding."

"Well, that's good, Jake. Because I surely do hate being in the middle."

Jake watched as Su Ling hurried to the table where Tok Loy Hong sat quietly sipping tea. Two of his huge bodyguards stood behind him with their backs to the wall. As she approached them, bowing deferentially, Jake wondered what was going on. Then he saw Kaz Bochek and Horace McCafferty push through the swinging doors and head to the bar.

Every time Jake saw Bochek, the hair stood up on the back of his neck. Why, he couldn't be sure. It was just a sixth sense. Jake left the table and walked to where the two men stood at the bar. Rupert set a whiskey in front of Bochek and drew McCafferty a beer.

"Megan says she's got somethin' real special for you, Kaz." Rupert flashed a knowing grin.

McCafferty glanced at Bochek, smiled, and glanced around the room, looking for the pretty little redhead.

Jake walked up beside them. "Thought you didn't care for the consistency of our whiskey, Bochek." Pointing a finger at McCafferty's beer mug, Jake motioned Rupert to draw him a brew as well.

Bochek downed the shot in front of him. "You

want me to do my drinkin' somewhere else, Weston?''

"Your money's as good as the next man's," Jake said, returning Bochek's hard look.

"Better than most," Bochek grunted.

"Where's Megan?" McCafferty asked Rupert.

Without waiting to hear Rupert's answer, Jake turned his back on them and crossed the room toward the table occupied by Tok Loy Hong. As always, Tok Loy was dressed in a simple black silk robe, with a matching skullcap that perched at the top of his long braid. A thumb-sized pearl scarf pin, his one concession to Western ways, adorned the robe just below the neckline. As Jake drew near, Tok Loy's bodyguards eyed him coldly.

"To what do we owe the pleasure of this visit, Tok Loy?" Jake asked.

"Ah, Mr. Weston. I have come to pay my respects to the daughter of Henry Taggart."

"She's quite a woman. I think her father would have been proud." Jake glanced away as he remembered her beautiful body stretched out beside him on the deep feather mattress. He felt a tender stirring at the thought.

"I am sure she honors her father's memory."

Jake shifted uncomfortably. "Does she know you're here?"

"The young *mui jai* who works for you has informed her."

"I sure she'll be along soon then. Would you like more tea?"

"No, thank you."

"I don't imagine you've heard anything interesting about the wreck of the *Memphis Cloud*?" Jake asked, trying to keep his tone casual.

"As you know, I am of the Gum San tong, Mr. Weston. That question might be better asked of the Auspicious Laborers of the Sea."

"Perhaps, Tok Loy, perhaps. Enjoy your tea."

Jake turned and headed upstairs to his office. He nodded at Paddy, who waited near the door leading to the attic. Only Paddy had taken notice of Jake's early-morning exit from Jessie's room. Although the big Irishman hadn't said a word, he'd looked at Jake accusingly, and Jake didn't blame him.

A hand on the heavy brass doorknob, Jake paused and glanced back to the attic door. He'd been a fool last night. He'd taken Jessie's virginity, made love to her knowing that his intentions were far from honorable, then left because he couldn't face her in the bright light of day.

He felt like a scoundrel of the worst sort, and he dreaded the look of condemnation he was sure to see on her face. You've let Henry down, he thought. You treated his daughter like a two-bit whore. Then a second voice broke in. She wanted you as much as you wanted her. She enjoyed making love to you. But making love to Jessie had been more than just a roll in the hay. Afterward he'd felt contented and closer to her than he'd ever been to a woman.

Although he hated to admit it, the voice that bothered him the most was the one that reminded him that Jessie wouldn't marry him even if he asked. Jake set his jaw. Women! By God, they'd be the death of him yet!

From habit, Jake swept a last glance over the saloon as he opened his office door. Megan O'Brien and Kaz Bochek stood at the rear of the room, near Mormon Pete's vacant piano. When Bochek glanced up and saw Jake watching them, he sat down on the piano stool and pulled the girl onto his lap, giving her a lusty kiss and caressing her derriere. Bochek laughed, but Megan seemed a little uneasy.

If you've got something special for the boy, Jake thought, get him up to your room and give it to him, or get on to another customer. He slammed the door behind him. Somehow it galled him to think of Bochek getting special treatment from any of his girls. Then he remembered it was Bochek who'd suggested they hire Megan in the first place.

They must be *special* friends, Jake thought. But just as he'd said, Bochek's money was as good as the next man's, and Kaz seemed to have plenty of it. Jake sat down at his desk and filled out the voucher for the whiskey being delivered downstairs.

Wearing a rust silk day dress cut just a little low in front, Jessie descended the stairway to the saloon, Paddy a few steps behind her. As usual, the room fell quiet for a second as the men looked in her direction, then the din of voices and female laughter resumed.

Su Ling waited at the bottom of the stairs. She bowed again and again as she waited for Jessie, who paused and spoke to several customers along the way.

When Tok Loy rose to his feet, Jessie smiled and extended her hand. "I presume you are Mr. Hong?" she said, while Paddy pulled up a chair at the next table to trade stares with Tok Loy's bodyguards.

"Yes, Miss Taggart. Tok Loy Hong of the Gum San tong. I appreciate your indulgence in my unexpected arrival."

Jessie was surprised at the strength of the man's voice, in contrast to his reedy hand and thin, weathered face. "It's my pleasure, Mr. Hong. What can I do for you?" Jessie took the seat offered by Tok Loy, who dismissed Su Ling with a glance and sat back down.

"I have been remiss in not calling on you sooner, Miss Taggart," Tok Loy said. "Your father was an old and valued friend of the Gum San tong."

"Mr. Weston has told me something about the tongs, but I'm afraid I still know very little about your ways."

"Would you care to join me in some tea, Miss Taggart?"

"Thank you, that would be nice."

Tok Loy gestured to Su Ling, who stood out of earshot but carefully watched the table. "The tongs are nothing more than social organizations, Miss Taggart. We have some . . . influence . . . with the Celestial population."

"And with the Occidental business community, and the political community, and the financial community, if what Mr. Weston says is true."

"Mr. Weston's estimation of our influence is overstated, Miss Taggart. We are a humble group of workingmen . . . visitors to your country." His expression changed to one of concern. "But, if we can be of help to you in any way, you can be assured of our assistance. As I said before, your father was a valued friend of our humble organization, and the Gum San never forgets a friend. You will find that we Celestials believe strongly in the bonds of friendship and in our ancestors. We would never shame their memories, and their debts and obligations pass from one generation to the next."

Su Ling set the tea in front of Jessie and refilled Tok Loy's cup. He waited until she had finished and retreated. "Please understand, Miss Taggart. We owe you a debt of honor. If you are ever in need, do not hesitate to call on us."

"That's very kind of you, Mr. Hong. I don't know what you could possibly do for me, but thank you."

Tok Loy rose. "You have honored me by your presence, Miss Taggart."

"There is one thing you might be able to help me with, Mr. Hong."

"Anything."

"Tell me who murdered my father."

"I can only say that I do not believe the Celestials had anything to do with it, Miss Taggart."

"You think a white man killed my father?" Jessie

felt the color drain from her face. "What about the tong hatchet and the red silk garrote?"

"I believe those were used to divert suspicion away from the real killer. No Celestial would disobey the humble wishes of the Gum San. Although modest by Occidental standards, we are the largest of the Celestial organizations, and the most respected."

Tok Loy raised his eyes, and Jessie followed his line of vision to where Jake Weston rested against the upper floor handrail, watching them. The sounds around her seemed to grow dim and fade away, leaving only Jake's imposing presence. The sudden memory of their heated lovemaking seemed to block all other thoughts, and a tingling raced up her spine. Her cheeks flamed, and she had to look away.

With iron control, she forced her attention back to her guest and the subject of her father. "What white man, Mr. Hong?"

"Again I must tell you that I do not know. The answer lies in discovering a motive. Who had the most to gain? Who would want him dead, and why? Those answers will lead you to the man who killed Henry Taggart. But rest assured, if I find out, I will leave his body to be picked by the scavengers until his bones bleach in the sun." Tok Loy came around the table, and Jessie forced a smile and stood up too.

"Just remember, Miss Taggart, you can rely on the Gum San tong as a true friend."

"Thank you again, Mr. Hong," Jessie said.

His robe trailing softly behind him, Tok Loy Hong left the saloon, followed closely by his bodyguards.

After exiting through the bat-wing doors, Tok Loy walked half a block and stopped in his tracks. Hatchets suddenly in hand, his bodyguards encircled him. Tok Loy stood face to face with Charley Sing, wearing a hat and carrying a walking stick. Charley's own hulking bodyguards stood at his back.

In the Mandarin dialect of the upper class, Tok Loy addressed the equally surprised Sing. "I see you still wear the dress of the white devil."

"And you, old man, frequent their whorehouses."

As Tok Loy listened, his wise old eyes searched the street. Along with Charley's two bodyguards, four Chinese men stood on the far side of the road and three more walked twenty paces behind.

"You have dishonored all Chinese, Charley Sing. You too owe a debt to Henry Taggart, and the destruction of the *Callie Sue* was no accident. The red silk garrote was a clumsy ploy to cover your own deceit."

"The AL of S had nothing to do with that, old man. If you and all members of the Gum San were not sired by monkeys, you would know that."

Tok Loy's bodyguards took a menacing step forward, while Charley's brandished their hatchets.

"Save your lies for another time and another place," Tok Loy said quietly. "Then your worthless AL of S will feel the sting of Gum San blades."

Tok Loy and his bodyguards took a few steps backward, then they turned and strode down the street.

"It is a great honor to be called upon by the honorable Tok Loy Hong," Su Ling said to Jessie after the wizened old man had left.

"I'm sure it is, Su Ling." Jessie found it hard to concentrate on the girl's words. *Motive*, her mind kept repeating. Who would benefit from her father's death? Unconsciously, her eyes rose to the tall man standing at the upstairs rail. Did Tok Loy suspect Jake? This time the shiver that raced up her spine was one of apprehension.

Su Ling nodded. "I go back to work now, missy?"

Jessie nodded, and Su Ling hurried among the men lining the bar. As promised, Jake had given the girl her contract, but Su Ling had politely refused. No amount of argument could sway her—she had a debt to pay. They compromised by allowing her to work off the debt as she chose, which meant she no longer had to work the cribs. Su Ling was extremely grateful, and became more loyal than ever.

"You ready to sell this joint yet?"

Startled, Jessie looked up at the sound of Kaz Bochek's gravelly voice. He jerked a chair out and straddled it backward. With a momentary glance at Paddy, who returned his hard look, he focused again on Jessie. His dark eyes raked over her from top to bottom before coming to rest on the curve of her bosom. For the first time, Jessie wished she were wearing one of her high-necked dresses. Bochek gnawed on his cigar, awaiting her answer.

"Good morning, Mr. Bochek." She glanced at the clock above the piano. "I mean good afternoon."

"That's not an answer, Miss Taggart."

Jessie brushed past him. "If I decide to sell, you'll be the first to know, Mr. Bochek. Nice to see you."

"I understand you had a little accident," Bochek called after her as she walked away, but Jessie ignored him.

Kaz watched the sway of her hips, then finished off his drink and left the saloon. As he sauntered along the board sidewalk, he chuckled, thinking of the information Megan O'Brien had given him.

The Taggart woman had suggested that the Jackson bullion shipment be hauled in the guise of a homesteader's wagon. Not a bad idea and not a bad piece of information to have. Weston had apparently disagreed, but the girl had a knack for getting her way. Kaz would pass the word on to Portigee Santos Silva. No matter how the gold was shipped, Silva would be waiting. It paid to have friends in the right places. Megan had earned herself a double eagle with that special piece of news. All he needed to know now was the route they would take and the time of departure. He had no doubt Megan would find out—really, she had no other choice.

His thoughts on the coming shipment, Kaz bumped into a dark-suited man, almost knocking him down. He picked up the bowler the man had dropped, then looked up to see Charley Sing standing in front of him, his two big bodyguards at his side. Glancing down at the hat in his hand, he grinned and sailed it into the muddy street, where it was promptly flattened by a milk wagon.

"Why don't you watch where you're going, you yellow slant-eye?" Kaz taunted.

"It is you who should watch yourself, Mr. Bochek." Charley brandished his walking stick with its brass dragon-head handle.

"Don't get smart with me, coolie." With his ham-like hands balled into fists, Kaz stepped forward, only to feel the cold metal blade of a dagger pressing beneath his chin, another against his ample belly. Charley's bodyguards eyed him coldly.

"You owe me a hat, Mr. Bochek," Charley said in a low voice.

"I'll have your head and feed it to the dogs," Kaz threatened as he stood frozen.

Charley stepped around him, only the rapid tapping of his ebony walking stick on the rough wooden walk betraying his anger. When he was several steps away, the bodyguards withdrew their blades from Kaz's person and followed Charley Sing down the street.

"You sons a' swines!" Kaz yelled after them. "Someday, I'll hang you all with the braided queues of your own yellow scum."

Trembling in anger, Kaz stomped off toward his office. Then he calmed down and smiled to himself. Nothing would spoil his day. In fact, the yellow dogs had given him another idea.

* * *

Jessie brushed past several of the girls on her way back up to her room. Everyone seemed friendly as always, no one looked at her askance. At least it appeared Jake had been discreet when he left her room early that morning. At that thought, Jessie glanced toward his office, wondering if he was there. He had certainly been conspicuously absent. Apparently, he didn't want to see her any more than she wanted to see him.

As if by magic, her thoughts seemed to conjure up his tall frame when he opened his office door. His eyes shifted almost instantly away from her face, but she didn't miss how handsome he looked. Clean-shaven, he wore a fresh white shirt, four-in-hand tie, and snug brown breeches that defined his lean hips and muscular legs. Their night of passion had obviously done wonders for *his* constitution, Jessie thought, while she felt out of sorts and more than a little melancholy.

"I . . . I thought I'd take a nap before we get any busier," she said, then felt her cheeks grow hot. Why had she said that, of all things? It wasn't as if Jake didn't know exactly why she was tired.

"Jess . . ." Glancing at the women in the hall, and at Paddy a few feet away, he grabbed her arm and pulled her into his office. "I think we should talk."

She waited until he had closed the door. Instead of a smug expression, Jake wore a definite look of remorse, which was almost worse.

"I don't think there's much left to say, Jake. What happened last night was . . . was . . . an unfortunate accident. Nothing more."

"An *accident?*" he repeated, incredulous. "I'd hardly call it that."

"Then just exactly what would you call it?"

Jake clamped his jaw. "Look, Boston, I know you're upset with me, and I don't blame you. I took advantage of you. I betrayed your father's trust. I—''

"You made love to me, which is exactly what I wanted you to do. My father, God rest his soul, had nothing to do with it. We were both pursuing our . . . natural urges. Something I'm certain *you* have every intention of continuing to do. I, on the other hand, will use more prudent judgment on the next such occasion."

"I don't consider what happened between us a matter of urges—and *what* 'next occasion'?"

"I found I quite enjoyed myself," Jessie told him, determined to brazen her way through the encounter. "I assumed you did, too." In truth, every time she looked at him, she remembered the things they'd done, the way he'd made her feel—the abandon with which she'd responded. But she'd be damned if she let him see her uncertainty. "Now that I know the pleasures one can experience with a member of the opposite sex . . . well, should the right man come along . . ."

"The right man? What does that make me?"

"In case you've forgotten, you, Mr. Weston, are my partner. You also happen to be the man who initiated me into the act of love. The latter relationship, you'll note, is in the past tense. Our partnership remains."

"A fact of which I'm more than well aware." Jake took a deep breath, watching her closely. She certainly wasn't condemning him, as he would have expected. Instead, she was thanking him—which galled him more than a little. She looked lovely this morning. Maybe the others hadn't noticed, but Jake hadn't missed the bloom in her cheeks, her slightly pouty lips still tender from his kisses. To Jake she appeared the way every woman should in the morning—Miss Boston Taggart looked very well loved.

"All right, Jess, we'll play this game any way you want. But I'm warning you, don't try your schoolgirl experiments on somebody else. You might not like the consequences.''

''Meaning?''

Jake's voice softened. ''Meaning . . . it isn't always the way it was between us last night. With some people it's different, better than with others—a lot better.''

For the first time Jessie smiled. It was a small, tenuous smile, but a smile just the same. ''Thank you, Jake, I'll remember that.'' She pulled open the door, paused, and glanced at him over her shoulder. ''But's there's really no way of knowing which man will be the right one until I have . . . experimented, is there?''

Before she could leave, Jake kicked the door closed with a booted foot. ''Now, you listen to me, Jessica Taggart.''

''I listened to you last night, Jake Weston.''

He stepped closer. ''You just forget about experimenting, and behave like the lady you are.''

She opened the door. ''I'll behave as I see fit.''

Jake kicked it closed. ''Don't try it, Jess. I'm warning you.''

Jessie opened the door. ''What's good for the goose is good for the gander.''

Jake kicked it closed. ''The first sonofabitch you drag up those stairs is a dead man.''

Jessie just smiled. She pulled open the door and swept from the room, leaving Jake raging silently behind her.

Charley Sing searched the crowded room for the woman he hoped to recognize from Henry Taggart's funeral. Of the fifteen woman he counted, he didn't see her, so he found a vacant table and took a seat. Speaking softly to his bodyguard, he sent the man over to talk to the bartender.

Rupert waved over Lovey. ''Another Chinese to see Jessie. What's she doin'? Fixin' to join the Women's Occidental Board, or runnin' for queen of Grant Street?''

"If she was," Lovey muttered, "she wouldn't need any help from the likes of you, Rupert Scroggins." Lovey waddled to the stairway, climbed it with some effort, opened the attic door, and yelled up the stairs. "Another Chinese gentleman to see you, Jessie. This one's dressed like a Harvard professor."

Lovey turned to Paddy, who sat on a chair near the door. "She's busier than a one-legged man at a rump-kickin' contest," she said.

So much for her nap, Jessie thought, slipping back into the high-top shoes she had just taken off, redoing the buttons with her tiny metal hook. As she headed down the attic stairs, she wondered who in the world had decided to call on her this time. Paddy fell in behind her as she closed the hallway door.

At the same table Tok Loy had occupied earlier sat another Oriental. His two large bodyguards stood nearby. Dressed in a dark, expensively tailored suit and carrying an ebony walking stick, he came to his feet as she approached.

"Miss Taggart, I'm Charley Sing, president of the Auspicious Laborers of the Sea." When they sat down, Su Ling hurried over with tea.

"I came to assure you that the AL of S had nothing to do with either your father's death or the mysterious accident involving your scow. I also wish to offer you the allegiance of the AL of S. Your father once saved my life. I have not forgotten. Your father was a friend of me, as he was to all Chinese."

"Then, Mr. Sing, why was he killed with a tong hatchet and a Chinese silk garrote?"

For a moment Charley Sing didn't answer. "The red silk garrote is the mark of the Gum San. I cannot speak for them, but only for myself and the AL of S. And I promise you, if it is the Gum San, they will pay."

Beneath the table, Jessie gripped the folds of her skirt and carefully watched the handsome Chinese man from beneath her lashes. "Do you really believe the Gum San was responsible?"

The look on his face said he most certainly did, but he merely shrugged his shoulders and replied, "We shall see."

"Could it have been a white man?" Jessie asked.

"Possibly." Charley Sing shoved back his chair and rose to his feet. "As a friend, I will tell you to watch your back, Miss Taggart. Whoever wanted your father dead may also wish you dead. Trust no one, but remember you can depend upon the AL of S."

With a slight bow, he headed for the door, his bodyguards following behind him. Jessie sat in silence. The two tong leaders had left her in a state of confusion, renewing old doubts, but telling her nothing new. Feeling suddenly depressed, she finished her tea and headed toward the stairs. Along the way, she couldn't stop the terrible thought that kept echoing in her mind—Jake had the most to gain from her father's death. Jake had the motive, and the means to accomplish it. He knew her father's habits, and although he'd been out of town at the time, he could easily have hired someone to do it and placed the blame on the Chinese.

Jake stopped Jessie and Paddy as they reached the landing.

"Go get something to eat, Paddy," he said. "I'll watch over Jessie." Paddy retreated down the stairs. "You don't so good," he said to Jessie.

"I'm fine, Jake, just a little tired." She tried to brush past him, but he caught her arm.

"Every time I looked over, you were talking to one of those Chinamen."

"They both seemed like gentlemen to me, Jake. They're extremely intelligent men."

"Oh, they're smart all right. But they're capable of anything. They profit from the barracoon and the cribs and the opium trade."

Jessie nodded absently, her thoughts still whirling. She needed time to sort things through, time to consider what the tong leaders had said. "I think I'll get some rest."

Jake walked her to her door and pulled it open. "Tok Loy and Charley Sing are dangerous men, Jess. Don't ever forget that. You're better off staying away from them. Your father was their friend. He went to their ceremonies and even learned some of their language, but we still can't be certain they had no part in his death."

"No, we can't. We can't be certain about *anybody*," she said pointedly.

Jake stiffened. "What the hell does that mean? And it better not mean what I think it does."

"It means that you had a motive—and you had the means." Jessie felt the sting of tears, but she blinked them away. "It means . . . it means, I just don't know anymore!"

"We've been through all this," Jake warned her, his eyes dark with anger.

"I want to believe you had nothing to do with his death, but . . ." Jessie faltered.

"But what?" he pressed. "But those Chinamen convinced you I'm to blame?"

"Not exactly." She moved past him and headed up the steps, Jake on her heels.

"I'm tired, Jake," she said when she reached her attic bedroom. "I'd appreciate it if you'd leave."

Jake's face turned red, and a muscle worked in his jaw. "I'll leave, Miss Taggart, because I'm liable to throttle you if I stay."

His descending footsteps sounded angrily on the steps, then the door slammed with a ringing note that reverberated up the narrow stairway. Jessie sank down on the bed, trying to stifle her tears. She didn't know what to believe. Jake had been good to her— he'd cared for her, protected her, been gentle and loving. How could she doubt him? He hadn't even been in San Francisco when her father was killed.

Still, he had the most to gain; he could have hired someone to do it.

Again her woman's intuition told her that it couldn't be true. Brushing the tears from her cheeks with the back of her hand, Jessie descended the narrow stairway and pulled open her door. She could just see the back of Jake's brown split-tail coat disappearing through the bat-wing doors.

"Did Jake say where he was going?" she asked Paddy.

"No, mum, 'fraid he didn't."

Jessie hesitated a moment. She thought of going after him, then remembered Monique and the Golden Thorn just across the street—and decided against it. Her shoulders sagged. "Paddy, please tell everyone I'm resting. I don't want to be disturbed."

"Yes, mum."

Jessie made it back inside her door and up the stairs before she started to sob in earnest.

Chapter 16

Women! Jake thought as he stalked up the hill
away from the Tenderloin. Last night the little minx had been warm and loving—today she'd
accused him of murder! If he lived to be a hundred,
he'd never understand the fairer sex.

Spotting the open doors of the Double Eagle saloon, Jake made his way inside. The late-afternoon
crowd was just beginning to arrive, mostly dock-
hands and carpenters who got an early start on the
day and an equally early start on the evening. Jake
downed a quick Scotch, hoping that alcohol would
dull his senses and calm his raging temper.

Henry Taggart had been his friend! He thought
Jessie understood that. After the closeness they'd
shared, he found it almost unbelievable that she
could think him capable of murder. Jake flipped a
coin on the bar and headed out the door.

Walking up the hill, he stopped at Tadich's and
moved through the crowd to the stand-up bar, ordering another Scotch. Before he'd taken his first
sip, four bar girls walked in, laughing and giggling.
Just what I need, he muttered to himself—more
female companionship.

"Hello, Jake honey," one of the girls said, stopping in front of him. She leaned over and straightened his collar. "You remember Dolly, don't you?"

"How could I forget?" He reached up and re-curled his collar. "I like it that way." Dolly arched a brow and walked away from him. Jake shrugged, downed his drink, and left.

He continued up the hill until he was out of breath, then turned into Brannigan's. A dingy place, Brannigan's smelled of tobacco and sweat. Jake took a seat, and the old three-legged chair nearly toppled him over.

"That's to test ya balance," the round-cheeked barmaid teased. "What be ya pleasure?" She tucked a stray tendril of brown hair into the rag she'd tied around her forehead to keep the unruly mop out of her eyes.

"I'll have three fingers of the best Scotch whiskey in the house."

"Don't be sayin' that so loud," she cautioned, but three burly freighters standing at the bar had already turned to see who the interloper was.

"You don't have any Scotch?" Jake pressed.

"Hush man, this is Brannigan's. I'll bring ye a spot of the Irish."

"No, thanks." Jake shoved back his chair. As he headed for the door, one of the freighters stepped in front of him.

"There be something wrong with the tears of St. Patty?" He puffed out his barrel chest and stood with his feet apart, his beefy hands on his hips.

"Look, mister, I just came in for a drink."

The Irishman chuckled, but he didn't move out of the way. "As Patty ran the snakes from blessed Ireland, me and the boys has taken an oath to keep them out o' this wee spot o' the old country."

Jake bristled. The man was itching for a fight, and considering the mood Jake was in, he might just give him one. "If you're lookin' for trouble—"

"Here ye be," the barmaid interrupted, handing him a glass half full of Irish whiskey. "Give this a try." Glancing from Jake to the Irishman, she flashed a nervous smile.

"Now," the freighter said, "there be a glass o' whiskey."

His temper barely in check, Jake smiled thinly and lifted the glass. After taking a long slow draw, he wiped his mouth with the back of his hand. "Tastes like . . . let me see, tastes like . . ." He set the glass back on the bar while the Irishman smiled at the anticipated compliment.

"St. Patty's tears, eh?" Jake repeated. "Tastes more like the sweat off his kelly-green hide."

The man's jaw dropped. His mouth opened and closed, but no words came out. He pulled back his right arm, but before he could launch the blow, Jake hauled off and hit him in the jaw. He fell back against the wall, and leaned there, dazed.

His two drinking companions slid off their stools and walked over to Jake, who stood facing them, unconsciously flexing his slightly bruised knuckles.

"Mike, me little brother, be the youngest and the kindest o' the O'Herlihys, me friend. Don't be judging the rest o' the family by him."

The man lunged forward, his fist hitting Jake in the midsection and knocking the breath from his lungs. Jake sidestepped the next smashing blow and landed two jabs to the man's chin. He threw a right, but the Irishman ducked with surprising quickness and gave him a punch in the stomach that doubled Jake over. He grabbed a chair and tossed it between them, fighting for time to regain his breath. The Irishman stumbled over the chair and went to his knees.

Jake ducked a whiskey bottle thrown by the other Irishman, and it shattered on the wall behind him. It was time to end the battle. He punched O'Herlihy as the man tried to get up, knocking him backward into his friend. He looked up to catch just a flash of the shillelagh being swung by the bartender before it crashed into the side of his head. As he hit the floor, he saw the copper ceiling and heard the bartender's brogue.

"It's a fine blackthorn cudgel from Stol Eiligh Town in County Wicklow. An' blessed St. Patty would be proud we slew another snake with it." Then all went dark.

Jake awoke to Paddy's smile, which almost reached his ears. "Boss's coming 'round."

Jessie bent over him next. "The mademoiselle must have improved her aim," she said. Before he could focus on her face, she had disappeared into blackness.

"It was an Irish girl took Paddy to him, Jessie," Lovey said quietly.

"Irish, French, mongrel, I'm sure Mr. Weston has quite a variety."

Jake tried to rise but the room swam, and he had to lower his head back down to the pillow.

"He'll be fine," he heard Lovey's reassuring voice.

"Sooner or later," Jessie added. "In the meantime, I'm stuck running this place by myself. If he'd stayed at work where he should have been, this wouldn't have happened."

"He could use some soup," Lovey said, ignoring Jessie's outburst.

"Well, I certainly don't intend to hand feed him," Jessie said. "Why don't you go get his little Irish girl?"

Jake winced as the slamming door shook the room, making his head throb even more.

"She talks tough now," Lovey said, "but she was sure worried about you when Paddy brought you in. She was snapping orders like a drill sergeant till she seen you was gonna be all right."

Jake just grunted.

"Could you take a little soup, Jake?" Lovey asked.

"Later," he whispered. "How did I get here?"

"The barmaid from Brannigan's came to get Paddy. He found you lying in the street."

"Yeah, boss. She told me who done it. Do you want me to go up there and return the favor?"

Recalling the events in the bar, Jake shook his head, and the pounding momentarily increased. As he massaged the egg-sized lump, he managed a lopsided smile.

"I was in a foul mood when I went in there," he said, forcing his eyes open to look at Paddy. "I remember making a disparaging remark about St. Patrick. I was asking for trouble, and by the feel of my head I got it in high style."

"It's a wonder those boys didn't break your skull, boss," Paddy told him. "And talkin' about St. Patty . . ." He shook his head. "I'll be lightin' a candle for yer immortal soul."

"Doc Bedford said you probably got a concussion," Lovey added, patting his shoulder. "You'll have to stay in bed fer a few days."

"And let Miss Boston Taggart turn the place upside down?" Jake tried to sit up.

Lovey shoved him back down, this time with less tenderness. "Jessie'll do just fine, Jake Weston. You mind the gettin' well. Paddy and I'll watch over Jessie and the Tin Angel."

"Humph," Jake grunted, but his head hurt far too much to argue. He closed his eyes and heard Paddy's heavy steps as he headed out the door.

Again he felt Lovey's pat on his shoulder. "I'll bring you up some soup after a while," she said. "Right now you get a little more sleep." She crossed the room and closed the door quietly.

Jake was asleep in a heartbeat.

It took Jessie three tries to work up the courage to go to Jake's room. She still felt angry and hurt at the way they'd parted, but now that she'd had time to think things over, she knew she was mostly to blame.

She should never have made those wild accusations of murder. Jake had done nothing to earn her distrust, far from it. Everything he'd ever said or done had been forthright and sincere. She knew he could not have killed her father, as surely as she knew her own name. She owed him an apology and, difficult or not, she would give him one.

Almost hoping he wouldn't hear her, Jessie rapped softly on the door.

"It's open," came his terse reply. He was lying on his back, the covers pulled over his chest. It was hard not to notice the muscles rippling across his bare shoulders, or the way his tousled black hair curled softly on his forehead. A late-evening beard darkened his jaw.

"I didn't mean to bother you."

"You aren't bothering me."

"I . . . I . . . came because . . ."

Jessie shifted her gaze from his forehead to his eyes, even bluer than she remembered. She raised her chin and faced him squarely. "I want you to know right off, I don't approve of your drinking and brawling and . . . and . . . God only knows what else."

"I appreciate your concern," he said sarcastically.

Jessie swallowed hard and glanced away. He wasn't making this easy. "How do you feel?" she finally asked, trying a change of tactic. She hadn't come to antagonize him, but thoughts of the Irish girl Paddy had mentioned kept taunting her.

"Like a freight wagon hit me."

Jessie's gaze swung back to his. "I suppose you think it's my fault."

"Now, why would I think that? Calling a man a murderer after you made love to him hardly seems reason to be angry."

"All right," she conceded, trying to ignore his reminder of their intimacy. "I'm sorry for what I said. I didn't really mean it; I was just a little confused."

Jake propped himself up in bed, drawing her attention to the dark hair covering his broad chest. "I don't want an apology, Jess. I want you to know—without a shadow of a doubt—that I did not kill your father."

Jessie sank down on the chair beside his bed. "I know you didn't do it. I didn't believe it even when I said it. But the Chinese . . . well, they think a white man killed my father. I was upset, so I took it out on you."

Jake reached for her hand, but Jessie pulled it away and came to her feet.

"I'd better be going," she said. "You need to get some rest."

Jake watched her for a moment, as if assessing the uneasiness she couldn't quite conceal.

"There's something else," he said. "What is it?"

"Nothing," she answered, a little too quickly.

"Damn it, Jess! Tell me what's going on in that crazy mind of yours."

"The Irish girl," she blurted out, unable to stop herself. "Is she another one of your mistresses? I know what happened between us doesn't give me the right to ask, but I need to know."

Jake propped himself on an elbow and pinned her with his eyes. "There was no Irish girl," he said. He covered her hand with his, and this time she let him. "The girl who came for Paddy was a barmaid, a girl I've never seen before. Actually, she looked like she needed a good scrubbing."

Jessie felt the pull of a smile, and a rush of relief so poignant it made her dizzy. "I'd better get back to work," she said. "The doctor says you'll be back on your feet in no time, and I want things running smoothly."

Jake lay back down and closed his eyes. "Stay out of trouble," he said with a teasing smile.

Feeling lighthearted for the first time in days, Jessie closed the door behind her.

She awoke the following morning, eager to face the day. With her partner laid up, Taggart Enterprises was her responsibility. She intended to handle the job the very best she could.

Before heading downstairs for Jake's usual eleven-thirty meeting with Alec Abernathy, she checked with Lovey on Jake's condition. He was sleeping, Lovey told her, but earlier he'd eaten some biscuits and mush. Apparently his head still ached, and the lump had turned a vicious black and blue.

"Thanks, Lovey," Jessie said when she'd finished her report. "Keep an eye on him, will you?"

"Course, Miss Jessie. Don't you worry about a thing."

Jessie nodded and continued downstairs. When the freight manager entered, he walked straight to the table where she sat in her partner's chair.

"Mornin', Miss Jessie. Jake running late?"

"Jake won't be running anywhere for a while, Alec. He's got a concussion."

"What happened?"

"You'd have to ask him. He looks as if someone danced a jig on his head."

"What?"

"It doesn't matter, Alec. He'll be in bed for a while, but he'll be fine. Now, what is the status of the Consolidated Jackson shipment?"

"On schedule for day after tomorrow." He sat back in the chair and watched her uncertainly, while Su Ling poured him a cup of coffee. "Jake knows all about it."

"Jake is out of commission, Mr. Abernathy, and you work for me, fifty-one percent."

"Jake said you two had a new understanding."

"Oh he did, did he? Well, let me set you straight. Even if Jake Weston were here, which he is not, I have the final say on what happens with Taggart Enterprises. That's *Taggart* Enterprises, in case you've forgotten.''

''I haven't forgotten, ma'am. Still—''

''You've got to make up your mind, Alec. You can work with me, or you can work someplace else.''

Alec sat quietly. Even in booming San Francisco, good jobs were hard to come by. Jessie figured that he might want to quit out of pride, but his common sense would warn him to do as he was told.

''Surely you can't expect me to ignore Jake's wishes,'' he finally said. ''He's been my boss for years.''

''I didn't say that. Jake is still ramrod around here, until I say differently.''

Alec sighed resignedly. ''All right, ma'am, whatever you say.''

''That's better. Now, I figure if we leave within the hour, we should make Sacramento City by nightfall.''

''Sacramento City?''

''That's what I said.''

Alec swallowed dryly and glanced away.

Jake slept all afternoon. Finally, as the plinking of Mormon Pete's piano wafted upstairs, he rubbed his eyes and managed to sit up. Still a little shaky, he pulled on his breeches and shirt. Then, steadying himself, he walked out the door to the railing and stood surveying the saloon. From below, Lovey saw him and puffed up the stairs. She turned him around and shoved him through the doorway and onto the bed.

''Jake Weston, I told you the doctor said a few days.''

''It'll be a few weeks, Lovey, if you keep pushin' me around like that.'' Lovey's meaty fingers worked the top button on his breeches. ''Wait a damned minute, woman," he growled as she ignored him and tugged his pants down around his ankles.

"Don't get schoolmarm-modest with me, Jake Weston. Ain't nothin' you got I ain't seen a hundred times over. Now how 'bout some supper?"

"That suits me," Jake said, climbing back under the covers. "By the way, where's Jessie?"

Lovey turned in the doorway. "She said she had some shoppin' to do."

"What about Paddy?"

"Paddy's with Jessie."

Jake nodded. "Well, how about a slice of sourdough with my supper?"

"That I can handle." She laughed as she left the room.

Jake shoved his hands behind his head. Although he hated to admit it, the lump on his head still throbbed, and he was dizzier than a drunken drover trying to focus on Fatima's belly. He was almost glad Jessie hadn't come back to see him. He could hardly think straight as it was, and that woman always had the damnedest effect on him. Although he'd willed himself not to, he'd dreamed about her—torrid dreams of their passionate lovemaking. He'd been kissing her in his sleep—in places he hadn't dared that first night. She'd been too damned innocent then.

Jake smiled inwardly. If Miss Boston Taggart thought she knew everything there was to know about lovemaking, she was most sorely mistaken. Jake Weston had just begun. The next time he intended to taste every inch of her luscious little body—every inch!

Jake groaned aloud. What in God's name was he thinking? He had to quit torturing himself with what could never be. Making love to Jessie meant nothing but trouble. What he needed was another woman like Monique, a passionate woman he could bed without entanglements.

He liked his carefree existence—didn't he? He liked living alone and counting on no one but himself—didn't he? A woman like Jessie meant marriage, settling down, raising a family. It meant having a wife and children, people who needed him, cared for him. Those responsibilities were the last things Jake needed—weren't they? Of course they were!

Besides, the girl was a worse pain in the breeches than riding bareback on that ridge-backed stallion he used to own. She was spoiled, willful, outspoken . . . but she was also intelligent, caring, and thoughtful. Jessie worked hard, never shirked responsibility, had grit and determination. She was like no other woman he'd known. She was turning out to be a damned fine partner, he admitted.

He chuckled as he conjured up memories of the most luscious pink-tipped breasts he'd ever seen. He could still remember how tiny her waist was, the smooth round curves of her bottom. God, how he'd felt when he'd been inside her . . .

Fool! Jake slammed his hand down on the lowboy beside the bed. Fool, fool, fool! Maybe he should make peace with Monique. A woman of experience had tricks sweet little Jessie had never dreamed of. He'd leave it to Monique to get his mind off Jessie— he'd just have to be careful to call her the right name.

At dawn the following morning Jake awoke clear-headed. He rubbed the lump on his crown, pleased to note that it had shrunk to robin's egg size. After pulling on his breeches and shirt, he headed toward the back stairs that led to the kitchen. Since no one was awake, he'd heat some water to shave. As he moved along the hall, he paused for a moment in front of Jessie's door.

If she were anyone but Henry's daughter, he'd open that door, climb those stairs, and give Miss Boston Taggart a lesson in love she wouldn't soon forget. Jake grew hard at the thought. Damn, he swore, grinding his teeth. He had to get that kind of thinking out of his head.

Jake lit the cookstove, heated some water, and returned to his room. After a wash-up and a nice hot shave, he felt better. Wearing clean clothes, he walked downstairs—a little disappointed to find everything in order even though he'd been laid up for two days—and headed over to Tadich's for breakfast.

As he downed a platter of steak and eggs, he read a copy of the *Chronicle*. A recent international court decision had resulted in a fifteen and a half million dollar judgment against Britain in favor of the United States for supplying the South with ships during the rebellion. The vast amount of money brought to mind the gold shipment due in San Francisco in the next few days. His morning meeting with Alec would supply last-minute details.

By the time he arrived back at the Tin Angel, the doors were open and Rupert was sweeping the boardwalk in front of the saloon.

"Mornin', boss." He tipped his hat as Jake approached and quickly went back to his sweeping.

"Is Jessie up yet?" Jake asked as he headed toward the door.

"I dunno," Rupert answered without looking up. "She didn't stay here last night, or the night before."

Jake stopped in his tracks. Visions of Jessie in bed with Rene La Porte flashed across his mind. "And just where in the hell *did* little Miss Boston Taggart spend the night?"

"I dunno, boss," Rupert mumbled, still not looking up.

Jake stepped into the path of his sweeping, the broom coming to rest against the toe of his shiny black boot. "You know." He said the words with menacing slowness. "Now, where is she?"

"I . . . I ain't lyin', boss. Lovey was havin' a real to-do with Jessie before she and Paddy left, day before last. Jessie said not to say nothin' to no one."

Jake was through the front door before Rupert could start his next sentence. He took the stairs two at a time and didn't pause until he stood directly in front of Lovey's door. He hammered loudly.

"Who is it?" Lovey answered, as if she hadn't already guessed.

Jake threw open the door. "Where the hell is Jessie?"

"I told her you'd be mad as the fourth shoat from a three-titted sow when you found out she was gone."

"Where is she?" he demanded, his hands balled into fists. It was all he could to do keep from shouting.

"She went to Jackson with Paddy and Alec."

"Jackson?" He felt a momentary wave of relief that she wasn't with Rene, then a bolt of white-hot, murderous rage. "To escort that bullion shipment?"

"Far as I know."

"If somebody hasn't done it already, I just may kill her myself!" Jake looked at Lovey so hard she had to glance away. "What in God's name possessed you not to tell me?"

Lovey seemed contrite. "You know Jessie has a mule-strong will. You were down sick and Jessie said—"

"You and Rupert mind the store. I'll deal with the both of you when I get back."

"Jake, you shouldn't. You ain't up to it," Lovey cried, but he slammed the door so hard the room shook.

Pausing only long enough to pull on his denim breeches and leather boots, Jake rolled up his blanket. He shoved his sawed-off .36 under his flannel shirt and into his pants at the back. He pulled his Leech and Rigdon .44 from where it hung on his bedpost and started to check the load, then decided he would have plenty of time on the paddle-wheeler to Sacramento City.

He left the Tin Angel at a run, heading for the livery where he kept his saddle horse. The big gray stallion danced nervously as Jake saddled and mounted him, taking the city streets leading to the wharf at a clattering gallop. He and Faro barely made the noon boat as it left the docks.

Dressed in simple calico, her hair in a tight chignon beneath a wide sunbonnet, Jessie stood beside Paddy and Alec Abernathy inside Superintendent Howard Collier's impressive office at the Consolidated Jackson Mining Company, half a day's ride east of Jackson. They'd traveled eight hours by steamship to Sacramento City, then thirteen hours by wagon, including an overnight stop.

Alec signed the receipt for twenty-two thousand, seven hundred and fifty-two dollars in gold bullion—fourteen hundred and twenty-two ounces, or a little over eighty-eight pounds. Collier accepted the paper and slid it into his desk drawer.

The slender, bespectacled superintendent cleared his throat and pulled a sack of Bull Durham tobacco from his pocket. With a worried expression, he rolled a cigarette as he spoke.

"I want you both to know that hiring Taggart Freighting wasn't my idea. I've always worked with Wells, Fargo. They're a fine old company. The *Alta California* says they've made good on every loss they ever suffered. That's over four hundred thousand dollars since they started in '52." He pulled a match from his waistcoat pocket with a shaky hand and eyed Jessie nervously. "You don't mind, ma'am?"

"Not at all, Mr. Collier." Jessie had said little since their two-wagon caravan had arrived a little after noon. Alec and a shotgun guard had ridden aboard the freight wagon with Taggart Freighting painted boldly on the side, while she and Paddy had traveled in a patched and tattered covered wagon she'd had the freight master in Sacramento purchase. The homesteader's wagon bulged under its dingy canvas covering, stuffed to overflowing with secondhand household goods.

Collier blew a plume of cigarette smoke in her direction while Alec gave him a confident look and extended his hand. "Taggart Freighting is a fine company too, Mr. Collier. And we guarantee our losses just like Wells, Fargo."

"Saying it's guaranteed and actually making good are two different things, Mr. Abernathy." His nervously constructed cigarette began to unravel. "Damn," he muttered, glancing up. "Pardon me, ma'am."

Jessie smiled and turned her gaze out the window. Earlier, she had watched the bars of gold being loaded beneath the bed of the wagon, then carefully covered with a false floor. Now, as the men reloaded the last of the furniture on top of the hidden gold, she began to doubt her plan for the very first time. What if they lost the bullion to thieves? The loss of this one shipment would sink Taggart Freighting, and probably take the Yuba City Riverboats and the Tin Angel down with it.

"Well," Alec said, "if that's all, we'll get started."

The men shook hands, and the three of them left the office. Outside, Alec turned to Paddy. "Remember, if you hear shots up near the freight wagon, get turned around and head in the opposite direction. We'll take care of ourselves."

"Yes, sir, Mr. Abernathy."

They mounted the wagons and headed out. The freight wagon left the smelting plant yard, taking a five-minute headstart. Then a mounted guard followed, carrying a shotgun, a Winchester in his saddle scabbard, and a Colt on his hip. Another Colt hung from his saddle horn. Jessie and Paddy followed in the homesteader's wagon, pulled by four strong mules. Behind them, a second guard followed just out of sight.

With five well-armed men and the freight wagon as decoy, it seemed a foolproof plan.

As Paddy finished checking the loads in his scattergun and whipped up the mules, the butterflies in Jessie's stomach settled down. But each time they met someone on the narrow Mokelumne River road, the butterflies fluttered with a vengeance.

Chapter 17

The wagon ride along the river road and across a range of sharp-shouldered hills to the town of Jackson took the rest of the afternoon.

The caravan had worked its way through granite outcroppings, digger pines, and forests of scrub oak to reach the outskirts just before dusk. Since it was too risky to travel by night, they'd decided that Jackson would be the safest place to stop. The men would sleep in the Taggart Freighting yard with the wagons, alternating guard duty, while Jessie checked into the National Hotel.

Jessie was pleased. The trip from the mine had been uneventful. By noon tomorrow they'd be out of the hills and on their way to Sacramento City. And Jake had said they'd be safer once they reached the flats.

Leaning on the bar off the small lobby of the hotel, Portigee Santos Silva and four hired men watched Jessica Taggart check in.

"Right on schedule," Silva said to the man on his right. The man grinned and downed his whiskey. Silva bought one more round of drinks, using part of a double eagle he'd been paid for the wreck of the *Callie Sue*. He smiled to himself. He could afford it. Soon he'd have all the gold he could spend.

Silva chuckled aloud. That dumb Pole Bochek

thought he was planning to share. He would have, too, if the sonofabitch had paid him what he owed.

You were too damned greedy, Bochek.

The passes over the Sierras were open at this time of year, and Virginia City would be a good place to stop on his way East. After that he'd head for Chicago, hit New York, then Lisbon, or maybe the Azores—first-class all the way.

Silva drained his drink and stood up. "Come on, boys. We got a little riding to do before we bed down. We John Chinamen got to be up and at 'em," he said, winking at the others, none of whom were Chinese, "by the time the rooster crows."

It was an ink-black moonless night when Jake finally unloaded his horse from the paddle-wheeler and headed toward town. Even as angry and worried as he was, he knew it would be crazy to try the road in the dark. Laming his horse would do no good. He'd sleep in Sacramento City, then leave at first light for Jackson.

The way he had it figured, Jessie's cockamamie homesteader's wagon—if he knew Jessie, and he was beginning to wish he didn't—would lay over in Jackson and leave in the morning for Sacramento. Jake could cover the distance to the foothills faster than they could, so he'd intercept them well before they reached the valley. That should be somewhere between Dry Town and Michigan Bar.

By the time Miss Jessie Taggart got her wagon seat warmed up, he would be there to do a little seat-warming of his own!

In the darkness, Jessie slapped the clanging alarm clock she'd borrowed from the desk clerk and fumbled for a match to light the chimney lamp on the bedside table.

After the second sleepy try, the lamp blazed to life, casting a warm glow over the room. She used the pitcher and basin to wash up, then she combed her hair and twisted it into a bun. Finally she donned her calico dress and bonnet.

Downstairs, she handed the desk clerk her key and paid the bill. "Is there somewhere I can get a cup of coffee?"

He yawned and pointed toward the kitchen. "Cook starts baking at three in morning. He's always got a pot goin'."

Jessie smelled the aroma of cinnamon rolls as soon as she entered.

"Can I help you?" the cook asked, turning away from the stove.

"How about selling me cup of coffee and a dozen of those rolls?"

"I bake 'em for the whole town," he said. "I can spare a dozen." Pulling a cheesecloth from under the dry sink, he quickly bundled them up. "That's twelve cents, pay at the desk."

By the time Jessie had walked the three city blocks to Taggart Freighting, the men had the mules harnessed and were backing them into the traces. "Did the men get breakfast?" she asked Alec.

"We had beans and sowbelly," he answered, "and some kind of varnish the freight master called coffee."

Jessie passed the rolls among the men, getting wide grins for her trouble, and headed toward her wagon. In the distance, the first light of dawn pinkened the sky over the Sierras. Paddy helped her climb up to the seat, and they watched the freight wagon roll out, Alec and the shotgun guard waving good-bye. The mounted guard followed some distance behind. A few minutes later, Paddy whipped up the mules and they headed down the road. The final guard waited the appropriate length of time, then fell in too.

By the middle of the morning, when they reached Dry Town, Jessie was convinced that all her worrying had been for naught. Only three more miles and they would be out of the foothills and onto the gently rolling plain that led to Sacramento City. There the homesteader's wagon would be loaded onto the paddleboat for the trip downriver to San Francisco.

They passed through Dry Town without incident and turned off north to Placerville, the town that had decided its original name, Hangtown, wasn't respectable enough for a thriving community. A little farther on, the road swung due west toward Michigan Bar and Bridgehouse, where they would pick up some food to eat along the way.

Jessie yawned and stretched and closed her eyes to daydream a little. Life was rich, the sun warm on her face. Birds sang happily in roadside trees, and the gold shipment was almost safe. Jake would have to admit her plan had been a good one after all. He'd take her interest in the businesses more seriously. She knew he'd be angry at first, but afterward, she hoped he'd be pleased.

"By the saints!"

Hearing Paddy's voice, she opened her eyes to find a fallen oak limb blocking the road.

"How'd you s'pose Alec got the freight wagon around that?" Paddy asked. A raven circled above, cawing ominously, but Jessie didn't heed its warning.

"Maybe it just fell down," she said as Paddy began to climb from the seat. Then she noticed that the end of the limb had been cut with an ax, and grew wary. She reached down to the floorboards for the shotgun.

"Don't be gettin' no weapon out of that wagon, missy," a voice rang out from the rocks.

Fear trickled down her back like melting ice. Jessie straightened, searching desperately for the man behind the voice.

"Put yer hands on yer lap, missy."

Paddy looked stunned. He started to climb back

into the wagon just as three men stepped out of the brush dressed in the black robes of Chinese coolies, skullcaps perched atop their heads. Their faces were covered with masks, but Jessie could see that the men weren't Chinese.

"Yer about to take a back full of buckshot, mister," the first man shouted. Paddy paused and looked helplessly up at Jessie. The men walked slowly up behind him, and one of them brought his heavy revolver across Paddy's bowler with a hollow thump. The hat flew into the brush, and Paddy sagged to his knees.

"Paddy!" Jessie screamed. She reached blindly for the shotgun and swung it up and around, but one of the men jumped onto the wagon wheel and caught the gun before she could aim. It fired wildly into the air, knocking her back on the seat. The man pried her fingers loose and tossed the gun to his companion. Then he grabbed her roughly around the waist and dragged her kicking and screaming from the seat. Her bonnet fell off when he dumped her unceremoniously into the dust at his feet.

"What . . . what do you want?" Jessie asked, forcing a show of bravado.

"You know damned well what we want," one of them said.

"My mother gave me that furniture," Jessie told him.

"We ain't after no junk furniture," the man said. Before he could speak further, the ground shook with the force of a blast up ahead. Jessie stifled the scream that was caught in her throat. What in God's name had happened to the freight wagon? Determined to remain calm, she clenched her trembling hands in the folds of her skirt.

The man who appeared to be the leader turned to his companions. "Get back down the road and take care of the guard coming up from the rear." The two men ran to the bend in the road and hid in the rocks.

Jessie could hear gunfire ahead, and feared for Alec and the guard in the freight wagon. Then she heard the rapid hoofbeats of the man riding rear guard. *Oh God, no!* Leaping to her feet, she raced toward the man about to be ambushed.

"Look out!" she yelled. "They're in the rocks!" But as soon as the words were spoken, a deafening shotgun blast blew the man from his saddle.

Jessie glanced at the outlaws, who were now running toward her. She knew the guard was dead before he hit the dusty road, but his horse continued at a gallop. Jessie bolted in its direction, hoping to slow the animal long enough to mount it and ride away. A flying tackle from the man behind landed her just inches away from the horse's churning hooves.

Struggling frantically against her assailant, Jessie beat at his chest furiously. The man smiled down at her, enjoying her futile efforts, and pinned her wrists to the ground beside her head.

"Take her over to that oak tree and tie her up," the leader instructed. She was jerked roughly to her feet, the last of the pins holding up her hair scattering and her heavy curls tumbling across her shoulders.

"You'd best stay quiet, missy," the leader warned, "if you know what's good for you."

Lying near the wagon, Paddy struggled to his feet. "Get away from her!" he bellowed.

The leader drew the gun he carried at his waist and fired in a single easy motion. Jessie screamed and tried desperately to break free. Clutching his chest, Paddy staggered backward into the ditch beside the road, his shirtfront covered with blood.

Wild with anguish, Jessie tore free and raced toward the man holding the still-smoking gun. She tried to wrench the weapon away, but he only laughed at her. Fury blinded her, as her open palm connected with his cheek in a stinging slap that snapped his head back, surprising them both. With a sneer, he shoved his gun back in the holster, doubled his fist, and punched her hard in the jaw. The last thing Jessie remembered was the salty taste of blood.

Riding at a steady pace, Jake had been churning up the dusty road for hours. The gray was lathered; it was time for rest and water. Jake figured he could use a little grub too, but he'd settle for a bite of beef jerky for now. Seeing the sign for Bridgehouse, only a mile away, he headed toward the way station, the only building at the Consumnes River crossing.

He reined up and loosened the cinch, then led the horse to a trough near the barn door. The animal pushed aside some floating moss and drew deeply on the water.

A dark-skinned youth approached from the shadows of the building. "You want I should feed your horse, mister?"

"No time. We've still got some ridin' ahead of us."

The boy nodded and headed back into the barn. Jake brushed the dust from his breeches and shirt and raked a hand through his hair before he settled his black flat-brimmed hat back on his head.

After giving Faro a few more minutes to cool, he tightened the cinch and mounted. Again they took up a steady, mile-eating gait.

Jessie woke up with the stark realization that her hands and ankles were bound. She focused on the three men she remembered. They were now joined by another two, busily loading the gold bars into the packsaddle of a big hammerheaded mule. Furniture lay strewn all over the road. One man stood aside while the other four worked. Glancing over, he noticed that Jessie was awake.

"You shouldn't have slapped me, missy," he said

as he walked up beside her. "I hated to bruise your pretty face."

"You won't get away with this."

"I already got away with it, Miss Taggart."

"You know me?"

With the toe of his boot he shoved her skirt up to her knee, leaving a portion of her stockinged leg exposed.

"Not as well as I'm going to."

She tried to jerk free, but her hands were tied behind her back and she only succeeded in hitching her skirt and petticoats up higher. Her face burning, she glanced away, but not before she caught the lewd smile in his eyes. He turned and walked back to where the men were working.

"That's all of it, Silva. We each took what we was promised," one of them said.

The first man walked to his horse, dug into a saddlebag, and came out with a tong hatchet. With a resounding crack, he drove it into the side of the homesteader's wagon.

They all laughed.

"Tie Miss Taggart across a saddle, Hank. I'll be taking her with me so she won't be telling a posse where we've gone. You fellas ride out the way we planned. You'd be wise to stay clear of the Barbary Coast for a while."

One of the men turned toward Jessie, his dark eyes scanning her from head to foot. "I think I'd rather ride with you, boss, if it's all the same."

"It ain't all the same." Silva rested his hand casually on the butt of the gun at his waist. The man shrugged his shoulders and walked to where the horses were tied, leading one over. He hoisted Jessie up and tossed her facedown across the saddle. He hiked her skirts up, exposing her legs as he tied her bound ankles to a stirrup with a rawhide thong. Then he tied her wrists to the stirrup on the other side.

"I'd say that's a mighty pretty sight." He chuckled, running a hand along Jessie's calf. She tried to kick him, but only managed to wiggle her backside enticingly.

"You little hellcat, keep that up and we'll all take a turn at you right here and now."

"Get going," the man named Silva ordered.

The other man grumbled as he walked to his horse and swung into the saddle. The other three joined him. "Have your fun, Portigee," the mounted man said, "but remember, she knows it wasn't no John Chinaman did this."

"You just get down the road and away from here. I'll take care of whatever else needs handling."

A shiver raced down Jessie's spine. *He's planning to kill me!* He couldn't afford to leave her alive. Remembering Paddy, she glanced over her shoulder and saw him lying facedown in the ditch. The guard was sprawled a few feet away. Oh, God, what have I done? She felt like crying, like giving in to the feminine instinct that told her she was no match for them, but instead she took a deep breath. It was too late to save the others, but not too late to save herself. Sooner or later, he'd have to cut her loose. When he did, she would find some way to escape.

Without another word, Silva took up her horse's lead rope and tied him behind the pack mule. The thunder of horses' hooves marked the other men's departure. Silva kicked his own horse into a trot, and Jessie jounced up and down across the saddle, wincing with every jolt and praying for a chance to escape.

Jake had been riding for over an hour when he spotted two horses trotting down the road in his direction. His heart began to pound, and he spurred the gray, sparing the team only a glance as he passed them on the road. As he'd feared, they carried the

Taggart Freighting TF brand on their rumps. A knot of worry tightened his chest.

Before he'd gone another mile, he found the overturned freight wagon. Dismounting, he searched for some sign of the men it had carried, but he found no one. A quarter mile down the road from where the team had apparently dragged the abandoned wagon, he came upon the bodies of Alec Abernathy and the man who'd been riding shotgun. They sprawled in the road just in front of a landslide that completely blocked the narrow lane.

Checking to be certain both men were dead, Jake found that the guard had been shot in the back with a high-caliber rifle, and Alec had been shot twice through the chest. Jake muttered an oath beneath his breath. Alec had been a good man, and he had a wife and children back home. They would miss him—Jake would miss him.

The knot of dread moved to his stomach. He walked to the twenty-foot pile of rocks in the road below where the dynamite had been placed.

Then he saw the woven leather rein that led out of the rock pile, the booted foot that was twisted at a gruesome angle. He wondered if the man beneath the rocks was friend or foe. Jake swallowed hard. So far he'd been able to keep his thoughts under careful control, but as the minutes slipped by, images of Jessie overwhelmed him. The freight wagon had to be on the other side of the debris. Maybe the men who'd attacked the wagon hadn't discovered Jessie's ruse. Maybe Paddy'd had sense enough to turn around and hightail it back to the nearest town. Maybe Jessie was safe.

The knot in his stomach twisted tighter. *Why wasn't he convinced?*

After studying the hillsides on either side of the trail, Jake mounted and began working his way up and around the hill. When he reached the top, he spotted the homesteader's wagon and its mules. The animals were grazing along the roadside among piles of broken furniture.

The gray slipped and slid as Jake urged him down the incline to the road. When he reached the wagon, he reined up and dismounted. Terrified of what he might find, he forced himself to stay in control.

A quick search turned up only a few more pieces of furniture and the boards that had been used to line the bottom of the wagon. A tong hatchet was embedded in the side of the wagon. A forlorn sunbonnet lay in the road—and a trail of blood marked the ground.

It was all Jake could do to force himself to walk along the trail. A few feet ahead, he spotted a body in the ditch beside the road. He knelt down, and with shaking hands gently turned Paddy over and wiped the dust from his face. A low moan from Paddy's dirt-covered lips gave Jake a moment of relief. He checked Paddy's wound, stuffing a piece of his own shirt into the bullet hole in his friend's shoulder to stop the bleeding. Then he continued his search for Jessie.

A look around the grounds failed to turn up any sign of her, as he'd been fairly sure it would. With Paddy out of the way, Jessie would have had little protection. And women were at a premium—especially one as pretty as Jessie. He could have bet the men would take her along. They'd use her well and hard before they killed her. The thought sliced through him like the hatchet blade just a few feet away.

Forcing himself to stay calm, he began looking for signs. Three animals had headed north, four south. He'd pick up the trail as soon as he took care of Paddy. Since they weren't far from Dry Town, Jake tied the gray to the now-empty wagon and loaded Paddy into the back. He then hitched the mules up and clucked them into a trot. He stopped only once— when he came upon another body. It didn't take long to discover that the man was dead—his face blown away by a shotgun blast.

Within the hour, Jake was back at the site of the robbery, having left Paddy with the Dry Town doctor. A wagon had been sent for Alec's body and those of the guards, and the sheriff was busy appointing deputies, who would soon be following.

Jake left immediately, riding a big buckskin gelding and leading a well-muscled sorrel mare. He'd left the tired gray at the livery where he'd purchased these two. He didn't know how far he would have to ride to find Jessie, but he wouldn't stop until he did. He prayed to God he wouldn't be too late.

Again Jake studied the signs marking the road. What would he do if he had a load of gold and a beautiful woman? One set of the tracks heading north looked shallower than the others. Logic, and a sixth sense that had rarely failed him, told him Jessie was riding that lightly loaded horse.

Since the other group of tracks revealed no significant clues, Jake took the only lead he had. With a quick prayer that he was right, he rode off down the trail, the sorrel following behind. It wasn't long before the tracks veered east. Jake figured they were headed for the rugged hill country. With a second horse in tow, Jake could maintain a fast pace without worrying that the animals would tire. He thought of Jessie and prayed she'd keep her wits about her—and her temper in check—long enough for him to get there.

Four hours after he'd headed out, Portigee Santos Silva left the trail that led into the high country and trotted off into an area of steep granite cliffs. Anyone following them would be hard-pressed to track them across this rugged stretch of land. He planned to keep moving, hoping to reach the cabin he'd found up above Placerville. He had plenty of food

stashed away, as well as firewood and blankets—
now he even had a pretty bed partner for the night.

Portigee glanced back over his shoulder and
smiled. Watching the girl's calico-clad bottom
bounce up and down in the saddle stirred a chord
of desire, and his manhood pressed urgently against
his trousers. He chuckled softly. *Later, my friend.
Later you will enjoy her.* For now he would concentrate on getting safely away.

Jake followed the tracks until they disappeared.
Then he went carefully over the trail trying to discover where the animals ahead of him had moved
off the path. What would *he* do if he thought he
might be followed? he asked himself again. Surveying the countryside around him, he suddenly knew.
Somewhere across the rocks, his adversary's trail
continued. The only problem was—where?

Knowing it would cost him valuable time, Jake
headed for the divide at the mountaintop. From
there he could see for miles in every direction.
Thankful for the spyglass he'd had the foresight to
buy in Dry Town, along with a smattering of other
supplies, he figured he might just get lucky enough
to spot his prey.

The sun was high in the afternoon sky by the time
Jake reached his goal. He tied the horses beneath a
sugar pine, settled among the fallen pine cones, and
began to scan the mountain. Since some of the ter-
rain was just too hostile to climb on horseback, his
job would be easier. He leaned against the tree
trunk, his back propped against the rough bark, and
began his methodical search. He knew it wouldn't
be easy, but as long as the sun was up, he had a
chance.

Two hours later, he spotted them far across the
canyon. Jake's hand tightened on the telescope and
a muscle bunched in his jaw. A single man was lead-

ing a heavily laden mule and a saddle horse. His mouth went dry as he focused on a woman in calico skirts draped across the saddle. He couldn't see her face, but he'd know that bottom a hundred miles away.

Jake slipped the bridle off the buckskin and slapped him on the flank, knowing the animal would eventually find his way to the livery in Dry Town. Speed counted now. He would make better time on the fresh sorrel.

He glanced back across the canyon. Mentally plotting the course the man was following, Jake calculated that if he crossed at an angle, taking the steeper route through the ravine, he'd cut their trail and soon be less than an hour behind them. Only an hour.

But for a woman alone with a killer the likes of this one, an hour was a very long time.

Chapter 18

Teeth tightly clamped against the jolting, jarring ride and her mounting need to relieve herself, Jessie was just about to put aside her pride and beg Silva to stop when he pulled the animals to a halt in the cool shade of a pine tree.

Wordlessly, he untied her from the stirrups, cut the rope that bound her feet, and helped her down. It was all she could do to remain standing.

"You behave yerself," he warned, "and I'll give you a minute's privacy."

Jessie's eyes closed in relief. "Thank you." She saw that he'd discarded his coolie disguise. He was a muscular man with kinky black hair and hard gray eyes. When she stepped toward the boulder to her right, he caught her arm.

"Not so fast." He tied a length of rope around her already bound wrists. "Try to go farther than the end of this rope, and I'll jerk you on yer pretty little arse."

Jessie just nodded. The thought of escape had crossed her mind, but her immediate problem seemed more important at the moment. She skirted a large boulder, took care of her needs, and returned to the horses.

"You give me yer word you won't make trouble," he said, "and I'll let you sit that horse, 'stead of being slung across it like a sack a' rolled oats."

Giving her word would be a lie, but Jessie didn't hesitate. What was all that balderdash about honor among thieves? So far she'd seen none of it. "You have my word," she said meekly. If she could trick him into trusting her, she just might have a chance.

They remounted and Silva tied her hands to the saddle horn. Her ribs ached, her back hurt, her jaw felt bruised and swollen, and her hair hung in tangled strands around her face. At least the blood no longer rushed to her head.

She wondered if anyone had discovered the wagons and the bodies of Paddy and the Taggart Freighting men, wondered if anyone even knew she was missing. What would Jake do when he found out? What would he be thinking? He would come after her, she was sure—if only because she was his partner. But Jake was still in San Francisco, any other attempt at rescue hours behind. By the time someone found her, it would be too late.

Jessie shuddered at the thought. She'd gotten herself into this mess—now she'd have to get herself out. She'd never felt more alone in her life.

The rest of the afternoon passed in a blur of aches and pains, escape plans made and discarded and thoughts of Jake. At least she wouldn't end her life without knowing the joys of being a woman. She could still remember Jake's hard body thrusting into her, the overwhelming sensations he'd stirred, the closeness she'd felt. She just wished the experience had meant more to him.

Over the next hour, her thoughts sank lower. She kept remembering Paddy lying dead, the others bleeding and dying on the dusty road. It's all my fault. They're all dead because of me. Tears gathered, but she refused to let them fall. She was a Taggart, by damn! She couldn't afford to cry, couldn't afford to let her guard down even for a moment. She wouldn't give up, not yet. She'd fight till she breathed her last.

* * *

Dusk was falling when the horses rounded a bend in the trail and Jessie spotted a cabin. Low roofed, made of logs chinked with mud and bark, the place looked abandoned. Silva reined up, tied up his horse and the pack mule, then returned for her. After helping her down, he tied her to a tree, led her horse away, then went into the cabin.

Beginning to tremble from the evening chill, Jessie noticed a thin tendril of smoke coming from the low rock chimney. Maybe someone will see it, she thought with a surge of hope. Then she realized her captor had laid his plans so well that he had little to fear. Fighting a wave of despair, she sagged against the ropes that bound her.

"I got some grub on the stove," Silva said as he approached, drawing her attention. "But there's somethin' I need more than food." With a hungry look that left no doubt as to his intentions, he pulled a knife from the inside of his boot.

Jessie closed her eyes and felt her stomach roll. He meant to use her; he wouldn't wait until later. Any chance for escape had to be now. As Silva sliced through the ropes, Jessie jerked free. She shoved him as hard as she could, then raced toward the forest, hoping to lose herself in the darkness.

Silva was on top of her before she reached the edge of the clearing. "Let me go!" she screamed as they crashed into the dirt and rolled into a tumble of pine needles. Breathing hard, Jessie lay pinned beneath him, her hair tangled wildly around her face.

Silva just laughed. "Still got plenty of spirit. I like that." He jerked her to her feet and dragged her kicking and screaming back toward the cabin. Twice he slapped her, but in her fear, she hardly noticed.

Inside the cabin, he shoved her toward the make-shift bed. His hands were on her in an instant as he pressed her down on the cornhusk mattress. Jessie pulled his hair and tried to bite him, clawing and scratching his face. He slapped her, two hard ear-ringing blows that nearly knocked her out. She could taste blood in her mouth, and the room spun crazily. By the time she regained her senses, her skirts were hiked up, the bodice of her dress torn to her waist, her chemise open, and her breasts exposed. Jessie moaned low in her throat.

Groping desperately, trying to find something to use as a weapon, she closed her hand over an earth-enware chamber pot beside the bed. With all her might, she smashed it against the side of her assail-ant's head. Silva sagged on top of her. She tried to shove him away, but only succeeded in prying her-self free. She came to her feet, gasping for air and clutching the front of her dress over her bare bosom. She took a single step toward the door before Silva's fingers closed around her ankle, jerking her off bal-ance and dragging her toward him.

Jessie waited until he let go of her foot and grabbed her waist to pull her into his arms. Dou-bling up her fist, she punched him in the nose as hard as she could. Blood gushed over his face, and a look so hard it could have bent nails distorted his features.

"You're really something," he muttered, his eyes narrowed to slits. He strategically placed himself be-tween her and the door. "I'm gonna pleasure my-self with you in ways I've only dreamed. Wouldn't do it if you'd acted like a lady. Even considered tak-ing you with me." As he spoke he circled her, wip-ing the blood from his nose. Jessie looked frantically from the door to the single hide-covered window.

"Before I'm through with you, there won't be an inch of yer pretty little body that ain't been used."

Jessie swallowed hard. "You'll have to kill me first," she said softly.

"You ain't gonna be that lucky."

"You a bettin' man, mister?" The familiar deep

voice and the ominous click of a revolver swung Jessie's gaze to the open doorway. Bathed in the flickering light of the fire, Jake Weston looked more dangerous than her assailant—and more dear than she could have imagined.

"Jake," she whispered.

Silva stood frozen, Jake's gun just inches from his temple.

"Hello, Boston,"

She heard the catch in his throat, the gentleness, and wished she could see his eyes, shaded by the wide brim of his hat. "Jake," she repeated, as if saying his name would ensure he was really there.

"Think you could use a little help?" he baited her, his voice no longer soft. "Or would you rather handle this by yourself, too?"

"Jake, I—"

"Move," he ordered Silva before she could answer. "Nice and easy. We're going outside." Silva inched slowly toward the door, his hands poised midway between his shoulders and the gun he wore near his waist.

"I know what you're thinking," Jake said. "I wouldn't advise it. There's nothing I'd like better than to put a bullet through your head."

Silva raised his hands a little higher. "Take it easy, mister. Let's talk this out. Maybe we can make a deal."

"Sorry, friend. The lady you've been manhandling is my partner. I take that relationship seriously, even if she doesn't." He cast her a hard glance. "I won't argue she deserved a good beating, but I prefer to do my own dirty work."

"I'm sorry, Jake. I know I should have—"

"For once in your life, Jessie Taggart, keep your mouth shut."

Jessie's jaw snapped closed.

"Outside." Inch by inch, Jake moved Silva into the open. They'd just cleared the doorway when

Silva spun, knocking Jake's gun aside as he drove an elbow into his ribs.

With a low growl, Jake punched Silva in the stomach, doubling him over. Another punch sent him sprawling in the powdery dirt. Jake grabbed the front of Silva's shirt, hoisted him up, and hit him full in the face. Jake forgot where he was, forgot his intentions. All he could see was Jessie's torn dress, the blood on her face, the terror in her eyes—and he wanted to kill the sonofabitch with his bare hands.

He kept throwing punches until the man was unconscious. His own exhaustion and Jessie's hand on his arm finally stopped him.

"Jake?" she said tremulously, holding up her dress with shaking fingers.

Jake forced his thoughts back to the man at his feet. He was breathing, but his eyes were closed, his body limp.

Jake turned to look at Jessie, and found her staring at him as if she'd never seen him before. Unable to stop himself, he pulled her into his arms. "God, Jess, I was so worried," he whispered against her hair.

"How did you find me?" she asked, a catch in her voice. "How did you know where I'd gone?"

"I guess I'm beginning to understand how that crazy mind of yours works." He tilted her chin, saw the bruise on her face and her uncertain look. "Stay here," he ordered. "I want him trussed good and tight."

Jessie stepped away from him and watched as Jake went to his horse and loosened a length of rope tied to the saddle. She'd never seen him this way—coldly detached, grimly resolved, a man perfectly capable of killing. As he bent over Silva, she could sense the tension in his body, the rage he was barely keeping under control. Watching Jake work with such cold determination, Jessie almost forgot Silva's knife.

Then she caught the flash of silver and realized that Jake was about to die.

"Jake!" she screamed, diving for the gun he had lost earlier in his struggle with Silva. She grabbed it as Jake dodged away from the slashing blade, and pulled the trigger. The revolver bucked in her hand, and Silva was blown back into the dirt and brush, where he lay deathly still.

Jake was beside her instantly, helping her to stand, then lifting her into his arms. Her tears came with a vengeance this time.

"It's all right, honey," he said. "He can't hurt you now." Jake tightened his hold, carrying her into the cabin and placing her gently on the cornhusk bed. Finding a bucket of water near the fire, he dampened his shirttail and gently washed her face.

"You were right, Jake. A . . . a woman has no place in business. Paddy and the others . . . they're dead, and it's all my fault." Jessie broke into fresh sobs, turning her face into the mattress. Jake eased her into his arms and she pressed her cheek against his chest.

"Paddy isn't dead," he told her. "He's pretty badly hurt, but the doctor says he'll live. As for the others, somebody knew your setup. They knew the road you would follow, your schedule—their timing was perfect. Somebody on the inside tipped them off."

Jessie sniffed back her tears. "Somebody told them? Who, Jake? Who could have known?"

"I don't know, but I intend to find out."

"They were dressed as Chinese, Jake. But they weren't."

"They left a tong hatchet—Auspicious Laborers, I think. They must have been covering their bets with the clothes. Protection in case someone saw them from a distance, or some poor sucker lived."

"It was awful," Jessie whispered. "There was so much blood. He said he was going to do . . . *things*

. . . to me. Pleasure himself in ways . . ." She glanced up at him. "What did he mean? I thought what happened the other night between us . . . I thought that was how it was done."

For the first time in what seemed like years, Jake smiled. "You're one helluva woman, Jessie Taggart, but when it comes to making love, you're sorely in need of an education."

"But we made love, didn't we?"

"There are hundreds of ways to make love—some not so gentle."

She digested that for a moment. "I see. . . . Could you explain—"

"Jess, I don't think now's the time to be talking about this." Helplessly, Jake felt his eyes drawn to the tempting flesh barely covered by her torn calico dress.

"No, I suppose not," she said, "but if no one explains, how does a woman ever know?"

"Damn it, Jess! You're not supposed to know until you're married. Then your husband's supposed to teach you."

"I might be old and gray by then. I want to know now."

Jake clamped his jaw shut. If he didn't get her off this subject quickly, she was going to find out, whether she wanted to or not. "Look, Jess, I'm trying to keep things straight between us. It's like you said—we're poorly suited, we don't love each other, we don't belong together. But I'm warning you, you keep sitting there asking questions, wearing near nothing and lookin' so damned pitiful, and I swear you're gonna get another lesson. One I'm trying damned hard not to give you right now."

Jessie watched him from underneath her lashes. She wanted him to kiss her, to hold her, to make her forget the horrors she'd seen this day. She wanted to feel protected, as close to him as she had before. "I thought about you today," she told him.

"I was glad I wasn't going to die without knowing . . . without ever making love."

Jake glanced away.

"I remembered the way you made me feel." She turned his face with her hand. "I want to learn more, Jake. Will you teach me?"

"Jess," he said, "you don't know what you're doing to me." But he knew it was already too late. Cupping her face between his palms, he kissed her, a feather-soft touch against her bruised and swollen lips. Her arms slipped around his neck, her fingers laced through his hair, and he heard himself groan.

"I want you, damn it. I want you so bad it hurts." As battered as she was, he wanted to possess her, own her, he wanted to drive any thoughts of other men away. He didn't question the reason—he didn't want to know.

She increased the pressure of the kiss, and Jake felt the tentative touch of her tongue. He didn't want to hurt her, but his control was beginning to slip. She moved her mouth across his as if she felt the same.

It took only a second to part the tattered bodice of her dress, only an instant for his hands to lift the silken weight of her breast, for his finger to tease the pink softness into a pebble-hard bud. When Jessie moaned and arched against him, Jake lowered his mouth to her nipple, licked it with his tongue, then circled the peak with his lips and tugged it gently. She mewed softly, while her trembling hands worked the buttons on his shirt. He felt a gust of cool air as it opened, then her fingers gliding through his curly black chest hair.

"I still can't believe you're here," Jessie whispered. His skin felt so warm, the crisp hairs curled so deliciously that she wanted to explore more of him. She felt his hands on her body, sliding the torn dress down, tugging the cord of her petticoats and drawers, dropping the whole dusty pile at her feet.

Then he was removing his boots, his breeches sliding down his lean hard thighs, his shirt joining the growing mess of discarded clothes.

She hadn't had the courage to look at him before. Now she couldn't take her eyes off him. She could see the faint line of an old war wound on his chest, while another marked his thigh. His shaft was huge and swollen, thrusting forward as if it sought her touch. Tentatively, her fingers brushed his flesh, and he groaned.

"Easy Boston, we've got the rest of the night."

Jessie flushed with embarrassment. Was her desire that obvious? He pressed her back on the mattress, settling himself between her legs. He kissed her then, gently but urgently, moving along the line of her throat as he stroked her breasts. He kissed each peak till she moaned, then slid down her body. She didn't realize his intentions until she felt his mouth close over her most private place.

"Jake!" She tried to draw away from him, but he held her immobile.

"You wanted a lesson, honey. I'm about to give you one." His hands held her buttocks as he lowered his mouth again, tasting her, nibbling her sensitive flesh and driving her insane. She felt his tongue slip inside her and knew she was close to that starry burst of pleasure she'd known before. He didn't stop until she moaned and fell into that deep chasm of exquisite sensation.

Then he was above her, lean and strong and powerful. The wondrous sensations heightened as he kissed her and drove himself inside, the hardened length of him filling her, renewing a flood of desire. He moved against her, and her body responded with a will of its own. He was holding back, she sensed, working slowly to heighten her pleasure. Knowing that he cared about her increased the fire of her passion, and again she spiraled over the edge.

His own release followed, his body tensing as he

whispered her name. They both lay silent while they drifted down, a fine sheen of perspiration covering their naked flesh. He snuggled her against him.

"How do you feel?" he finally asked.

"Warm and content. I ache all over, but for a while you made me forget." Even in the darkness, she felt his smile.

"What am I going to do with you, Jessica Taggart?"

Her own smile faded. What indeed? He didn't love her, he'd come right out and said it. And she probably didn't love him. Probably. Possibly. Well, there was still a chance she hadn't completely lost her mind.

"Maybe the real question is: What am I to do with you?" she said.

Jake chuckled. "One thing's sure. If we don't stop your education soon, we'll both be in the soup. You'll find yourself with child, and I'll wind up a married man."

The thought sparked a surge of joy that Jessie didn't expect. Then her common sense returned. "Somehow it's hard to imagine you as a husband."

Jake turned to face her. "What's that supposed to mean?" His voice, gentle just moments before, suddenly sounded hard.

"It means you're not exactly the marrying kind."

Jake rolled to his back and shoved his hands behind his head. "My father was married; unfortunately, not to my mother. I guess I didn't have much of an example. I figure if a man takes a wife, he ought to stand by her. If he can't . . . well, he ought to stay single."

"So that's what you've done?"

"Never met a woman I could spend a lifetime with."

"I guess she'd have to be someone pretty special."

Jake didn't answer, and his silence caused an ache in Jessie's heart.

Finally he asked, "What about you, Jess? You said you weren't ready to settle down. What do you want if it isn't a home and family?"

Jessie propped herself on an elbow, her long dark hair spreading like a glossy fan across Jake's shoulder. "In the beginning I wanted adventure. I thought coming to California would be the most exciting thing in the world."

"Well, you were certainly right about that."

"I'm afraid I got a little more than I bargained for."

"And the businesses?" he asked.

"I wanted to prove myself. In the beginning, probably more for my father than for myself. After I got started, I discovered I really enjoyed the challenge. Now, well . . . I still want to accomplish things, but . . ."

"But what?"

"But it would be nice to have a family, someone to care about. Sometimes I get lonely. I guess if the right man came along . . ."

The muscles on Jake's chest grew taut. "I hope you aren't including La Porte in that category."

He sounded jealous, and Jessie's heart soared. Maybe he cared more than he was willing to admit. "Rene has been very kind to me," she said, goading him further. "Of course, I haven't really had a chance to find out how I feel about him."

Jake rolled on top of her, pressing her into the lumpy cornhusk mattress. "I warned you before, Jess. Stay away from La Porte."

"Jealous?" she asked lightly.

"Hardly! I owe it to your father to see that you don't wind up with a man like him."

"Or a man like you?" she said, his denial hurting more than it should have.

Jake growled low in his throat. "Unfortunately, I haven't done much to protect you from myself."

"Rene is a successful businessman who has played the gentleman far better than you," Jessie said, beginning to get angry. How dare Jake criticize Rene! He didn't want her for himself, but he was certainly willing to bed her, and keep her from finding someone who might love her.

"He isn't the marrying kind."

"Neither are you," she reminded him coldly.

Jake made no response.

"Let me up," she said, pressing her hands against his chest. "You can have this miserable excuse for a mattress."

"You're not going anywhere," Jake said.

Jessie gasped. She could feel his manhood, hard again and throbbing against her flesh. "I think I've had enough education for the evening," she told him.

"It seems to me it was you who was begging for a lesson."

"Why, you—" She tried to jerk free, but he caught her wrists and pinned them beside her head. "You're . . . you're impossible, Jake Weston!"

"If anyone in this gawd-awful partnership of ours is impossible, it's you!"

"Get off me, you bully. I won't put up with this one minute more." Squirming beneath him, she tried to break free, but succeeded only in moving down his body until his manhood pressed against the inside of her thigh. "Don't you dare," she warned as she saw his satisfied smile and guessed his intentions. "I won't let you. I'll fight you this time, I swear it."

"Hush, Jess," he said, his voice soft and low. "We've both done enough fighting for one day." Then he dipped his head and kissed her, stilling her protests. She kissed him back and let him slide inside her, stirring a fiery warmth she couldn't deny.

I'm lost, she thought. I'm lost and there's nothing I can do. Accepting her fate, and grudgingly admitting it was exactly what she wanted, she let her body take over while she slid helplessly into the depths of passion.

Morning brought the cold light of dawn. Jessie opened her eyes. A fire blazed in the hearth, and she smelled fresh coffee. Jake was nowhere to be seen. She was climbing out of bed to gather up what was left of her clothes when the door opened and he walked in. One corner of his mouth tilted into a lazy smile when he saw her standing there naked.

"I'd appreciate it if you'd wait outside while I dress," she told him frostily, trying to retain some small measure of her dignity, although after the wanton way she'd responded last night, that was nearly impossible. She'd sworn she wouldn't be another of his conquests, but she'd failed to consider her own treacherous desires.

"So, my sweet Jessie has disappeared already. I have only my waspish partner to escort down the mountain."

"Waspish?"

"Maybe shrewish would be more appropriate." He took a step in her direction, and Jessie grabbed her torn calico dress and backed away, holding it in front of her.

"I am not being shrewish," she said indignantly. "I'm merely trying to put our relationship back on a businesslike basis."

"By all means, Miss Taggart. Let's keep things businesslike. We're partners, nothing more. That wasn't you in bed with me last night. It wasn't you with the lovely breasts and tiny waist, with the soft sweet skin I kissed and caressed until you begged for more?"

"Stop it, Jake! I don't want to hear it. You and I

are partners, and that's all we can ever be. We can't let last night happen again."

"Just like that? *We* can't let it happen? Well, what if *I* want it to happen?" He stepped toward her, his flashing blue eyes pinning her where she stood.

Her bravado withered. One kiss and she'd be flat on her back, kissing him wantonly, and asking for more. He's not the marrying kind, she told herself firmly. To him a wife is a burden.

"Please, Jake," she said softly. "You don't want to be tied to me any more than I want to be tied to you. When we get back, I'm moving out of the Angel. It was a mistake to stay there in the first place. If I hadn't, we would never have . . . gotten into this situation," she finished weakly.

Jake's anger fled. She was right, of course. The last thing he needed was a know-it-all schoolgirl millstone around his neck. "You're right. I'm sorry." His hands dropped to his sides, and he turned and walked out the door. When she opened it a few minutes later, dressed in her torn clothes, he was leaning against the porch, one booted foot propped behind him, smoking a thin cigar.

"Please don't be angry," she said quietly.

Jake chuckled softly. "I'm not angry. Though I damned well ought to be. That was a fool stunt you pulled, not telling me where you were going."

"I know." One hand clutched her torn bodice. She glanced down shyly. "I have a little problem," she told him.

"So I see." His eyes focused on the bare skin showing through the front of her dress. He tossed the cigar away and moved to where the horses were tied. He'd already reloaded the stolen gold onto the pack mule and had readied the animals for the trip down the mountain.

Searching his saddlebag, he pulled out a white cotton shirt and tossed it to Jessie. She caught it easily, but gave him a glimpse of her lush, pink-tipped breasts as she did.

Jake stifled a groan. What was there about the woman that kept him in a constant state of arousal? This hadn't happened with any another woman he could remember.

She pulled the shirt on over her dress. "Thank you."

"You're welcome."

"I've been thinking, Jake."

"With you, that's always dangerous."

She ignored his barb. "I was wondering if maybe that man I killed had something to do with my father's murder. After all, he was dressed as a Chinese, and they left that tong hatchet to try and pin the blame on them."

"I've been thinking the same thing. But it doesn't make sense. What motive would the man have?"

"I wish I knew." Jessie glanced to the base of the tree, where Silva had lain. "Where . . . where did you put him? Shouldn't we take him back to town or something?"

"I've got him rolled in a tarpaulin. We'll take him down to Dry Town. Maybe the sheriff can trace him down. You say his name is Silva?"

"One of them called him Silva. Another one called him Portigee."

"With a distinctive name like that," Jake said, "somebody ought to know who he is. In the meantime, how about rustling us up something to eat? It's a long way back to San Francisco."

"All right." Jessie went back inside, moving a bit woodenly, it seemed to Jake.

Killing never comes easy, Jake thought. Little Miss Boston Taggart had probably saved his life. He chuckled softly and wondered why the idea of taking care of her didn't sound half bad.

* * *

They left Silva's body in Dry Town, checked on Paddy, who was awake and restless, then sent a telegram to Benny Hodges, Alec's assistant, informing him of the robbery, Alec's death, and Hodges's promotion to manager. They also sent a wire to the Tin Angel, telling everyone they were all right.

While Jessie sat with Paddy, Jake picked up his big gray stallion and the horse he'd set loose on the mountain. They told no one but the sheriff of the recovered gold. Jake simply switched the packsaddle from the mule to one of the horses he'd purchased and headed home. He noticed Jessie never once complained about having to ride astride instead of sidesaddle, as any proper Boston lady should have preferred.

Chapter 19

L ate in the afternoon of the following day, Lovey, Rupert, and the girls greeted Jake and Jessie at the back door of the Tin Angel, all asking questions at the same time.

"Are you two all right?" Lovey wanted to know.

"How's Paddy?" Annabelle asked.

"Did you get the gold back?" Rupert pressed.

"We're fine," Jessie said. "Paddy will be all better in a day or two, and yes, we got the gold—most of it anyway. A man named Portigee Silva stole it. Jake caught up with him and I . . . he was killed."

She felt bone tired, but she was touched by their concern. She and Jake had spent the night on the trail, then stopped in Sacramento City and bought a dress for her to wear aboard the *Bonanza Lady* for the trip back home. Although it was a day excursion, they'd both had staterooms on the cabin deck of the paddle-wheeler, Jake wanting a place to secure the gold, Jessie hoping to get some sleep.

On the trail, she and Jake had carefully avoided each other, saying little and sleeping on opposite sides of the campfire. Although Jessie had enjoyed making love to Jake, she knew that it was certainly not the proper thing to do. And as Jake had pointedly reminded her, there could be unwelcome consequences.

Unwelcome for him, she amended, but not for her.

She hadn't considered the possibility before, but having Jake's baby would be more a blessing than a curse. Jessie sighed at the unsettling thought.

The girls dispersed to mingle with the late-afternoon customers, and things began to settle down.

"I was so worried," Lovey said when they reached the office and closed the door. She hugged Jessie and gave Jake a contrite look. "The story of the robbery is all over town." She shook her head. "Poor Alec, and those other lost men."

Jessie looked away.

"Before anybody gets the wrong idea," Jake said, "it wasn't Jessie's plan that cost those men their lives. The outlaws knew her movements ahead of time. She never had a chance to succeed."

Jessie threw Jake a look of surprise, then a grateful smile.

"You mean somebody tipped them off?" Rupert asked, incredulous.

"Somebody over at the freighting office—or somebody right here."

"Surely nobody here would do a thing like that," Lovey said.

Jake set his jaw. "I sure as hell hope not, but I intend to find out."

"You ain't the only one in town with that in mind," Lovey told him. "Alec Abernathy was a member of the Masonic Order and a respected member of the community. I heard tell they's several vigilante meetings bein' held. The sheriff has already been to one of 'em, trying to calm folks down. Way he tells it, didn't do a whole lot a' good. I'd be surprised if Chinatown ain't up in flames before morning."

"That's ridiculous, Lovey," Jessie said. "The men who held us up weren't Chinese."

"They weren't?" Lovey looked surprised. "That's right, you mentioned a fella named Silva."

"The sheriff was out with the posse when we brought the body in," Jake said. "Somebody must have found that damned tong hatchet and wired ahead. I'd better get over to Handley's office, then I'll go on to the *Chronicle*. By tomorrow, we'll have this thing all straightened out."

"I'll go with you," Jessie said.

"Oh no you won't. I promised you the hottest bath in San Francisco and I want you to have it. Lovey, get her up to her room." Jake laid a hand on Rupert's shoulder. "You start heating the water. Jessie's earned a long, hot bath."

"I thought you were mad at the lot of us," Lovey said.

Jake pinned her with a glance. "I was, and I am. But we'll have plenty of time to talk about that later. In the meantime, I've got to straighten out this mess before a lot of innocent Chinese pay for somebody else's dirty work."

Jake pushed through the swinging double doors and headed into the street.

For the better part of an hour, Jessie soaked in the leather tub Paco had brought up to her. By the time she had finished, she felt ten pounds lighter and glad to be back at the Tin Angel, happy to be home. It was strange that a saloon could feel like home, she thought, but it did.

She knew it was partly because Jake lived there. Jake. She'd told him she was moving out, but she didn't want to. She liked being near him, even if he was a stubborn, mule-headed *male* most of the time. She just wished that Jake cared half as much for her as she had come to care for him.

She knew he thought they were ill-suited. So had she in the beginning. But now she saw that he was caring, thoughtful—protective almost to a fault. He was loyal to his friends and steadfast in his beliefs.

Jake had a stubborn sense of right and wrong that Jessie had come to admire.

The more she got to know him, the more she realized why her father had made him her partner. Jake was a hard worker and a darned good businessman. He was doing a good job running their affairs. He'd been making them money until this last string of accidents. And more and more those accidents were beginning to look like sabotage.

Dressed in a dusty-rose satin gown edged with black Belgian lace, Jessie left her room. The nap she'd taken aboard the *Bonanza Lady* had refreshed her more than she'd believed. She was looking forward to the evening, anticipating her usual verbal jesting with Jake, and wishing there was a way she could eliminate the rest of the females competing for his attention.

Of course there was one small snag she would have to mend—Jessie wasn't about to become one of Jake Weston's mistresses. Either he wanted her enough to give up other women and make some promises—or he would rapidly discover he'd been replaced. There were hordes of men in San Francisco. Surely she could find a man who attracted her as much as Jake did—a man who would love her and want her for his wife.

The thought brought an end to her buoyant mood. Jake Weston was not a man who could easily be replaced.

Jessie squared her shoulders. One thing was certain—the next man she fell for would be the marrying kind.

Reaching the top of the second-floor stairway, Jessie saw Rupert standing behind the bar, talking with a Chinese coolie who waved his arms and gestured wildly up the stairs. Rupert glanced up and motioned her down.

The bar was only half full, but from now until closing the raucous crowd would increase. She noticed several miners in slouch hats standing at the opposite end of the bar, and saw Horace McCafferty talking to Megan O'Brien in the corner. Mormon Pete had just lifted the lid on the upright and was getting ready to begin the evening's entertainment.

"What's the matter, Rupert?" Jessie asked as she reached his side.

"If it ain't one thing . . . This man's with Charley Sing's bunch." He pointed to the little Chinese. "He works down at the docks. Near as I kin make out, he overheard some of the *Fair Wind* hands talking about coming here tonight. *Fair Wind*'s the clipper ship your friend, Bull Haskin, is first mate aboard. She's been sailing the coast, picking up trade goods fer her next trip to China."

"What's that got to do with us?"

"Seems Bull is bringing her whole crew over to redecorate the Angel, 'cause of how he was treated the last time he was here. Say's he's gonna give us a going-away present." Rupert shuffled his feet and glanced away, as if he had something more to tell her but wasn't quite sure he should.

"Go on," Jessie urged.

"Well, ma'am, he was braggin' he still had a brass token he was gonna leave on your dresser."

Jessie's lips thinned to a stubborn line. "How soon does this man expect them to arrive?"

"Chinaman here says he ran on ahead. They's headin' this way right now."

"Oh, dear." Jessie glanced around the bar. "Is Jake back yet?"

"No, ma'am, an' with Paddy gone . . ." Rupert walked down the bar, reached under and pulled out the scattergun he kept there, then checked the ammunition.

"I don't want anyone shot, Rupert," Jessie said sharply. "I'm not the same naive schoolgirl I was the last time I tussled with Bull Haskin. I'll meet them at the door, but I won't let him near me.

Somehow I'll convince them to go on down to the Golden Thorn to have their fun."

"Miss Jessie, I wouldn't count on talkin'—"

"I'll handle it, Rupert. You run out back and get Paco. Send him and Lovey to see if they can find Jake."

"Now that's a sensible idea." Rupert hurried toward the kitchen, and the little Chinese left through the front door in a loping run.

Jessie stepped behind the bar and poured herself a shot of whiskey. She tossed it back as she'd seen Jake do, coughed and sputtered and wiped the tears from her eyes. Then she walked to the bat-wing doors to watch the street that led to the waterfront. Lovey and Paco hurried around her and up the street in the opposite direction, splitting up when they reached the corner. Rupert took up his position behind the bar.

In minutes, Jessie's vigilance was rewarded. She took a deep breath and glanced over her shoulder at Rupert. "There must be twenty of them," she told him, "and they look ready for all kinds of trouble."

"I wish Jake was here." Rupert picked up the scattergun.

Jessie looked up to see a row of girls scantily clad in stockings, filmy negligees, and lacy black corsets lining the upstairs railing. They all faced the door clutching a variety of weapons, from pistols to six-inch hatpins. Their clients, in varying degrees of disarray, were busily fastening cuffs and collars as they headed down the stairs. At their approach, many of the customers gambling below shoved back their chairs and moved toward the door. Others grinned stupidly, in gleeful anticipation of the coming entertainment.

Moments later, the sounds of heavy footsteps on the boardwalk out front echoed into the saloon. Jessie pushed her way through the doors.

At the front of the group, Bull Haskin strode up

to greet her. Jessie swallowed hard, having forgotten just how tall he was, how thick his shoulders were, how hamlike his fists.

He looked her up and down. "You're even prettier than I recollected, girl." Bull dug into his pocket and came up with the brass token. "I came to collect."

"Sorry, Bull." Jessie looked him straight in the eye. "We're closed to you and your men. We don't want any trouble."

"Well, you'd better open up, girl. This be the crew of the proud ship *Fair Wind*, and we've come to drink till dawn an' whore like a hurricane afore we set sail for Macao."

"Sorry, Bull. Go on down to the Golden Thorn. I'm sure they'll be happy to take your money."

"What's that?" Bull pointed into the saloon and Jessie turned to follow the line of his finger. She gasped as she felt Bull's shoulder against her midsection. Not again, she thought as he hoisted her off her feet. He slapped her soundly on the bottom, roared with laughter, and spun around to face his crew. "Well, boys, it be whiskey and women and a table-chuckin' contest."

"Set me down, you big bohunk!" Jessie commanded. A hearty burst of laughter and another slap on the derriere were all she got for her trouble as he pushed through the swinging double doors.

She was pounding his back, prepared to unleash a stream of unladylike oaths, when she noticed the shocked expressions on the faces of the men who had followed Bull into the saloon. They fell silent, standing stock-still as they stared straight ahead. To her surprise, Bull set her carefully on her feet. She turned to see Rupert Scroggins's scattergun, both barrels cocked, laid across the top of a table. The girls stood in a semicircle behind him, pistols, kitchen knives, and hatpins in hand. The sight warmed her heart.

"Now, Mr. Haskin," Rupert said quietly, "I suggest you take your men on down to the Golden Thorn like Miss Jessie says."

"Why, sure," Bull said, his voice easy and light. But as he turned to leave, he grabbed Jessie's arm and jerked her in front of him. He held her with her back to his chest, his cheek alongside hers, a powerful hand wrapped around her slender neck. "I can pop this neck as easy as squeezin' the life out of a cod. You step back and find a table to set that goosegun on, and the rest of you girls pile those trinkets alongside it."

"Don't do it, Rupert," Jessie managed, wincing as Bull Haskin tightened his hold.

The girls had quietly begun to place their weapons on the table alongside Rupert's when Jessie heard feet pounding down the wooden walk.

"Leave her be, Haskin." Jake's voice, low and menacing, cut through the muffled sounds in the room.

Bull loosened his grip on Jessie's throat, but he didn't release her. Jake stood twenty feet away, his expression carefully controlled, his hand resting on the butt of the .44 at his hip.

"I would suggest you do as he says," said another voice from behind Jake, drawing not only his attention, but that of the *Fair Wind* crewmen. Bull searched the crowd for the owner of the voice.

"I'll be damned," he muttered. Suddenly, the street outside the bat-wing doors had filled with scores of Chinese, each holding a hatchet. Standing in silence, they carefully watched the men from the clipper ship.

"As I said," Charley Sing repeated in his clear, concise English, "do as Mr. Weston instructs and release Miss Taggart."

Bull released Jessie, and she moved to Jake's side. He wrapped an arm around her shoulders.

"Well, now," Bull said softly, scanning the group

of Chinese. "I guess the Golden Thorn don't sound so bad after all. Let's go get us a drink, boys."

"Don't come back to the Tin Angel, Bull," Jake warned as the big sailor and his men moved out the door. "You're no longer welcome here."

Bull stopped and reached into his pocket. Jake's hand moved back toward his gun, but Bull produced the brass token and flipped it to Jake, who caught it in mid-air.

"Guess I won't be needin' this."

Jake nodded, and Bull's loud guffaw echoed through the quiet street.

As the *Fair Wind* crew disappeared down the boardwalk, the black-robed men stowed their hatchets under their clothes and began to disperse. Jessie stepped away from Jake's arm and ran after them. "Mr. Sing, wait."

Charley Sing turned and bowed.

"Please accept my gratitude, Mr. Sing, for what you and your people did just now."

"It was a small thing, Miss Taggart. Your father did much for us. We can do very little to repay him."

"Would you like to come in for some tea?" she asked. "Or maybe something stronger?"

"I am sorry. There is much for me to do."

"As Jessie said," Jake added, "we both thank you."

Charley Sing bowed again, turned, and continued down the street.

"You all right?" Jake asked.

"I'm fine," she told him, but he didn't seem convinced.

"I think you're right about moving out," he said. "Sooner or later, you're going to get hurt around here."

Jessie stiffened. "I'll move out, if that's what you want, but not because I'm afraid I'll get hurt. I was doing just fine without your help. Besides, Mr. Sing would have stopped Bull Haskin, even if you hadn't arrived.''

"A saloon's no place for a lady. It wasn't when you came, and it isn't now.''

Jessie cast him a defiant glance. "You just want me gone so Monique and the others can return to your bed. That's all you really care about—your damnable lust!''

"You little idiot,'' Jake snapped. "That isn't it, and you know it.''

But Jessie stormed off, heading upstairs to pack her bag. If he wanted her gone—well fine, she'd be gone by morning!

Jake took a deep breath and headed over to the bar. He'd done the right thing, hadn't he? She'd move into some nice, refined boardinghouse, and he'd go back to running the Tin Angel by himself, as he had before. She could handle the ledgers, if she wanted, and maybe manage some of the riverboat operation.

They wouldn't be thrown together so much. He'd be able to stop thinking about making love to her. He'd go back to the life he'd led before, renew his relationship with Monique, or maybe start one with that pretty little widow who lived down the street from the freight office. She managed to corner him nearly every time he went near the place. The Widow McKinsey was known for her discretion, and rumor was she was back on the prowl.

"Pour me a shot of Who Hit John,'' Jake told Rupert. "Make it a double.''

"You and Miss Jessie at it again, boss?''

"She's a handful, Rupert.''

"She's got more grit than a Feather River sandbar. Kinda makes the rest of 'em seem like watered-down soup, don't she?''

"I can't believe her father would want her running a place like this.''

"Don't seem so unlikely to me. Old Henry never

done nothing by the book in his life. Look how he took in them Chinese when nobody else would. Weren't considered real respectable, but that didn't stop ol' Henry."

"When you put it that way . . ."

"Seems to me Miss Jessie takes after ol' Henry a whole lot more'n we thought. Better watch out, boss, she'll have you wearin' blinders like a tinker's jackass before you even know what hit you."

"That's exactly what I'm trying to avoid." A woman like Jessie meant marriage, something Jake had scrupulously avoided. He'd been a drifter most of his life, changed jobs whenever he got the urge, and loved every minute of his freedom. After Henry had hired him, he'd discovered he liked running the Taggart businesses, relished the responsibility and the challenge—and he was good at it.

He enjoyed living in one place, too. Liked the people he worked with, found he cared what happened to them. Now Jessie Taggart had entered his life with a vengeance. She seemed to occupy his thoughts day and night. *Especially* at night, he amended. Did he want to be rid of her?

The Widow McKinsey seemed like watered-down soup, all right. Comparing her to Jessie was like comparing flat beer to fine Napoleon brandy.

"Have Paco fetch me a bath," Jake told Rupert, then he headed up to his room.

Jessie packed for the better part of an hour, refusing to cry, desperately wishing things could be different. A wolf can't change the color of his fur, she thought. Jake was trying to put some distance between them. He wanted her out of his life. If that was the way he felt, she'd be more than happy to oblige.

A knock on the door interrupted her. Lovey called up from the bottom of the attic stairs, "Su Ling wants to talk to you. She says it's important."

"Send her in."

Clutching her silk robe around her, Su Ling headed up the stairs. Jessie indicated a seat in front of the tiny fire that warmed the room, and her friend sat down.

"What is it, Su Ling?" Jessie asked, noticing the girl's pale face.

"Su Ling not want to cause trouble, only want to help her people."

"Go on."

"My respected countrymen," she said, "the Chinese who were here . . . ?"

"Yes?"

"They told me another Auspicious Laborers tong hatchet was found. It was left by the men who took your gold. Is that not right?"

"We know it wasn't the Chinese, Su Ling. Jake has already been to the sheriff and the newspaper with that information."

"You are sure?"

"Very sure. Why?"

"Charley Sing believes the Gum San is responsible, since they are the ones who would profit most by discrediting the AL of S."

"But the crime was committed by white men," Jessie repeated.

"Charley Sing does not know that."

"What does he mean to do?" Jessie asked, beginning to worry.

"I have been told there will be an attack on the Gum San tonight. There will most certainly be a tong war."

"That's absurd! Tok Loy wasn't responsible. Portigee Silva was."

"Someone must tell them, Miss Jessie. Someone they trust. They trusted your father. They will trust you. We tell Mr. Jake, and he take us there."

"Mr. Jake is busy," Jessie said, although she had no idea if that was true. "You can take me."

"Oh no, missy. Too dangerous. No, no. I find Mr. Jake." She headed for the door.

"Mr. Jake won't take us, Su Ling. He doesn't think I belong here. He thinks I'll get hurt. He won't help us, and I'm not going to stand by and let your people get killed. Now, either you take me, or I'll go by myself. Someone in Chinatown will be able to help me find Charley Sing."

Su Ling chewed her bottom lip nervously. "Mr. Jake not like this. He be hot as firecracker. But I am *mui jai* to you too, Miss Jessie, and I must help my people. We go."

Before they left, Jessie changed into a simple navy-blue dress and hooded cloak and loaned Su Ling a cloak. Then they headed down the back stairs.

Under a cloud of tobacco smoke in the Sons of Liberty meeting hall, two hundred men sat on wooden benches while dozens more lined the walls. The whiskey and beer had been flowing for hours, carried by buxom serving girls, while men in canvas pants and homespun shirts argued about the Chinese problem in San Francisco.

One man, named Skinner, shouted above the others. "We got the eight-hour day, but what good does it do us? The Chinese sonsabitches work from dawn to dark for practically nothing. They live on rice and fish heads, take our jobs, then steal and kill besides." The speaker, a red-haired gangly hostler, stood atop a ladder-backed chair. His knotty-knuckled hands extended from too-short shirt-sleeves, accentuating his gaunt appearance as he held the attention of the rough-and-tumble group of freighters, muleteers, and longshoremen.

"They steal our jobs!" he yelled, a mug of beer in one hand, a bowie knife in the other.

Seated in the chair beside him, Kaz Bochek tilted his head to look up at him. "Then they send their earnings home to China," he added so softly that only his rabble-rousing head freighter could hear.

"Then the blackguards send their money to their scum-sucking brothers in China!" Skinner shouted, speaking with the mesmerizing conviction of a traveling preacher.

Seated across from him, Horace McCafferty watched with fascination as Kaz manipulated his employee. Bochek's hatred of the Chinese exceeded even his desire for wealth and power, Horace thought. Horace figured the Pole's prejudice was a sort of cockeyed retribution for the discrimination he had suffered as a Polish immigrant.

"Alec Abernathy was a fine Christian man who left a widow and three children," Skinner said, then took a draw on his beer. The foam clung to the stubble of a day's growth of beard. He raised his mug high. "Here's to a fine man, a fine white Christian man. A thirty-second degree Freemason. A Son of Liberty!" He downed the beer in one long continuous swallow, then wiped the foam from his lips with the back of his hand.

"I, for one, know what to do with the yellow heathen and their poxed whores!" he said, spittle flying as his voice climbed yet another octave. "Who's with me?" Skinner raised his big bowie knife. The men leaped to their feet, downing their drinks and waving their weapons.

With a rousing whoop, he jumped from the chair and charged through the cheering men. Fifty pressed behind him, more gathering in his wake, pushing and shoving as he neared the door. By the time he got outside, all the men in the room save two had followed him into the street.

Kaz and Horace sat quietly in the suddenly vacant, barnlike room, sipping their drinks and watching as the waitresses gathered glasses and rearranged chairs. One swept up a broken mug near Bochek's feet.

"There'll be hell to pay tonight, guv'nor," the girl said.

"Looks that way," Bochek agreed with a satisfied smile. Gaining his feet, he stretched and yawned and finished the last of his beer. As the girl wiped the table in front of him, he eyed the bulge of her heavy breasts beneath her tight cotton bodice. "Yes girl, hell to pay. A wise soul would stay inside and off the streets. I suppose you have a place to get out of the chilly night air?"

McCafferty looked away, embarrassed.

"Why, I'm a married woman, guv'nor."

Kaz spat on the sawdust floor. "Then I suggest you git home to the beggar." He ground out the butt of his cigar on the tabletop while the girl hurried away without a backward glance. Kaz pulled another cigar from his waistcoat pocket.

"So Weston recovered the gold." He puffed a billow of smoke in McCafferty's direction.

"Most of it," Horace said. "If that fool Silva hadn't taken the girl, he'd probably have gotten away."

"His pecker always was as hard as his head."

"How about some supper?" Horace asked.

"Not good for us to be seen together too often. Why don't you get over to your office and figure a way to convince the Taggart girl to sell out. I want that business. With my connections, I'll be able to triple the profits in weeks."

"I've tried everything I know. I'm not sure what else I can do," Horace said.

"The girl's your client, isn't she? Do your job. Advise her of what's in her best interests. I'll take care of Weston."

McCafferty adjusted his bowler. "Well, good night, Kaz."

"Yeah," Bochek managed. As he watched the pudgy, sallow-faced attorney thread his way through the chairs and tables, he wondered if the crowd outside had cleared away enough so he could catch a hansom. Dinner at Anton's, high on Nob Hill, would provide a good view of Chinatown. He chuckled to himself. With luck, the burning buildings would be a pretty sight.

Chapter 20

❦

"What's the matter?" Jessie asked as the cabbie reined in the horse. Outside, the streets were dark and empty. A thick layer of clouds covered the moon.

The driver leaned over from his seat at the rear of the hansom and spoke through the hole in the roof. "This is as far as I go, ma'am."

"But we need to get to Auspicious Laborers of the Sea headquarters."

"Beggin' your pardon, ma'am, but only Chinamen and fools venture into Chinatown at night, and I, for one, am neither . . . no offense intended."

Jessie and Su Ling climbed from the cab into the darkened street. Jessie dug into her reticule for some coins, holding her purse up to the lantern on the side of the carriage to find them. She flicked the driver a look of contempt as she handed him the silver. The carriage clattered away, taking the lanterns with it and leaving the street in eerie darkness. The *clip-clop* of the horse's hooves on the hard-packed earthen street faded into the night, replaced by a hollow echo as the carriage disappeared into the fog below.

Roads empty of the thousands of Chinese who crowded them in the daytime were now dank, quiet, and dark. Cast-iron shutters, tightly closed, sealed off vegetable and poultry shops, herb stores and noodle stands. Shadows played over the garbage-littered street from the few coal-oil lamps that dimly lit some of the upper-story windows.

"Is it too far to walk, Su Ling?" Jessie pulled her hooded cloak around her and quelled the second thoughts she was having.

"Only few blocks, Miss Jessie. But I think we should have brought Mr. Jake."

"I told you, Jake wouldn't approve."

"Then we go this way." Su Ling pointed up the narrow street. "Pardon, Miss Jessie—" Su Ling reached up and pulled the hood of Jessie's cloak so it almost covered her face. "Occidental girl very valuable in the barracoon."

"You don't mean they would . . . ? Oh, my God," she whispered.

"They would take you to Macao or Hong Kong. Please keep face down so they cannot see."

Jessie glanced nervously down the street. "Let's hurry," she said, attempting to convey a confidence she didn't feel. Su Ling shuffled off, Jessie close behind her. As she glanced into the first alley they passed, she made out the dark figures and glowing smokes of a few huddled men. The odor of garbage rotting in the gutters assaulted her nostrils, so strong she could taste it.

With her hood partially blocking her view, she collided with a man on the walk. "Excuse me."

He brushed on by with an odd look and a sing-song Chinese curse.

"Please, Miss Jessie, no talk. Let Su Ling talk for you in Chinatown."

As they moved deeper into the darkness, a huge carved Chinese dog resting on a dais startled her just before she collided with it. She stepped away, glancing around to regain her bearings and thinking: *Why didn't I listen to Su Ling?*

"Hurry, Miss Jessie."

So far, she decided, this hadn't been a smart idea. She shouldn't have come without Jake; she could certainly see that now. He would be furious, and this time she couldn't blame him. Even mad as a hornet, and raging at her as she knew he would be, she'd give her last dollar to have him here now.

Still . . . if she could stop needless deaths, she would probably do it again.

"Lovey, have you seen Jessie?" Jake asked. "She isn't in her room, and I can't find her downstairs."

"Are you sure?"

"I saw her going down the back stairs with Sugar Su," Annabelle called from down the hall. "They were dressed to go out. I kinda wondered where they were headed."

"Oh, my God," Lovey said. "I knew I should have taken Su Ling to see you first, but I thought you might be sleeping. You looked so durned tired, I didn't want to bother you."

"What does Su Ling have to do with this?" Jake asked, his sixth sense pulsing with danger signs.

"She came to me with some cock-'n'-bull story about a tong war eruptin' tonight. Said Charley Sing thought the Gum San had robbed your gold. She wanted to talk to you and Jessie about it."

"A tong war." Jake groaned. "That's all we need. The whole damned city's ready to come down on Chinatown. Right or wrong, the whites are up in arms over Alec's killing. They're determined to take it out on someone. Surely Jessie isn't crazy enough to go to Chinatown."

But he knew the answer even before he said the words. Without waiting for Lovey's reply, he headed down the hall, pushed open the door to his room, and took his holstered .44 down from the coat tree in the corner.

With jerky movements that betrayed his anger, he strapped the leather belt around his hips and knotted the rawhide tie at his thigh. After stuffing his cutdown .36 into the waistband of his breeches, he put his black frock coat on over it. Grabbing his flat-brimmed hat from a peg beside the door, he settled it over his thick black hair and headed toward the back stairs that led out into the street.

As angry as he was at Jessie for going without him—and he was nail-spitting furious—he knew he was partly to blame. She hadn't come to him because she knew he would have said no. He'd have told her it was too dangerous for her to go—which it was. She had gone without him, just as she'd done before, because he was so damned unbending. By constantly trying to protect her, he kept forcing her to take the very risks he meant to save her from.

Damn it, when would he learn? Jessie wasn't like other women. She wouldn't knuckle under to him, or to anybody else. He admired her for it—and right now he wanted to thrash her within an inch of her life!

Tok Loy Hong handed a small gold coin to the man who'd just informed him that members of the Auspicious Laborers of the Sea were gathered at the wharf, preparing to descend upon the Gum San joss house from three different directions.

"You have done well," Tok Loy said, then turned to his bodyguards. "Send runners to gather the tong. We will meet at Chin Lo's warehouse. Then get all the servants and concubines out of the house by way of the tunnels." As his men hurried away, Tok Loy settled into his massive carved chair.

It has finally come, he thought. The day of reckoning. Charley Sing was young and impulsive, a man who acted before he took time to think. It could mean the end of the world for the Chinese in San Francisco, and all because Sing did not have the benefit of age and reason.

Tok Loy felt sure there was someone else behind the atrocities being blamed on the Celestials. But who? Surely a white man who hates the Chinese, he thought. Or one who has something to gain from their downfall, or the downfall of Taggart Enterprises. Tok Loy sighed. If we Celestials do not kill each other, then the white devils will probably do it for us.

He knew about the vigilante meetings. Rumors had been running rampant ever since the news of Alec Abernathy's murder had reached the city. The whites were up in arms. Most of the Chinese had gathered their belongings and were prepared to flee on a moment's notice.

It was as it had been for the last twenty years.

The Chinese were subject to the whims of the white man, and worse, their ridiculous and prejudicial laws. *Guests*, the law called them. Tok Loy smiled sardonically. They were barely tolerated, let alone treated as guests.

But then, honorable guests did not fight among themselves.

Tok Loy rose when his bodyguards reentered the room. They fell in behind him as his measured steps carried him to the door.

"We are almost there, Miss Jessie."

Jessie nodded and picked up her pace, just as three black-garbed men stepped from a darkened doorway to block their path.

Su Ling stopped in her tracks, forcing Jessie to do the same. One man spoke to Su Ling in a low voice, and Su Ling answered, sounding anxious. The man shook his head, and her tone became more urgent. Jessie could tell things weren't going the way the Chinese woman intended.

When the man turned Su Ling around and pointed back down the street, Jessie stepped forward. "We have business in Chinatown. Get out of our way."

"Don't—" Su Ling cried as the man reached forward and swept the hood from Jessie's head. Her dark mahogany hair tumbled around her shoulders.

Pinning him with a glare, Jessie forced a tone of authority into her voice that she didn't feel. "I said, get out of our way." The tall man looked at her hard, and the other two stepped closer, encircling her. I'm seconds from a trip to Macao, Jessie thought, a knot of dread tightening in the pit of her stomach.

The tall Chinese studied her a moment more, then took a step backward. "You are the daughter of the honorable Henry Taggart?"

"Henry Taggart was my father."

"You should not be on the streets in the black of night."

"We are looking for Charley Sing."

"He is busy tonight. You should flee from here, now. Just as we are."

"I must talk to Mr. Sing."

"I cannot help you. Is there another you would see in his place?"

Jessie hesitated only a moment. "Tok Loy Hong."

"The Gum San joss house is not far; Su Ling can show you. But you should heed my warning and return to your home."

"I can't do that."

The man stepped aside. "If you do not fear the stench of the dragon's breath, you invite the caress of his tongue and teeth."

"Listen to him, Miss Jessie," Su Ling said, her voice thin with fear. "We are too late. We must not go on."

"We've come too far to stop now," Jessie said with renewed confidence, since the men seemed to respect her.

"Then we must hurry." Su Ling's footsteps thudded softly on the walk as she headed into the darkness. Behind them, Jessie heard the mutterings of the three Chinese who hurried away. She couldn't understand their words, but their tone was apprehensive—and they were headed in the opposite direction.

* * *

"This is the time we knew would come!" Charley Sing stood atop a hogshead barrel addressing the hundred men who were gathered around him.

"Even now, the Occidentals prepare to burn your homes and businesses, and it is all the fault of the Gum San tong. Tok Loy Hong and the worthless dog droppings he calls his followers have brought discredit to all Celestials. They have shamed your honorable ancestors. They must be stopped."

His voice rose an octave, and he lifted his hatchet high overhead. "It is a mission for the honorable warriors of the AL of S. A mission we must accomplish."

He was shouting now, the others waving their hatchets in the air. "Kill the Gum San. Kill the Gum San. Everyone in the joss house must die. Kill the servants, kill the miserable concubines who give the Gum San pleasure. Kill them!" he screamed. Jumping from the barrel, he charged through the crowd of men, who followed at a trot, waving their gleaming hatchets in the air and chanting, "Kill them, kill them, kill them!"

Jessie and Su Ling hesitated in front of the three-story building with the bright red double doors. Even in the darkness, the intricately designed brass hinges caught the reflection of what little light came from upper-story windows across the street.

Jessie took a shaky breath. Grasping a heavy dragon's head door knocker, she rapped loudly. A face appeared in a window of the house next door, then as quickly disappeared. The lights in several of the neighboring upper-story windows went out, and the street sank into darkness.

Jessie waited for a moment, then knocked again. Still no one came.

When she tugged at the door, it opened with an

eerie creak. Glancing back over her shoulder, she looked at Su Ling. "Are you sure this is the place?"

"Yes, Miss Jessie, but we must not go in."

Ignoring Su Ling's plea, Jessie turned and entered. The interior was dimly lit by two single-candle wall sconces, which provided enough light to make out the wide stairway. The pleasant odor of incense was almost a shock after the putrid gutter smells.

As her eyes ran over a wide silk screen intricately painted with trees and brilliantly colored birds that hung from one wall, and a beaten brass relief of several Chinese warriors fighting a huge red dragon that hung from another, Jessie hesitated. Two life-sized ceramic warriors guarded each side of the stairway. Eyes of translucent glass reflected the candles and warned her away.

"H-hello," Jessie called out, but her voice caught. She cleared her throat. "Hello!"

"No one home," Su Ling said. "We come another time." She turned and started back outside.

"I'm going upstairs. They probably can't hear us."

"Oooh" was all Su Ling could manage, but she followed Jessie up the stairway.

Tok Loy split his men into three groups. Charley Sing would lead his rabble to the Gum San joss house, and when they found no one there, would destroy the building. It did not matter. Before this night was through, the AL of S would be a thing of the past. The Gum San tong would control all of the *mui jai* and opium trade in the city.

Tok Loy's men left Chin Lo's warehouse and quietly headed back toward the joss house. Tok Loy planned to trap Charley Sing inside, to meet him on the Gum San's own ground, where his men knew every nook and cranny of the house and the streets beyond.

While Sing and his men were busy wreaking

havoc, half of the Gum San would enter the building from the rear, and half from the front. Ten men would climb to the top of the building next door and jump to the roof. Sing's men would be trapped inside.

Tok Loy smiled at his wisdom and reflected that his venerable age would make the difference between victory and defeat.

Reaching the top floor of the joss house, Jessie and Su Ling entered the dimly lit, eerily shadowed chamber just in time to hear a rapidly building commotion in the streets outside. Jessie fought down a wave of panic.

"We go now, Miss Jessie," Su Ling said, her eyes wide with fear.

Jessie brushed by her, past a huge gilded chair, and made her way toward the windows, which turned out to be a set of glass doors behind filigreed panels that opened onto a narrow veranda. Outside, the din of noise built to a crescendo, and Jessie's already racing heart pounded even harder.

She pulled open the doors and moved out on the deck until she could see the street three stories below her. A crowd of men, armed with knives and hatchets, stretched from building to building, filling the road.

"Please, Miss Jessie," Su Ling pleaded, "let us run from here."

"I think it's too late to run." Jessie watched as the men hesitated in front of the house, waving their hatchets and knives, the sound of their blood-chilling screams echoing up and down the street. In seconds they had thrown open the heavy double doors and were charging into the building.

"Quick, we hide." Su Ling tugged on Jessie's sleeve, pulling her back inside the main chamber.

"We came here to talk to them. Now we have no choice."

Striding toward the stairway, Jessie heard the sound of breaking glass and the heavy thud of furniture being smashed against the walls, then a fresh wave of shouts coming from the street. Dashing back out on the veranda, she saw a second group of men charge into the building. On the roof next door, men with hatchets in hand, red silk garrotes at their waists, jumped to the roof of the joss house and onto the verandas.

Jessie stifled a scream and turned toward the door, but five men carrying torches in one hand and weapons in the other blocked the doorway, their eyes locked on the first group of men.

"Wait!" Jessie yelled across the now well-lit porch, tearing her cloak from her head to expose her Occidental features and thick reddish-brown hair—and praying that someone would know who she was. All eyes turned in her direction. Although she tried to sound calm, her mouth felt so dry she could hardly talk.

"I must speak to Tok Loy Hong or Charley Sing." More men arrived behind the men in the doorway. No one moved or breathed.

"I'm Jessica Taggart. My father was Henry Taggart. I'm here to see Charley Sing and Tok Loy Hong." She did her best to remain in control, but her voice wavered with every word. Still no one moved, each man debating whether to retreat with her message as she asked, or continue his assault. Jessie's heart pounded so loudly she almost didn't hear the clatter of hoofbeats on the street below. Then a shot rang out, breaking the stillness. A huge brass gong at one end of the porch sounded with a reverberating clang, a wide hole marring its once smooth surface.

"The first man who moves dies!" His voice steely, Jake sat astride his big gray stallion, his revolver aimed at the men on the veranda.

Jessie felt a rush of relief so poignant it made her head swim.

Tok Loy stepped from the shadows on the street, his bodyguards behind him. "Stay out of this, Mr. Weston," he advised.

"There's nothing I'd like better—if you'd get *her* out of it." Jake pointed up, and Tok Loy's eyes rose to see Jessie standing by the rail.

"Miss Taggart?" Tok Loy said, surprised, then his gaze shifted from the porch to the red brass-trimmed double doors. A group of men whom he recognized as AL of S burst out, some of them already bloodied from clashes with Gum San men. Tok Loy spoke to Jessie but watched Charley Sing, who stood on the steps in front of the joss house. "Miss Taggart, you have wandered into the jaws of death."

"Miss Taggart is here?"

Jessie recognized Charley Sing's voice, but she couldn't see him until he and his bodyguards walked across the street to look up at the veranda. Jake sat on his big gray, who pawed the street nervously between the two tong leaders and their bodyguards.

"Get down here, Jessie," Jake ordered. "Now!"

Struggling to make her voice work, Jessie leaned over the rail. She couldn't see Jake's face, but she'd know that angry voice anywhere. It didn't matter how mad he was. She was darned glad to see him.

"First I have something to say to our friends," she called down to him, and thought he muttered something beneath his breath. "Gentlemen, could we all meet in the street?"

Tok Loy and Charley Sing exchanged venomous glances, then nodded. "As you wish," Tok Loy said.

With Su Ling close behind her, Jessie gathered her skirts and hurried through the group of black-robed, hatchet-wielding warriors, down the stairs, and out the doors into the street.

Su Ling waited beside the building while Tok Loy and Charley Sing, leaving their bodyguards behind, walked to where Jessie waited. Jake holstered his .44, dismounted, and tied Faro to a hitching post before joining them.

Jessie flashed him a brief smile, received a scowl in return, and cleared her throat to speak. "I have come to know both of you," she said, hoping to find the right words. "And through you and Su Ling, I have come to respect your ways."

Jake listened, but his eyes kept shifting from one group of men to the other, from the street to the veranda and back again.

"I speak to you now as my father would have," Jessie said softly. "I speak to you as a friend. I saw the men who robbed the gold shipment, the men who killed Alec Abernathy. Those men were not Chinese. Mr. Weston has told this to the sheriff and also to the newspapers. It will appear in the *Chronicle* tomorrow. You must stop this fighting between you. Trouble in Chinatown will only bring disaster on yourselves and your people." As a new sound caught her attention, Jessie turned to look up the street.

"It appears your wisdom has come too late," Tok Loy said dryly. Quickly, he motioned to the veranda, signaling his men to come down. Charley Sing did the same. Half a block away, the street suddenly brightened with torchlight and rang with the sound of shattering glass.

Two hundred white vigilantes rounded the corner.

Jake groaned aloud. "Damn you, Jessie. One of these days you're going to get us killed—and that day may very well have come!"

"I had to do it, Jake. It's what my father would have wanted. You wouldn't have let me go, so I came by myself."

"If we get out of this alive, you and I are going to have a talk."

Jessie stifled an inward groan. Jake was even madder than she thought. She glanced toward the joss house. Hundreds of Chinese poured into the street from the house and alleyways, massing behind their leaders, who together now faced a greater threat.

Jessie turned on her heel and strode away from them, up the street toward the sweeping crowd of men. Jake stared after her in disbelief. "That has got to be the craziest female ever put on the face of the earth," he exclaimed to no one in particular, then turned and stalked after her.

"Jessie," he grumbled beneath his breath as he drew alongside her, "you've had the luck of the Irish so far, but even Robert E. Lee knew when to retreat."

"I've always been lucky, Jake, and right is on my side. I'm going to stop this," she informed him tersely, her eyes fixed straight ahead.

"Who the hell do you think you are—bloody Joan of Arc?"

"I'm Henry Taggart's daughter. I mean to see this through."

Up ahead, the tide of white laborers made out the armed Chinese, and their shouting abruptly ceased. Torches blazed while hatred filled their eyes. Hank Skinner, a head taller than the rest, led the group.

"Well, boys," he said, breaking the silence, "it looks like we've found the yellow bonanza."

"Wait just a minute!" Jessie's voice rang out in the street. Skinner focused on the diminutive shape approaching the crowd like St. George approaching the dragon.

"What's this?" he cackled at Jessie, who had stopped twenty feet in front of the crowd.

"The Chinese have done nothing," Jessie told them. "You men go on home before there's real damage done."

"Get back to your mending, woman," Skinner commanded, his voice ringing down the street to where the Chinese waited in silence.

"You men better listen to her," Jake said, a hard edge to his words. "White men killed Abernathy. You can read all about it in tomorrow's paper."

"We've come to burn the yellow scum out." Skinner snatched a torch from a short, stocky man next to him.

Jessie took a step forward. "All the Chinese want is to work and live in peace."

"No, miss, what they want is our jobs." The crowd grew more restive and surged forward. Jessie instinctively fell back.

"Get the heathens!" a man shouted.

"Burn them out!" another yelled.

"Stop this!" Jessie screamed.

"We'll stop," Skinner warned, "when all the yellow scum is in the sea!"

He turned to throw the torch onto a stoop bordering the street, but Jake's .44 roared and the flaming torch flew from the man's grip. He clutched his shattered hand to his chest, a trail of blood turning the front of his white shirt crimson.

The street went as quiet as it had been noisy.

"You bastard," Skinner whimpered.

"Let's string up these Chink lovers along with their yellow scum friends!" someone shouted.

The last of Jessie's courage fled. My God, they were going to kill the Chinese and her and Jake along with them! Instinctively, she stepped closer to Jake, until she could feel the tension in his body, see the whiteness of his knuckles as he gripped the handle of his gun.

With a shrill neigh from one of the horses, a wagon careened around the corner, followed by another, then another. The shields on their chests reflecting in the torchlight, men wearing city marshal's office uniforms leaped from the wagons even before they slid to a halt. Behind them, a wagonload of sheriff's deputies climbed down. Half the men faced the Chinese, half of them faced the vigilantes. All of them carried deadly scatterguns.

Isaac Handley strode up beside Jessie, his hard gaze fixed on the crowd of angry men. "You men go on home to your wives and families." He motioned with his double-barreled shotgun. "I'd hate to have you missing work tomorrow 'cause you were waiting for the judge to let you out of jail."

The men murmured to each other, standing their ground for a moment. A few muttered words were spoken, then they began to disperse. Jessie sagged against Jake, and his arm went around her shoulders.

Isaac cast them an uncertain glance. "How the hell did you two get caught in the middle of this?"

Jake exhaled a deep breath. "This crazy female has a way of winding up in the middle of a cockfight." He glanced down at her and tried to look stern. Although part of him was furious with her, the other part was so damned glad to find her unhurt, he couldn't stand the thought of letting her out of his sight. "She could spark a gunfight in the middle of the Holy Sisters' Convent." Reaching down, he took her arm and, with a firm hand at her waist, started toward the hitching rail where Faro was tied.

"What about Su Ling?" Jessie asked, hurrying to keep from stumbling as he tugged her along.

"Isaac," he yelled back, "can you give Sugar Su a ride to the Tin Angel?"

"You got it, my friend."

"Jake!" Jessie dug in her heels. "What are they doing to Tok Loy and Charley Sing?" She jerked her arm free and started in their direction. Jake clenched his fists in frustration as he watched her go over to where a group of deputies were talking to the tong leaders.

"The two of you climb into the back of that wagon," one of the deputies ordered, motioning with the scattergun.

"Why?" Jessie asked indignantly, facing the deputy, shoulders squared.

"Because they're under arrest, that's why," the man said.

"Why didn't you arrest that bunch of white rabble?"

"Who are you?" the deputy demanded.

"She's got a good point," Jake said, strolling up behind her.

"Good evening, Mr. Weston," the deputy said.

"Let's just let everything cool down here," Jake suggested, extending a hand to the deputy. "It's good to see you, Jedediah." The deputy accepted Jake's handshake, and a broad grin flashed across his face. Jessie saw the man discreetly pocket the handful of brass tokens Jake had passed him.

"If you think so, Mr. Weston." Jedediah smiled and turned to the rest of the deputies. "Let's clear out of here."

Jake took Jessie's arm again. "Now, if just once in a while you would let me handle things . . . See how a little reasoning works? When it comes man to man." Jake herded her toward Faro. "Man's work is man's work," he told her.

"Jake Weston, you solved that piece of man's work by giving away several pieces of woman's work."

For the first time, Jake grinned. "You saw that, huh?"

"I saw it."

"Then do you think we could go on home?"

"You mean back to the Tin Angel? It isn't my home anymore, remember? I'll be moving out in the morning."

Jake pulled her into the shadows. She could feel his breath, warm against her cheek.

"Why don't you stay a little longer?" he said. "It's obvious you're going to get into trouble no matter where you live. At least at the Angel I'll be close by."

"Too close by," Jessie retorted.

He tilted her face with his hand until she looked him straight in the eye. "Next time, come to me first. I promise I'll listen." He looked down at her. Even in the darkness she could read his concern.

"You never listened before," she said softly.

"Maybe I'm beginning to understand you. As much as I hate to see you take chances, I've got to admire your courage. You believe in people, believe in doing what you can to help. You're one helluva woman, Jessica Taggart. Your father would have been proud."

His hands circled her waist and he pulled her close. She started to tremble even before his mouth came down on hers. The words he'd spoken sang in her ears as his tongue slid into her mouth, and she moaned. Mindlessly, she slipped her arms around his neck and buried her fingers in his hair, pulling him closer. She felt weak and disoriented and hot all over.

Finally, Jake broke away, although she didn't want him to.

"This isn't the place," he said, his voice husky. "Will you stay at the Angel?"

"For a while" was all she said.

Chapter 21

"**P**lease, don't kiss me." Jessie pushed against Jake's wide chest and felt his muscles flex. They stood at the bottom of the attic stairs, just inside the doorway.

Jake smiled indulgently. "I ought to wring your pretty little neck."

"I thought maybe you would."

"I guess I was just so damned glad you weren't hurt, I forgot to properly thrash you."

Jessie fought the pull of a smile. "Thank you for coming."

"I wouldn't have wanted to miss all the fun."

He was looking at her with more affection than anger. He'd said he admired her, and the words rang dear to her heart. He looked so handsome standing there with his thick dark hair a little mussed, and his black flat-brimmed hat in his hand. She wondered if he remembered their kisses, wondered if he wanted to touch her again, to hold her as she wished him to, although she knew she shouldn't. She wanted him to make love to her again, she realized. When she looked into his eyes, his expression had turned hungry, and she knew with a jolt of certainty that he wanted her, too.

Nervously, Jessie wet her lips and fought to push her thoughts in a safer direction. "Do you think we'll ever find out who killed my father?"

"I don't know, Jess. It could very well have been Silva."

"I know," she said. Jake's gaze fastened on her mouth until she had to glance away. "I'd better go on up. It's getting late and I . . . we don't want to . . ." She swallowed hard. "Good night, Jake."

He watched her for a moment. "Good night, Boston." He started to leave, one hand on the doorknob, then turned, sweeping her into his arms and kissing her, his lips hot and demanding, his tongue plundering her mouth.

When he spoke again, his voice was gruff. "Stay out of trouble for a while, will you?" Without giving her time to respond, he was gone.

Jessie fought to still her pounding heart. What in God's name was she going to do? There was no use denying it—she was in love with Jake. Helplessly, hopelessly, mindlessly in love with him. How long had she been lying to herself? Hours? Days? Weeks?

It was time she faced the truth. Now that she had, she had to win his love in return—or leave. There were no other choices. How did he feel about her? she wondered. He'd said he admired her. That was a start. He desired her, of that she was sure. But did he care for her enough to give up the other women in his life? Would he marry her?

For the first time, Jessie admitted marriage was exactly what she wanted from Jake. But not because he felt obligated to do the right thing. Not because he felt some past loyalty to her father. She wanted him to marry her because he loved her desperately and wanted to be with her for the rest of his life.

Jessie sighed and climbed the stairs. Why had she ever come to California? Why had her father gotten her into this mess in the first place? Hearing a soft knock on the door, Jessie called down permission to enter and saw Megan O'Brien coming up the stairs.

"Jake said ya might be needin' some help with your dress," she said.

"Thank you, Megan." Jessie presented her back to the pretty red-haired woman, grateful Jake had sent her up. Then an unwanted thought came to mind—had Megan been one of Jake's conquests? He'd said he kept business strictly business, but still she wondered. And the fact that she wondered made her feel more uncertain than ever.

"How long have you been at the Tin Angel, Megan?" Jessie asked.

"A bit o'er a year, Miss Jessie."

"Do you like working here?"

Megan paled. She swallowed and glanced away.

"Why, Megan, what's the matter?"

"Nothing, Miss Jessie . . . really. It's just that . . . When I first came here, I didn't know anyone. I didn't trust anyone. I was lonely. I ne'er had a place I could call me home. Jake and Lovey and the girls, they've been good to me and I . . ."

"What, Megan?"

"Nothing, ma'am." She helped Jessie out of her petticoats and chemise.

"It isn't Jake, is it? I mean, he hasn't . . . mistreated you or . . . anything?"

"Oh, no, Miss Jessie. All the girls love Jake. He treats us like ladies. Not like whores, I mean. Jake's a gentleman."

Jessie arched a brow. "I've thought of him as a lot of things, but hardly a gentleman."

"Oh, but he is. He ne'er comes to our rooms. He ne'er talks dirty to us, like some gents do. And he's always there when ya need 'im. That's why I . . ."

"You what?"

Megan sighed. "It's nothin'." She glanced at Jessie and gave her a watery smile. "I'm believin' he cares for ya, Miss Jessie. He ne'er looks at any o' us the way he looks at you."

It was Jessie's turn to smile. "I hope you're right, Megan."

Megan finished helping Jessie undress, then quietly left the room. Jessie wondered why she seemed so forlorn, but decided that if she herself were forced to work in a house of ill-repute, she'd probably be forlorn, too.

It was five o'clock in the morning by the time Jessie realized sleep was not going to come. The Angel had been quiet for almost an hour, the rabble-rousers gone home for the night, the girls finished working and quietly tucked in bed. Jake would be sleeping. *Jake.* Was he asleep, or tossing and turning just as she was? She could still recall the fiery kiss he'd left her with, the hard arousal he'd mercilessly pressed against her.

For the hundredth time, she shoved the same thought aside, but it wouldn't leave her. *Go to him. Love him. If you give your love freely, you can win his love in return.*

A thousand doubts assailed her. Jake was a dedicated bachelor, a man who'd never be happy with just one woman. Jake didn't care for her in the least; he just enjoyed her body. Jake was using her, making a fool of her. Still, she wasn't convinced. *I've got to try,* her heart said. I love him. I won't give up without a fight.

Her heart won out. Jessie threw on her ruffled silk wrapper, brushed her hair, and tiptoed softly down the stairs. Pulling open the door to the hall, she glanced around, but saw no one. They wouldn't be up and about for hours.

Her slippered feet padding against the rough wooden floors, Jessie walked quietly down the hall and pulled open Jake's door. Moonlight streaming through an open window cast a beam of light on his naked chest. He was sleeping after all, she saw, disappointed. Then with a jolt that sent her head spinning, she spied the dark-haired woman in the bed beside him.

The beautiful girl propped herself on an elbow, the sheet falling away to reveal a bare breast as she

smiled in Jessie's direction. But Monique Dubois
didn't say a word. Instead she wet the end of a long-
nailed finger and circled Jake's flat copper nipple.

Jessie stifled the low moan that caught in her
throat, and with trembling fingers quietly closed the
door. *Fool!* her mind cried out. Naive, silly schoolgirl! Jake had been right all along!

With the back of her hand, she wiped hot tears
from her cheeks, but she couldn't stop a fresh flood
from coming. Blindly she found her way back to her
room and raced up the stairs. She couldn't leave the
Tin Angel now; it wasn't even light outside. But as
soon as the hour turned respectable, she'd be gone.
She prayed Monique wouldn't tell Jake about her
visit to his room—she couldn't bear the humiliation.
Then, without doubt, she knew the beautiful French
girl wouldn't say a word. Monique didn't want competition any more than Jessie did. A cord of despair
wrapped around her heart. She was getting less naive by the minute!

Jessie sank down on the edge of the bed, her gaze
fixed on the gray sky outside her window. It would
be overcast today, windy and cold. She shivered as
if she were cold already, and in her heart she was.
She remembered the time she'd spent with Jake, the
angry words, usually spoken more from concern
than outrage; the laughter they'd shared; the tears
she'd shed in front of Jake that few others had seen.
She'd come to trust him, and that had led to love.

A vision of Monique's smug expression flashed
across Jessie's mind, and she wondered how she
could have been so completely fooled. Just a few
hours earlier, Jake had asked her to stay at the Tin
Angel, had looked at her with such warmth and caring, she'd believed he meant it. How he must have
laughed, knowing he'd be sleeping with Monique
the very same night! Jessie blinked hard, but she
couldn't stop a fresh flood of tears. Fool! Fool! Fool!
she repeated.

Giving in to her sobs, Jessie rolled onto her stomach, buried her face in her pillow, and cried in earnest. Tomorrow she would go to Rene and sell her interest in the Tin Angel. She wouldn't sell to Jake if he were the last man alive! She'd leave for Boston, go back where she belonged—get as far away from Jake Weston as she possibly could. She'd forget him, she vowed, and find somebody new to love. She pulled the pillow against her cheek, trying to find some comfort from the dreary gray light in her room and the darkness in her heart.

What a stupid, silly fool she'd been to ever believe he cared.

Jake felt the gentle tug of small sharp teeth on his nipple, the wetness of a delicate tongue as it teased and coaxed, stirring his arousal. Slim fingers laced through the hair on his chest, and a rush of blood surged to his loins.

"Jess," he groaned softly, pulling the girl's naked body into his arms. Rolling on top of her, he pressed her into the soft feather mattress, kissing her urgently while his hand cupped her heavy breast. It was the practiced kiss he received in return, the taste of a woman's breath more sensual than sweet, that brought him fully awake.

"Monique!" he roared, pulling away from her as if she were a viper. "What the hell do you think you're doing?"

"I 'ave missed you, *chéri*. 'Ave you not missed Monique, just a little?"

Jake swung his long legs to the side of the bed and grabbed his breeches, sliding them over his hips and fastening the buttons. "I thought you understood. What we had is over, Monique. You have other men. Why don't you pay one of them a visit?"

Monique sat up in bed, her long black hair falling seductively across her shoulder, to hide one luscious, pink-tipped breast. Oddly enough, the sight did nothing to arouse Jake's interest, which had died the minute he'd discovered the woman in his bed wasn't Jessie.

"I do not want another." Monique pouted. "I want you. That woman has poisoned your mind. I will scratch 'er eyes out."

"I wouldn't try it if I were you. She can be one tough lady." He tossed her the lacy chemise that lay at his feet. "Go on home, Monique."

Monique watched him from beneath her silky black lashes. "You are in love with 'er. I can see it in your eyes."

Jake didn't answer.

Monique let out a long resigned breath. "Love is something we French understand, *chéri*. If that is what you feel . . ." She shrugged.

Jake pulled on his shirt.

"I do not envy you," she continued. "I 'ave been in love. It is sometimes beautiful, sometimes ugly. But always it is painful." She picked up her chemise and began to dress. "I wish you luck, *chéri*."

Jake pulled on his boots and headed downstairs, leaving her alone.

He had some thinking to do. His fear for Jessie this evening, and his reaction to Monique, had stripped away the last of his doubts. He didn't want Monique. He didn't want any other woman. He wanted Jessica Taggart.

It was all he could do to keep his hands off her, all he could do to keep from tearing off her clothes and making passionate love to her. Although she often tested his patience, he felt fiercely protective of her, and wildly jealous of other men. He loved her, all right. Any fool could see it. Beyond that— and this was the crazy part—he wanted to marry her, wanted her to bear his children, to grow old with him.

But did she love him? Would she marry him if he asked her?

Jake headed down the back stairs toward the cookstove, the kettle of coffee on the top still warm although the fire had turned to glowing coals. There was no way to find out unless he asked her. His chest tightened as he considered the strong possibility she would say no. His earnings from Taggart Enterprises were enough to keep her in style, assuming the company had no more losses, and he would like nothing better if she'd give him the chance. Still, he was a gambler, a man who ran a saloon full of whores, not some Boston dandy.

Jake released a long, exasperated breath and poured himself a cup of the thick black coffee. Sooner or later he'd have to tell her how he felt. Sooner or later.

Thinking about her reaction, how he would feel if she said no, he decided later was plenty soon enough.

"Lovey?" Jessie called into the hallway. "Would you ask Paco to come up here for a moment?"

"Sure." Lovey threw Jessie a curious look and waddled toward the back stairs. In minutes Jessie heard a knock and invited Paco inside.

"I want you to take a message to Mr. La Porte," she said tersely, handing him a sealed white envelope. "Tell him I said it was important, and wait for his reply."

"*Sí*, Señorita Jessie." He seemed uncertain for a moment. "You are not angry with Paco, are you?"

Jessie's expression softened. "No, Paco. This has nothing to do with you." She ran a finger along his cheek, and he smiled.

"I do as you wish, Señorita Jessie." Turning, he bolted down the attic stairs.

She would miss him, she thought. She'd miss him and the others more than she would have guessed. "And Paco," she added, "this is none of Mr. Weston's affair, do you understand?"

"*Sí*, Señorita Jessie."

"Hurry now."

Paco nodded and scrambled off. Jessie paced the floor until he appeared half an hour later. Accepting Rene's return message, she thanked Paco and handed him a fifty-cent piece.

Paco looked up at her as if she'd given him the moon. "*Gracias*, Señorita Jessie."

"*De nada*," she answered, using a phrase he'd taught her. "Remember what I told you."

He put a finger to his lips, then grinned and slipped out the door.

Jessie ripped open the envelope.

> Be assured, *chérie*, my supper invitation still stands. I will await your arrival at the Palace, as you wished. I look forward to our evening and the business discussion you mentioned. Until tonight.
>
>   Your devoted admirer,
>   Rene

Jessie took a breath of resignation and slipped the note back into the envelope. All day long she'd felt sick at heart, angry, hurt, and used. Anger had won out. She needed her anger to get her through these next few days.

Jake was an ill-bred, uncouth, womanizing . . . whoremonger! She was lucky she'd found out before she'd made a bigger fool of herself than she already had. Jessie continued to fume as she got dressed. Finally she left the saloon, hailing a hansom cab to carry her along the ocean. She needed to clear her thoughts and gain control of her wayward emotions. Tonight she would face Rene, offer him her interests in Taggart Enterprises—at a more than equitable price—and she would leave for Boston on the morrow.

By the time Jessie returned to the Angel, she'd

fallen into a numb calmness. Using the back staircase, she scrupulously avoided Jake and headed up to her room. As tired as she was, she found she still couldn't sleep, so she ordered a bath and soaked for as long as she dared. Then she dressed and left for the Palace Hotel, the only neutral territory she'd been able to think of on the spur of the moment.

She'd worn her favorite gown, an emerald silk with a sweeping polonaise of heavy gold brocade. Although the low-cut bodice revealed a little more bosom than was proper, the green accentuated her eyes, and the gown showed off her figure to its best advantage. If only she could disguise the smudges beneath her eyes and the wan look that had replaced her usually blooming complexion.

Jessie sighed and clutched her reticule a little tighter as the hansom cab jolted along the streets. Would Jake notice she'd gone out? She doubted it. He hadn't come near her all day, and that was probably a darned good thing. As determined as she'd been to pretend nothing had changed between them, she was afraid she would have lost her temper and tried to murder him instead.

How could he? she asked herself for the hundredth time. But thinking of the beautiful dark-haired French girl who had shared his bed, she knew the answer even though she wished she didn't.

"Good evening, *chérie,*" Rene said solicitously as he greeted her in the lobby of the elegant Palace Hotel.

"Good evening, Rene." He brought her gloved hand to his lips, and she could feel the warmth through the gold cloth. As he guided her into the salon beneath crystal chandeliers, she heard the eloquent strains of violins. A four-piece orchestra played softly from a small, velvet-draped stage in one corner. Once they were seated, Rene summoned a waiter.

"A glass of sherry?" he asked. "Or would you

prefer champagne?'' He looked handsome in his black evening clothes, his blond hair combed away from his face, his skin lightly tanned. With his straight nose, dark eyes, and sensuous mouth, it was easy to see why women found him attractive. Still . . . Rene wasn't Jake.

"Sherry would be fine.'' They exchanged pleasantries, Rene's eyes drifting continually toward her bosom. She probably should have worn something more conservative, she thought, then chided herself for being a fool. Rene was handsome and solicitous, and she owed Jake Weston nothing!

While they enjoyed a sumptuous dinner of mock turtle soup, baked filet of trout, and braised quail larded with jelly, including three different kinds of wine, and, of course, champagne, they discussed the weather, city affairs, and the events in Chinatown the previous night. It wasn't until the conversation turned to business that things began to get awkward.

"Why have you suddenly decided to sell?'' Rene asked. "It was not long ago that you were adamantly opposed to selling. Has business fallen off so badly?''

Jessie took another long sip of her champagne and tried to swallow the bit of plum pudding that had suddenly lodged in her throat. "I've just decided I don't belong here. I'm going back to Boston.'' She took another drink of champagne.

"And what of Monsieur Weston? Has he not expressed an interest in buying your share?''

Jessie drained her glass and Rene refilled it, his eyes watching hers until she glanced away. "Mr. Weston has caused me considerable inconvenience. I do not wish to do him any favors. You, on the other hand, once saved my life. Let's just say I want to repay you.''

"I see.'' They finished the meal, Jessie barely touching the delicious food, but nervously sipping champagne, emptying her glass as fast as Rene filled it. When she finally knocked over the stemmed crystal, shattering it against the marble floor and drawing the curious glances of people at nearby tables, Rene smiled indulgently and took her hand.

"It slipped," she said, embarrassed, then she hiccupped.

"I think it is time to go," he told her, his eyes sparkling with amusement.

Jessie could barely make out his words. "That's a very good idea," she told him with a giggle and a hiccup. She felt warm all over and heady with excitement. "Where shall we go from here?"

Rene smiled. "You, *chérie*, should go home."

Jessie vehemently shook her head. "I'm not ready to go home. I don't even have a home." When Rene helped her from her chair, she swayed against him and he took her arm, guiding her through the restaurant and out through the lobby. His coach and driver were waiting beneath the wide covered portico in front of the hotel.

"I'm not going home, Rene," she warned him, affecting what she hoped was a most becoming pout. "If you're tired of my company, I shall go back inside and find someone who isn't."

"It is rare that I tire of a beautiful woman's company." He helped her into the carriage and motioned to the driver, who picked up the reins and clucked the horses into a trot.

Jessie sat back against the seat, feeling dizzy and disoriented, but better than she had since she'd opened the door to Jake's room. "How about another glass of champagne?"

"You will make yourself sick," Rene said. "Why do you not tell me what this is about?"

"You wanted to take me to supper, didn't you? You wanted to buy out my share?"

"I also wanted to make love to you, but I wanted it to be your idea as well."

"Fine," she said, slinging her arms around his neck.

Rene gently unwrapped her arms. "What did Weston do?"

"I don't want to talk about it. I just want some more champagne."

They reached Rene's beautiful Victorian mansion on Pacific Street a few minutes later. The carriage rolled to a stop. Rene's strong arm around her waist was all that kept her from falling to the floor.

The door opened, and the driver helped her down. Rene was beside her in an instant. "Come, *chérie*." He pulled her cloak more tightly around her. "You will catch a chill out here." Jessie let Rene guide her inside and seat her on a pale brocade sofa.

"We will get you some coffee," he suggested. "You will be fine. Mrs. O'Clanahan," he called out. "Coffee, if you please. Very strong and a great deal of it." The buxom housekeeper took one look at Jessie, rolled her eyes, and disappeared into the kitchen.

"I don't want coffee," Jessie said, pouting. "I want some more champagne. I thought we were having fun."

Rene smiled and tilted her chin with his hand. His mouth came down over hers in a feather-soft kiss. "There will be other times, if you wish it. But now, *chérie*, tell me what is wrong. Believe it or not, I am your friend."

Jessie's bottom lip trembled. She glanced away and blinked furiously, but great tears rolled down her cheeks. "I love him so much," she blurted out, although she wished she could call back the words. "I thought he cared about me. I thought I meant something to him. I'm such a fool, Rene."

"We are all fools at one time or another. It is nothing to be ashamed of."

"I thought you were the scoundrel, but it was Jake all along."

"We are both rogues, I think."

"I've got to get away from here. Go back to Boston. I can't think straight anymore." She let him pull her into his arms and cried softly against his chest. "I'm so tired, Rene. So tired." She nestled against him. Her eyes fluttered closed, and then she was asleep.

Morning arrived with a vengeance. Jessie awoke with a pounding headache and a rolling stomach. She looked up to a canopy of gleaming pale gray satin trimmed with peach, and wondered for a moment where she was. Across the room, a carved wooden armoire stood open to reveal a row of men's suits and shirts. Starched white celluloid collars sat on the matching rosewood dresser beside a man's gold pocket watch and fob.

Jessie's heart began to pound. Her gown lay across the chair, her lacy chemise and pantalets folded neatly beside it. When she glanced down at herself, she discovered she was wearing another of Rene's nightshirts, and stifled a moan.

Oh, God, she was in Rene's bedroom! How had she gotten there? What had she done? Although she tried to convince herself it wasn't so, Jessie remembered just enough of the evening to know the truth. *I'm not ready to go home . . . I want some more champagne . . . I thought we were having fun.* She could remember his hands at her waist, even remember him kissing her—a not entirely unpleasant sensation.

Trembling inside, her head pounding even harder than her heart, Jessie climbed from the huge canopied bed. She dressed quickly in her slightly wilted evening clothes, and stumbled over to the mirror. Her thick dark hair was a mass of tangled curls. She searched the bureau fruitlessly for a brush, then quickly pulled out her few remaining hairpins and tried to comb the heavy mass with her fingers.

Maybe Rene had been a gentleman, realized how drunk she was, and carried her upstairs. *Not a chance*, Jessie thought ruefully. The man had been trying to seduce her for weeks. Last night he had seen his opportunity and taken it. She had only to think of the way he'd undressed her the last time to be sure. On board his yacht, she'd been injured. This time she'd been drunk, and practically begged him to take her to bed. He was a man, wasn't he? And she'd learned in no time at all that men couldn't be trusted.

Fool me once, you're the fool. Fool me twice, I'm the fool. Rene had made love to her last night, and she'd probably even enjoyed it. Jessie shuddered at the thought. He certainly hadn't forced her—there were no bruises, no telltale marks on her body. She wished she could convince herself it hadn't happened, but she'd drunk so much and her memory was so foggy, anything could have occurred. And the way she'd felt when she awakened—she certainly felt guilty about something!

How in God's name would she face him? The thought stirred a wave of despair that matched her rolling stomach. She had to get out of his house and go back to the Tin Angel.

With that goal in mind, she grabbed her cloak, checked her disheveled appearance in the mirror, and opened the door to the hall. Seeing no one, she headed for the leaded-glass front door. She didn't breathe a sigh of relief until she'd reached the corner and hailed a passing hack.

Chapter 22

"Take me to the Tin Angel," she ordered. "Let me off in back."

The driver grinned knowingly, and Jessie stifled a groan. If anyone saw her, dressed as she was, they would know exactly what kind of night she'd spent. Please, God, she prayed, let me get back to my room without being caught. I promise I'll return to Boston and lead the quiet life my mother always wanted.

But she wasn't that lucky. She hadn't gotten five steps up the back stairs when she heard Jake's booming voice.

"Where the hell have you been?" he demanded. He was standing at the top of the stairs, his expression a mixture of worry and rage. "I told you to stay out of trouble. I actually believed you listened to me."

Clutching her full silk skirts so she wouldn't trip, her evening cloak billowing out behind her, Jessie tried to brush past him, but he caught her arm in a grip so hard she winced.

"I asked you a question. Where the hell have you been?"

"Take your hands off me! You have no right to question me. I'm leaving this place, selling out to Rene La Porte and going back to Boston."

"What?" Jake seemed incredulous. "What are you talking about?"

Feeling his hold loosen, Jessie jerked free and headed up the attic stairs. Jake climbed the steps behind her, his footfalls ringing in the silence. When he reached the top, he turned her to face him. For the first time he got a good look at her wrinkled evening clothes, the tangled mass of her hair.

"Were you with La Porte last night?" he demanded.

"What do you care? I know all about you, Jake Weston. I know you don't care the least bit about me. I saw Monique in your bed. I was a fool, Jake. But I'm not a fool anymore."

Jake clenched his jaw and swore beneath his breath. "I'm sorry you saw her, Jess, but it wasn't the way you think. I didn't ask her to come. I was asleep. When I woke up, she was wrapped around me like a gopher snake on a mouse. I didn't make love to her, Jess, I swear it. I sent her home."

"You didn't make love to her?" she repeated, incredulous.

"She didn't even arouse my . . . interest. I'm in love with you, Jess. I want to marry you."

Jessie backed away from him, shaking her head. Her emerald eyes had grown huge in her pale face.

"You're lying! You . . . you have women all over the city. You couldn't be happy with just one."

Jake gripped her arms and pulled her in front of him. "That's what I thought before I met you. I've had my share of women, I won't lie about that. Not as many as you believe. . . . But it's you I want, not them. I'm telling you the truth, Jess."

"You can't be." She swallowed past the growing lump in her throat. "You were with Monique. I saw you. I . . . I . . ."

"Nothing happened, Jess. I love you."

Jessie just shook her head. How she had longed to hear those words, yearned to see the tender expression on his face—now it was too late.

"No," she whispered, shaking her head. Her

throat was so dry she couldn't speak. She could see the candor in his face, the way his eyes begged her to believe him, the forthright curve of his mouth. He confronted her squarely, hiding nothing, knowing he had nothing to hide, while she couldn't face him at all. She wanted to doubt him, but she couldn't—Jake was telling the truth.

"Why didn't you say something sooner?" she said, her voice still a whisper, the tears running freely down her cheeks. "Why did you wait until now?"

"Marriage isn't something a man cottons to right off. I wanted to be sure. I'm sure now, Jess. More certain than I've ever been in my life."

Jessie lifted her chin to meet those bright blue eyes whose honesty had just destroyed her world. "You were right," she said, her tone suddenly flat. "I spent the night with Rene. I don't really remember everything that happened. I got drunk. He wanted to take me home, but I wouldn't go. It wasn't really his fault. I . . . I practically begged him to take me to bed." She delivered her speech in a monotone, her heart so bleak and aching that she could barely choke out the words.

Jake's expression hardened to a cold, taut mask. "I'll kill him," he said hoarsely, turning to leave.

Jessie caught his arm, her touch as soft as the sound of her voice. "No," she said. "Please don't bring Rene into this. It isn't his fault, it's all mine. I'm the one to blame, not Rene. I'll sell out to you, of course. I'll have Horace draw up the papers. It shouldn't take more than a couple of days. Any price you and Horace think is fair is all right with me." She studied the toes of her muddy satin slippers. "If I could change things I would, but I can't."

Jake just looked at her.

"Until we get things settled, I'll be staying at the Palace," she added.

"Jess . . ."

"Don't say anything, Jake. Please. I have a knack for messing things up. You've said so yourself, a dozen times at least."

"Maybe we can work things out."

Jessie just shook her head, fresh tears rolling down her cheeks. "It would always be between us. You couldn't forgive me for sleeping with Rene any more than I could have forgiven you for sleeping with Monique. We're all or nothing kind of people. We never do anything halfway." She turned from him then, trying hard to be strong when what she wanted was to go to him, feel his arms around her, hear him tell her things would be all right.

"I want you to know I appreciate all you've done for me," Jessie said, amazed her voice could sound so strong when her heart was breaking in two. "The way you've looked out for me and all. I want you to know I'll never forget you."

"You're sure this is what you want?"

"I made my choice last night."

Jake bristled. "So you did." He turned to leave, and she heard his footsteps pounding down the stairs.

"Jake?" she called after him, unable to stop herself, but he didn't answer, just stopped and looked up at her, his expression remote. "There's one more thing I want you to know." His eyes seemed even brighter than she remembered. "I . . . I . . ." but she couldn't say the three painful words. Just thinking of how much she loved him made her heart ache unbearably. "I'm proud you were my partner," she said instead. "I know my father would have been proud of you, too."

Jake's dark expression pinned her where she stood. "Would you have said yes?"

"What?" she asked, uncertain of his meaning, the room beginning to whirl around her.

"If this hadn't happened, would you have married me?"

Jessie couldn't bear to look at him, couldn't bear to hurt him any more than she already had. "No," she lied, forcing a tone of disinterest that tortured her heart. "We weren't well-suited. It never would have worked."

His hands balled into fists, Jake strode back up the stairs, taking them two at a time until he reached her side. "I don't believe you," he said, grabbing her arms and pulling her roughly against him.

Jessie moaned when he kissed her, his touch both punishing and yearning at the same time. She could feel his hand at her neck, his fingers raking through her tangled hair.

"I love you," he whispered harshly beside her ear, as if the words were wrenched from his soul. "I can't have been that wrong."

Jessie broke away, trembling all over, wanting him to hold her, wanting him and knowing he was already lost. "But you were," was all she said.

Jake let her go and backed away. "I'll send Su Ling up to help you pack," he said, his voice low and gruff. His eyes moved over her face. "You won't be easy to forget."

"I won't forget you, either."

"Good-bye, Boston."

Jessie studied him for a long moment, wanting to remember the dear line of his jaw, the width of his shoulders, the dark hair curling on his chest. "Good-bye, Jake."

She memorized the sensuous play of muscle across his wide back and narrow hips as he pulled the door closed behind him.

Jake fought the knot of despair that tightened in his stomach. He banged on the mahogany door until he thought the leaded-glass panes would certainly shatter. "La Porte!" he yelled, and the door swung wide.

"Ah, Monsieur Weston. I have been expecting you."

"I'll bet you have." Jake clenched his fist and punched La Porte in the jaw. The Frenchman flew backward, knocking over a small rosewood table and sending a Chinese cloisonné vase crashing to the floor. La Porte came slowly to his feet, massaging his jaw and scowling.

Jake stood in the doorway and rubbed his skinned knuckles with anticipation. He wanted to enjoy the beating he was about to give this French dandy.

"Our little rendezvous has been coming for some time," Rene said softly, a hard look in his eyes. "I will be happy to beat you senseless, monsieur, but I would prefer to do it outside. These are imported tartan carpets. You have already cost me an expensive Chinese vase." He turned his back, shrugged out of his coat, and tossed it over a chair. Then he headed toward the French doors that led onto a terrace at the rear of the house.

Jake followed, his jaw clamped tight while he too removed his coat. Rene crossed the terrace, unfastening the links on his cuffs. Jake unbuttoned the top two buttons on his shirt while Rene carefully rolled up one shirtsleeve, then the other. Jake took a step forward. Ignoring his advance, Rene removed his waistcoat, carefully emptying the slim cigars from his pockets and placing them on a small wrought-iron table next to a matching, equally intricate chair.

"Are you sure you're ready?" Jake asked sarcastically.

"As you wish." Rene moved onto the grass and lifted his hands in the Queensbury stance.

Jake stepped in front of him and threw a roundhouse right which Rene blocked easily. He received two quick jabs in the face as the Frenchman danced away. A little surprised, Jake stepped back. Although he tried to remain cool, the image of a masterful French lover spreading Jessie's pretty thighs, her mahogany hair fanned across the pillow, flashed through Jake's mind, and his already heated temper began to boil. He rushed La Porte, swinging wildly, and again Rene sidestepped and gave him two quick snapping jabs. La Porte moved in with a right, and the blow rocked Jake to his boots. He could taste the blood in his mouth, and for a moment, his vision dimmed.

"You bastard." Jake stepped back and eyed the Frenchman, who bobbed and weaved, never standing still, never dropping his Queensbury stance.

So the Frenchman could fight. He wouldn't underestimate the man again. Concentrating on La Porte's aquiline nose, he threw a right, straight from the shoulder. They traded solid blows to the head and body, then separated.

This time it was Rene who shook off the blows. A trickle of blood ran from one nostril. "Swine," La Porte muttered.

Jake's lip curled in a triumphant half smile. He moved in again. Rene sidestepped and dropped to the ground, entangling Jake's legs in his as he passed. Jake fell heavily onto the grass. Rene was over him before he could rise, dealing several hard blows to his face. Jake dropped to his back and struck out with his own booted feet, driving the Frenchman backward.

Jake struggled to his feet, blood flowing freely from his nose, his eye beginning to swell. The sonofabitch was tougher than he thought.

Rene swung a roundhouse blow; Jake ducked, but caught Rene's knee square in the face for his effort. By now both men were staggering, breathing heavily.

"You've . . . done some . . . fighting," Jake said, trying to catch his breath, a tinge of respect in his voice. Moving inside, he swung a blow that caught Rene on the chin. They fought for several minutes, each man gaining the advantage, then losing it.

"I paid . . . my dues . . . on the docks . . . at New Orleans." Rene gasped, fighting for air. "Many a . . . longshoreman, black . . . brown . . . and white . . . found he could not best the Frenchman."

"Yeah? Well . . . this time the Frog gets whipped," Jake growled.

They battled back and forth, winding up on the terrace, where they rolled onto the bricks, sending the wrought-iron table and chair flying.

They traded blows on the ground, both men breathing so heavily that words wouldn't come. Too winded to do anything else, they fought on their knees, their blows now little more than shoves. Finally, gasping for air and bleeding, they sprawled on the terrace, each too exhausted to stand.

"You bastard," Jake finally said. "You took advantage."

"Of you? How?"

"Of Jessie."

Rene managed to sit up, his legs out in front of him, his finely tailored trousers torn at both knees. "And you did not?"

Jake, too, managed to sit up. "That's different."

"Why? Because you love her?" Rene struggled to his feet. Limping over, he set the chair and table upright.

Jake hesitated. Then he too climbed to his feet. "You got her drunk."

"She got herself drunk. I had little to do with it."

"She didn't know what she was doing. You've got a helluva lot more experience with women than she's got with men."

"Ah." Rene's mouth curved in a sarcastic grin. "So you believe I have ruined her. The owner of a whorehouse tells Rene La Porte that he is a despoiler of women. That is amusing, monsieur."

"Not to me, Frenchy."

"Let us continue our disagreement after a glass of

burgundy." Rene picked up his waistcoat and hob-
bled toward the terrace doors.

"One glass, then back outside." Jake stumbled after him.

Rene removed his shirt before he entered the
house, and mopped the blood from his face. He tore
the tail off and handed it to Jake. "Press this against
your nose, Weston. You will bleed on my carpet."

Jake flashed him the dirtiest look he could muster,
but tipped his head back and held the shirt to his
nose until the bleeding ceased. He wiped his face
with the rest of the cloth, then threw it onto the
terrace.

Rene cast him a disparaging look as he crossed the
room to the sideboard. He pulled the cork from a
wine bottle and poured a liberal amount into two
crystal glasses. Jake picked up a glass and took a
long, reviving drink. Then his eyes met La Porte's.

"She's going back to Boston," Jake said.

"I know. It's probably for the best." Jake didn't
answer. "Surely you are pleased to be rid of her?"

"Truthfully?" Jake said. "No."

"But your honor has been sullied. You would not
ask her to stay—surely you would not want a ruined
woman." Rene shook his head.

"That's not the point."

"It makes so much difference that she slept with
me?"

"Now that I've had time to think about it," Jake
said, "it wouldn't make a damn bit of difference if
she'd slept with Attila the Hun."

Rene laughed aloud and Jake cast him a murderous look.

The Frenchman held up a placating hand. "I feel
as you, Monsieur Weston. If I loved a woman, I
would take her from an Algiers brothel."

With a sigh, Jake leaned against the wall. "I don't
think she'd stay even if I begged her."

"I have a hard time imagining the great Monsieur

Weston on his knees, although Mademoiselle Taggart would be worth it." Rene raised his glass. "Here's to love."

Jake drained his wineglass. "I guess there's no need for us to continue beating ourselves to death."

"Part of this was between us, but the rest is between you and your lady."

"Thanks for the wine." Jake headed toward the door.

"There is one more thing before you go."

Jake turned to face him, his hand on the heavy brass doorknob.

"Mrs. O'Clanahan," La Porte called out. "Would you come down here a moment?"

Jake looked up to see a buxom gray-haired woman descending the sweeping staircase, a mobcap atop her head and a starched white apron over her crisp black uniform.

"Yes, Mr. La Porte?" Her brows rose as she scanned their torn and bloody clothes, and her nose wrinkled in disapproval.

"Would you tell my friend here where Miss Taggart spent the night?"

"Hold on, La Porte. Enough is enough."

"Miss Taggart slept in Mr. La Porte's room, since that is the finest room in the house. Mr. La Porte went out for the evening—the entire evening."

"But Jessie said—"

"Surely Mademoiselle Taggart did not give you a detailed description of my masterful lovemaking."

"No. She just said she got drunk and . . ." Jake looked over at La Porte, who was smiling. A slow grin lifted one corner of Jake's mouth. "She said she didn't remember."

"I assure you, monsieur, that if Jessica had spent the night in my bed, she would remember."

"Mr. La Porte is a gentleman," the housekeeper declared.

Jake's grin broadened. "I'll be damned! You

know, La Porte, I think I'm gonna wind up liking you after all.'' Jake crossed the room and extended his hand. ''No hard feelings?''

La Porte accepted the handshake. ''Give her my regards.''

When he reached the door, Jake paused. ''She said she practically begged you to take her to bed.''

''Actually, she told me how much she loves you. It was not an auspicious beginning for an evening of seduction.''

Jake watched La Porte for a moment, then nodded. Pulling open the door, he stepped out onto the porch. He couldn't remember when the San Francisco air had ever smelled so sweet.

Jessie had shed all the tears she'd allow. She had no one to blame but herself. Now it was up to her to get on with her life, to make a fresh start somewhere else. There'd be another man to love, she told herself staunchly. Someone who wouldn't try to bully her all the time. Someone who'd let her run her life the way she wanted. A man who wouldn't be able to use her passions to drive her wildly out of control.

Someone who wasn't Jake.

Jessie blinked back a fresh wave of tears and straightened the cuffs of her dark gray day dress. She'd chosen the dress to match her mood, then wondered if Horace McCafferty would catch the subtle innuendo. Earlier, she'd had Paco deliver her message, a short note advising Horace of her decision to sell and asking him to begin the paperwork. The note she'd received in return had suggested she come to his office at his earliest convenience, that being five o'clock this afternoon.

The hansom cab rounded the corner onto Battery Street, where the offices of Brace and McCafferty, Esquires were located in a sturdy two-story building of tan brick with twin Corinthian columns flanking double mahogany doors. The structure bespoke solidity and confidence. Brace and McCafferty catered to the financial and shipping trade.

With a sigh of resignation, Jessie looked out the cab's isinglass window and up at the building. She hadn't seen Jake since their confrontation that morning, and she didn't want to. In fact, if she never had to face him again it would be too soon. She'd remember his stunned expression till the day she died—a look that said he just couldn't believe Jessica Taggart would betray him. Obviously, Jake didn't know her as well as he thought.

The door to the carriage opened, and the driver helped her down to the cobblestone street. She paid him, and, forcing a smile she didn't feel, opened one of the heavy mahogany doors. A tiny bell above signaled her arrival and the round-cheeked young man she recognized as Horace's secretary led her upstairs to his offices. Horace looked up from his paperwork as she approached.

"Please sit down, Miss Taggart," Horace said as he dried his quill pen with a scrap of paper and returned it to its pewter holder. "I'm sorry to hear you'll be leaving us, although I believe you're making the right decision."

Jessie just nodded. Horace hooked a thumb in his waistcoat and leaned back in his chair. "I took the liberty of inviting another interested party, Miss Taggart. After all, I am your legal adviser. I want you, as my client, to receive the best possible offer for your share in Taggart Enterprises."

"I'm sorry, Horace, I should have been more specific. I'm not interested in entertaining offers."

Behind her, the door opened and Kazimir Bochek entered the room. "Good afternoon, Miss Taggart."

Jessie bristled. "This meeting was supposed to be between my attorney and myself. I could have saved you the trouble of coming over. My offer to sell is not open to anyone other than Mr. Weston. It's what my father would have wanted, and it's what I want."

"Your father was a hardheaded old fool," Bochek said, and Jessie sprang to her feet.

"Don't you dare speak like that about my father! Henry Taggart was a fine, upstanding man."

"A little too upstanding for his own good, it appears to me," Bochek said. "Upstandin' way he cottoned to those China boys up and got him killed."

"Mr. McCafferty," Jessie said, turning in his direction, "I'd appreciate it if you would kindly ask Mr. Bochek to leave us."

McCafferty sputtered and glanced in Bochek's direction.

"Sit down, McCafferty," Bochek ordered, and the rotund attorney dropped into his seat as if his legs had been severed at the knees.

"I, for one," Jessie said, "have had quite enough of your rudeness. Horace, after today you may reach me at the Palace Hotel. I'd appreciate your immediate attention to the matter in question."

Bochek leaned back against the door. "Sorry, Miss Jessie, you aren't goin' nowhere. I've been patient for far too long. I want those shares, and I want them now."

"Sorry, Mr. Bochek, that isn't possible."

"I don't think I'm gittin' through to you. I'm gonna own your interest one way or another."

Jessie felt the first real prickle of alarm. "And what exactly do you intend to do if I refuse to sell?"

"I intend to arrange another accident. This one I assure you will be fatal."

Jessie stared at him, incredulous, his words finally beginning to register. "My God—you're the man who killed my father!"

Bochek shrugged his wide shoulders. "It was an accident, really. I was pressin' ol' Henry hard, tryin' to force him to sell. Things got heated. Henry always did have a temper. He hit me. I hit him back a little harder than I intended. He was dead when he hit the ground. Figured the heathen Chinese were as good as any to take the blame, so I made it look like the tongs did it.''

''Why are you telling me this now?'' Jessie asked, tears of rage at her father's murderer stinging her eyes.

'' 'Cause I want you to know I mean business.''

''What about those men who robbed the freight wagon? Were you responsible for that, too?''

''If I'd handled the job myself, you would never have wound up with the gold.''

Her tears stopped as quickly as they'd started, and a steely resolve settled over her. ''You killed all those men just to get your hands on Taggart Enterprises?''

''That's about it.''

''So what am I supposed to do now?''

''Sit down and shut up.''

Jessie didn't move.

Bochek turned to Horace. ''Git that boy downstairs to deliver a message to Weston. Tell him I got the girl and if he wants her back, he'd better git here fast. Tell him to come alone and unarmed, and be prepared to sign off his share of the Taggart businesses.''

Horace swallowed hard. ''I don't know about this, Kaz. Maybe we should—''

''You just do as you're told—unless you want the whole damned city to know about you and your pretty little houseboy.'' Kaz smiled sardonically.

Horace flushed and Bochek smiled. He'd been blackmailing McCafferty for the better part of two years, ever since he'd steamed opened a letter containing a generous draft to a Moroccan firm that supplied mideastern ''houseboys.'' The letter had spelled out Horace's very specific requirements, including the exact duties the young boy would perform. Kaz had copied the letter in his own hand, then sent the copy and draft, keeping the original locked in his safe. Eight months after the boy's arrival, Bochek had used the letter to obtain McCafferty's "cooperation."

Horace glanced at Jessie. His face was red, and he wouldn't meet her eyes. She didn't quite understand what hold Bochek had over her attorney, but it was obviously a powerful one.

"We had an agreement," Horace pleaded to Bochek.

"And you promised to deliver Taggart Enterprises. Now that I have to accomplish that task myself, we start a new agreement."

McCafferty wet his lips, nodded, and headed toward the door.

Jessie listened to their exchange while her mind raced over her options. There were still a few people downstairs. If she screamed, someone might come to her rescue—or Bochek might shoot her where she stood.

As if reading her thoughts, he pulled out a big revolver and began toying with the hammer. "Might as well make yourself comfortable, Miss Jessie."

"Don't call me that."

Bochek chuckled softly. "You got fire. I like that. If you were smart, you'd think about sidin' up with me. Together we could have half the politicians in this town in our pocket. They'd stand up and take notice, I promise you. Mr. and Mrs. Kaz Bochek would be a force to reckon with."

"You're a pig, Bochek. I wouldn't spit on you if you were roasting in hell."

Bochek stiffened. "You got fire, but you ain't too smart. From now on, you'll do good to keep your mouth shut—before I decide to take a piece of you right here on ol' Horace's desk."

Jessie paled and glanced toward the door.

Bochek chuckled and pointed the gun in her direction. "I'm a good shot, Miss Jessie. And I'm beginning to feel a mite randy."

Lifting her chin, Jessie marched toward a chair against the wall and sat down. Clasping her hands in her lap, she didn't say another word.

Feeling as if he'd been trampled by the entire Union cavalry, Jake shoved open the Tin Angel's bat-wing doors.

The place was beginning to fill with the evening crowd. Jake could hear murmurs of curiosity as people turned in his direction. Holding his torn and bloodied shirt together across his chest, he was surprised to see Paddy leaning against the bar, his arm in a sling, talking to Rupert.

"What the hell happened to you?" Rupert asked as Jake joined them, quickly pouring him a generous portion of whiskey.

Jake downed it in a swallow. "Rene La Porte beat a little sense into my thick skull."

"From the looks of you, it took a while. How's Rene?"

"Let's put it this way, we gained some mutual respect." Jake turned to Paddy and shook his good hand. "Welcome back, my friend. We missed you."

Paddy looked a little sheepish. "Doc told me to stay in bed, but he were a Scotsman, and I wondered about his advice. Figured him for a horse doctor. I kinda wanted to get on home."

Rupert poured Jake another whiskey. "There's a boy from McCafferty's office waitin' fer you. I sent him on upstairs."

"Where's Jessie?"

"She had an appointment with Horace late this afternoon. She ain't come back yet."

"When she gets here, tell her I want to see her."

"Sure enough, boss."

"I'm gonna clean up before I talk to the boy." He turned to Paddy. "Tell him I'll be with him in fifteen minutes." Jake headed for the stairs. Paddy followed him up, going into the office while Jake went into his room.

He came out wearing a fresh white shirt and clean breeches, his hair damp. He was still sore all over, but he felt a whole lot better.

The boy waiting in his office jumped to his feet as Jake entered. Paddy sat in a chair across the way. He looked a little pale, but it was obvious he was glad to be home.

The young man handed Jake a wax-sealed note. "I'm Mr. McCafferty's secretary. I'm to give this to you and no one else, but I don't have to wait for a reply. I'm done for the day and headed home." The youth flashed Jake a smile and stepped into the hall.

Jake closed the door behind him, then tore open the note. His jaw tightened as he read.

Weston—

If you wish to see Miss Taggart again, come to the offices of Brace and McCafferty. Mr. Bochek will release her into your care as soon as he obtains your signature on the deed to Taggart Enterprises. You must come unarmed.

Bochek! On several occasions, Bochek had expressed an interest in buying the businesses, especially Taggart Freighting. Jake didn't blame him. With Bochek's connections, no one could make the freighting company, and even the scows, more profitable than Kaz. Now that Jake thought back on it, Bochek had tried to get Henry to sell too. They'd argued about it more than once.

"Anything wrong, boss?"

Jake looked at his wounded friend, his shoulder still far from healed. "Nothing you can help me with, Paddy."

Paddy started to protest, but Jake stopped him. "If I'm not back by eight o'clock, fetch Sheriff Handley. Tell him I went to Horace McCafferty's office.

He should look for me there and bring a few deputies.''

''You sure you don't want me to come with you?'' Paddy asked.

''Just do as I say,'' Jake said, a little more sternly than he intended. He tossed the note on his desk. Paddy looked confused but said nothing more.

Jake glanced at his Leech and Rigdon hanging on the coat tree. The note said Bochek was holding Jessie and that he must come unarmed. An ominous statement. Regretfully, he left the big revolver hanging, but he reached into a drawer and pulled out his modified .36. Stuffing it into his boot, Jake hurried out the door and down the stairs.

Paddy reached across and picked up the crumpled piece of paper. He'd had only a few short reading lessons since Miss Jessie had discovered he couldn't read. Right now he wished he could—Jake had looked awful upset. Paddy clutched the paper in his fist and scanned the letters he was only beginning to recognize.

Jake had gone to McCafferty's law office. That's where Rupert said Miss Jessie was. Jake had told him to wait until eight, then fetch the sheriff. But a lot could happen between now and eight.

Paddy scratched his balding head and wondered if he should show the note to Rupert. If he did, Jake would surely be mad. If he didn't . . . Paddy sat down in Jake's chair, trying to decide what to do. If Jake didn't get back in an hour, he'd go to McCafferty's himself. He glanced at the clock above the desk, hearing the *tick-tock* of the heavy brass pendulum. An hour was an awful long time to wait.

Chapter 23

J ake quickly paid the driver, adding a two-bit tip.

The old black horse that had pulled the carriage up the hilly streets at a gallop fought to catch its breath while a lamplighter standing on a nearby ladder lit a tall gas streetlamp. The glow cast ominous shadows as Jake looked up at McCafferty's second-story window. Wondering if he should enter from the rear, Jake hesitated, then he decided the direct approach was better. He still wasn't sure exactly what Bochek's message meant, and until he was certain Jessie was safe, he'd play by the big Pole's rules.

Although the offices were closed for the day, the double mahogany doors were unlocked. Jake stepped into the entry, scanned the downstairs to familiarize himself with the layout, then headed up to McCafferty's second-floor office. Pausing outside the etched glass door, he took a deep breath. Then he turned the knob and stepped in.

The door to the inner office stood open. Behind McCafferty's big oak desk, Kaz Bochek sat waiting, a long cigar locked between his teeth. Jake cut his glance to the nickel-plated revolver resting near Bochek's left hand on the desktop.

"Come on in, Weston." Bochek motioned him forward.

As Jake stepped into the room, he spied Jessie sitting in a straight-backed chair near the corner. She

rose to her feet when she saw him. Horace Mc-
Cafferty stood with his back to the wall.

"What the hell is going on, Bochek?"

"He's the man who killed my father," Jessie burst
out.

"Sit down and shut up," Bochek ordered. He
pulled his right hand from beneath the desk to reveal the second Remington he'd had trained on Jake
since the moment he'd entered the room.

"Do as he says, Jess." Jake cast her a look of reassurance. Even under the perilous circumstances,
he felt a rush of warmth at seeing her. She wore a
somber gray walking dress, and Jake figured that if
she felt anywhere near as rotten as he had before
his meeting with Rene, it matched her mood. With
a worried look at his bruised and battered face, Jessie glanced nervously from him to Bochek, and back
again. Then she sat down.

"Search him," Bochek ordered McCafferty, who
looked pale.

"I don't like this, Kaz."

"Do it."

"Turn around," Horace said, his voice strained.

Jake complied, unwilling to start anything with
Jessie in danger. Horace quickly patted him down,
missing the gun in his boot.

"Show him the papers," Kaz instructed. Mc-
Cafferty handed him three legal-sized sheets of onionskin written in a precise hand.

Jake carried them across the room and took a seat
next to Jessie, covering her cold hand with his.

"Are you all right?"

She nodded. "What about you? What happened
to your face?"

"A lesson in the Queensbury tradition." He
touched her cheek, then turned his attention to the
document.

"No need to read it." Kaz pushed the inkwell to

the front edge of the desk. "You're selling out, receiving ten thousand for Taggart Enterprises."

Jake raised his eyes from the paper, past the muzzle of the .46 aimed at his chest, to Bochek's smiling face. "A little on the cheap side, don't you think, Kaz?"

"It doesn't matter, Weston. You won't be getting a dime, much less the ten. Sign it!"

Jake cut his eyes to McCafferty. "Are you part of this deal?"

"I've . . . I've got no choice, Jake. I'd suggest . . ." Horace cleared his throat. "My advice is to sign it."

Jake squeezed Jessie's hand and looked her directly in the eye. "Jess, you *know*," he emphasized, "how much I enjoyed Wall Eye Wong's sea slug, and the scow trip, and how much I liked you going into Chinatown." Jessie stared at him, puzzled. "Now I want you to stay in that chair and away from the door." He tipped his head toward it. "No matter what."

Kaz furrowed his brow. What the hell was Weston talking about? The man had lost his mind. "Sign it, both of you," he ordered impatiently.

Jake rose and crossed the room to the desk. Kaz palmed the second Remington and backed his chair up against the narrow oak table behind him, as far as he could get from Weston, careful to keep both guns leveled on him. Jake dipped the pen in the inkwell and shuffled through the papers.

"Where?" He glanced at Horace, who hurried to his side. When Horace pointed at the signature line on the last page, Jake gripped the man's wrist, hooked his other arm behind his back, and threw the pudgy man across the desk in front of him, shouting, "Run, Jess!"

Both Remingtons discharged with a roar that rocked the room. McCafferty's body slammed into Jake, then slumped against the top of his desk. Jake vaulted over McCafferty's body toward Bochek.

Jessie made the doorway before she heard the ominous click of Bochek's Remingtons being cocked. They were leveled at Jake.

"Stop where you are, Miss Taggart, or I'll kill the fool."

Jessie stopped short, turning to look at them. Jake backed away from Bochek, and McCafferty's body slid to the floor.

"I said, I'll kill him," Bochek repeated with conviction.

Jake sidestepped, blocking Bochek's line of fire to Jessie. "He's got to kill us after we sign the agreement, Jess. Do as I said—"

"I'll kill him right now if you don't get back here. You both sign the agreement, and I'll leave you tied up here—alive." Bochek extended his arm, leveling one of the big revolvers at Jake's head.

"Put it down, Mr. Bochek," Jessie said. "I have no intention of running out on my partner."

"Damn it, Jess."

She walked back to Jake's side. "I'm sorry, Jake. You know I couldn't do a thing like that."

"No," he said. "I don't suppose you could." Jessie looked at him oddly.

"Now, Weston, pick up that pen and sign those papers."

Fighting to control his helpless rage, Jake dipped the pen in the inkwell and signed the onionskin with a flourish.

"Now you, Miss Taggart."

Jessie did as she was told.

"To show you I'm a man of my word, Weston, go pull the sash on those drapes and use it to tie her to a chair."

Jake walked to the windows, jerked the heavy gold braid free, and pulled the straight-backed chair away from the wall. He glanced at Bochek, looking for another opening.

"I wouldn't advise it. You try anything, and this time she gets the first bullet."

Jake looked down at McCafferty, his mouth and eyes open in shocked surprise. There was no doubt Bochek meant what he said. And there was no doubt he was lying about letting them live.

As instructed, Jake bound Jessie to the chair, leaving her bonds as loose as he dared. His eyes never stopped moving as he watched for another opportunity, some mistake that would give him the chance he needed.

"Now, pull that other chair over here, turn it around, and sit down facing the wall. Put your arms behind you."

Jake did as he was told. His hand crept toward the .36 in his boot, but he would have to raise his pant leg to get it, and he knew he'd never make it in time.

"I said arms behind you."

Jake felt the sash go around his elbows. It was now or never. He put both feet on the wall and shoved as hard as he could, crashing into Bochek, who stood behind the chair. As Jake rolled to the floor, he dug for his .36 and caught the reflection of light on Bochek's heavy nickeled Remington just before it smashed against the side of his head. Fighting for consciousness, Jake hit the floor and pain shot up his spine. Then all went black.

"Don't kill him," Jessie pleaded.

Bochek ignored her, hoisting Jake into the chair in a surprisingly easy motion that confirmed his strength. Jessie felt a chill run down her back as Bochek tied Jake, pulling mercilessly on the sash.

"You'll never get away with this," she said.

"Oh? I've gotten away with damned near everything else I've ever tried, except getting promoted in that damned pious Wells, Fargo. Now I won't have to worry about it. I've got my own freighting company, scows, and the Tin Angel as a little bonus." Kaz finished tying Jake, who slumped unconscious in his chair. Then he went to Jessie and tightened her bonds.

"You're a piss-poor knot-tyer for the ex-owner of a freighting company, Weston," Bochek said to Jake's unconscious form. The big Pole laughed. "And to tell you the truth, you were right. I can't afford to leave you alive."

Jessie swallowed hard. "You've got what you wanted. If you'll let us live, we'll say a burglar came in while we were signing the contracts. We'll say he killed Horace."

Bochek chuckled. "Sorry. You should have sold out when you had the chance. I'd shoot you both right now, but there's no use stirring up more suspicion than necessary. Besides, I got no stomach for shootin' a woman." He stepped in front of Jessie and stuffed his handkerchief in her mouth. Tearing a strip from her petticoat, he tied the gag in place.

Walking to the desk, he picked up the document and examined the signatures, then he slipped it into the pocket of his coat. Next he blew out the coal-oil lamp on Horace's desk, leaving only the dim light of a single wall sconce. He emptied the kerosene over Horace's body, around the edge of the room, and beneath the heavy draperies at the window.

"I'll tell them I left you three here, celebrating the sale of Taggart Enterprises." Kaz kicked Jake's chair over, sending him crashing to the floor. He walked to Jessie and lowered hers to the ground, sliding it around to back up against Jake's, binding them together with braided sash. "Too bad about you," he told her.

Bochek walked to the door, and his look hardened. "I have no idea how the fire started, sheriff," he said mockingly. "I left them celebrating." He laughed sardonically. "As promised, I'm leaving you both alive." The door slammed, and Jessie felt its reverberation as a deadly chill raced down her spine.

Kaz entered the general office directly below McCafferty's private office. By the light of the gas streetlamp filtering through the window, he heaped some papers together between the oak file cabinets and a scarred oak desk. A coat tree and two oak chairs joined the pile. Retrieving two more oil lamps, he opened them and dribbled kerosene across the file cabinets. Once they were empty, he tossed them into the heap.

Pulling a cigar from the pocket of his waistcoat, Bochek bit the end off and spit it onto the pile. He lit the cigar, took several satisfied puffs, and dropped the still-burning match into the papers.

By the time he left the general office and stepped into the entry, flames were licking at the ceiling directly below where Jake and Jessie were tied. Damned shame, he thought. A waste of good real estate and a damned fine-lookin' woman. If he hadn't already negotiated contracts with four different mining concerns and three different shipping companies to haul their bullion and freight, he'd have bought out some other operation. Of course, none of them suited his interests so perfectly.

Eager to put some distance between himself and the red glare lighting the building behind him, he headed into the street. Killing the girl was the part he liked the least. Pity she weren't smarter. She and Weston could have sold out fair and square. Stupid as her old man, that girl. In fact, he thought, they would both die of stupidity. She could have had me, money, everything.

Kaz walked to the corner and turned back. Smoke billowed from the lower-floor windows. As the glow began to light the street, a few people were beginning to take notice. He decided he would stay and watch, just to make sure.

Besides, he always enjoyed a good fire.

* * *

His coat thrown lightly across his shoulders to accommodate his sling, Paddy jogged around the corner and stopped to stare at the growing crowd in front of the two-story brick building. He knew this was the block that McCafferty's office was on, but he wasn't sure which building. Paddy felt the hair rise on the back of his neck. Lord, he hated fires. During a fight in South Dakota, he'd almost been trampled by a half-crazed mob when the tent went up in flames.

He pushed through the crowd. As he reached the middle of the street, the lower windows on the south side of the building blew out and tentacles of flame licked upward. A fine-looking building, too, Paddy thought. A second set of windows blew, and a horse's shrill neigh came from the livery stable next door, where men were working feverishly to lead the prancing beasts to safety. A gray jerked free and bolted and the men in the street scrambled out of the way as the horse clattered by, his eyes rolling in fear.

Paddy dodged the horse and moved closer, feeling not only the prickle of fear he always suffered during a fire, but also a wariness that told him something more was wrong. He walked closer, the heat bringing beads of sweat to his forehead as he studied the letters on the sign beside the door. One of words was the same as in the note—the message he'd finally shown to Megan, who'd started to cry and told him he should go after Jake now, before it was too late. He recognized the word on the sign because it had a big letter C in the middle. *McCafferty*, she'd told him.

This was Horace McCafferty's office, he realized with a sickening jolt of despair. Jake and Miss Jessie were up in that building.

A bucket brigade gathered, rapidly draining the two wooden water troughs in front of the livery. Paddy glanced from the men to the fiery building and made his decision. As he raced to the water trough, he sent two onlookers sprawling. With clumsy haste, he stripped the coat off his shoulders and dunked it into the water. He was working his way back toward the building when the sound of men shouting and the rapid clatter of hooves announced the arrival of the horse-drawn steam pumper from the Embarcadero Fire, Drum, and Bugle Contingency. The shiny red and brass firewagon charged up the street from one end of the block, while the Hilltop Vigilant Fire Protection Brigade's green hand-pumper clattered down the street from the other direction.

For a moment, Paddy felt relieved. Then he realized that by the time the firemen had set up and started pumping, it would be too late.

Fighting his urge to flee, and the powerful fear that gnawed his insides, Paddy charged up the wide brick stairs to the double mahogany doors. He heard men yelling, warning him not to be a fool, but he covered his face with his soggy wool coat and stepped into the entry. Heat from the office on the right seared his skin. Flames were charring the glass door. The varnish bubbled, the glass exploded inward, and the wind sucked at him as he rushed by. Glancing into the room on his left, he saw no one, so he headed toward the stairs. Smoky tears blurred his vision, and he mopped at them with the sleeve of his wet wool coat. His heart pounded with fear and thoughts of the grisly fate that might be his, but he forced one foot in front of the other up the staircase.

As he rounded the landing, he saw smoke seeping from under a door with the word *McCafferty* etched into the glass.

Paddy kicked the door on the run, smashing it off its hinges and cracking the glass. He charged into McCafferty's outer office, but it was empty. The inner door shattered with a second tremendous kick. Paddy mopped at his eyes, barely able to make out

the shapes in the smoky room. The floor on one side
smoldered from the heat below, and the flames licking past the front windows cast eerie flickering
shadows.

Paddy charged across the room, tripping over a
heavy object and falling painfully on his injured
shoulder. He saw that it was a body, but it was Horace, not Jake, so Paddy hurried over to the figures
he could just make out on the floor.

He could see Jessie's eyes above the top of her
gag, and the terror he saw hastened his movements.

Jessie had almost given up hope. Jake was still
unconscious, and the floor beneath her was blister-
ing hot. Only the thick Persian carpet had so far
saved her from burns, and the edges of the rug were
flaming beneath the drapes. She glanced up at
Paddy. Since he didn't have a knife, he had stripped
his sling away, grimacing with pain, and his massive fists were wrapped around the thick gold cord
binding her to the chair. His face reddened with the
effort as his powerful biceps bulged. The sash parted
with a sudden rending. Her hands now free, Jessie
pulled the gag from her mouth with trembling fingers and rolled to her knees beside Jake, tearing furiously at his bindings.

"We've got to hurry," she said, her voice shaking
with fear. She coughed and fought the sash, but before she could loosen the knot, the cord gave way
to Paddy's mighty hands, and he flung the chair
across the room. Jake groaned as Paddy jerked him
to his feet. Jessie flashed the big Irishman an uncertain glance, which he ignored as he hefted Jake
across his one good shoulder. By the time they
reached the stairs, Jake was coughing, ordering
Paddy to put him down.

Gaining his feet, Jake shook his head to clear it
and grinned. "You're a damned welcome sight, my
friend," he gasped.

Paddy smiled weakly, but his eyes darted toward

the office floor, which had just burst into flames. Pushing Jessie in front of them, they reached the mid-stair landing, but stopped beside a tall frosted-glass window etched with an egret in a pond. Hair-curling heat blocked the stairs below, while orange-red flames roared into the stairwell above them.

Jessie gasped when Paddy covered his face with his coat and charged the glass. It shattered as he crashed through and disappeared into the smoke beyond. Jake climbed onto the sill. Paddy stood in the swirling smoke on the roof of the livery, four feet below, his outstretched arms awaiting them.

"Your turn, Boston," Jake said, helping her onto the sill beside him. His hands at her waist steadied her until she jumped toward Paddy, who caught her but winced in pain. By the time Jake landed safely on the rooftop, Paddy had pulled her to safety near the rear of the building.

Jake followed Paddy and Jessie and they leaped off the roof onto a haystack. Then they rolled out of the stiff straw and made their way to the alley. Leaning against a tall brick fence for support, they wiped the tears from their eyes, coughing and gasping. With a crash that sent flames, smoke, and fiery debris exploding into the clear night sky, the second floor of the building caved in on the first.

Jake pulled Jessie into his arms, pressing his cheek against hers. "Thank God, you're all right." Even with her face smudged with smoke, her hair in tumbled disarray, she looked beautiful. She clung to him, her slender arms wrapped tightly around his neck, her body pressed against the length of him as if she'd never let him go. He felt her tremble and held her tighter.

When she looked up, tears had washed paths in the soot on her cheeks. "I always cause you trouble," she whispered.

"You didn't cause this, Bochek did." Jake worked a muscle in his jaw, then grinned down at her. "Besides, you're worth it.'' He turned to Paddy and extended a hand. ''Thank you, Paddy. If it hadn't been for you . . . You're a damned fine friend, Paddy Fitzpatrick.''

Jessie stepped over and threw her arms around Paddy's thick neck, giving him a hug that said more than words ever could. His tentative smile broke into an embarrassed grin when she placed a big kiss on his cheek.

Then Jake's resolve hardened. ''Bochek.'' He spat the word and fixed his gaze on Jessie. ''I'm going after him.''

''Leave him to the sheriff,'' Jessie pleaded as they hurried down the alley. ''You've been through enough, Jake.''

''A trial and a rope's too good for him, Jess. Besides, there's always a chance he'll get away. You go on back to the Tin Angel.''

''I'll take her, boss,'' Paddy said weakly.

''I want to go with you,'' Jessie said.

''No,'' Jake said, and kept on walking. Jessie and Paddy trailed behind. As they reached the end of the alley, Jake turned to Jessie. ''I'm not dragging you along, Jess. Paddy, take her back.''

''You said before that you'd listen the next time. Kaz Bochek killed my father! If you're going after him, I am too.''

He *had* said those words, although right now Jake couldn't fathom why. Knowing he was making a mistake, Jake conceded. At least he could keep an eye on her. God only knew what she'd try if she set out on her own.

''Just stay out of the way,'' he said quietly, and Jessie's brows arched in surprise. She looked so damned good to him he found it hard to concentrate. God, how the woman had gotten under his skin! ''You're a damnable distraction, Jessie Taggart.'' He swept her into his arms and kissed her, something he'd been wanting to do since the moment he'd seen her in McCafferty's office. "Try not to make me think of that instead of Bochek, will you?"

Jessie's cheeks flamed prettily, although her expression was a bit puzzled at his response. Ignoring her questioning look, he bent down and pulled up his pant leg to retrieve the .36 he hadn't been able to reach before. Shoving his gun into his belt behind his back, Jake turned his attention to the crowded streets.

"Paddy!" Jessie shrieked, and Jake saw that Paddy had slumped to one knee. Blood stained his shirt through the dressing on his shoulder.

Jessie knelt beside him. "It's been too much for him!"

"He needs a doctor, Jess." Ignoring Paddy's weak assertion that he was all right, they hoisted him to his feet and draped one of his arms across each of their shoulders. A hansom cab was parked nearby, the cabbie watching the fire.

Jake shoved Paddy into the cab and, with a firm grip on her waist, hoisted Jessie in beside him.

"I'm watching the fire, mate." The cabbie impatiently waved Jake away.

Jake pulled his .36 out and leveled it between the man's eyes. "You're gonna be watchin' out of *three* eye sockets if you don't get this man to a doctor."

The cabbie's face paled. He grabbed for the reins, and Jake stepped away.

Jessie stuck her head out of the window. "Aren't you coming with us?"

"I've got something to do first." He'd said she could go, but now there was Paddy to think of—it was as good an excuse as any to keep her safe. "I'll see you back at the Angel." He threw her a warning glance. "I expect you to be there when I get back. There are some things we need to discuss."

Her gaze shifted away from him, and he read the guilt in her expression. Let her squirm, he thought.

The little baggage deserves every blasted minute of misery. But, he admitted, he'd be glad when this business with Bochek was behind them, glad when they'd set things straight. Glad when he had a ring on her finger and her pretty little backside firmly installed in his bed.

As the cab clattered away, Jake set out for the boardinghouse where he knew Kaz lived. He hadn't gone six paces when he saw Bochek beneath an awning on the opposite corner, intently watching the blaze. The sonofabitch! Jake cursed and started toward him.

Bochek spotted Jake at almost the same instant. His eyes widened in disbelief. Standing in the open, he had no choice but to go for his revolver, just as Jake did. Both men leveled their guns at the same time, and both fired too quickly. Jake's shot slammed into the brick wall behind Kaz, and Bochek's shot pinged off the gas streetlamp next to Jake. Then Bochek slipped into the crowd.

Hearing the sharp crack of gunshots over the noise and commotion, Jessie leaned out of the window and searched the throng that was rapidly disappearing behind the cab.

"Pull up!" she commanded the driver, seeing Jake bolt down the street, his gun in hand. The cabbie drew rein, but before the rig had completely stopped, Jessie was out of the carriage. "Take him to the Tin Angel on Montgomery Street. They'll pay your fare and a dollar tip. Tell them Jessie sent you." She searched the street behind them and saw Jake's dark-haired head above the crowd. He was running, and she knew which man he was after.

"Be careful, mum!" Paddy called out.

Jessie nodded, gathered her skirts, and ran back to the intersection. The carriage disappeared down the street.

Chapter 24

Up ahead, Jake saw Bochek pushing and shoving through the crowd. Men yelled and shook their fists at him, only to be shouldered aside again by Jake.

Once clear of the throng, Bochek stopped and leveled his revolver, forcing Jake to take cover behind a stairway. When Jake leaped out to fire, the man had disappeared.

Sprinting to where the big Pole had been standing, Jake figured he must have ducked into the alleyway. He raced along the wall until his boot hit something slick and he almost went down. He felt the slap of the wind from Bochek's bullet as it pinged loudly against the wall above his head.

"Jake!" Jessie screamed, running toward him.

Jake dove to his right and grabbed her waist, pulling her to the ground beside him an instant before Bochek's second shot whistled above their heads. Careful to stay in darkness, they huddled against the cold brick wall.

"Are you all right?" Jessie whispered, touching his cheek with a trembling hand. "I saw you go down and I thought you were hit."

"Lucky for me, I just slipped." They could hear running footsteps, fading away as they disappeared down the alley. "Stay here." Jake was on his feet and moving. Jessie gathered her skirts and followed at a run. At the alley entrance, Jake stopped and Jessie hurried up beside him.

He pushed her farther into the shadows. "Jess, I wish you'd go back to the Angel."

"And I wish you'd let the sheriff handle this, but since you won't, I'm going with you. I only wish I had a gun."

With a sigh of resignation, Jake nodded. "All right, but let me see where he's gotten to first." He rounded the corner and moved up the street in the direction Bochek had taken, a street with no gas lamps. He waited at the end of the block for Jessie to catch up with him. "He's heading for Chinatown," Jake said without looking back at her.

"If he gets into that maze, we'll never find him."

"That's the idea," Jake said, "but it isn't going to work." With grim determination, he slipped around the corner, this time holding Jessie's hand.

"Look out!" she screamed, and Jake pulled her into a basement stairwell beside him. Half a block away, fire spit from the muzzle of Bochek's heavy .46, splintering a railing that ran along the stairs.

"He's in a doorway up ahead," Jessie said breathlessly.

Jake spotted him rounding a well-lit corner onto a busy street lined with cribs, each decorated by brightly colored rice paper lanterns hanging near the openings. A variety of men strolled the boardwalks, bottles in hand, a few with tiny Oriental girls nestled beneath their arms. Kaz Bochek was nowhere to be seen.

"He could be in any of these cubbyholes," Jake said as he and Jessie made their way from opening to opening. Whores called out to Jake in their vulgar pidgin English, and Jessie's cheeks turned red. He pulled her into a deserted doorway. "I thought you'd be used to that sort of talk by now."

"I guess I'll never get used to it."

"Once a lady, always a lady," he teased, but his

eyes searched the street. Bending down, he brushed her lips with a kiss. "I told you that before."

Jessie looked at him a moment, blinked hard at a sudden rush of tears, and glanced away. "If I were truly a lady, I wouldn't have done what I did with Rene—or you for that matter."

He turned her face with his hand. "Jess—"

A black-robed Chinese man stepped in front of them, and Jake's hand fell away. His other hand tightened on the butt of his revolver.

The man bowed deferentially and gestured toward a warehouse in the middle of the block. "The man you seek is in there, Mr. Weston." He pointed with a thin-fingered hand, then faded out of sight into a crib.

"Come on." Jake pulled Jessie toward the darkened warehouse. After making a cursory survey of their surroundings, he shoved open the heavy plank door. A bullet splintered the jamb, sending chips of wood flying into the air. "Damn," Jake cursed. Jessie touched his face, wiping away a fine line of blood where a wood chip had hit him.

"We should leave this to Sheriff Handley," she whispered.

"Probably," he agreed. But he had no intention of doing anything that sane. Bochek had murdered Henry and done his best to burn him and Jessie alive. That made the matter personal.

Jake dropped to his knee and leaned into the opening. His .36 spat flame. They could hear feet moving through the rows of crates and boxes that were dimly visible inside. A shout rang out as Bochek fired back at them, then they heard a scraping sound and the crash of a crate coming down.

"He's knocked something over," Jessie whispered.

"Maybe it fell on top of him, and we'll find him squashed like the bug he is."

The building was a full block deep, they discovered as they moved carefully inside, and the rear doorway opened onto the next street. Just before they reached the back, Jake caught a reflection out of the corner of his eye and slid to a stop in front of Jessie. One of Bochek's Remingtons lay on the floor. He must have dropped it when he fell, but there was no other sign of him. Jake checked the gun and shoved it into his belt.

"I wish you'd let the sheriff handle this," Jessie said again.

"And I wish you'd get the hell back to the Angel."

Jessie just shook her head.

Like the street in front, the one out back was lined with Chinese lanterns and bustling with Chinese coolies.

"Damn," Jake grumbled, peering into the throng. "We've lost him again."

Two black-robed Chinese approached from a few feet away. The man said something in Chinese, pointing first to the gun in Jake's belt, then down the street.

"What's going on here?" Jessie whispered over Jake's shoulder.

"It looks like we're getting a little Celestial assistance, Jess. The Chinese don't like Bochek any more than he likes them. They won't interfere directly, but we can use any help they're willing to give us."

When they reached the corner, another Chinese stood pointing. They took the corner at a run. Another Chinese stood at the alley. He stopped Jake with a raised hand.

"Like a rat into a trap," the man said, "the scum has gone into the barracoon."

Located in an abandoned warehouse, the slave-trading house opened off the alley. Jake had only been inside one time. There was an entry, he remembered, with a bar and tables, which opened onto a larger room where the auctions were held.

The stagelike dais where the girls were paraded had doors at either end. Those doors, Jake had been told, opened into the communal quarters for the women.

Jake paused at the entrance. Painted jade-green, with polished brass hinges, it looked out of place in the otherwise dismal alley—an alley as grim and dark as the business of the barracoon.

Jake pulled open the heavy door, and its hinges creaked loudly. The moon had risen, but it did little to brighten the entry. One hand holding Jessie's, the other pointing his .36 upward, Jake stepped inside, hesitating until their eyes adjusted to the darkness.

Across the way, beneath the auction room door, dim rays of light seeped in. Jake stumbled against a chair as he maneuvered across the expanse, and he heard a noise from inside the auction area. Pulling open the door, he realized the room had skylights, something he hadn't remembered. Moonlight sent shafts of white onto the floor, dimly outlining rows of chairs.

"Stay here," Jake ordered. "I can't watch him and you at the same time."

Jessie nodded and backed against the wall. Jake dove through the opening and rolled, knocking two chairs aside. A shot rang out, but slammed harmlessly into the wall behind where he crouched. He'd never be able to get an accurate shot off in the darkness, but then Bochek couldn't see him either.

Hearing a shuffling sound near the stage, Jake moved forward, keeping low. He tracked the sound up the stairs with the muzzle of his .36. Four shots left, he thought. He heard Bochek's footfalls, hollow on the raised wooden floor. Catching a shadow, he fired; and Bochek, using the blast to locate his target, fired in return. When Jake pulled the trigger again, Bochek's return shot tore though his coat. Jake heard the big Pole trip and land heavily on the floor—and prayed he had hit him.

Feeling a hand on his shoulder, Jake jumped half

out of his boots. "Damn!" he growled beneath his breath. He pulled Jessie to the floor as another shot rang out and the bullet whizzed over their heads. "You, woman, are without a doubt the most senseless female I could have picked to fall in love with." Jake aimed carefully and fired in the direction of the muzzle blast.

"I thought maybe if you gave me Bochek's gun, I could draw his fire and you could figure out where he was."

"That's not a bad idea, Jess. Except Bochek's gun is empty."

"Oh."

"Now stay down, and this time, do what I say." Jake rolled to the side and came to his feet. He had one shot left. He'd better make it a good one.

Suddenly, both doors leading from the dais opened up, and the light of a dozen torches lit the stage. Bochek stood in the middle. Glancing from left to right, he raced toward the nearest opening, but Jake's bullet tore into his chest before he even got close. He hit the floor and rolled onto his back, gasping for breath. Blood seeping though his fingers, Bochek clutched his coat where the bullet had entered.

A black-robed figure appeared in one doorway and a black-suited figure in the other. As their bodyguards stepped out of the openings behind them, Jake recognized Charley Sing and Tok Loy Hong. Bochek clawed at the Remington on the floor beside him, but Charley Sing reached down and picked it up, holding it away as if it were a piece of garbage off the street.

"I don't think so, Mr. Bochek," he said politely, then he walked down the stairs to where Jake and Jessie stood.

"Bochek is the man who killed my father," Jessie told him.

Sing didn't seem surprised. "After our last unfor-

tunate . . . encounter, Miss Taggart, the honorable
Tok Loy and I began to investigate that possibility.
We had both heard certain . . . rumors. We were
still not sure until we learned of the fire tonight. We
thought you were both dead until one of our people
saw you chasing Bochek into Chinatown."

He offered the Remington to Jake. "A keepsake?"

"Thank you." Jake accepted the heavy revolver
and handed his empty .36 to Jessie. "You said you
wanted a gun. As soon as things settle down, I'll
show you how to use it."

Jessie glanced up at him. "I hardly think we'll
have time for that." Her suddenly taut expression
said that nothing had changed between them. "I'm
leaving for Boston on the noon train."

Jake turned her around to face him. "If I had a
lick of sense, I'd probably help you pack. But—"

"He has gone to meet his ancestors," Tok Loy
Hong interrupted from the dais, where he knelt beside Bochek, his bony fingers pressed against the
Pole's thick neck. "It will be a sad day in Occidental
heaven." He smiled sagely. "If there is such a
place."

"More likely he'll be headed in the other direction," Jake said. Taking the stairs two at a time, he
crossed the stage with long strides. Reaching down,
he pulled the ownership document from Bochek's
blood-soaked pocket. Returning to Jessie's side, he
unfolded it, and realized there were two documents,
each marred by three round holes, where Jake's single bullet had perforated the folds.

"Burn it," Jessie said.

"I can burn ours," Jake agreed, "but Don Gutierrez would probably like to have his mortgage back.
His home will be free and clear again. At least for
as long as we can keep him away from the tables."

Thinking of the proud Califronio she had met
when she first arrived at the Tin Angel, Jessie
smiled. "I have a feeling the don may have learned

his lesson. The few times he's been in lately, he hasn't gambled at all."

Jake smiled. "I'm glad something good came of all this."

"Me too." Jessie agreed a bit forlornly.

"Thank you both for all your help," Jake told the two Chinese men.

"Yes," Jessie added. "You've both been good friends."

"As have you," Tok Loy said.

Jake turned his attention to Jessie. "Let's go home, Boston. We'll get a message to the sheriff, wash off this soot, and then we'll talk."

Jessie just looked at him. "I don't know what there is to talk about. Nothing's changed between us, and I can't undo what I've done."

"Home, Boston. We'll talk about it at home."

Jessie wanted to say the Tin Angel hadn't been her home since the night she'd slept with Rene. Instead, she breathed a sigh of resignation and let him lead her to the door.

They reached the Tin Angel to find the place in an uproar. Paddy was in his basement room with Doc Bedford, who proclaimed that with rest he'd be fine. Lovey and Rupert were in the office with a weeping Megan O'Brien.

"She says Bochek's been blackmailing her for information," Lovey told them. "Says she didn't mean for nobody to git killed, but she's got this little baby girl over at the Sisters of Redemption school. Bochek knew about the child, and threatened to do her harm if Megan didn't cooperate."

"Sounds like something he'd do," Jake said.

"He was blackmailing McCafferty, too," Jessie told them. "He said something about Horace's houseboy, and Horace looked as if he might faint." Jessie glanced at Lovey, who chuckled softly.

"I always knew there was somethin' about that man."

Jessie turned to Jake, who didn't seem surprised at all, but flashed her an amused half grin.

"I can see I'm missing something," she said. "Would one of you care to explain?"

"It's all right, Jess," Jake said. "A lady isn't supposed to know about things like that."

"Well, this lady intends to find out." Jake's grin grew broad, and Jessie's cheeks began to burn. "But later will be soon enough."

When his smile softened, Jessie felt a bit uneasy. Why was he being so sweet to her after what she'd done with Rene?

"Megan," Jake said softly, a hand on the girl's slender shoulder, "you were a victim, just the same as the rest of us."

She hiccupped and fought to stop crying. "Then ye won't be turnin' me over the sheriff?"

"No."

She gripped his hand and kissed it. "Saints be praised! You've me undyin' thanks, Jake Weston. Miss Jessie, you'll not regret it, I promise ye."

Jessie smiled at Megan, pleased with Jake's decision. Turning, she left the room to bathe and change her clothes.

Jake sent a message to the sheriff, and when Isaac arrived, filled him in on the details of the evening. Since Jessie hadn't come down yet, Isaac agreed to come back for her statement in the morning. Once things had returned to some semblance of order, Jake headed gratefully to his own hot bath and a shave.

Jessie relaxed in the narrow bathtub in front of her tiny fireplace. The flames flickered in the hearth, and she thought of the terrible fire at Horace's, imagining the grim consequences if Paddy hadn't come to their aid. At least her father's ghost was at rest, which was more than Jessie could say for herself. There'd be no peace for her until she left San Francisco and got as far away from her memories as she could.

She tried to imagine herself back in Boston, but she couldn't. She could scarcely remember what the streets looked like; the shops and stately buildings. She had no home there. She'd be starting over, living in some very proper boardinghouse for single ladies, making a life on her own. There'd be no Lovey McDougal to mother her, no Rupert to entertain her, no Paddy Fitzpatrick to protect her. The life she faced sounded so lonely that Jessie felt the sting of tears.

You have no home here either, she reminded herself sternly. This is Jake's home. You intruded for a while, caused him nothing but grief, and now it's time to go. He wanted to speak to her tonight, although the hour was late and both of them were exhausted. She wasn't sure what he wanted to discuss, but she was worried that he might ask her to stay.

The gentle looks, the kisses he'd stolen, the hugs she would always remember, hinted at a forgiveness she couldn't accept. It made her love him all the more—and more determined than ever to leave.

As the water in the tub cooled, Jessie dried off and dressed. She was sitting before the fire wearing a prim white cotton nightgown and a warm pink velvet robe, her freshly washed hair only slightly damp, when she heard a knock on her door.

"Come in," she called from the head of the stairs, and Jake stepped through the door. Even with the bruises on his face, he had never looked more handsome, and certainly never more dear. I love him so, she thought, and felt her determination falter. Dressed in spotless black breeches and a crisp white linen shirt, his dark hair still damp and curling above his collar, he mounted the stairs two at a time, the echo of his booted feet ringing across the room. He was smiling, she noticed, a smile so warm and tender it broke her heart.

She found herself going against all her resolute vows to leave him, praying he would ask her to stay, and knowing that if he did she would, no matter what heartbreak it might cause them later.

He took her cold hands between his warm ones, leaned over and kissed her mouth. It was a soft kiss, gentle and undemanding.

"Hello, Boston."

"Hello, Jake." She fought to still her pounding heart.

He led her over to the small settee and sat down beside her. "Are you all right?"

"Yes," she answered softly. "Just a little tired."

"I wish this could wait, but I don't think it can." She didn't answer.

"I want you to marry me," he said bluntly. "I love you so damned much I can't think straight."

Her bottom lip trembled. There they were—the words she had prayed for—the words she dreaded to hear. She only shook her head.

"Do you really believe we're not suited?"

"I didn't really mean what I said that morning. I just felt so guilty. . . . I still do." Jessie lifted her eyes to his. "You deserve a woman who won't betray you," she said softly.

"And you think you would?"

"I already have."

"You thought I had betrayed you."

"I should have trusted you; I should have had more faith."

"And you think that under the same circumstances I would have believed you were innocent?"

Jessie smiled at that. "No, I don't suppose you would."

"I think we've both learned a valuable lesson." He squeezed her cold hands. "Marry me."

She glanced away. "Earlier I told myself I would leave no matter what, because I believed that sooner or later what happened with Rene would destroy us. Then I prayed that you would want me to stay, and I knew that I would. Now that you're here and you're asking, I don't know what to do."

"Jess . . ." Jake tilted her chin with his hand. "This afternoon I went to see La Porte."

Jessie felt the blood drain from her cheeks. "That's what happened to your face, isn't it? You argued with Rene."

"We had a . . . discussion of sorts."

"I asked you not to, Jake. How could you do such a thing?"

"Listen to me, Jess. You didn't sleep with him."

"Is that what he told you?"

"Yes."

"Well, what did you expect him to say?"

Jake took a deep breath and leaned back against the settee. "He said he didn't sleep with you, and I believe him."

"Well, I don't."

"All right. If you're still unconvinced, let's clear the air. Tell me how you felt when Rene made love to you."

Jessie brows shot up. "That's perverse, Jake Weston. What on earth can you be thinking?"

"What I think is, if we get things out in the open, you'll know the truth and so will I."

"So you do have doubts," she said accusingly.

"Let's just say both of us will feel better knowing the truth."

Jessie watched him a moment while she toyed with the folds of her robe. "Maybe you're right," she said at last, but she wasn't really sure. Leaning back against the settee, she began to search her memory. "Rene and I started the evening at the Palace. We had dinner. I . . . I drank some sherry, then some champagne." She swallowed hard. "Lots of champagne. I remember breaking a glass in the restaurant, and Rene said I should go home. I told him I didn't have a home." She saw Jake shift uncomfortably. "He took me to his house and ordered his housekeeper to make me some coffee. I told him I wanted more champagne. I . . ."

"You what, Jess?" Jake asked softly.

She didn't look at him, but she could feel his gaze on her face. "I told him I was in love with you. . . ."

"And then?"

"Rene said something about you both being rogues, and . . . he kissed me."

Jake straightened. "Go on."

"I . . . I . . ." A tear rolled down her cheek and Jake swept it away with the tip of his finger.

"Go on, Jess."

"I can't remember the rest." She focused on her hands, folded tightly in her lap.

"You can't remember because it didn't happen. Rene wasn't even in the house."

Jessie looked up at him. She could read the truth in his eyes, see that he loved her so much that it wouldn't have mattered anyway. Sliding her arms around his neck, she pressed her cheek against his as a soft sob caught in her throat.

"Marry me, Jess," he said.

"I love you so much," she told him, clinging to him and knowing there wasn't a man alive who could take his place. His arms enfolded her, and she felt his lips against her cheek, his fingers smoothing back her hair.

Jessie kissed him then, a kiss so sweet and loving she hoped he would know what he meant to her. He responded with a kiss a lot less sweet and a lot more demanding. She felt the heat of it all the way to her toes.

When the kiss ended, she pulled away just enough

to look at him. ''I'd be proud to marry you. I don't think I could have left you even if I'd tried.''

''Soon, Jess. Tomorrow, if you're ready. We'll buy a house—big enough for a family. We may have to sell the Tin Angel and turn respectable, but we've got plenty of time to make that decision, and we'll still have the freighting and shipping business even if we do. I love you, Jess.''

''Oh, Jake. I love you so.'' He kissed her again, his mouth warm and possessive. Pulling her to her feet, he lifted her into his arms and carried her to the bed. When he let go of her, she slid down the hard length of his body. Through his snug black breeches, she could feel his hardened arousal pressing against her.

''I'll wait until we're married, if that's what you want,'' he told her.

''What I want, Jake Weston, is another of your lessons.''

With a tender smile and a hungry look, Jake captured her mouth and slid his tongue inside. Jessie felt a jolt of desire so powerful it nearly buckled her knees. His hands moved to the ribbon that closed the front of her robe; he pulled it, and slipped the robe off her shoulders. The nightgown fell away with little more effort, pooling in a soft cotton swirl at her feet.

''God, you're beautiful,'' he whispered as he lowered his head to her naked breast.

''Not so fast,'' she teased. With trembling fingers, she worked the buttons on his shirt. He grinned, pulling off his boots and shrugging out of his shirt, then he slid his breeches down the length of his sinewy thighs. Jessie's fingers swept over his muscular buttocks, and she heard him groan.

''Little baggage,'' he whispered against her ear as he pulled her into his arms. She felt his fingers in her hair, tipping her head back, then the demanding force of his mouth. He kissed her for so long that she felt weak. Then his lips moved along her neck and down her shoulders, until his tongue circled her breast and his mouth drew her nipple into a hard bud. He lifted her up on the bed and lay down beside her, kissing her so thoroughly she could barely breathe.

Her fingers slipped through the stiff hair curling on his chest, ran over the scar that marked one shoulder and down along his flat stomach until she felt the thick shaft of his manhood. She circled it with her fingers and felt his body tense.

"I want to please you," she told him. "Show me a way."

In the glow of the firelight, she caught his breathtaking smile. Before she knew what had happened, he had lifted her and settled her astride him. Her eyes widened as she felt his hardness pressing insistently between her legs.

"You wanted a lesson, wife-to-be. Do you think you understand where this one is going?"

Leaning forward, Jessie kissed him, sliding full length along his shaft. His hardness filled her, stirring the blood in her veins until she felt hot, wet, and dizzy. "I think so," she teased breathlessly, and felt his muscles tighten.

"You always were more than a pretty face."

When she arched her back, tossing her thick mahogany hair over her shoulder, and started to move against him, all conversation ceased. One hand stroked her nipple, sending gooseflesh rippling along her skin. She could hear his rapid breathing, feel the pounding of his heart against her hand.

She knew his desire was building at a pace that matched her own; she could feel it in the way the muscles in his legs tensed beneath her, the thrust of his thighs as he met each rotation of her hips. Her body felt hot, yet shivery; the place between her legs pulsed and tingled. She controlled him with her body, felt his response, and exalted in the power she held. She had almost reached her peak when his hands gripped her buttocks, forcing her even more firmly against him.

He held her immobile, taking control, driving himself inside, and Jessie felt her desire surge hotter with every pounding thrust. She couldn't think, couldn't breathe, could only feel. As he buried himself deeper, she cried out and careened over the edge. Jessie called his name, dug her fingers into his shoulders, and ground her hips against his hardened shaft. Shivers of pleasure danced up her spine, and the world spun away in a crescendo of heat and joy and swirling delight. Jake tensed and shuddered and spilled his seed as he followed her to release.

Jessie slumped against him, the sheen of their bodies lit with a satiny glow. "I love you," she whispered.

"I love you too, Boston. I think maybe I always have."

As she nestled into the curve of his arm, Jessie thanked God for the blessings He'd given her. Their life would never be simple—they just weren't that kind. But neither would it be dull. She loved him, and he loved her. The problems they would share would only bring them closer. She smiled and kissed his cheek.

"Do you think tomorrow's too soon?" she asked.

"We'll get married tonight, if you've still got the strength."

"Tomorrow will be fine," she told him, perfectly content. When her fingers brushed against him, his arms went around her and she smiled into the darkness. Tomorrow would be soon enough to begin her life with Jake.